About the Authors

New Zealander **Alison Roberts** has written more than eighty romance novels for Mills & Boon. She has also worked as a primary school teacher, a cardiology research technician and a paramedic. Currently, she is living her dream of living – and writing – in a gorgeous village in the south of France.

There was never a time when **Elle Wright** wasn't about to start a book, wasn't already deep in a book – or had just finished one. She grew up believing in the importance of reading, and became a lover of all things romance when her mother gave her her first romance novel. She lives in Michigan.

Marie Ferrarella is a *USA TODAY* bestselling and *RITA®* Award-winning author who has written more than two hundred books for Mills & Boon, some under the name Marie Nicole. Her romances are beloved by fans worldwide. Visit her website at www.marieferrarella.com

D0807735

Irresistible Bachelors

Irresistible Bachelors:
One Night to Change her Mind

ALISON ROBERTS

ELLE WRIGHT

MARIE FERRARELLA

MILLS & BOON

First Published in Great Britain 2021
by Mills & Boon, an imprint of HarperCollins*Publishers* Ltd,
1 London Bridge Street, London, SE1 9GF

www.harpercollins.co.uk

HarperCollins*Publishers*
1st Floor, Watermarque Building,
Ringsend Road, Dublin 4, Ireland

IRRESISTIBLE BACHELORS: ONE NIGHT TO CHANGE HER
MIND © 2021 Harlequin Books S.A.

Daredevil, Doctor...Husband? © 2015 Alison Roberts
It's Always Been You © 2018 Leslie Wright
Lassoed by Fortune © 2014 Harlequin Books S.A.

Special thanks and acknowledgement are given to Marie Ferrarella
for her contribution to the *Fortunes of Texas: Welcome to Horseback
Hollow* continuity.

ISBN: 978-0-263-30058-1

MIX
Paper from
responsible sources
FSC™ C007454

This book is produced from independently certified FSC™ paper
to ensure responsible forest management.

For more information visit: www.harpercollins.co.uk/green

Printed and bound in Spain
by CPI, Barcelona

DAREDEVIL, DOCTOR... HUSBAND?

ALISON ROBERTS

CHAPTER ONE

HE WAS NOTHING like what she'd expected.

Well, the fact that he was tall, dark and ridiculously good-looking was no surprise for someone who'd been considered the most eligible doctor at Auckland General Hospital a couple of years ago but Summer Pearson had good reason to believe this man was a total bastard. A monster, even.

And monsters weren't supposed to have warm brown eyes and a smile that could light up an entire room. Maybe she'd made an incorrect assumption when she'd been given the name of her extra crew for the shift.

'Dr Mitchell?'

'That's me.'

'*Zac* Mitchell?'

'Yep. My gran still calls me Isaac, mind you. She doesn't hold with names being messed around with. She's an iceberg lettuce kind of girl, you know? You won't find any of those new-fangled fancy baby mesclun leaves in one of her salads because that's another thing that shouldn't get messed with.'

Good grief…he was telling her about his granny? And there was sheer mischief in those dark eyes. Salad greens and names were clearly only a couple of the many things Zac was more than happy to mess around with. Summer could feel her eyes narrowing as the confirmation of her suspicions became inevitable.

'And you used to work in Auckland? In A&E?'

'Sure did. I've spent the last couple of years in the UK, though. As the permanent doctor on shift for the busiest helicopter rescue service in the country.'

The base manager, Graham, came into the duty room, an orange flight suit draped over his arm.

'Found one in your size, Zac. And here's a tee shirt, too. I see you've met Summer?'

'Ah...we hadn't got as far as a proper introduction.'

Because she'd been grilling him like a prosecution lawyer in a courtroom—making sure of the identity of the accused before firing the real ammunition? Summer felt her cheeks getting pink.

'Sorry,' she muttered. 'I'm Summer Pearson. Intensive Care Paramedic. I've been with the rescue service for nearly three years now.'

'I've heard a lot about you.' An eyebrow lifted and his tone dropped a notch. 'And it was all good.'

No...was he trying to *flirt* with her?

I've heard a lot about you, too. And none of it was good...

Pretending she hadn't heard the compliment, Summer turned to Graham. 'I'll do the usual orientation while we're quiet, shall I?'

A groan came from the doorway as another man entered the room. 'Oh, no...did she just say the Q word?'

'She did.' Graham shook his head. 'What's your guess?'

'Eight minutes.'

'I'll give it six.' Graham grinned at Zac. 'Running

bet on how long till a job comes in after someone says the Q word. Worst performer of the week restocks the beer fridge. Meet Monty, Zac—one of our pilots.'

The men shook hands. Then they all looked at Summer and she tried to erase the expression that felt remarkably like a scowl from her face.

'Three minutes,' she offered reluctantly. Wishful thinking, maybe, but how good would it be if what was likely to be a complicated winch job came in and an untrained doctor had to be left on base in favour of experienced crewmen? 'So I guess we'd better get started on the orientation.'

'Just show him where everything is,' Graham said. 'Zac, here, is the most highly trained doctor we've ever had joining us. Fully winch trained. He's done HUET and he's even part way through his pilot's training.'

Summer could feel the scowl creeping back. She refused to be impressed but it was difficult. Helicopter Underwater Escape Training was not something for the faint-hearted.

Zac was shrugging off the praise. 'I'm passionate about emergency medicine, that's all. And the challenge of being on the front line is a lot more exciting than working inside a controlled environment like an emergency department. Maybe I haven't really grown up yet, and that keeps me chasing adventures.'

Immaturity was no excuse for anything. It certainly didn't mitigate ruining someone's life and then walking away. Summer tried to catch Graham's eye. Could she tell him she really wasn't comfortable working with this new team member?

She didn't get the chance. The strident signal from

the on-base communication system told them a job had come in.

Monty checked his watch. 'Two minutes, ten seconds. You win, Summer.'

She picked up her helmet and jammed it on her head. She didn't feel as if she'd won anything at all.

She was nothing like what he'd expected.

Well, she *was* small. No more than about five foot four at a guess. Her head barely reached his shoulder and that was including the spikes of her short blonde hair. *Pocket rocket*, his ED colleagues had told him. *But don't be fooled. She's as tough as. And one of the best paramedics in the business.*

But they'd also told him she was Summer by name and sunny by nature. And that she was great fun to work with. *You're a lucky man*, they'd said.

He'd been expecting summer and he'd got winter instead. Funny, but he didn't feel that lucky.

Or maybe he did. Here he was in a chopper again and he hadn't realised how much he was missing the excitement of being airborne and heading for the unknown. Not only that, he was doing it over the sparkling blue waters of his home town instead of the grey British skies he'd become so familiar with. And they were heading for even more spectacular scenery on the far side of the Coromandel Peninsula—one of his most favourite places on earth.

'Car's over a bank,' he heard through the speakers built into his helmet. 'On the 309, between the Kauri grove and Waiau Falls. Ambulance and fire service are on scene.'

'The 309's still a gravel road, I presume?'

'You know it?' Monty sounded surprised.

'Spent most of my childhood holidays on the Coromandel. I'm into water sports.'

'Talk to Summer.' Monty chuckled. 'Queen of the paddleboard, she is.'

Zac would have been happy to do exactly that but it only took a glance to see that she had no desire to chat. Her face was turned away and she gave the impression of finding the view too fascinating to resist.

She still looked small, with the wide straps of her harness across her chest. The helmet looked too big for her head and while someone might be excused for getting the impression of a child playing dress-up, they'd only need to see her profile to sense a very adult level of focus and...what was it...judgement?

Yeah... He felt as if he'd been tried and judged and the verdict had not been favourable.

But he'd never even met the woman before today so what was he being judged on?

Was she some kind of control freak, perhaps, who didn't appreciate having someone on board who had a medical authority higher than hers? Or did she require confirmation that a newcomer's ability was what it appeared to be on paper?

Fair enough.

What wasn't acceptable was making said newcomer feel less than welcome. Undesirable, even.

As if she felt the force of his frown, Summer turned her head. Her gaze met his and held longer than could be considered polite.

Yeah...she was fierce, all right. Unafraid.

Who was going to look away first? Defusing tension was a skill that came automatically for Zac. He might

have had to learn it for all the wrong reasons when he
was too young to understand but shades of that ability still came in handy at times. All it usually took was
turning on the charm. He summoned his best smile and,
for a split second, he thought it was going to work because she almost smiled back. But then she jerked her
head, breaking the eye contact.

A deliberate snub? Zac tamped down a response that
could have been disappointment. Or possibly annoy-
ance. Neither would be helpful in establishing a good
working relationship with this unexpectedly prickly
young woman.

'You should get a good view of the Pinnacles on your
side in a few minutes,' Summer said.

'Might get a bit bumpy going over the mountains,'
Monty added. 'I'll get an update on scene info as soon
as we get over the top.'

When he'd first started this kind of work, Zac would
be using this time to go over all the possible medical
scenarios in his head and the procedures that might be
needed to deal with them. A chest decompression for a
pneumothorax, perhaps. Management of a spinal, crush
or severe head injury. Partial or complete amputations.
Uncontrollable haemorrhage. But the list was long and
he'd learned that there was no point expending mental
energy on imaginary scenarios.

He'd also learned that it was better to start a job without assumptions that could distract him from the unexpected. And that he could deal with whatever he found.
This time was better used to relax and centre himself.
The view of the spectacular bush-covered peaks below
them was ideal—and definitely better than trying to

make conversation with someone who clearly had no intention of making his life any more pleasant.

'ETA two minutes.'

'Roger.' Summer leaned forward in her seat to get a better view of the ground below. 'Vehicles at eleven o'clock. I can see a fire truck and ambulance.'

'Copy that,' Monty said. 'Comms? Rescue One. On location, on location.'

The chopper tilted as they turned. Monty was using the crew frequency now. 'Turning windward,' he advised. 'I think the road's going to be the only landing place.'

'Got a bit of a tilt to it. No wires, though.'

'No worries,' Monty said. 'Be a bit dusty, folks. Okay…right skid's going to touch first.'

They had the doors open before the dust cloud had cleared. Zac released the catch of his safety harness first and hoisted one of the backpacks onto his shoulder as they climbed out.

Summer picked up the other pack and a portable oxygen cylinder and followed. Weirdly, it felt like she was used to working with this guy already. Maybe that was because he seemed to know exactly what he was doing and he wasn't waiting to follow her lead. At least he stood back when they reached the knot of people standing by the side of the road near the fire truck so it was Summer that the fireman in charge of the scene spoke to first.

'We've got the vehicle secured but haven't got the driver out. It's a bit of a steep climb.'

'Single occupant?'

'Yes. An eighty-three-year-old woman. Frances.'

'Status?'

'I'd say two.' An ambulance officer joined them. 'GCS was lowered on arrival. She's confused and distressed. Airway seems to be clear but we haven't got close enough to assess her properly yet and, given the MOI and her age, there's every probability she has serious injuries.'

'Access?'

'Ladder. It's a few metres short of the target, though. You'll have to be careful but there's plenty of trees to hang on to.'

'Cool. We'll go down and see what's what.' Summer glanced at Zac. Tall and broad-shouldered, his size and weight would make the climb and access to the vehicle much harder than it was for her. It would probably be sensible for him to suggest waiting up here on the road while she did an initial assessment and made their patient stable enough to be extricated by the fire crew.

'Want me to go first?' he asked. 'And test the ladder?'

'If you like.' Summer passed her backpack to a fireman who was ready to secure it to a rope and lower it down. Not that it was needed, but she had to give him points for thinking about her safety.

Looking at the narrow ladder lying on the crushed and probably slippery ferns of the bush undergrowth on an almost vertical cliff face, she had to acknowledge those points.

'Yeah...you going first is a good idea, Zac. There'll be less damage done if I land on you rather than the other way round.'

'Impersonating a cushion is one of my splinter skills.' Zac handed his pack to the fireman and then turned without hesitation to climb onto the ladder. A rope attached to the top and anchored to the back of the fire truck was preventing it sliding downwards but it couldn't control any sideways movement. Another rope was attached to the back of the small car that could be seen protruding from the mangled scrub and ferns a good fifteen metres down the bank.

'She was lucky the scrub cushioned the impact,' the fireman said. 'Probably why she's still alive.'

Zac was halfway down the ladder now and climbing carefully enough not to make it swing. Summer caught the top rung and turned her body to find a foothold. She loved the kind of challenge this sort of job presented. The ladder was easy. Getting down the last stretch when you had to slide between trees was harder. There were fire crew down here but it was Zac who was moving just ahead of her and every time he caught himself, he was looking back to make sure she'd reached her last handhold safely.

It was Summer who needed to take the lead as they got close enough to touch the car. A small hatchback well buried in undergrowth left virtually no room for a large man to see much. The front passenger window had been smashed. Summer put her head in the gap.

'Hi there... Frances, is it?'

The elderly woman groaned. Her voice was high and quavery. 'Get me out. *Please*...'

'That's what we're here for. My name's Summer and I've got Zac with me. Are you having any trouble breathing, Frances?'

'I...I don't think so.'

'Does anything hurt?'

'I...I don't know...I'm *scared*...'

Summer was trying to assess their patient visually. Pale skin and a bump on the head that was bleeding. She could see the woman's chest rising and falling rapidly. The more distressed she was, the harder it would be to assess and try to move her.

The window on the driver's side was broken too and suddenly there was movement as the prickly branches of scrub got pushed aside. The face that appeared was wearing a helmet. How on earth had Zac managed to get down that side of the vehicle?

Not only that, he was reaching in to touch the woman. To put a calming hand on her forehead, probably to stop her turning her head to look at him in case she had injured her neck.

'It's okay, sweetheart,' he said. 'We're going to take good care of you.'

Sweetheart? Was that an appropriate way to address an eighty-three-year-old woman?

'Oh...' Frances didn't seem offended. 'Oh... Who are you?'

'I'm Zac. I'm a doctor.'

'Do I know you?'

'You do now.' He leaned in further, a lopsided smile appearing as he make a clicking sound like someone encouraging a pony to move. The sound was accompanied by a wink.

'Oh...' The outward breath sounded like a sigh of relief. There was even a shaky smile in response. 'Thank you, dear. I've been *so* scared...'

'I know.' His voice was understanding. Reassuring. Was he holding a hand or taking a pulse in there? 'Summer—are you able to open the door on your side? It's jammed over here.'

With the assistance of a fireman and a crowbar, the answer was affirmative.

With the new space, Summer was able to ease herself cautiously into the car. The creaking and slight forward movement of the vehicle made her catch her breath but it terrified Frances.

'No…help…'

This time it was Summer as well as their patient who took comfort from Zac's confident tone. 'The ropes just needed to take up the extra weight. You're safe. There's a great big fire engine up on the road that's not going anywhere and the car is very firmly attached to it. Relax, sweetheart…'

There it was again. That cheeky endearment. Summer wouldn't want to admit that skip of her heart when it seemed like the car was beginning to roll further down the cliff. She most definitely wouldn't want to admit that warm feeling the use of the endearment created. How powerful could a single word be? It could make you think that someone genuinely cared about you.

That you were, indeed, safe.

Suddenly, it was easy to focus completely on the job she needed to do. Summer unhooked the stethoscope from around her neck and fitted it into her ears.

'Take a deep breath for me, Frances.'

There was equal air entry in both lungs and a pulse that was a little too fast and uneven enough to suggest an underlying cardiac condition, although Frances denied having any. The worst bleeding from lacerations in papery skin needed pressure dressings for control because blood pressure was already low and Summer

eased a cervical collar in place as Zac held the head
steady.

'Sorry, Frances. I know this is uncomfortable but
it's to protect your neck while we get you out. We can't
examine you properly until we get you up to the ambulance.'

'That's all right, dear.' But it was Zac that Frances
was looking at for reassurance. His hand she was holding through the window as Summer worked quickly
beside her in the car.

'Are you sure nothing's hurting, Frances?'

'My chest is a bit sore. And my arm...'

'We can give you something for the pain.'

But Frances shook her head. 'I can bear it, dear. It's
not that bad...'

Summer glanced up at Zac, who was still supporting
the elderly woman's head and neck. 'We can reassess
after we move her but I think we can probably wait till
we get up to the top before worrying about IV access.'

'Absolutely.' Zac nodded. 'The tubing and trying to
carry a bag of fluids will only create a complication we
don't need. Bit of oxygen might be a good idea, though,
do you think?'

'Sure.'

They explained how they were going to get her out
of the car, using a backboard to slide her towards the
passenger side and then turning her to lie flat as they
lifted her out onto a stretcher.

'You'll be quite safe,' Summer said. 'We've got lots
of strong young firemen to carry you up the hill.'

'Oh... I've caused everybody so much trouble,
haven't I?'

'It's what we do,' Zac told her. 'If people didn't have

accidents or get sick, we'd be out of a job.' He was smiling again. 'And we *love* our job, don't we, Summer?'

This time, she really couldn't help smiling back so she tilted her head towards her patient. 'Indeed we do. Okay, Frances. You ready to get out of here?'

Getting her out of the car had to be done as gently as possible because there could be fractured bones or internal injuries that hadn't been recognised due to position and limited access but if there had been any increase in pain during the procedure, Frances wasn't complaining. Cocooned in a blanket and strapped securely into the Stokes basket stretcher, she looked almost relaxed as the rescue team began the slow process of inching the stretcher up to the road.

In the relative safety of the ambulance, it was Zac who led a more complete examination while an ambulance officer filled in some paperwork.

'Next of kin?'

'I haven't got any. Not now.'

'Is there anyone you'd like us to call?'

'Maybe my neighbour. She'll take care of the cats if I don't get home tonight. Oh…that's why I was driving today. There's a special on in the supermarket at Whitianga. For cat food.'

Zac got an IV line through fragile skin with a skill that was unlikely to leave so much as a bruise and Summer hooked up the IV fluids, aware of how meticulous and gentle the rest of his survey was, despite being rapid enough to get them on their way as soon as possible. ECG electrodes, blood pressure and oxygen saturation monitors were in place and Zac was keeping an eye on all the readings. A raised eyebrow at Summer had her nodding. The heart rhythm wasn't dangerous but was definitely abnormal and would need treatment.

'You don't get dizzy spells, do you, Frances?' Zac asked. 'You weren't feeling sick before the accident?'

'I don't think so. I really can't remember...'

'What medications are you on?'

'I don't take anything, dear. Apart from my calcium tablets. I'm as healthy as a horse. Haven't needed to see a doctor for years.'

'Might be a good thing that you're going to get a proper check-up in hospital then. Bit of a warrant of fitness.'

'I don't like bothering a doctor when I don't need to.'

'I know. My gran Ivy is exactly the same.'

'How old is *she*?'

'Ninety-two.'

Summer found herself sliding a quizzical glance in his direction as she gathered dressings and bandages to dress some of the superficial wounds more thoroughly. It wouldn't occur to her to think about, let alone tell others, anything about her own family. What was it with him and his grandmother? Nobody could miss the pride in his voice and it just didn't fit with the whole cheeky, bad boy vibe. And it certainly didn't fit with his reputation.

'She still swims every day,' Zac added. 'Has done her whole life. Reckons she's half-mermaid. Does it hurt if I press here?'

'Ooh...yes...'

'Can you wiggle your fingers?'

'That hurts, too... Have I broken something?'

'It's possible. We'll put a splint on it and keep it nice and still till you get an X-ray. We might give you something for the pain, too. You don't have to be brave and put up with it, you know. Sometimes, it's nice to just let someone else take care of you.'

Frances got a bit weepy at that point but the transfer to the helicopter and their take-off a short time later was enough of a distraction.

It didn't quite distract Summer. Was Frances stoic and uncomplaining because there was no point in being anything else? Was there really nobody who needed to know she'd had a bad accident other than her neighbour?

The thought was sad.

Maybe more so because it resonated. As the chopper lifted and swung inland to head back to Auckland, Summer watched the people on the ground get smaller and a cluster of houses in the small township of Coromandel where Frances lived become visible. They vanished just as quickly and Summer turned, wondering if the elderly woman was aware and distressed by how far from her home they were taking her.

'Morphine's doing its job.' Zac's voice sounded loud in her helmet. 'She's having a wee nap.' His eyes were on the cardiac monitor. 'She's stable. Enjoy the view.'

But Summer still felt oddly flat. What if she'd been the one to have an accident in such an isolated location? Who would she call if she was about to be flown to an emergency department a long way from her home?

It was moments like this that she noticed the absence of a partner in her life with a sharpness that felt increasingly like failure since she'd entered her thirties and everyone her age seemed to be getting married and starting families. There was nobody to call her 'sweetheart' and really mean it. No one to make her feel cherished and safe. It wasn't that she hadn't tried to find someone—relationships just never seemed to work out.

If she was really honest, though, she hadn't tried that hard. She'd told herself that there was plenty of time and her career had to take priority but it went deeper than that, didn't it? Moments like this always made the loss of her mother seem like yesterday instead of more than fifteen years ago and what she'd been taught about not trusting men was as much a part of those memories as anything else.

Would she put her father down as next of kin? Not likely. She hadn't seen him since her mother's funeral and there was still anger there that he'd had the nerve to turn up for it.

She'd probably do what Frances had done and opt to put a call in to a neighbour to make sure her pet was cared for.

No. Her life wasn't that sad. She had a lot of good friends. The guys she worked with, for starters. And her oldest friend, Kate, would do anything to help. It was just a shame she lived in Hamilton—a good hour's drive away. Not that that was any excuse for the fact they hadn't seen each other for so long. Or even talked, come to that.

And, boy...they had something to talk about now, didn't they?

With Zac monitoring Frances during the flight and clearly happy that the condition of their patient was still stable, there was no reason why Summer shouldn't get her mobile phone from her pocket and flick off a text message.

Hey, Kate. How's things? U home tonite?

The response came back swiftly.

Late finish but home by 10. Call me. Be good 2 talk.

It would. Her friend might need some prior warning, though.

You'll never guess who's back in town!

CHAPTER TWO

'Zac...when did you get back into town?' The nurse wheeling an IV trolley through the emergency department was overdoing the delighted astonishment just a tad when she caught sight of the helicopter crew coming out of Resus.

'Only last week. Didn't see you around, Mandy.'

'I was on holiday. Giving my new bikini a test run on a beach in Rarotonga.'

'Nice.'

'It was. Is. Pink—with little purple flowers. Might have to give it another outing at Takapuna on my next day off.'

It was no surprise that Mandy chose to assume he was referring to the bikini rather than the Pacific island. Confident and popular, she had flirting down to a fine art. There were rumours that it went further than flirting but Summer preferred to trust her own instincts and Mandy had always been willing to help when their paths crossed at work and good company at social events. The smile was as friendly as ever right now, but somehow it struck a discordant note. Maybe it had been the tone in Zac's voice. Or the warm glance that had flashed between them.

No surprise there, so why was it so annoying?

Because her instincts had been trying to convince her that Zac wasn't the monster she'd heard about? That someone who could treat a frightened elderly patient as if she was his own beloved granny couldn't possibly be that bad? They'd just finished handing Frances over to the team in Resus and Zac had promised to come and visit to see how she was as soon as he was back in the department again. There had been tears on her wrinkled cheeks as she'd told Rob, the ED consultant taking over, that this 'dear boy' had saved her life.

'That's our Zac.' Rob had grinned. 'We're lucky to have him back but we're letting him out to play on the helicopters every so often.'

It was a reminder that she was on Zac's turf now because his primary job was as another one of the department's consultants. After three years of working in Auckland, both on the road and in the rescue service, Summer felt as much at home in this environment as she did on station or at the base but something subtle had just shifted in unspoken ratings. Zac was the person Frances considered to be her lifesaver. He was also a doctor and clearly not only respected for his skills but well liked. Probably more popular than Mandy, even?

Did none of them know what she knew about him?

She'd been close to doubting the truth herself but seeing the way he and Mandy had looked at each other was a wake-up call. She'd been in danger of being sucked in by that charm. Like countless other women, including Mandy. And Kate's sister, Shelley. Had she really been prepared to dismiss how Shelley's life had been wrecked?

'Hey, Summer.' Mandy was still smiling. 'Have you guys stolen Zac away from us?'

'Wouldn't dream of it.' She kept her tone light enough for her words to pass as a joke. 'I'm sure he'll get sick of us soon enough and he'll be all yours again.'

Mandy's sigh was theatrical. 'Dreams are free,' she murmured.

A curtain twitched open nearby. 'We need that trolley, Mandy. When you're ready?'

'Oops.' Mandy rolled her eyes, blew a kiss in Zac's direction and disappeared with her trolley.

It was only then that Summer felt the stare she was receiving. A level stare. Cool enough to be a completely different season from a few seconds ago when Mandy had been present.

Had he guessed that she hadn't been joking? That she'd been wishful thinking out loud? Did she care?

No.

Then why was she suddenly feeling like a complete bitch? Helicopter crews were notoriously tight teams. They had to be. This was Zac's first day on the job and, under any other circumstances, he would be a welcome addition to the team. Perfect, in fact. She'd never gone out of her way to make a newcomer feel unwelcome. Ever.

She got a glimpse of how she must be coming across to Zac and she didn't like what she saw.

And that was even more annoying than feeling as if she had a running battle between her head and heart about what sort of person he really was. Or watching him confirm his 'bad boy' reputation by encouraging Mandy.

Summer was being someone she didn't even recognise.

'We'd better take this stretcher back upstairs. Monty'll be wondering where we've got to.' She couldn't meet his gaze any longer. Was this unfamiliar, unpleasant sensation what it felt like to be ashamed of yourself? She needed to find some way to rectify the situation. But how?

She manoeuvred the stretcher into the lift. They would be airborne again within minutes, either on their way back to base or onto another job. They had to work together so, at the very least, she had to be professional and to stop letting anything personal get in the way of that.

She broke the awkward silence in the lift just before the doors opened at roof level. 'Great job, by the way… with Frances.'

Talk about being damned by faint praise.

And she'd all but announced to Mandy that she'd be delighted if he decided he'd rather stay within the four walls of the hospital's emergency department from now on. How long would it take for that message to get dispersed amongst his colleagues?

He'd been looking forward to this. Coming into the department as a uniformed HEMS member to hand over his first patient. Showing everybody that this was where his passion lay and that he was good at it. This was supposed to be the start of the life he'd dreamed of. A job that used every ounce of skill he possessed and challenged him to keep learning more. A balance of the controlled safety of a state-of-the-art emergency department with the adrenaline rush of coping with the unexpected in sometimes impossible environments. The chance to do exactly the job he wanted in the place he'd always wanted to do it in—close to the only family he had, in a city big enough to offer everything, a great climate and, best of all, the sea within easy reach. Beaches and boats. The perfect playground to unwind in after giving your all at work.

But the blue sky of that promise of fulfilment had a big cloud in it. A dark cloud that threatened rain. Possibly even hail and thunder.

How ironic was it that her name was Summer?

'Yes?'

Oh, Lord...had he said something out loud? The microphone on his helmet was so close to his mouth, it could easily pick something up, even with the increasing roar of the rotors picking up speed to take off. Like the ironic tone of her name. He had to think fast.

'Cute name,' he offered. 'Can't say I've ever met a Summer before.'

'My parents were hippies. Apparently I got conceived on a beach. After a surfing competition.'

Monty's laugh reminded him that this conversation wasn't private. 'I never knew that. No wonder you've got sea water in your veins.'

It was the first piece of personal information Summer had offered. Monty's amusement added to a lighter atmosphere and Zac wanted more.

'A summer memory to keep, then?'

'Yeah...'

'Not many people know where they were conceived. I wouldn't have a clue.'

'Maybe you should ask your mother.'

'My mother died in a car accident when I was seven and I never knew my dad. I got brought up by my gran.'

'Oh…' She caught his gaze for a moment, horrified that she'd been so insensitive. 'Sorry…'

'No worries. It's ancient history.' Zac was happy to keep the conversation going. 'You got any siblings? Spring, maybe? Or Autumn?'

'Nope.'

The word was a snap. She could offer personal information but he wasn't welcome to ask for it.

Zac suppressed a sigh. Maybe he should have a word to the base manager about being assigned to a different shift on the rescue service.

The call coming in meant that wasn't going to happen any time soon.

'Missing child,' Comms relayed. 'Six-year-old boy. Red tee shirt, blue shorts, bare feet. They think he's been swept off rocks at St Leonard's beach. Coastguard's sending a boat and the police chopper's on its way but you're closest.'

A six-year-old boy.

How long would he last in the water? How frightened would he be?

He was close to the same age Zac had been when he'd lost his mother. Summer could only imagine how frightened *he* would have been. He would have had the same soft dark curls by then. And big brown eyes.

Heart-wrenching.

She didn't want to feel sorry for Zac, any more than she wanted his charm to get under her skin.

Maybe this kid could swim. She'd been able to at least keep herself afloat by the time she was four but

Monty was right—she had sea water in her veins and life had been all about the sun and sand and surf back then. Happy days.

They were circling above the cliffs and rocks surrounding one of the many bays on Auckland's north shore now and she could see the knot of people anxiously staring at the sea. Others were climbing the rocks, staring down into the pools where a small body could wash up with the incoming tide. In the distance, as they circled again, she could see a coastguard boat leaving a foamy wake behind it as it sped out from the inner harbour.

Her heart was sinking. It was too hard to keep feeling optimistic that this search would have a happy ending.

And one glance at how pale Zac was looking, with that fierce frown of deep concern on his face, and it was too hard to keep believing that he was some kind of monster.

Round and round they went. Monty focused on keeping them low and moving slowly over a small area, his crew peering down, trying to spot the smallest sign of anything in the soft blue swells of water or the whiteness as they broke over rocks.

Emergency vehicles were gathering at a nearby park above the beach. A police car and then a fire engine. An ambulance…

'What was that?'

'Where?'

'I think I caught a flash of something red.'

'*Where?*' Summer narrowed her eyes, willing something to show up on the water below. The coastguard boat was there now. And a civilian dinghy. Even someone on a paddleboard.

'Not in the water. Up the cliff. Take us round again, Monty.'

Another slow circuit but Summer couldn't see anything.

'I swear I saw it. About halfway up, where that pohutukawa tree is coming out sideways.'

Monty stopped their circling and hovered. Took them in a bit closer. A bit lower.

'*There*...' Excitement made Zac's voice reverberate in her helmet. 'Two o'clock. There's a bit of an overhang behind the trunk. There's something there. Something *red*...'

They hovered where they were as the information was relayed to emergency crews on the ground. A fire truck got shifted and parked at the top of the cliff, facing backwards. Abseiling gear and a rope appeared and then someone was on their way down to check out the possible sighting. For an agonisingly long moment, the fire officer disappeared after climbing over the trunk and crawling beneath the overhang.

Summer held her breath.

He reappeared, backing out slowly so it took another couple of seconds to see that he held something in his arms. A small child, wearing a red T-shirt and shorts. And then he held up his hand and, despite the heavy gloves he was wearing, it was clear that he was giving a 'thumbs-up' signal that all was well.

The boy was not injured.

The relief was surprisingly overwhelming. It was instinctive to share that relief with someone, as if sharing would somehow confirm that what she was seeing was real. Maybe Zac felt the same way because their eyes met at precisely the same instant.

And, yes...her own relief was reflected there. Zac had probably dealt with the same kind of heart-breaking jobs she had in the past, where a child's life had been lost. The kind of jobs you would choose never to repeat if it was within your power—something they both knew was too much to hope for. But this time they'd won. The boy's family had won. Tragedy had been averted and it felt like a major triumph.

The momentary connection was impossible to dismiss. She and Zac felt exactly the same way and the depth of a bond that came from the kind of trauma that was part of what they did was not something everybody could share. Even amongst colleagues, the ability to distance yourself from feeling so strongly was very different. Summer still couldn't breathe past the huge lump in her throat and she suspected that Zac was just the same.

But he wasn't supposed to have an emotional connection to others like this, given what Summer knew about him. It was confusing. Not to be trusted.

The radio message telling the rescue crew to stand down broke the atmosphere. Monty's delighted whoop as he turned away and swept them back towards base added a third person to the mix and suddenly it became purely professional again and not at all confusing.

'How lucky was that?' They could hear the grin in Monty's voice. 'The kid decided to go climbing instead of getting washed out to sea.'

'Small boys can climb like spiders.'

'Only going up, though. It's when it's time to go down that they realise they're stuck.'

'He must have been scared stiff,' Summer put in. 'Good thing there was the overhang to climb under.'

'He probably knew he'd be in trouble. No wonder he decided it was safer to hide for a while.'

'He won't be in trouble.' Zac's voice was quiet. 'Or not for long, anyway. I'd love to have seen his mum's face when she gets to give him a hug.'

This time, Summer deliberately didn't look at Zac but kept her gaze on the forest of masts in the yacht marina below. She didn't want to see the recognition of what it was like to know you'd lost someone precious and what a miracle it would be to have them returned to you. Zac must have dreamed of such a miracle when he was the same age as that little boy in the red tee shirt. How long had it taken to understand that it was never going to happen?

She'd known instantly. Did that make it easier?

If she'd met his gaze, it might be a question that was impossible not to ask silently and maybe she didn't want to know the answer because that might extend that connection she'd felt.

A connection that felt wrong.

Almost like a betrayal of some kind?

Life didn't get much better than this.

A quiet, late summer evening on Takapuna beach, with a sun-kissed Rangitoto island as a backdrop to a calm blue sea. The long swim had been invigorating and it was still warm enough to sit and be amongst so many people enjoying themselves. There weren't many people swimming now but there were lots of small boats coming in to the ramp at the end of the beach, paddle-boarders beyond where the gentle waves were breaking and people walking their dogs. A group of young men were having a game of football and family groups were picnicking on the nearby grassed area.

It was the kind of scene that was so much a part of home for Zac he'd missed it with an ache during his years in London. This beach had been his playground for as long as he could remember. He loved it in all its moods—as calm as an oversized swimming pool some days, wild and stormy and leaving a mountain of seaweed on the beach at other times. Little room to walk at high tide but endless sand and rocks to clamber over at low tide. Kite surfers loved it on the windy days and paddleboards reigned on days like this.

Funny that he'd never tried that particular water sport. Maybe because it looked a bit tame. For heaven's sake—it was so tame, there was somebody out there with a dog sitting behind the person who was standing, paddling the board.

A big dog. A small person. They were attracting attention from some of the walkers and Zac could see the pleasure they were getting from the sight by the way they were pointing and smiling. More than one person was capturing the image with a camera. He took another look himself. The dog was shaggy and black. The paddler was a girl in a bikini and even from this distance she was clearly attractively curvy.

He'd finished rubbing himself down with his towel so there was no reason not to head back to the house for a hot shower but there was still enough warmth in the setting sun to make it pleasant to stand here and that pleasure certainly wasn't dimmed by watching the girl on the paddleboard for a few more moments as she headed in to shore. How would the dog cope with the challenge of staying on board as they negotiated even small waves?

It didn't. As soon as the board began to ride the swell, it jumped clear and swam beside its owner, who stayed upright and rode in until the board beached itself on the sand. It was only then that Zac realised who he'd been watching.

What had Monty called her?

Oh, yeah…the queen of the paddleboard.

Who knew that that flight suit had been covering curves that were all the sweeter when there wasn't an ounce of extra flesh anywhere else on her body? The muscles in her arms and legs had the kind of definition that only peak fitness could maintain and she had a six-pack that put his to shame.

Zac found himself sucking in his stomach just a little as he moved towards where she was dragging the huge board out of the final wash of the waves. He couldn't pretend he hadn't seen her and maybe this was a great opportunity to get past that weird hostility he'd been so aware of today. There'd been a moment when he'd thought it was behind them—when they'd shared that moment of triumph that they no longer needed to try and spot a small body floating in the sea—but it hadn't lasted. Summer had been immersed in paperwork when he'd signed off for his first shift and she'd barely acknowledged his departure.

He summoned a friendly smile. 'Need a hand?'

'Zac…'

He was possibly the last person Summer might have expected to meet here on the beach. The last person she would have *wanted* to meet? She was having to share yet another patch of her turf. First the base where she worked. Then the emergency department that was also part of her working life. Now this—not exactly her home but a huge part of when she spent her downtime and a place that was very special to her. And he was... he was almost *naked*.

Oh...my... The board shorts were perfectly respectable attire for the beach but the last time she'd seen him as he left the base that afternoon he'd been wearing real clothes. Clothes that covered up that rather overwhelming expanse of well tanned, smooth, astonishingly *male* skin. He'd obviously towelled himself off recently but droplets of water were still clinging in places. Caught in the sparse hair, for example, between the dark copper discs of his nipples.

'I've been swimming.'

Oh, help... He'd noticed her looking, hadn't he? Hastily, Summer dragged her gaze upwards again. His hair was wet and spiky and his expression suggested that he was as disconcerted as she was by their lack of clothing. Suddenly, it struck her as funny and she had to smile.

'No...really?'

'I'd offer you my towel but it's a bit damp.'

'I've been standing up. I'm not actually that wet.'

Just as she spoke, her dog emerged from his frolic in the waves, bounded towards them, stopped and then shook himself vigorously. It was like a short, sharp and rather cold shower.

'*Flint*... Oh, sorry about that. My bag's just over here. I've got a dry towel in there.'

'No worries.' Zac was laughing. He reached out his hand. 'Hey, Flint...'

The big dog sniffed the hand cautiously, wagged

a shaggy tail politely and then sat on the sand, close enough to lean on Summer's leg. He looked up and the question might as well have been a bubble in the air over his head.

Friend of yours? Acceptable company?

Summer touched the dog's head.

Yes. He's okay. I'm safe.

Maybe it was the genuine laughter that had made a joke of something many people would have found annoying. Or the way he'd reached out to make friends with Flint. She might not let people *too* close but she'd always trusted her instincts about their character and there was nothing here to be ringing alarm bells. Quite the opposite, in fact.

'So, do you need a hand dragging this thing somewhere? It looks heavy.'

'No. Jay'll come and get it soon. He's busy giving someone a lesson at the moment.' Turning the board sideways on the soft sand close to her brightly coloured beach bag, she sat down on one end. 'I'll just look after the board until he's done.'

'Jay?'

'He runs a paddleboard business. I hired one the first time I came to this beach and fell in love with it. I've been coming back ever since.'

'And Flint? He fell in love with it too?' Zac sat down, uninvited, on the other end of the board but somehow it felt perfectly natural. Welcome, even.

'He was in love with me.' The memory made Summer smile. 'Jay was going to look after him while I went for a ride, the first time I brought him here as a pup, but Flint wasn't having any of it. He just came after me. Luckily, Jay shouted loud enough for me to hear so I could fish him out of the water before he got so exhausted he sank. He fell asleep on the board coming back in and that's been his spot ever since.' She laughed. 'You're sitting on it right now. That's why he's standing there glaring at you.'

'Oh...my apologies.' Zac shuffled closer to Summer and Flint stepped onto the end of the board, turned around and then lay down in a neat ball with his nose on his paws.

Zac was so close to Summer now that she could feel the warmth of his skin. His *bare* skin. His legs were bent and she could see sand caught in the dusting of dark hair. The legs of his board shorts were loose enough to be exposing skin on his inner thigh that looked paler than the rest of him. Soft...

She cleared her throat as she looked away. Maybe that would clear inappropriate thoughts as well. 'So why Takapuna? Auckland's got a lot of beaches to choose from when you need an after-work dip.'

'It's been my backyard for ever. That's my gran's house up there.' He was pointing to the prestigious row of houses that had gardens blending into the edge of the beach. Multi-million-dollar houses. 'The old one, with the boat shed and the anchor set in the gate.'

It was impossible not to be seriously impressed. 'You *live* there?'

'I know...' Zac pushed his wet hair off his face. 'It's a bit weird. I'm thirty-six years old and I'm still living with my gran. But the house is on two levels. Gran's upstairs and I rent the bottom half and it's always just worked for both of us. She'd deny it but I think she's relieved to have me back. I'm relieved too, I have to admit. I worried about her while I was away. She's a bit old to be living entirely on her own.'

'A *bit* old? Didn't you say she was in her nineties?'

'Ninety-two. You wouldn't think so, though, if you met her. She reckons ninety is the new seventy.' Zac turned his head. 'She'd love to meet you. Would you like to come in for a drink or something?'

Summer turned her head as well and suddenly their faces were too close. She could see the genuine warmth of that invitation in his eyes. What was the 'something' on offer as well as a drink?

Whatever it was, she wanted it. The attraction was as strong as it was unexpected. She could feel the curl of it deep in her belly. A delicious cramp that eased into tendrils that floated right down to her toes.

She'd been fighting this from the moment she'd first seen this man this morning, hadn't she?

He was—quite simply—gorgeous…

It wasn't just his looks. It was his enthusiasm for his work. His charm. That smile. The way he loved his grandmother.

She couldn't look away. Couldn't find anything to say. All she could do was stare at those dark eyes. Feel the puff of his breath on her face. Notice the dark stubble on his jaw and how soft it made his lips look…

The board beneath her rocked a little as Flint jumped off. Maybe he'd knocked Zac slightly off balance and that was why he leaned even closer to her. It was no excuse, though, was it?

You really shouldn't kiss somebody you'd only just met. Somebody who you were probably going to be working with on an almost daily basis.

Summer couldn't deny that she'd been thinking about

kissing him. Couldn't deny that sudden attraction. Had it been contagious?

Who actually moved first or was it just the result of that movement on top of already sitting so close?

Not that it mattered. Nothing seemed to matter for the brief blink of time that Zac's lips touched her own. The touch was so electric that she jerked back instinctively. She'd never felt *anything* like that...

Flint's deep bark couldn't be ignored. Jay was walking towards them. The random sound of a frog croaking from her beach bag was another alert. She had a text message on her phone.

Real life was demanding her attention but, for a crazy moment, Summer wanted it to just go away. She wanted to sit on the sand as the sun set.

She wanted to kiss Zac again.

Properly, this time...

'So...' Zac had noticed Flint's enthusiastic greeting and must have guessed that it was Jay coming to collect the board. 'How 'bout that drink?'

Summer was also getting to her feet. She'd scooped up her bag and was checking her phone. It could be an emergency call-out.

Except it wasn't. It was a text from Kate.

It's driving me nuts trying to guess. You don't mean Zac M, do you? OMG. If it is, stay AWAY.

Somehow Summer managed a friendly introduction between Jay and her new work colleague despite the chaos in the back of her mind as memories forced themselves to the surface.

Driving Kate up to Auckland late that night because

Shelley had been hospitalised after an attempted suicide. Listening to the hysterical account of the man
she'd been abandoned by. The father of her baby. The
monster who'd tried to push her down a staircase when
he'd learned that she was pregnant...

So many buttons could be pushed by memories that
could never be erased.

And she'd actually wanted to *kiss* him again?

'I'll give you a hand closing up,' she heard herself
saying to Jay as he picked up her board. She barely
glanced over her shoulder. 'See you later, Zac.'

CHAPTER THREE

HE HAD NO one to blame other than himself.

How stupid had he been?

Even now, a good twenty hours after the incident, the realisation that he'd *kissed* Summer Pearson was enough to make him cringe inwardly. Or maybe it was an echo of the flinch his current patient had just made.

'Sorry, mate. It's just the local going in. It's a deep wound.'

'Tell me about it. As if it wasn't bad enough getting bitten by the damn dog, I had to rip half my leg open on the barbed wire fence getting away from it. Bled like a stuck pig, I did.'

'I'll bet.' Zac reached for the next syringe of local that Mandy had drawn up for him. 'Almost there. We can start stitching you up in a minute.'

'You won't feel a thing,' Mandy assured him. 'You've got the best doctor in the house.'

'At least he's a bloke. D'you know, there were two *girls* on the ambulance that came to get me?'

'Hadn't you heard, Mr Sanders?' Mandy's tone was amused. 'Girls can do anything these days. Can't we, Zac?'

'Absolutely. I'd say you were a lucky man, Mr Sanders. Can you pass me the saline flush, please, Mandy? I'd like to give this a good clean-out before we start putting things back together.'

He took his time flushing out the deep laceration. He'd do the deep muscle suturing here but he had every intention of handing over to Mandy to finish the task. It might do his patient good to realise that girls could be trusted to do all sorts of things these days.

Like fly around in helicopters and save people's lives. Not that he'd seen Summer do anything that required a high level of skill yesterday but he was quite confident that she had the capability to impress him. He was looking forward to a job that would challenge them both.

At least, he *had* been looking forward to it.

What had he been thinking on the beach yesterday evening? That because she seemed to be thawing towards him he'd make a move and ensure that she actually had a good reason to hate working with him?

Idiot…

Except it hadn't been like that, had it?

Zac reached for the curved needle with the length of absorbable suture material attached. He touched the base of the wound at one side.

'Can you feel that?'

'Nope.'

'Okay. Let me know if you do feel anything.'

'Sure will.'

Zac inserted the needle at the base of the wound and then brought it out halfway up the other side. Pulling it through, he inserted it in the opposite side at the same level and then pulled it through at the base again. This meant he could tie it at the bottom and bury the knots to reduce tissue traction, which would give a better cosmetic result.

His patient was happy to lie back on his pillow, his hands behind his head, smiling at Mandy, who was happy to keep him distracted while Zac focused on his task.

'What sort of dog was it, Mr Sanders?'

'No idea. Horrible big black thing. Bit of Rottweiler in it, I reckon, judging by the size of those teeth.'

Zac tried to tune out from the chat. Tried not to think about big black dogs. But the suturing was a skill that was automatic and it left his mind free to circle back yet again to how things had gone so bottom-up on the beach.

He'd been enjoying himself. Taking pleasure in sitting beside an attractive young woman, sharing his favourite place with someone who loved it as much as he did. Feeling as if he was making real progress in forging a new professional relationship because of the way Summer had been telling him about part of her personal life. Loving the idea of such a faithful bond between owner and dog that a bit of ocean wasn't about to separate them.

And suddenly something had changed dramatically. He'd been shoved sideways by the dog and Summer had been looking at him and it felt as if he was seeing who she really was for the first time and he'd liked what he was seeing.

Really liked it.

But he didn't go around kissing women just because he found them attractive. No way. He would never force himself on a woman, either. *Ever.* Being made to feel as if he had done that stirred feelings that were a lot less than pleasant.

The needle slid in and out of flesh smoothly and the wound was closing nicely but Zac wasn't feeling the satisfaction of a job being done well. He was in the same emotional place he'd been left in last night, when Summer had virtually dismissed him and walked away without a backward glance.

If it wasn't beyond the realm of something remotely believable, he might have decided that it was Summer who'd initiated that kiss but the way she'd jerked back in horror had made it very clear that hadn't been the case.

He felt as if he'd been duped. Manipulated in some incomprehensible way. Pulled closer and then slapped down. Treated unfairly.

The final knot of the deep sutures was pulled very tight. The snip of the scissors a satisfying end note.

Okay…he was angry.

He needed to put it aside properly before it had any chance of affecting his work. At least he was in the emergency department today. He was due for another shift on the helicopter tomorrow but maybe he'd find time to ring the base manager later and ask if he could juggle shifts.

With a bit of luck, he could find another crew to work with, without having to tell anybody why he couldn't work with Summer again.

The call-out had been more than welcome.

'Big MVA up north.' Her crew partner today was Dan. 'You ready to rock and roll, Summer?'

'Bring it on.'

It was very unfortunate for the people in the vehicles that had collided head-on at high speed on an open road, but Summer had been suffering from cabin fever for several hours by now. She needed action. Enough action to silence the internal conflict that seemed to be increasingly loud.

The usual distractions that a quiet spell provided hadn't worked. She should have made the most of the time to catch up on journal articles or do some work on the research project she had going but, instead, she'd paced around. Checking kits and rearranging stock. Cleaning things, for heaven's sake.

A bit like the way she'd acted when she'd got home last night and couldn't settle to cook or eat any dinner because she kept going over and over what had happened on the beach.

Trying to persuade herself that that kiss had been all Zac's idea. That she hadn't felt what she had when his lips had touched hers.

She was still experiencing those mental circles today and, if anything, they were even more confusing, thanks to that conversation she'd had with Kate late in the evening.

Of course he's charming. Why do you think Shelley fell for him so hard?

But it was more than a surface charm designed to lure women into his bed on a temporary basis.

Zac cared. About elderly patients. About small boys who might have been washed off a rock and drowned.

Small boys. Children. Presumably babies. And if he cared about other people's children, it just didn't fit that he'd abandoned his own. The story was getting old now. Maybe she hadn't remembered the details so well. Kate had been happy to remind her.

Yes...of course he knew Shelley was pregnant. That was why he tried to push her down the stairs.

So why hadn't Shelley pressed charges or demanded paternal support?

She was too scared to have anything more to do with him. And she planned to terminate the pregnancy, remember? Only, in the end, she didn't...

And Zac had been on the other side of the world by then. And Shelley had had one health issue after another. Always at the doctor's or turning up at the Hamilton emergency department Kate still worked in. Things hadn't changed much, either—except now it was her son who always seemed to be sick or getting injured. The whole family had to focus on supporting Shelley and little Felix and sometimes it was a burden.

'Are you going to tell Shelley?' she finally had to ask.

God, I don't know...I might have a chat to her psychiatrist about it. The new meds seem to be working finally, at the moment. It might be bad news to throw a spanner in the works...

It had been Summer who'd thrown the spanner. Not only at Kate but, potentially, at Zac, too. What if Shelley was told? If she took legal action of some kind and demanded a paternity test and back payment of parental support? Or, worse—if she went public with accusations of physical abuse? It could ruin the career Zac was clearly so passionate about. She would not only be responsible for things hitting the fan but she would be stuck in the middle having to work with him.

Why hadn't she just kept her mouth shut? It wasn't as if she saw Kate much these days and she hadn't seen Shelley since that night at the hospital.

But—if it was true—didn't he deserve to face the consequences?

That was the problem in a nutshell, wasn't it?

If it was true. She had no reason to believe it wasn't.

Except what her gut was telling her.

Thank goodness she could stop thinking about it for a while now. She had a job to focus on. A huge job. She could see the traffic banked up in both directions below them now. A cluster of emergency vehicles. She'd heard the updates on the victims. One patient was dead on scene. Another two were still trapped and one of them had a potential spinal injury. The other was having increasing difficulty breathing.

'He was initially responsive to voice,' the paramedic on scene told Summer. 'But he's become unresponsive, with increasing respiratory distress. We've got a wide bore IV in and oxygen on.'

'The passenger?'

'She's not complaining of any pain but she can't move her legs and they're not trapped. She's got a cervical collar on and someone holding her head still while they've been cutting the roof off.'

'And the van driver's status zero?'

'Yes. He was dead by the time we arrived, which was...' the paramedic checked his watch '...twenty-two minutes ago.'

The next few minutes were spent on a rapid assessment of the driver, who was the most critically injured. Summer took note of the jagged metal and other hazards as she went to lean into the car's interior.

'Any undeployed airbags?' Summer had to raise her voice to be heard over the pneumatic cutting gear the fire service were still using to open the badly crushed car.

'No.'

'Is the car stable?'

'Yes. We can roll the dash as soon as you're ready and then you can get him out. Passenger should be clear for extrication now.'

'Dan, can you coordinate that? I might need you in a minute, though. I'm going to intubate and get another IV in before we move the driver.'

He was already in a bad way and she knew to expect a clinical deterioration as soon as they moved him, even when it was to an area where it would be easier to work. Due to his level of unconsciousness, she didn't need any drugs to help her insert the tube to keep his airway safe. By the time she'd ensured adequate ventilation and got both high flow oxygen and some intravenous fluids running, Dan and his team had extricated the passenger and had her safely immobilised and ready for a slow road trip to the nearest hospital by ambulance.

Summer coordinated the fire crew to help lift the driver from the wreckage and get him onto the helicopter stretcher but she wasn't ready to take off yet. She crouched down at the foot of the stretcher so that she could see his exposed chest at eye level.

'Flail chest,' she told Dan. 'Look at that asymmetrical movement.'

'Here's his driver's licence.' A police officer handed it to Dan. 'His name's Brian Tripp. He's forty-three.'

They already had that information from his wife. There was paperwork the paramedics on scene first had completed. Summer had more important things to deal with. She could hear more clearly with her stethoscope now and she wasn't happy with what she could hear.

'I'm going to do a bilateral chest decompression before we fly,' she decided. 'Can you get the ECG monitor on, Dan? And start fluid resus.'

The only procedure Summer had to deal with a build-up of air in the chest that was preventing the lungs from expanding properly was to insert a needle. It was a temporary measure and it didn't help a lung to re-expand. It also didn't help a build-up of blood instead of air.

And that was the moment—in the midst of dealing with something that was taking her entire focus—that she thought about Zac again.

If only he'd been on board today instead of yesterday. He could have performed a much more useful procedure by actually opening the chest cavity. Not to put a drainage tube in, because that would take too much time, but it was the same procedure and left an opening that would be of far more benefit than the tiny hole a needle could make.

One that could—and did—get blocked when they were in the air only minutes later, even though Monty was keeping them flying low to avoid any pressure changes that could exacerbate the problem.

It was touch and go to keep her patient alive until they reached Auckland General and Summer was virtually running to keep up with the stretcher as they headed for Resus in the ground floor emergency department.

Who knew that Zac Mitchell would be leading the team waiting for them? The wave of relief was odd, given that she had yet to see how this doctor performed under pressure, but there was no denying it was there. Instinct again?

Was it Zac's expression as he caught her gaze? Focused. Intelligent. Ready for whatever she was about to tell him. Not that there was any time for information about what they'd found on scene—like the amount of cabin intrusion that had advertised a potentially serious chest injury. Even the name and age of their patient would have to wait.

'Tension pneumothorax,' she told Zac succinctly. 'Came on en route. He went into respiratory arrest as we landed.'

Within seconds, Zac was performing the exact procedure she had wished he'd been there to perform on scene. And he was doing it with a calm efficiency that—along with the evidence that her patient was breathing for himself again—made Summer even more relieved.

Her instincts about his skill level had not been wrong.

She wanted to stay and watch the resuscitation and assessment that would, hopefully, result in a trip to Theatre to have the major injuries dealt with but another call took her and Dan away with barely enough time to restock their gear.

This was a winch job to collect a mountain biker with a dislocated shoulder who was on a track with difficult access. A road crew were there to take over the care and transport of the patient so there was no return trip to hospital that would have given Summer the chance to find out what had happened to Brian.

She would have been happy to wait until tomorrow. Zac was due to fly with them again and they could have discussed the case. But the base manager, Graham, caught her when she was getting changed at the end of her shift.

'What did you do to Zac yesterday?'

'What do you mean?'

'I had a call. He didn't come out and say it directly

but he seems to think it might be better to be attached to a different shift. I told him there weren't any other slots and he said that was fine but...'

Monty was in the locker room at the same time. 'Summer doesn't like him.'

Graham gave her an odd look. 'What's not to like? He's got to be one of the best we've been lucky enough to have on board. What did you say to him?'

'I didn't say anything.'

'You didn't exactly roll out the welcome mat, Summer.' But Monty was smiling. 'And it's not like you to be shy.'

'It's got nothing to do with that.'

'What has it got to do with, then?' Both men were looking at her curiously.

What could she say?

That she knew things about Zac that they didn't know? She'd already caused disruption in other people's lives by telling Kate that he was back in town. How much more trouble would she cause by telling her colleagues? Word would get around in no time flat. She'd never been a troublemaker. Or a gossip, come to that. And it wasn't really any of her business, was it?

Or could she say that she'd met him on the beach last evening and ended up kissing him? That he was possibly so appalled at how unprofessional she'd been that he couldn't see himself being able to work with her again?

Things were getting seriously out of control, here.

'It's nothing,' she snapped. 'Leave it with me. I'll sort it.'

The excuse of getting an update on a major case was a good enough reason to pop into the emergency department on her way home.

Normally, it would be something to look forward to. A professional interaction and discussion that could well be of benefit in her management of similar cases in the future.

But what really needed discussing had nothing to do with her patient from the car accident. It was at the other end of the spectrum of professional versus personal. It felt like a minefield and it was one that had been created because she knew too much.

Or maybe not enough?

Summer felt ridiculously nervous as she scanned the department looking for Zac. He was at the triage desk, looking over Mandy's shoulder at something on a computer screen. When he glanced up and spotted Summer, he smiled politely.

She sucked in a breath. 'You got a minute?'

She looked different.

Maybe it was the clothes. He'd seen her in her flight suit and he'd seen her virtually in her underwear, given what that bikini had covered.

Even now, as he ushered her into his office, the memory gave him a twinge of appreciation that could easily turn into something inappropriate. Something to be avoided at all costs, given the way she had dismissed him so rudely on the beach last night.

It was easy enough to reconnect with the anger at being unfairly treated that was still simmering. Anger that had only received some new fuel by the demonstration of how Summer could blow hot and cold with no obvious encouragement.

He'd already been cool on greeting her. Hadn't said a thing, in fact. He'd just tilted his head with a raised eye-

brow in response to her request and excused himself to
Mandy before leading the way to his office. He'd seen
the surprise in Mandy's expression that he was taking
Summer somewhere private to talk. He was a bit surprised himself because there was no reason not to have
a professional discussion in front of others and he suspected Summer had come in to follow up on that serious chest injury she'd brought in earlier today.

Except that she looked different. Nervous, almost?

Nah…that seemed unlikely.

Easier to focus on what she was wearing. Leather
pants and a tight little jacket.

'You ride a bike?'

'Yeah… It's a requirement for employment on the
choppers that you can get to base fast. Even a traffic
snarl on the bridge is negotiable with a bike.'

'I know. I ride one myself. A Ducati.'

The quick smile was appreciative. 'Me, too. Can't
beat a Ducati.'

'No.' His tone was cool again. Zac wasn't ready for
another compass shift between hot and cold. It was
too confusing.

Her smile faded instantly. She looked away. 'I won't
take up too much of your time,' she said. 'I just came
in to…to apologise, I guess…'

Whoa…this was unexpected. And welcome? Was
she going to apologise for making him feel so unwelcome on shift yesterday?

She certainly looked uncomfortable. Zac perched on
the corner of his desk but Summer ignored the available
chair. She walked over to the bookshelf and looked as
if she was trying to read the dates on the thin spines
of the entire shelf of *Emergency Medicine Journals*.

'What happened last night was extremely unprofessional.' Her voice was tight. 'I just wanted to reassure you that it would never happen again.'

She was talking about the kiss rather than her treatment of him as a team member but this was a good start.

Better than good. So why did he have that dull, heavy sensation in his gut that felt remarkably like disappointment?

'And?'

Her head turned swiftly. Her jaw dropped a little. 'And…and I hope you won't let it influence you working on HEMS. Everybody's saying that we're very lucky to have you.'

'Everybody except you.'

Good grief…why couldn't he just accept her apology gracefully? They could shake hands and agree to make a fresh start in their new working relationship, which could solve the issue in the long run.

Because it would be shoving the issue under the carpet, that was why. Yes, they could probably find a way of working together but he'd never know *why* he'd made such a bad first impression.

Summer had bright spots of colour on her cheeks and her eyes were wide and uncertain. Almost…*fearful?* What the hell was going on here?

Zac stood up. He knew it was a bad idea the moment he did it because he was now towering over Summer. Intimidating her. To give her credit, however, he could see the way she straightened. Tilted her chin so that she could meet his gaze without flinching.

'What is it you don't like about me so much, Summer? You don't even *know* me.'

'I know *of* you.' There was a sharp note in her voice.

A note that said she was less than impressed with what she knew. Disgusted, even?

Zac's breath came out in a huff of disbelief. 'You amaze me,' he said slowly. 'And I don't mean that as a compliment.'

Anger flashed across her features. 'I grew up in Hamilton,' she snapped. 'I had a road job there as an intensive care paramedic. One of my oldest friends worked as a nurse in the emergency department. Kate, her name is. Kate Jones.'

'How nice for you.' Zac shook his head. 'I have no idea where this is going. Or who Kate Jones is. Or what relevance Hamilton has.'

'Kate has a younger sister who's also a nurse. Shelley Jones. Shelley used to work right here, in Auckland General's emergency department.'

Zac knew he was glaring at her. His eyes were still narrowed as something clicked into place.

'I remember her.' He could feel his mouth twisting into the kind of shape that came when you tasted something very unpleasant. 'She was a bit of a nuisance, in fact.'

'I'll bet she was.' Ice dripped from Summer's clipped words. 'I hope you don't have that kind of *nuisance* in your life too often.'

'What *are* you talking about?'

Her tone was sarcastic now. 'I guess getting girls pregnant could be seen as a bit of a nuisance.'

'*What?*' Time seemed to stop. Alarms sounded. He'd heard of men having their lives destroyed by false accusations of something like sexual abuse. His word against hers and the guy was always guilty until proved innocent. Sometimes it didn't make that much difference when the truth finally came out. Mud always stuck.

But...*pregnancy*?

'I never even went out with Shelley.' The words came out slowly. Cloaked in utter disbelief. 'The nuisance was that she had a fairly obvious crush on me. Kept bringing in gifts, like cakes or flowers. Leaving notes on my locker. Turning up in my street, even.' His anger was surfacing. 'If a guy did that to a girl, he'd be had up for stalking. She was a head case but everybody thought it was a joke.' He pushed stiff fingers through his hair. 'She was pregnant? She *told* people that *I* was the father?'

Shock like this couldn't be feigned.

Summer's mouth had gone completely dry. No wonder she'd been having so much trouble fighting her instincts. Zac was telling the truth.

'Only me and Kate.' She tried to swallow. Tried—and failed—to meet his gaze. 'It was when we had to go and see her when she got admitted to psyche after a suicide attempt.'

And she hadn't thought to query how stable Shelley was at that point? To even wonder if her story was accurate?

'Oh, this just gets better and better,' Zac snapped. 'Don't tell me—I was somehow responsible for this as well?'

He might as well know the worst. Would she want to, if she was in his position?

It was hard to get the words out, though. She really, really didn't want to make this any worse for him. She was only the messenger but a part of her knew she deserved to be shot. She'd treated him unfairly. Appallingly unfairly.

'She...um...told us you'd tried to push her down a flight of stairs. After...um...she'd told you about the baby.'

'And where was I when this was going on?'

'I think you'd left for London the day before.'

'How convenient.' Zac was pacing. Two steps in one direction and then an about-face for two steps back as if he felt the desperate need to go somewhere. Anywhere but here. He shoved his fingers through his hair, making the dark waves stand up in a tousled mess.

Then he stopped still and turned slowly to stare at Summer.

'And you *believed* her?'

She'd never felt so small. Strangely, he didn't look angry at the moment, although that would undoubtedly resurface. She could see disbelief. Deep disappointment. Anguish, even...

'As you said...I didn't know you. I'd never met you. All I knew was your name.'

'You met me yesterday.' Yes. There was anger there as well and the words were accusing. 'And you still believed it.'

Summer bit her bottom lip. Would it help to tell him how she'd had doubts from the first instant she'd set eyes on him? How she'd had to fight the feeling of being drawn closer? Of a connection that would have been exciting in any other circumstances? Of a confusion that had ultimately ended in wanting that kiss?

No. She had no excuses. For any of it. She closed her eyes.

'I'm sorry.'

'So am I.'

There was silence for a long moment. A heavy—
where do we go from here?—kind of silence that she
had no idea how to breach.

And then Zac sighed. He perched himself on the
corner of his desk again. Summer risked a glance but
he was staring at the floor.

'I guess it's better that I know about it,' he said finally. 'At least I'll be prepared for when she turns up
in the department again.'

'She gave up nursing. She's had a struggle with her...
um...mental health issues.'

Zac snorted.

'I haven't seen her since she was admitted that time.
I don't even see Kate much since I left Hamilton. Nobody else needs to know about this, Zac. I'm sorry I
knew. Or thought I knew. I wish she'd never mentioned
your name.'

'I'm sure you're not the only person she's "mentioned" it to. It's probably on some record somewhere.
Like a birth certificate? Oh, my God...' It was clearly
sinking home even deeper. 'She did *have* the baby?'

Summer nodded. Her cheeks were burning. 'She told
us she was going to have a termination but she didn't.
She went down south to stay with friends and apparently came back with the baby to land on her parents'
doorstep, asking for help. It was a boy. Felix. He'd be
about two and a half now.'

'So I'm probably on some social security list, somewhere. As a father who's failed to provide child support.'

Summer couldn't answer that.

'I hope I am,' Zac said surprisingly. 'A quick DNA

test will sort that out.' His huff was incredulous. 'I never even kissed her.'

He caught her gaze with those words. She completely believed that he'd never kissed Shelley.

But he had kissed her. And, for a heartbeat, that was all Summer could think of. That jolt of sensation that had been like some kind of electrical shock.

'It wasn't an immaculate conception,' Zac said dryly. 'It was an entirely imaginary one. Why, in God's name, would anybody *do* something like that?'

'I don't know,' Summer whispered.

Except—maybe—deep down, she did know. Zac Mitchell was the embodiment of a fantasy boyfriend. The ultimate husband and father for your baby. Something to dream about that was never likely to happen for real.

If you were desperate enough and maybe *sick* enough then, yes…she could imagine how somebody would do something like that.

But to make it so completely believable? That was what she really couldn't understand. Her instincts hadn't warned her about anything remotely off, that night. She'd still believed it after talking to Kate last night. Until she'd heard and seen the irrefutable truth in Zac's voice and body language.

'I'll tell Kate,' she offered. 'She can confront Shelley and get the truth out of her. She owes you one hell of an apology. We *all* owe you that.'

But Zac shook his head. 'I'd rather not rake it up any further. Not unless I have to. I'd rather move on and do what I came back here to do. Focus on my career and combine my ED work with as much time as possible in HEMS.'

'But you'd rather work with another shift?' Summer was trying to find what it was on the floor that had caught Zac's attention earlier. 'I could talk to Graham.'

'He said there weren't any other slots available.'

'I'm sure something could be juggled. A team has to be tight. It just doesn't work if there's a…a personality clash or something.'

Another silence fell. Summer finally had to look up and meet Zac's gaze. An unreadable gaze but the intensity was unmistakable.

'But we don't, do we?'

'Don't what?'

'Have a personality clash.'

She couldn't look away. She was being sucked in again. Like the way she had been when she'd been sitting beside him on the paddleboard last night. In that moment before she'd kissed him.

'No…'

'So why don't we just try and make a fresh start and see how it goes?'

Hope was something wonderful. A close cousin of both relief and excitement.

'You'd be okay with that?'

'If you are.'

It felt like the first time she was smiling at Zac. The first time it was a truly genuine smile, anyway.

Nothing else needed to be said because Zac smiled back.

The moment seemed to hang in time. And then it became just a little bit awkward. As though more was being communicated than either of them were ready for.

Zac cleared his throat. 'Do you want to hear about

the surgery on that tension pneumothorax guy you brought in?'

'Oh...' Summer's nod was probably a shade too enthusiastic. 'Yes, please...'

'Come with me. I'll show you the scans first. Man, that chest was a mess. I'm impressed that you got him here alive.'

Summer followed Zac out of his office. Their fresh start seemed to be happening now.

How good was that?

CHAPTER FOUR

ZAC'S BIKE WAS BIG, black and sleek.

It made Summer's smaller red model look feminine but the assumption would be deceptive. Only a certain kind of woman rode a machine like that.

Confident, feisty kind of women. And when they were wrapped up in a small package that could easily be seen as 'cute', it was a very intriguing mix. She must have arrived for work only seconds before he'd pulled into the rescue helicopter's base because she was standing beside her bike, pulling off her helmet. A glove came off next and the flattened spikes of her hair were fluffed up with a quick, spread finger comb-through—the feminine gesture at odds with the stance. With her feet apart and her helmet cradled under one arm making it look as if she had the hand on her hip, Summer Pearson looked ready to take on the world.

And she was watching him as he killed his engine and got off his own bike. Her gaze was…cautious?

Of course it was. This was the first time they were on base together after that extraordinary conversation in his office. And, yes, they'd agreed to make a fresh start and see how it went but how was that going to work, exactly? He'd had time to try and think it through but, if anything, he was finding it all increasingly disturbing.

Part of Zac—the angry part—wanted nothing more than to seek Shelley out and demand a retraction of accusations that were unbelievably malicious, but the voice of reason was warning him not to do anything without thinking it through very carefully. Yes, he could prove the child wasn't his but there were those appalling accusations of violence against a woman and that would be her word against his.

The people who knew him would never believe it but he didn't even want them to have to *think* about it. Imagine how upset his grandmother would be. It was something they never talked about these days—the way he'd seen his mother treated by the man who'd come into their lives when he'd been old enough to start remembering. Old enough to think that it was his fault and he needed to do something to defuse the tension that always ended with his mum bruised and crying.

Summer was taking his word for his innocence in regard to what she'd thought she knew about him. That was disturbing, too. Zac felt as though he still needed to prove himself in some way and he should never have had to feel like that.

There was a smudge of resentment in his mood and it was unfamiliar and unwelcome.

So maybe his gaze was just as cautious but they'd agreed to try a fresh start and Zac always kept his end of a bargain.

'Is that a Monster?'

'Yeah. A six five nine.' There was a definite note of relief in Summer's voice at the choice of an impersonal topic of conversation. A softening of her body language as she turned to look at *his* bike. 'About half the cc rating of yours, I expect.'

'Bet you'd still keep up. Maybe we should go for a ride one day.' The invitation was deliberately casual. A little forced, even? They were both trying to create a new base for a working relationship but the ice was potentially a little thin and they were both treading carefully.

'Sure. I like stretching out on the open road when I get a chance.'

They walked side by side into the building and Zac could feel some of the tension ease. Maybe it was more important than he cared to admit that he could prove himself to Summer. That it wasn't just his word she needed to trust but that she would get to know him well enough to understand just how impossible it would be for him to act in the way she'd believed he had acted. If he could convince someone who had believed the worst, he wouldn't need to fear any repercussions if the story became public.

Thinking about a place they could head to on a bike ride—like a beautiful beach, maybe—was premature, however. It was quite possible that Summer was just being polite, the way she was making it about the ride rather than his company. She'd had time to think things through in the last couple of days, too. Time to talk to her friend Kate again, perhaps. She might have changed her mind about taking his word for his innocence but was giving him the benefit of some doubt in the meantime. It wasn't just that she needed to trust him—he needed to trust her, as well. And right now his trust in women was justifiably fragile.

It certainly wouldn't be helpful to mention a beach.

To remind her of what had happened the last time they'd been sitting on a beach together. That had been even more premature. Unbelievably so, in fact. Zac still couldn't understand quite how that kiss had happened. Something else they needed to put behind them so they could move on with a more professional relationship? As far as building a base for their new working relationship, this was a minefield. Casual conversation was called for. The kind any new colleagues might have.

'You got four wheels as well as two?'

'No.' Summer gave him a quizzical glance. 'Why would I?'

'Doesn't it make things tricky when you want to take your dog somewhere with you?'

'We run.'

'*Everywhere?*'

Summer popped the studs on her jacket and started peeling it off. 'Everywhere we need to go, usually. If I have to take Flint to the vet or something, I'll get a friend to give us a ride. If I'm not at work or at home, we're generally at the beach. He gets a run there every day.'

'Guess I'll get to meet him again, then. I try and run on Takapuna beach every day.'

'Takapuna's our paddleboard beach. I have to use one of Jay's because it would be a bit tricky to carry one on a bike. If it's just a run or a swim we're after, we've got half a dozen beaches and bays to choose from. Or we can just jump overboard.'

'Sorry?' Zac was folding up his leather jacket. He couldn't see Summer because she was behind the open door of her locker now. He was sure he hadn't heard her correctly but then her face popped out and she was smiling. Really smiling. A real smile—like the one she'd given him in his office the other day, when they'd agreed to start again. A smile that could light up the darkest place.

'We live on a boat.'

'Oh…' Zac was lost for words. Just when he thought he was getting a handle on his new colleague, the rug got pulled out from beneath his feet. It wasn't just the unusual place to call home. That smile was doing something strange to his gut. It was more than relief that things seemed to be on a better footing. More, even, than the way it reminded him of what her lips had felt like for that brief instant. Maybe it was the impish quality—the hint of sheer *joie de vivre*—that made it impossible not to smile back.

'What sort of boat?'

'An old yacht. A thirty-foot Catalina. Her name's *Mermaid*. I'm not sure she'd be seaworthy to take out but I've been renting her to live in ever since I came up to Auckland. It's the only home Flint's ever known. He'd be a sad dog if he couldn't see the sea.'

'What does he do when you're at work?'

'Guards the boat. Or sleeps on the jetty. Everybody at the marina knows him. He's never wandered. Never needs a lead. He only wears a collar to hang his registration tag on and make him legal.'

Summer was pulling her flight suit on over her shorts and T-shirt. Her curves were disappearing beneath the shapeless garment and maybe that was just as well.

Zac was beginning to realise what an extraordinary woman Summer was. With the absence of the hostility with which they'd started working together, he was getting far more of a glimpse of what she was like. Fiercely independent, judging by her choice of lifestyle. Open-minded, maybe, given that she was prepared to take his word over that of a long-term friend. The relationship she had with her dog suggested a mutual loyalty and—a bit like her pet—maybe she was a free spirit who chose exactly where she wanted to be and who she wanted to be with. You couldn't lead Summer anywhere she didn't want to go.

But how privileged would you be if she chose to go with you?

Hang on a minute...she'd said 'we' live on a boat. He'd assumed she was talking about herself and her dog but what if there was another component to that 'we'?

That might go even further than both the misinformation on his past and prematurity in having made that kiss so shocking for her. No wonder this all felt so complicated.

Zac took a mental step backwards. Yep. He really did need to tread a little more carefully. There was still a lot more he needed to learn about Summer.

A trip to one of the inhabited islands right out in the Hauraki Gulf was always a bit of a treat. The longer flying time provided an opportunity to enjoy the spectacular views below. The harbour was busy, with ferries and yachts out enjoying the afternoon breeze. There was even a sleek cruise ship in the channel between Rangitoto Island and Takapuna beach.

'Tough day at the office.'

Summer laughed. 'You said it, Monty. And—even better—we're off to deliver a baby.'

'Might have arrived by the time we get there,' Zac warned. 'How far apart did she say her contractions were?'

'Five minutes. And Comms said she sounded a bit distressed.'

'I'm not surprised. It's an isolated place to give birth if something goes wrong.'

'She might be a bit earlier than full-term. It's usual practice for women to go to the mainland for delivery.' Summer was still enjoying the view. 'That's Tiritiri Matangi island. You ever been there?'

'No. Love lighthouses, though. It's a bird sanctuary, isn't it?'

'Yes. It's well worth a visit.' Summer took a breath, about to say something more, but then she closed her mouth.

Had she been about to suggest that they took a ride up to Gulf Harbour on their bikes the next time they had a day off at the same time? And then take the ferry and walk around the island, seeing things like the feeding stations that attracted hundreds of bellbirds and tuis?

Yep. Even now, the idea of spending a day like that with Zac was extremely appealing but he might have just been being polite, suggesting that they had a ride together. After all, it was a working relationship they'd agreed to make a fresh start on, not a personal one.

Wasn't it?

They were met at the landing site by a man called Kev, who was in charge of Civil Defence and the volunteer fire brigade for the small community. A retired fisherman with an impressive white beard, Kev had an ancient jeep to provide transport. The local nurse was unavailable to assist because she'd taken the ferry to the mainland to go shopping.

'Janine? Yep. I know where she lives. Haven't seen her for a while but she likes to keep to herself. She's sick?'

'In labour, apparently.'

'She's having a *baby*?'

Summer caught Zac's glance as he lifted the Thomas pack of gear into the back of the jeep. This was odd. In such a small community, surely a full-term pregnancy wouldn't go unnoticed?

Kev started the engine. It coughed and died so he tried again. This time it caught but he was shaking his head.

'A baby...well...how 'bout that?'

Summer climbed into the vehicle. 'You didn't know she was pregnant?'

Kev grinned. 'She's a big girl, is Janine. Can't say I noticed last time either, mind you.' He clicked his tongue. 'That was a sad business...'

'Oh? In what way?' Under normal circumstances, it might not be ethical to be discussing a patient with someone who wasn't a family member but the comment was ringing alarm bells. If the last birth had caused major problems, they needed to know about it.

'She did all the right things. Went to the big hospital in Whangerei to have the bub. Dunno what happened exactly, but it didn't come home. Janine was in bits. Broke her and Ev up in the end. He lives over on the mainland now but she goes off on the ferry to visit him sometimes so... Guess they must have decided to try again. She shouldn't be having it here, though, should she? Crumbs...what if something goes wrong again?'

'That's why we're here.' Zac's tone was calm. Reassuring. 'How far is it to her house?'

'It's not a house, exactly. More like a caravan with a bit built on. It's not too far. Up in the bush at the end of this beach coming up.'

'Does she have any family here?'

'Nah.'

'Friends?'

Kev scratched his beard as he brought the jeep to a halt. 'She gets on okay with everybody but, like I said, she keeps to herself pretty much. 'Specially since the trouble. Want me to come in with you?'

Summer caught Zac's gaze. There could be a reason why Janine had been keeping her pregnancy private.

'How 'bout you wait out here for us, Kev? We'll see what's happening and hopefully you can get us all back to the chopper pretty fast.'

Except that it didn't look as if they'd be moving their patient any time too soon.

Janine was inside the caravan, hanging onto the edge of the built-in table with one hand and clutching her belly with the other. She saw Summer and Zac ease themselves into the cramped space but clearly couldn't say anything in response to their introductions. Her face was contorted with pain.

'Contraction?'

Janine nodded, groaning at the same time.

'How long since the last one?'

Their patient shook her head. 'Dunno,' she gasped.

'Have your waters broken?'

A nod this time.

'We need to check what's happening,' Zac said. 'Would you prefer it if Summer examines you?'

Janine shook her head. 'You're the doctor. I'm...
scared...'

'Let's get you on your bed.' Summer took Janine's
arm to encourage her to move. 'We can help you. It
might help us if you can tell us about what happened
last time...'

But Janine burst into tears as she climbed onto the
narrow bed. She covered her face with her hands. Summer could see the swell of the young woman's belly now
that she was lying flat. She helped her bend her knees so
that Zac could find out how advanced the labour was.

He was frowning when he looked up a short time
later.

'No dilation whatsoever,' he said. 'No cervical softening, even.'

'Really?' Summer placed her hands on Janine's belly.
'Let's see if I can find out how Baby's lying.'

The swollen belly felt firm. And oddly smooth.

'Has Baby been moving?'

'Yes. Lots. Until this morning, anyway...'

Zac was unpacking the portable ultrasound unit.
'Have you been going over to the mainland for your
antenatal checks, Janine?'

'No...' She turned her head away from them. 'I didn't
trust the doctors at the hospital. Or the midwives. Not
after last time...'

'What happened, love?' Zac paused, the tube of gel
in his hands.

'It was all fine until I was in the hospital. They said
it was a knot in the cord and it...it stopped the oxygen.
I knew something was wrong but they were still telling
me to push and I...I...'

'It's okay, Janine.' Summer caught her hand. 'You're

having contractions now but you're nowhere near giving birth. We're going to get you to a safe place in plenty of time.'

Zac was pressing the ultrasound probe to Janine's belly, staring at the small screen of the unit. He was frowning again. He shifted the probe and tilted the screen so that Summer could see it. She stared too, totally bewildered.

'We just need some more gear,' Zac said calmly. 'We want to take your blood pressure and things, Janine. Be back in a tick.'

But... Summer stifled the word. They had all the gear they needed in the pack right beside them but she recognised the warning glance and followed Zac into the lean-to built onto the caravan that was a living area with armchairs and a potbelly stove.

She kept her voice low. 'There's no baby, is there?'

Zac shook his head.

'But she *looks* pregnant. She's having contractions. She's in *labour.*'

'She *thinks* she's in labour.' Zac spoke just as quietly. 'This is incredibly rare but I think it's a case of pseudocyesis.'

'Phantom pregnancy? Good grief...what do we do?'

'She needs help. When she finds out that she's not actually pregnant, it's going to be as devastating as losing her first baby. This isn't the time or place for that to happen.'

'So we go along with it? Transport her, believing that she's still about to give birth? Give her pain relief for the contractions?'

'What else can we do?'

There was no answer to that. Getting Janine to the

specialist psychiatric help she needed was a no-brainer. Making the situation even harder to deal with would have been a stupid option. It took a lot of persuasion to get Janine to agree to transport at all.

'I want to have my baby here. Where it's safe.'

'But it's not safe, Janine. You're too far away from the kind of specialist people and facilities that make it safe. And it's not going to happen for a while. We can't stay but we can't leave you here by yourself either.'

Finally, she agreed. She told Summer where the bag was with all the things she would need for the baby. A glance inside the bag showed some gorgeous hand-knitted booties and hats. A soft pink teddy bear. She was blinking back tears as they helped Janine into the jeep.

'You should've told us, love.' Kev looked worried. 'We were worried about you.'

'I'll be fine, Kev. I'll be back soon. With the baby.'

It was the strangest case Summer had ever had. She was still thinking about it that evening when she was walking on the beach with Flint.

She'd known there was a good chance of meeting Zac on Takapuna beach. It was easy enough to guess what time he was likely to be having a swim or a run. Maybe that was why she'd chosen this beach, despite not intending to go paddleboarding today. Maybe she wanted the chance to talk about such a puzzling case.

He'd been good to work with today. The fresh start was working well. Maybe there was even a pull to see him again that she wasn't about to admit to.

The excuse that this was where some of Flint's best dog friends came to play was a good cover. And Zac seemed happy enough to sit and chat.

'It was a good day, wasn't it? It's not often you get a "once in a lifetime" case like that.'

'I still can't believe that something imaginary could give rise to actual physical signs.'

'The power of the mind.' Zac nodded. 'It's extraordinary, isn't it?'

'The things she said when I was getting her history down en route. Like the date her periods stopped and the early nausea and breast changes. Feeling the baby starting to move at about sixteen weeks. Everything sounded so normal.'

'She'd been through it before. She knew what to expect.'

'But do you think she could actually feel what she thought was the baby moving?'

'I'm sure she could.'

'And the size and shape of her belly. I couldn't believe it when the ultrasound showed there was no baby.'

'I've read about it. They reckon it's due to changes in the endocrine system. When a woman wants to be pregnant so desperately, it can trick the body into believing it's pregnant, as well as the mind. That triggers the secretion of hormones like oestrogen and prolactin and that will stop periods and cause breast changes and nausea. And the weight gain and belly swelling. So, of course, there's no reason for her to stop believing she's pregnant—it just gets confirmed.'

'But for so many months? To actually go into an imaginary labour?'

'That's really rare. I think that psychiatrist that got called in looked quite excited about the case. He'll probably write it up for a journal article.'

'I just hope he takes good care of Janine. Poor thing.'

'Yeah... You have to feel sorry for her.'

They sat in silence for a while, then, watching Flint do the sniffing thing to greet a small black Spoodle. With an excited yap, the Spoodle ran in a circle and then dipped its head, inviting Flint to chase her. He complied and, a moment later, both dogs were splashing though the shallows at high speed against the backdrop of a pretty sunset over Rangitoto.

Summer felt her smile stretching. Life was good. Shifting her gaze, she found Zac smiling as well and, suddenly, there they were again. Looking at each other like they had been when they'd been sitting on her board the other night.

Only this time it felt different.

Relaxed.

The tension was gone and, just as suddenly, Summer thought she knew why.

'It's been bothering me,' she admitted. 'Why I believed Shelley. My instincts are usually so good about whether people are telling the truth. But it's like Janine, isn't it? What you said about the power of the mind.'

'Not sure I'm following you.'

'If we hadn't had that ultrasound with us, I would have believed Janine was pregnant.'

'She was certainly convincing.'

'So was Shelley.'

'But Shelley *was* pregnant.'

'I'm talking about the other stuff. About you being the father and...' No, she didn't even want to think about the accusations of violence. Zac had been so kind to poor Janine and the compassion in his voice had suggested he felt as sorry for her as others should. He'd made a terrifying situation bearable for Frances the other day. He adored his gran. It would be insulting to even voice something so unbelievable. 'But maybe she was believable because that's what she believed herself.'

Zac grunted. 'She's pretty sick, then.'

'Like Janine.'

'Janine's only hurting herself.'

'We don't know that for sure. There could be collateral damage for others—like her ex-husband? He might be involved enough to believe he's about to have another child.'

'I guess. You could be right. Maybe feeling sorry for Shelley is the best way to go.' Zac's sigh suggested that he didn't want to talk about it any more and that was fair enough.

Flint was shaking water from his coat as the Spoodle took off to rejoin its owner further down the beach. Any moment now and he'd probably come back, all damp and sandy, and she might have to excuse herself to go and finish their walk. Or maybe not. Zac might not want to talk about Shelley any more but he didn't seem annoyed when he spoke again.

'So you have good instincts, then?'

'I've always thought so.'

'Just out of interest—given what you thought you knew—what did those instincts tell you about me the other day?'

That was easy to answer. 'That you couldn't possibly be the monster I'd assumed you were.' She smiled. 'No one but an exceptionally nice person could start talking about his gran the moment he opened his mouth.'

Zac grinned and Summer found herself saying more than she'd intended to say. 'I liked you,' she admitted. 'It felt wrong but I... I *really* liked you.'

Zac was silent for a moment. It looked as if he might be taking a rather slow breath. Then he cleared his throat. 'Just for the record, I really liked you too. I still do.'

Another silence as Summer absorbed his words. Oh, yeah... Life was good.

'And what did those instincts tell you when we were on the beach the other night? When I...kissed you.'

'But *I* kissed *you*.'

'I don't think so.' There was amusement in his tone. 'At least, that's not the way I remember it.' He caught her gaze. 'You wouldn't have been so shocked if it had been your idea,' he added. 'You jumped like you'd got burned.'

'That was because it felt...weird...'

'Weird?'

'Yeah...' Summer had to break the eye contact. 'Different. Yeah...weird.'

'Hmm.' Another pause and then the query was interested. 'Good weird or bad weird?'

Summer tried to remember that odd jolt. To feel it again. But all that she was aware of was a growing warmth in her belly, spreading into her limbs. A tingly, delicious kind of warmth.

'I think...good weird.'

'But you're not sure?'

'No...' *Oh, my...* That look in Zac's eyes right now. The sheer mischief. The *intent*...

'I'm thinking there's only one way to find out.'

Did he mean what she thought he meant? That he would have to kiss her again?

Had he really thought he'd been the one who'd initiated the kiss the other night?

There could only be one explanation for that. That they'd both been thinking exactly the same thing. At the same time.

And they were doing it again right now. Summer's heart skipped a beat and picked up its pace.

Or maybe not.

'Not here,' Zac said. 'It's way too public.'

The disappointment was fleeting because the prospect of being somewhere more private was infinitely more exciting. Zac was already on his feet, ready to take her to that private place. Summer's heart was still thumping and now her mouth felt a little dry.

Or maybe not.

'Come and meet my gran.'

CHAPTER FIVE

HE'D WANTED TO take her home.

So he could kiss her again. Properly. Last time it had been a kind of accident that didn't count but even the memory of that brief brush of their lips gave him a twist of very powerful desire. And Summer remembered it well enough to think it was different? Weird but good?

She had no idea how good it *could* be…

It would have sounded crass to say that out loud and it could well have scared her off completely so he'd had to come up with another reason to get them away from such a public place.

But introducing her to his grandmother?

Now they were stuck. Flint looked happy enough on the terrace outside and Summer looked happy enough inside. Zac had come back from taking a quick shower and changing his clothes to find her helping his gran put a salad together—to go with the massive salmon fillet that just happened to have been baking in the oven this evening.

Ivy Mitchell had been thrilled to meet Summer.

'So you're the girl who has the dog on the back of the board? I watch you every time, dear. With my tele-scope.'

'Really?' Summer looked disconcerted. 'I had no idea people were spying on me.'

'Oh, I spy on everybody, darling. I'm ninety-two. Nobody's going to tell me off.'

'I might,' Zac growled. 'You can't go around spying on people, Gravy.'

'I'm not gainfully employed. I sit on my terrace and the telescope's right there. What's a girl supposed to do?'

Summer was laughing. And shaking her head. 'Gravy?'

Ivy smiled. 'I told Isaac's mum that I didn't want to be called Granny. I wasn't even sixty when he was born, for heaven's sake. Far too young! I said he could call me Ivy, like a real person, but she said I had to be Gran. So it was supposed to be Gran Ivy but it was too hard for him when he was learning to talk so it came out as Gravy. And it stuck.'

'I love it. The only grandmother I had was Nana, which seems terribly ordinary in comparison.'

'Had?'

'She died when I was quite young.'

'What a shame. The older generation is a blessing. Your family must miss that.'

'I don't have any family. My mum died when I was seventeen and my father was already well out of the picture.' Summer's tone was brisk and Zac recognised that it was not a topic open to further discussion. It reminded him of that first day in the chopper when he'd asked whether she had any siblings. The impression that she could offer personal information but he was not allowed to ask had been so strong he still hadn't tested those boundaries. He had boundaries of his own, didn't he? It might be unspoken but there was an agreement between them now that precluded any more discussion of Summer's friend Kate and her sister Shelley. Of the child he'd been accused of fathering.

Not that Ivy was likely to respect such boundaries. Except that this time she did. She opened her mouth but then closed it again, simply handing Summer a jar with a screw lid. 'Throw this dressing on the salad, darling. I make it myself and it's got a lovely garlic punch. So good for you, you know—garlic.'

'It's your secret to a long life, isn't it, Gravy?'

'That—and champagne, of course. Speaking of which, let's refresh our glasses, shall we, Summer? Champagne and salmon—a marriage made in heaven.'

Zac took a pull at the icy glass of lager he held. The view from the upper level of this old house was extraordinary—like a huge painting of a beach scene with the background of the sea and the distinctive volcano shape of Rangitoto Island placed perfectly dead centre. Right now, there were vivid streaks of red in the sky as daylight ended with a spectacular flourish. He had always loved the changing panorama of this living painting. He loved this house. Right now, he loved that a contented dog lay with his nose on his paws guarding the house and its occupants. He could smell good food and he was with the person who meant the most to him in the world—his beloved Gravy.

Could life get any better?

Maybe it could.

He was also with an extraordinary newcomer to his life. The idea of getting to know Summer a great deal better was exciting. Maybe—just maybe—this was the woman who could capture him enough to be the person he had yet to find. The one who could come to mean as much—or possibly even more—than his only family member.

The possibility was as breathtaking as the view.

Zac watched the conspiratorial grin between the two women as they clinked champagne flutes and he had to smile. Kindred spirits? They were certainly getting on very well together. He just hoped that second glass of bubbles wouldn't loosen his grandmother's tongue any further. Bad enough that she'd already admitted spying on Takapuna residents as they enjoyed their beach. How much worse would it be if she started on another favourite theme—that it was high time her grandson found a nice girl and settled down to start making babies?

As if she felt both the gaze and his smile, Summer turned her head and her gaze locked with his. And there was that kick of desire in his gut again. How long would it take them to eat dinner and escape? To find somewhere they could be alone together?

Maybe Summer was telepathic. He could see the way her chest rose as if she was taking a deep breath. The way her eyes darkened, suggesting that her thoughts mirrored his. When the tip of her tongue appeared to wet her lips, he almost uttered a growl of frustration. However long dinner took, it was going to be too long.

If Summer was lucky enough to live until she was in her nineties, she wanted to be exactly like Ivy Mitchell.

A little taller than Summer, Ivy was very slim but it would be an insult to call her frail. She had long silver hair that was wound up into an elegant knot high on the back of her head and her clothing was just as chic, white Capri pants and a dark blue tee shirt with a white embroidered anchor on it. As someone with sea water in her veins, maybe that was why she'd instantly felt at ease with Zac's grandmother.

Unusually at ease. Was it the age gap? Way too much to be a friend or a colleague. Too much, even, to be an age group that invited comparison to her mother, which was a good thing because Ivy's relaxed confidence, that was so like her grandson's, would have made her mother's constant anxiety seem awkward.

Or maybe it was because she had the same warm brown eyes as her gorgeous grandson. Whatever the reason, Summer was enjoying herself and feeling increasingly relaxed, which was ironic because the energy level emanating from Ivy was leaving her feeling rather breathless.

Or maybe that had something to do with the way Zac was looking at her every time she met his gaze. As if he really liked what he was seeing. As if he couldn't wait to see more.

And eating dinner with these two...

Oh, my...

Watching food going into Zac's mouth and the way he licked the corners of his lips occasionally to catch a drip of salad dressing was doing very strange things to her equilibrium.

This was crazy. She'd only met him last week. Summer Pearson did not go around jumping into bed with men she'd only just met. Especially men she hadn't even been on a date with. But what if time together counted, even if it hadn't been prearranged? Sitting on a beach with someone was *almost* like a date, wasn't it?

If Ivy had any idea of where her thoughts kept drifting, she wasn't bothered.

'So you live on a boat? I love that. But isn't it a bit cramped?'

'We manage. You do have to be tidy. And not collect too much junk.'

'We?' Ivy's eyebrows shot up. 'You have a *man* in your life, Summer?'

'Ah…' Summer kept her gaze firmly on the flakes of salmon she was spearing with her fork. 'Only Flint. He has to be tidy, too.'

'Of course he does.' There was a satisfied note in Ivy's voice and Summer looked up to catch the significant look she was giving Zac. There might have been an eyebrow wiggle involved as well.

It was cringe-worthy but then Zac grinned at her and winked and suddenly it was fine.

More than fine.

Summer grinned back. She had just fallen a little bit in love with Zac Mitchell.

'You know, I think I've been a bit of a pelican,' Ivy declared. 'My eyes held more than my belly can. Do you think Flint might be able to finish this for me? Salmon's not bad for dogs, is it?'

'It would be a huge treat for him.'

'Let's bring him inside, then.'

'Oh, I don't think you want to do that. You have no idea how much sand gets trapped in those fluffy paws.'

'Pfft…' Ivy waved her hand. 'What's a bit of sand between friends? I track it in every day myself.'

Summer went to invite Flint inside. Ivy insisted on giving him the salmon off her own plate and Summer shook her head but she was smiling. She had just fallen a little bit in love with Zac's grandmother as well.

'Where does he sleep?' Ivy asked. 'On the boat?'

'Yes. He has his own bed under the cockpit. A double berth, even.'

'Oh…I hope you have a double berth, too…'

Zac's sigh was clearly audible but Ivy winked at Summer. 'Don't mind me,' she said in a stage whisper. 'When you get to my age, you find you can get away with saying almost anything. Sometimes I might get a wee bit carried away.'

Summer smiled. 'I have a very comfortable double bed, Ivy. It's even got an inner-sprung mattress. Speaking of which…' she only had to straighten and look towards the door and Flint was instantly by her side '… I'd better get going. I've got an early start tomorrow.'

Zac pushed his chair back and got to his feet.

The air seemed to have disappeared from the room. What was going to happen now? Would he show her out and kiss her goodnight? How likely was that when Ivy would probably be peeping from a window?

'I'll give you a lift,' he said. 'It's too late to be jogging around the streets.'

'Thanks, but I don't let Flint run after a bike. It's a bit dangerous.'

'Ah…' Zac was almost beside her now. 'Unlike you, I keep four wheels as well as two. I have an SUV with a nice big space for a dog in the back.'

'It'll get full of sand.' But Summer's heart was doing that speeding up thing again. Zac was coming home with her? Would he want to stay for a while?

He was close enough to touch now. She could feel the heat of his body. Or maybe that was heat she was creating herself. A warmth that kicked up several notches as he grinned lazily.

'What's a bit of sand between friends?'

He kissed his grandmother. 'Leave the dishes,' he ordered. 'I'll pop in and do them when I get back.'

Ivy waved them off. 'That's what dishwashers are for. I'll see you tomorrow, Isaac. Don't do anything I wouldn't do, now.'

Zac groaned softly as he closed the door behind them. 'Sorry about that,' he muttered. 'She's incorrigible.'

He'd never been in a yacht that was being used as a permanent home. He'd been sailing, of course. Anyone who grew up beside the sea in Auckland ended up with more than a passing acquaintance with sailing boats.

'She's thirty feet? Feels much bigger inside.'

'It's a great design. Small but perfectly formed.'

Just like Summer?

Zac had to drag his gaze away from her. He'd only just stepped aboard *Mermaid* and, while the invitation to see her home had been freely given, he didn't want to push things too fast, here.

He didn't want to wreck something. Not when so many possibilities were floating so close to touching distance. Mind you, if his gran hadn't scared her off, he was probably in a good space right now.

An astonishing space. There was colour from the warm glow of all the woodwork. A rich blue cushion and padding covered the built-in bench seating around a narrow table and the colour was repeated in a strip of Persian-style carpet down the centre of the floor. The front of the boat's interior was almost closed off by a folding fabric screen but he could see a glimpse of a raised bed with a soft-looking white duvet and fluffy pillows.

Once again, he had to avert his gaze before what he was thinking got printed all over his face.

'Cute sink.'

'It works well, even if it's a single rather than a double. Gives a bit more bench room for cooking. I've got an oven here and even a microwave in this locker, see?'

'Mmm.'

What he liked best about this space was that there wasn't that much room for two people to move around, especially when there was a fairly large dog to avoid, and it was inevitable that they ended up standing extremely close to each other. He had to bend his head a little to admire the microwave oven tucked neatly into its storage space and that put his face extremely close to Summer's as well. Without looking up, he lifted a hand to close the locker and, as he lowered his hand, it felt perfectly natural to brush the spikes of her hair. To let his hand come to rest at the nape of her neck.

To bend his head just a little further so that he could touch her lips with his own. Just a feather-light touch for a heartbeat and then he increased the pressure and touched her lips with his tongue. He felt Summer's gasp as a physical change in her body—the kind of tension that a diver probably had in the moment before she launched herself into space to perform some dramatic series of tumbles and then slice cleanly into the deepest pool. And, as Summer's lips parted beneath his, he knew she had taken that plunge and she was ready to fly.

He had no idea how long they stood there kissing. Zac was aware of nothing more than the delicious taste and the responsiveness of this gorgeous girl. And that the ground was moving slightly beneath his feet. Because they were on a boat? It felt more personal than that. His whole world was gently rocking.

Time had absolutely no relevance because it didn't matter how long it took to explore this wonderful new world. The map was coming into focus and there was no hurry at all to find the right path. The way Summer took the lead to follow that path was possibly the most exciting part about it. She wanted this—as much as he did.

It was her hands that moved first, to disentangle themselves from around his neck to start roaming his body, and that gave him permission to let his own hands move. To shape the delicate bones of her shoulders and trace the length of her spine. To cup the deliciously firm curves of her bottom and the perfection of those surprisingly generous breasts.

It was Summer who took his hand and stopped him undoing another button on the soft shirt she was wearing and, for a moment, Zac had the horrible thought that she was asking him to stop completely. He could, of course, but man, would he need a cold shower when he got home…

It was time to get rid of the audience. A quiet command sent Flint to his bed. Her voice might have wobbled a little but Summer was still holding Zac's hand tightly. She led him to the other end of the boat. Past the screen and up a step to where her bed filled the whole space.

No. It was Zac who was filling this space. The only light was coming from a lamp on the table and the shadows being created gave shedding their clothes a surreal edge—like a scene from an arty movie. And then Zac was kneeling on the bed in front of her and she could flatten her hands against the bare skin of his chest as she raised her face for another kiss and she stopped thinking about the way anything looked. She could only *feel*...

No wonder she'd been shocked by that first ever touch of Zac's lips. She'd never known that arousal could be this intense. That nerve endings could be so sensitised by the lightest touch that the pleasure was almost pain. It was still weird because she'd never felt anything like this before but it was most definitely *good* weird.

Oh, yes...the best weird ever, and she could get used to this.

She wanted to get very, very used to it.

CHAPTER SIX

'Target sighted—two o'clock.'

The helicopter dipped and shuddered as Monty turned to circle the area. The stiff breeze made the top of the pine forest below sway enough to make an accurate estimation of clearance difficult.

'Not sure I like this,' Monty said. 'Might need to winch you guys in.'

'There's more of a clearing at five o'clock. Where the logging trucks are.'

'It's a fair hike. The guy's having trouble breathing.'

'Winch me down,' Summer said. 'I'll scoop him into the Stokes basket and we can transfer him to the clearing to stabilise him.'

'You happy for Zac to winch you?' Monty's query sounded casual but this was the first time they'd been in a situation like this. In rough weather like this. Yes, Zac was winch trained but Summer would be putting her life in his hands.

She caught Zac's gaze, and even through the muting effect of the visor on his helmet she could see—or maybe sense—the anticipation of her response and, in that instant, a seemingly casual query became so much bigger than being simply about the job they were all doing.

Did she trust Zac?

She *wanted* to. She had never wanted to trust anybody this much. Not with her life because she did that every time she took on a tricky winching job and she was used to putting that kind of trust in her colleagues.

No. This was about trusting a man with her heart and she'd never really done that before. But she *wanted* to. With Zac...

Monty was hovering over the area where the felling accident had occurred. An ambulance was bouncing along the rough track and stopped with a cloud of dust billowing from beneath its wheels.

'Let's wait and see what the crew thinks. We've only had the first aider's story so far.'

The small reprieve in decision-making gave Summer the chance to let her mind go further down that secret pathway.

She was more than a little bit in love with Zac Mitchell. Maybe it had started that night he'd winked at her across his grandmother's table last week. Or maybe it had started even before that—when he'd called that frightened elderly woman 'sweetheart' on that first job they'd ever done together.

The point of ignition didn't really matter now, anyway. What did matter was what happened next. She might want to take that next—huge—step of trusting him completely but it was debatable whether she was capable of it. Summer had no experience of going that far in a relationship but a lot of experience in pushing people away when she sensed any kind of a threat. She'd learned how to do that a very long time ago, when she'd only been a teenager. When she'd pushed her previously beloved father completely out of her life. She'd pushed other men away too, when they started to get too close.

That excuse of her career being more important wasn't really the truth at all, was it? She'd always had that whisper of warning that came in her mother's voice.

You can never trust a man. No matter how much you love them, it's never enough. They'll break your heart. Break you...

She was even pushing her best friend out of her life at the moment. There was a call she hadn't returned and a text message she'd brushed off with a breezy response that gave nothing away. Kate had no idea what was going on in Summer's life—that she was so far down the track of falling in love with the 'monster' who she believed had ruined her sister's life. Summer wasn't about to tell her, either. It was bad enough having the whisper of warning that was the haunting legacy her mother had left. Imagine adding the kind of poison that Kate couldn't help but administer, given her loyalty to Shelley? It would meld with that warning and she would have to start wondering if she was being as blind as her mother had been when she'd fallen in love so completely with her father.

That whole business with Shelley was a subject that she and Zac had put behind them by tacit consent and maybe she didn't want to hear what Kate had to say, anyway, because she wanted to trust Zac so much. She'd never met anyone remotely like him before and she instinctively knew that the odds of it happening again were non-existent.

This was her chance of finding out what it might be like. To be truly, utterly in love. And instinct was telling her more than how unique this situation was. Summer was also aware, on some level, that all it would require for her to take that final step of trust was to know that Zac felt the same way.

Telling Monty that she was prepared to put her life in Zac's hands on the end of the winch would have sent an unspoken response to that anticipation she'd sensed. It would have probably taken their newly forged bond to the next level—one that might have made it the right time to open their hearts a little further—but it wasn't going to happen today.

Another slow circuit in the blustery conditions and new information was available. The ground crew were going to scoop the patient and take him to the clearing. The patient was status two and was in respiratory distress but it wasn't a crush injury from the falling tree, as first reported.

It was far safer to land and preferable clinically, given that this was a chest injury and Zac could do more than any paramedic, but Summer was aware of a flash of disappointment. Had she wanted to publicly demonstrate the level of trust she had in Zac? Wanted the deeper kind of bond that would come from tackling—and winning—a tough challenge like this?

Never mind. It would no doubt come soon enough. And, in the meantime, they still had a challenge on their hands. A medical one.

'It's a penetrating wound,' the paramedic shouted over the noise of the slowing rotors as Zac and Summer ran, still crouching, towards the ambulance. 'The tree didn't land on him but it looks like he got stabbed with a branch or something. He's unresponsive. Now status one. Blood pressure's crashed and he's throwing off a lot of ectopics.'

This was an immediately life-threatening injury and it sounded as if a cardiac arrest was imminent. They worked fast and closely together as Summer intubated the young forestry worker and got IV fluids running as Zac performed the procedure she'd seen him do in Emergency on her car accident victim with the tension pneumothorax. But opening the chest cavity wasn't enough to allow the lungs to inflate, even when it had been done on both sides of the victim's chest.

'He's arrested.' Summer squeezed more oxygen in with the bag mask but this was looking hopeless. There was little point in starting external chest compressions when it was clear that there was some obstruction to the heart being able to fill and empty.

'The wound's within the nipple line on the left anterior chest.' Zac sounded calm but his tone was grim. 'It's not a pleural obstruction so it has to be pericardial. I'm going to open the chest with a clam shell thoracotomy.'

This was way beyond any procedure Summer could have performed. Beyond anything she'd seen in the emergency department, even. How confident would you have to be to actually open a chest in the field and expose a heart? But, if they didn't do something drastic, this young man was about to die.

Summer delegated the airway care to one of the ambulance paramedics so that she could work alongside Zac and pass him the necessary equipment. The sterilised strong scissors to extend the small opening that had been made in the hope of releasing trapped air or blood. The Gigli wire and forceps to cut through the breastbone. Rib spreaders to open the area and suction to clear it.

And then she watched, in amazement, as Zac used two clips to raise a tent of the covering around the heart and then cut a tiny hole before extending it. He used his gloved hands to remove massive blood clots. They could see the heart but it was still quivering ineffectually rather than beating.

Summer held her breath as Zac flicked the heart with his fingers. Once, then again, and she let her breath out in a sigh as she saw the heart contract. Fill and then contract again. She could feel the first effective beat as a pulse under her fingertips when she rested them on their patient's neck and a beep on the monitor behind them confirmed that a rhythm had recommenced. A movement of the whole chest was a first attempt by their patient to take a breath of his own.

Zac removed the rib spreaders and let the chest close.

'We'll put a sterile cover on this. We need to get him to Theatre stat.'

It still seemed like too big an ask to get their patient to hospital alive but, by some miracle, that was exactly what they managed to do. And, thanks to that achievement, the young forestry worker emerged from Theatre several hours later to go into intensive care. Still alive and looking as though he was going to stay that way.

It was all everyone could talk about, both in the emergency department of Auckland General and on the rescue helicopter base. It wasn't the first time such a major procedure had been attempted out of hospital but it was the first time it had had a successful outcome. Summer had never felt so proud of the job she did. Proud of the service she worked for. Proud of Zac...

'You're amazing, you know that?'

'So are you.'

They were still on base. Being professional colleagues. Nobody had guessed how close they'd become out of work hours yet and they were happy to keep it that way so all they could do right now was to hold eye contact long enough to communicate that the mutual appreciation went a lot deeper than anything professional. They would go over every tiny detail of this case, probably later this evening, and discuss the pros and cons of every choice and try to identify anything they could have done better. *Would* do better, if they were ever faced with a similar situation. She loved that they shared a passion for the same work. Being able to debrief a case in detail with Zac was taking Summer's clinical knowledge to a whole new level and she knew it was giving her an edge in her job that others were beginning to notice.

Maybe that wasn't the only thing that they were beginning to notice.

'What about me?' Monty sniffed. 'It wasn't exactly a ride in the park, flying in that weather, you know.'

'We couldn't have done it without you, mate.' Zac gave the pilot's shoulder a friendly thump as he went past. 'You're a legend.'

'We're all legends,' Summer said. 'How 'bout a beer after work to celebrate?'

'I've got a date already,' Monty said. 'You two go off on your own.' He returned Zac's friendly thump and grinned at Summer. 'You know you want to.'

'Um...' Summer could feel her cheeks redden. 'We just work well together.'

'Yeah...right. So how come you suck all the oxygen

out of the air for the rest of us when you stand around making sheep's eyes at each other?'

'Did he really say that we were making sheep's eyes at each other?'

'Mmm.' Summer tilted her head to smile up at Zac. 'I believe he did.'

Zac grinned back and tightened his hold on Summer's hand as he helped her over the boulders on the beach and back onto the track they were following. For a while, they were silent, enjoying the shade of the heavy canopy of native bush and the sounds of the bird-life they had come here to see.

The journey itself had been a joy. Being on the road with Summer, seeing her bike in his rear-view mirror, taking the corners like a faithful shadow. Riding a bike on the open road was always a pleasure but it could feel lonely. Being out with someone else changed the experience.

Being out with Summer Pearson changed everything. The sun seemed brighter. The smell of the sea as they stood outside on the ferry across to Tiritiri Matangi Island was fresher. Forgoing a guided tour so they could pretend they had the whole island to themselves had been a joint decision made with simply a heartbeat of eye contact. Walking hand in hand seemed like the most natural thing in the world. A pleasure shared being a pleasure doubled or something, maybe.

'What, exactly, *are* sheep's eyes?'

'Oh...you know...looking at each other for a bit too long, I guess. Like there's nobody else around.'

'I've always thought sheep were not particularly intelligent creatures.'

Summer laughed—a delicious ripple of sound that Zac immediately wanted to hear again.

'Are we being stupid, do you think?'

The glance he received was startled. 'How do you mean?'

'It's not against the rules, is it? To get involved with a fellow crew member? A colleague?'

Summer shook her head and her chuckle was rueful. 'If it was, you'd all be in trouble in the emergency department, wouldn't you?'

'It's a bit different on the choppers, though. Much tighter teams.'

'We're all adults. We get to make our own choices and deal with any consequences. The only trouble would be if you let something personal interfere with anything professional.' Summer dropped his hand as she climbed up a set of narrow steps that was part of a boardwalk. 'I'm surprised that anyone guessed about us so fast, though. I thought we were being really discreet.'

'Apparently we suck all the oxygen out of the room.' Zac's tone was light but he knew exactly what Monty had been referring to. Sometimes, it felt that way when he was looking at Summer. As if he'd forgotten how to breathe or something. A weird sensation that he'd never experienced before.

Good weird, though—he was pretty sure about that.

'Do you think Ivy knows?'

'Well…you know how you and Flint stayed around the other night, after we'd been out for that swim?'

'Mmm?' Something in her tone suggested that Summer was remembering how amazing the second time together had been. Any first time awkwardness had vanished and they had been ready to play. To get to know each other's bodies and revel in the pleasure they knew they could both give and receive.

'When I popped in to say good morning before I went to work the next day, she gave me a pile of new towels. Said that mine were old enough to feel like cardboard and they simply weren't suitable for delicate skin. I don't think she was referring to *my* skin.'

'But I snuck out well before dawn. It was still dark by the time Flint and I had jogged back to the boat.'

Zac threw a wry smile over his shoulder. 'There's not much that gets past Gravy. She's had ninety plus years to hone her skills, after all.'

'Oh... Do you think she disapproves?'

'If she did, I don't think she'd be supplying soft towels. She'd think that the cardboard variety would be a suitable penance. Oh...look at that.'

They had come to one of the feeding stations on the island. Cleverly designed platforms supported bottles of sugar water. This station had attracted both bellbirds and tuis and, for several minutes, they both stood entranced, watching. The bellbirds were small and elegant, the tuis much larger and more confident—the white ruff on their necks being shown off as they reached to sip the water from the metal tubes.

They saw stitchbirds and riflemen further along the track and then the highlight they would be talking about for days came when a group of takahe crossed their path. The huge flightless birds with their blue and green plumage and big red beaks were fascinating.

'They thought they were extinct, you know. Like the moas. There's only a few places you can see them now. This is a first for me.'

'Me, too.' Summer's face was alight with pleasure.

'This was such a good idea, Zac. And I thought we were just going for a bike ride.'

'I'm full of good ideas.' Zac caught her hand as they started walking again. 'Stick around long enough and you'll find out.'

'I might just do that.'

Her words stayed in the air as they walked on. Zac could still hear them when they finally sat on the grass near the lighthouse to eat the picnic they'd put together from the shop near the ferry terminal. They were hungry enough after all the walking to polish off the filled rolls and muffins and fruit and then they lay back in the long grass. They had some time to spare before walking back down the hill to catch the ferry back.

It was inevitable that they started kissing. They were lying so close together, well away from any other visitors to the island. It was a gorgeous day and they had been having the best time in each other's company. The kisses were sweet. Perfect. Was that why Zac was aware of a warning bell sounding?

'It feels like we're breaking the rules,' he finally confessed.

'But we only work together sometimes. It's not like we're even employed by the same people.'

'I didn't mean that.' Zac propped himself up on one elbow but Summer had closed her eyes against the glare of the sun, a hand shading her face. 'I mean my own rules.'

Summer spread her fingers and peered up at him. 'You have rules?'

'Kind of.'

'What kind of rules?'

'Like not getting in too deep.'

'Oh...' She was really looking at him now but he couldn't read her expression. If he had to guess, he might say she looked wary. Almost afraid?

He had to kiss her again. To reassure her. Or maybe he was trying to reassure himself?

'This feels different. Weird.'

Her lips quirked with a tiny smile. 'Good weird or bad weird?'

'I think...good weird.'

'But you don't know?'

Zac sucked in a breath. Had he ever been this honest with a woman before? 'I do know. I'm just not sure I trust it. Because it's...too good?'

A single nod from Summer. She understood.

'I've never had a good role model for what can be trusted,' Zac said quietly. 'My grandad died before I could remember him and my stepfather...well, I prefer not to remember him.'

Summer nodded again. 'My parents weren't exactly a shining example to follow either.' She sat up, as if even thinking about her family had disturbed her. Zac wanted to ask about what had gone so wrong but he didn't want to spoil this moment because it felt important. A step forward.

'But we're adults,' he said. 'We get to make our own choices, don't we? And live with the consequences.'

'How do you know if you're making the right choices, though?'

'I guess you don't. I think that maybe you have to do what feels right and then hope that you *have* made the right ones.'

Did she understand what he was trying to say here,

or was he being too clumsy? He didn't want to scare her off completely.

He didn't seem to have done that. If it had been a declaration of sorts, then Summer seemed to be in complete agreement. She stretched out her arms and linked them around his neck, pulling him towards her for another kiss.

'This feels right,' she murmured. 'Weird but good.'

Better than good. It felt as if they had agreed to make this choice. That there was a potential to trust on both sides. Almost an unspoken promise that they would both do their best for whatever was happening between them not to become an emotional disaster.

Inevitably, the real world had to intrude again. Zac checked his watch as he became aware that they really were alone here now. 'We've got two minutes and then we need to head back fast for the ferry. Gravy would be upset if we don't get back for the dinner she's cooking up for us.'

Her lips were moving against his. 'We'd better make the most of them then, hadn't we?'

'There you go, Gravy. A nice hot lemon drink to wash down that paracetamol. You'll feel better in no time.'

'I just hope I didn't give Summer this cold when she was here for dinner the other night after you'd been out to the bird island.'

'I think she's pretty tough. She'll survive.'

Ivy sniffed her drink. 'You know, I think a hot toddy might work faster. With a good slosh of whisky.'

'Hmm.' Zac took a mohair rug off the back of the couch and held it up but Ivy shook her head.

'Far too hot for that. Summer colds are the worst.'

Ivy blew her nose and leaned back in her chair but she was smiling. 'Summer,' she murmured. 'Such a lovely name. Conjures up the feeling of blue skies and sunshine, doesn't it? The sparkle of the sea and long, delicious evenings to enjoy it.'

'Is there anything else I can do for you before I head downstairs?'

'Sit and talk to me for a minute. Unless you're meeting your Summer?'

'Not tonight.' Zac settled himself on the couch beside his grandmother. 'She's doing some crew training. And we don't spend every minute of our time off together, anyway.'

'You'll have to bring her to dinner with me again soon. I ordered some new champagne online yesterday and it looks lovely. I could do your favourite roast chicken.'

'You're not to do anything for a few days except rest and get better. If that cough gets any worse, I'll be having a chat to your GP. You might need some antibiotics.'

'I'll be fine. I can't have been eating enough garlic, that's what it is.'

'Maybe you should stop swimming when the weather isn't so good. I saw you out in the rain the other day.'

Ivy snorted. 'You know as well as I do that the weather doesn't cause a viral infection.'

'Getting cold lowers your resistance.'

Ivy flapped a hand in his direction. 'I'll stop swimming when I'm dead, thanks very much, and who knows how far away that is? I intend to make the most of every day I've got.'

'Don't say that.' Zac frowned. 'I expect you to be around for a long time yet.'

Ivy's smile was unusually gentle. 'Nobody lives for ever, darling.'

Zac smiled back and took hold of one of her hands. When had her skin started to feel so papery and fragile? An internal alarm was sounding faintly. This was what it was like when you had somebody who was this important to you. You had to live with the fear of losing them. His gran was all the more precious because of that knowledge he'd come by too early in life.

'You could try.' There was a tight feeling in his throat. 'You're my touchstone, Gravy. I don't even want to think about what life will be like when you're not around.'

'Maybe you've found a new touchstone.' Ivy turned her hand over and gave his a squeeze. 'Your little ray of summer sunshine.'

'You wouldn't have thought that the first time I met her. She's not only tough. She can be quite fierce.'

'Good.' Ivy sipped her hot drink. 'Being fierce is an attribute. Sometimes you have to fight in life to get through things. And it sounds like she's had to get through more than her fair share. Not that she said much, but it sounded like her mum was the only family she had and she lost her when she was far too young.'

'Mmm…' He'd had the opportunity to ask more about her background when they'd been on the island but he'd held back. Boundaries were still being respected. On both sides? Was that a good thing—or another warning?

'She's got a heart of gold, that girl,' Ivy said quietly. 'And she loves you to bits.'

'You think…?'

'It's obvious from where I'm standing. And I think you feel the same way.'

Zac pushed his fingers through his hair. That would certainly explain why this felt so different. 'Maybe...'

'But?'

'Who said there was a but?'

'You only mess up your hair like that when you can't decide something. You've been doing it since you were a little boy, Isaac. I always had to carry a comb whenever we went out anywhere.'

'Hmm. It's early days, I guess.'

Ivy snorted. 'Nonsense. When something's right, it's right. You should know by now.'

'I don't want to rush into anything.'

'You're already into it up to your eyebrows, from what I can see.'

Zac couldn't deny it. He'd never felt this way about any girl before but... Yes, there was a but...

'Maybe it's her independence that bothers me,' he admitted. 'How different she is. How many girls live by themselves on a boat? Ride a motorbike and kick ass in a job that would be too much for most people to cope with?'

'*Language*, Isaac. Please.'

'Sorry. But she's amazing at what she does. She's got this confidence that makes you think she'd cope with anything by herself. And yes, she probably did have to cope with too much when she was young. But would she want to fight to keep a relationship together if times got tough or would she just walk away and cope all by herself again?'

Ivy sniffed. 'Sounds like the pot calling the kettle black, Isaac Mitchell. How many relationships have

you walked out on so far when they didn't go the way
you wanted them to? When they wanted more than you
were ready to give? You've broken your share of hearts,
you know.'

'It wasn't intentional.'

'I know that.' Ivy patted his hand. 'And you were always very kind about it.'

'I've just never found the person that makes me want
to give everything I could to.' But he had now, hadn't
he? The only thing stopping him was a fear of…what?
Having his heart broken? Again?

Ivy was giving him a look that said she understood.
That she remembered the small boy whose world had
crumbled when he'd lost his mother. But it was also a
look that told him it was time to be brave enough to
break his own rules. The ones about working hard and
playing hard and guarding your heart. That she knew
exactly who the person was. A look that suggested he
was being just a little bit obtuse.

Zac felt the need to defend himself. 'You only got
married once,' he reminded her. 'I'm cut from the same
cloth. If I give everything, it'll only happen once. I think
if the trust it takes to do that gets broken, you never find
it again. Never as much. So it has to be right.'

Ivy's gaze was misty. Was she remembering the love
of her life, who'd sadly been taken before Zac was old
enough to remember him?

'Nothing's ever perfect, darling. At some point you
have to take a leap of faith and hope for the best. I hope
you'll be as lucky as I was. But don't wait too long.' She
closed her eyes as she leaned her head back against a
cushion. 'I want to see you waiting for your bride at
the end of the aisle. I want to throw confetti and drink

a wee bit too much champagne and be disgracefully tipsy by the end of the reception.' She opened her eyes again and the expression in them gave Zac that tight feeling in his throat again. This time it felt like a rock with sharp edges.

'I want to know that you'll be living here in this house and there'll be babies playing in the garden and building sandcastles on the beach. Dogs tracking sand into the house and maybe a paddleboard or two propped up against that dusty old boatshed.'

Zac found his own eyes closing for a long blink. He could almost see it himself.

And it looked...perfect.

CHAPTER SEVEN

THE MORE TIME he spent with Summer, the more Zac could see that picture of a perfect future.

'D'you think you'll always want to live on a boat?' The query was casual. They were restocking gear during a quiet spell one afternoon.

'No way. I had no idea I'd be doing it for *this* long.' Summer turned to look at the pouch Zac was filling. 'Have you got plenty of size eight cuffed tracheal tubes in there?'

'Three. That's enough, isn't it?'

'Yes. Make sure we've got sizes three, four and five of the laryngeal mask airways, too. And we'll do the paediatric airway kit next.'

'Sure.' Zac checked the size printed on the sterile packages for the LMAs. 'So how long did you think you'd live on a boat, then?'

'As long as it took to save up a house deposit.' She snapped a laryngoscope handle into place to check the light and then folded it closed again. 'I was looking for a share flat when I moved up from Hamilton but then I heard about the boat and it was cheaper. I didn't expect house prices to go so crazy, though. It feels like

I'm getting further and further away. And living on the boat's not helping.'

'Even if it's cheaper?'

'I'm getting spoiled. I can't imagine living far from a beach now and they're always the pricier suburbs.'

'I know. My grandparents had no idea what a good investment they were making when they bought a run-down old house on the beach nearly sixty years ago.'

'It's a perfect house.'

Zac opened the paediatric airway kit. He ran his gaze over the shiny laryngoscope blades and handles, the Magill forceps and the range of tracheal tubes and LMAs. There didn't seem to be anything missing from the slots. He checked the pocket that held the tiniest airways that could be needed in resuscitating a newborn baby and sent out a silent prayer that they wouldn't be needing to use any of them any time soon.

A quick glance at Summer took in the way she was sitting cross-legged on the storeroom floor. She had another kit open on her lap—the serious airway gear that made things like scalpels and tracheal dilators available when all else failed.

Her words still echoed in the back of his head.

The house that he would inherit one day was *perfect*. Like the life that Ivy had imagined him living in it one day.

He'd always loved the house but how much better was it on the nights that Summer and Flint stayed over? When they could all go out at first light and run on the beach or brave the cold water for an early morning wake-up swim?

It was like his job. Perfect but so much better when he got to share it with Summer. The bonus of seeing the crew in their orange flight suits arrive to hand over a patient when he was on a shift in Emergency always added something special to his day. Days like today, when he was actually working on the rescue base as her crew partner, were the best of all.

Ivy's warning of not waiting too long had been surfacing more and more in recent days.

He was coasting. Enjoying each day as it came. Trusting that it would continue for as long as they both wanted it to. Trusting that it was safe to give more and more because it could become stronger and potentially last for the rest of his life.

And there was the rub. He might be confident that Summer felt the same way he did but he couldn't be sure until he heard her say it out loud. And maybe she was waiting for him to say something first? Something else Ivy had said had struck home. He was the pot calling the kettle black. Maybe he and Summer were more alike than he'd realised. They both had the kind of skills that came from putting so much effort into their work. They chose leisure activities like ocean sports and riding powerful bikes that meant they could play as hard as they worked. Perhaps Summer's fierce independence came from self-protection and it would take something extraordinary to persuade her to remove the barriers that were protecting her heart?

But what they had found together was extraordinary, wasn't it? Surely he couldn't be the only one feeling like this?

The buzzing of their pagers broke the silence. Kits were rolled up and stuffed back into the pack with swift movements. They were both on their feet within seconds. Strapped into their seats in the helicopter within minutes. Heading west.

'Piha Beach,' Monty confirmed. 'ETA ten minutes.'

'I've been there for near-drownings,' Summer said. 'And falls from the rocks. I can't believe someone's been attacked by a shark.'

'We're being followed,' Monty told them. 'Reckon you'll both be starring on the national news tonight.'

Zac knew he would recognise the landmarks below with ease. Lion Rock was famous. Lying forty kilometres west of the city, Piha was the most famous surf beach in the country.

'I used to surf at Piha when I was a kid,' he told Summer. 'When I got my first wheels when I was seventeen, I chose an old Combi van and me and my mates were in heaven. We'd load up the boards and wetsuits before dawn and we'd get home, sunburned and completely exhausted, well after dark. There was always a big roast dinner on offer when we got back. It was no wonder I was so popular at school.'

The look he was getting from Summer suggested that there were other reasons he might have been popular. Her gaze held his with a tenderness that made something ache deep in his chest and her smile made it feel like whatever it was had just split open to release some kind of hitherto untried drug.

Love. That was what it was, all right.

Summer *did* feel the same way he did—he was sure of it. And he'd never loved anyone this much. Never would ever again. It was time he did something about making sure he never lost it. For both their sakes, he needed to be brave and be the first one to take those barriers away. To put his heart on the line.

The first chance he got—tonight—he was going to tell Summer how he felt. Maybe even ask her to move in with him.

Marry him...?

Whoa...where had *that* notion come from? And now that it was here, it was the weirdest thought ever— maybe because it felt so right. The knowledge was fleeting, however. It couldn't claim even another second of headspace as the distinctive shape of Lion Rock— the formation that separated the two beaches at Piha— loomed larger.

Zac could see the knot of people on the beach below, including the red and yellow uniforms of the lifeguards, and many more were watching from a distance. Several bystanders were waving their arms, urging the rescue crew to land as quickly as possible. There was nobody in the water, surfing or swimming. It could be a while before this popular beach could be deemed safe, despite a shark attack in New Zealand being an extraordinarily rare occurrence.

One of the lifeguards met them as they raced from the helicopter over the firm sand they'd been able to land on.

'We've got the bleeding under control with a pressure bandage but he's lost a lot of blood. And his leg's a real mess, man... I hope he's not going to lose it.'

'Is he conscious?' The priority was keeping this patient alive, not discussing a potential prognosis. It sounded like preservation of blood volume was likely to be the key management, along with as swift a transfer to hospital as possible.

'He swam in himself with his board, yelling for help, but he was barely conscious by the time we got him onto the beach. We've got oxygen on and put some blankets over him to try and keep him warm and he's woken up a bit. He's in a lot of pain.'

The knot of people—including a skinny lad gripping a surfboard that had obvious tooth marks and a chunk bitten out of its end—parted to let Zac and Summer into the centre and place their packs on the sand. Summer immediately dropped to her knees to open the pack and start extracting gear they would need, like a blood pressure cuff and IV supplies. She reached for the man's wrist as Zac crouched by the patient's head.

'No radial pulse palpable,' she said.

The man looked to be in his early fifties and he was deathly pale but breathing well and Zac could feel a rapid pulse beneath his fingers from the carotid artery in his neck. It was a lot fainter than he would have liked and if it wasn't reaching his wrist it meant that his blood pressure was already dangerously low. Hypovolaemic shock was a life-threatening emergency and they might have to fight to keep this man alive. From the corner of his eye, Zac could see Summer unrolling the IV kit. She would be putting a tourniquet on and aiming to get a cannula in and IV fluids running as quickly as she could.

'Hey, buddy.' Zac shook the man's shoulder. 'Can you open your eyes for me?' Response to voice was a good indication of level of consciousness and he was relieved to see the man's eyelids flutter open and get a groan of verbal response.

Zac glanced up at the onlookers. 'Does anyone know his name?'

An affirmative chorus sounded from all sides.

'It's Jon,' one of the lifeguards told him. 'He's one of us—a Patrol Captain.'

'Jon Pearson,' someone else called. 'He's fifty-two. Lives locally.'

Pearson?

Startled, Zac's gaze swerved towards Summer and—just for a heartbeat—his focus was broken by regretting not taking that opportunity he'd had to find out more about her background. He really needed to know more than he did right now.

What little information he had flashed through his brain with astonishing speed. Her parents had been hippies. She'd been conceived on a beach in the wake of a surfing competition. She had no siblings. Her mother had died when she was seventeen and her father was already 'well out of the picture'. Her parents had not been 'a shining example' of something to follow as far as relationships went. What had she meant by that? *Dear God...*had there been violence involved? Had she had to cope with the same sort of fear in her childhood as he had?

More importantly in this moment, however, if this man *was* Summer's father—and that seemed quite likely given that he was a surfer—how was she coping, seeing him for the first time in so many years, let alone in a life-threatening emergency? Having to treat him? It was a paramedic's worst nightmare, having to treat a loved one. How much harder could it be if the relationship was complicated and emotionally distressing anyway?

She seemed to be coping. She had a tourniquet around their patient's arm and was swabbing the skin on his arm.

'You'll feel a sharp scratch,' she warned. 'There. All done.' The cannula slid home into the vein and Summer released the tourniquet and reached for the connection so that she could hook up the bag of IV fluid she had ready.

And then she looked up and caught Zac's steady gaze as he did his best to communicate silently.

I understand, he tried to tell her. *I'm here for you. I'll do whatever it takes to help.*

She could do this. She could cope.

She *had* to.

It had almost done her in, though, that first instant she'd seen their patient's face. Of course she had recognised him—despite the differences that fifteen years had etched onto his face. For one horrible moment, she had frozen—assaulted by a flashback of the grief she'd had to deal with all those years ago when he'd chosen to walk out of her life.

The only way to deal with it had been to blank out those memories. The visceral knowledge that this was her only living relative. He had to become simply another patient. A man with hypovolaemic shock who was in urgent need of fluid replacement. All she had to think about was putting a large bore cannula into his arm and to get fluids running. Probably two IV lines— except that it was equally important to find out whether the loss of blood was actually as controlled as the first aiders had led them to believe.

'I don't like the staining on that pressure bandage,' she told Zac. 'It could be soaking up volume.'

Zac nodded. 'Have a look at what's going on.' He

was still crouching beside her father's head. 'Jon? You still with us, mate? Open your eyes…'

'*Hurts*,' Jon groaned. 'My *leg*…'

'I'm going to give you something for the pain.'

Summer used shears to cut away the bandage. The ripped flesh on Jon's thigh was horrific. She could see the gleam of exposed bone in one patch and…yes… there was a small spurt of an arterial bleed still going on. She clamped her gloved fingers over the vessel and pressed hard.

Jon groaned and then swore vehemently. Summer had to close her eyes for a heartbeat as the cry of pain ripped its way through the emotional wall she had erected.

This was just another patient. *Jon*. Not Dad. Sometimes you had to cause pain to save a life. It didn't make it harder because he was her father. He wasn't her father any more. He hadn't been for fifteen years…

She opened her eyes as she sucked in a new breath, to find Zac looking up from where he was filling a syringe from an ampoule. He was giving her that look again. The one that told her he had somehow made the connection the moment he'd heard their patient's name and that he knew exactly how hard this was. How much he wanted to make it easier for her.

He knew nothing about her history and yet he was prepared to take her side and protect her from someone who had the potential to be some kind of threat. Funny how she could still be so focused on what she had to do but be aware of how much she loved this man. How easy it would be to put her emotional safety in his hands for ever.

'The femoral artery's been nicked,' she said. 'I'm putting some pressure on it.'

'We might need to clamp it. I'll get some pain relief on board first.'

Yes. Knock him out, Summer thought. The pain of what she was doing had roused him. Any second now and he was going to look to see what was happening and...

'*Summer?*' The word was shocked. Disbelieving. Jon pulled at the oxygen mask on his face as if he wanted to make his speech more audible. 'Is that...*you*?'

'Keep your mask on, mate.' A lifeguard crouching at his head pushed the mask back into place.

The guard holding the bag of IV fluid aloft crouched to catch his arm. 'Keep your arm still, Jon. You don't want the line to come out.'

During the flurry of activity, Zac injected the pain relief and Jon relaxed, his arms dropping and his eyes closing. A flash of eye contact told her that Zac was relieved that things hadn't got any more difficult but it did nothing to interrupt his focus on what they had to do as soon as possible—to get this bleeding under control so that pouring fluids in to maintain blood pressure wasn't a futile exercise.

Forceps were a good enough temporary measure to close the artery. Sterile dressings covered the wound. It took only a few minutes to have their patient packaged onto the stretcher and stable enough to fly.

'Any family or close friends here?' Zac asked.

Summer deliberately avoided making eye contact with anybody. How many people had heard him say her name? The name that was embroidered on her overalls for anybody to check. A name that was unusual enough to be an accusation if someone knew that Jon had had a daughter in a previous life. It was normal to find out whether there was anyone who might want to travel with a patient who was seriously injured, anyway. These could be the last moments they had together.

'Me.' The skinny kid who'd been standing there, silently gripping the damaged surfboard, spoke up. 'I'm Dylan. He's my dad.'

She didn't manage to avoid Zac's glance this time. He was hiding it well but he was shocked. Did he think she'd known she had a half-brother? *Oh, man...* he couldn't be as shocked as she was. A half-*brother*?

She tried to shove the thought aside. This was her father's new family. It didn't have to have anything to do with her, other than as a professional. They couldn't just take a boy who didn't look any older than about ten or eleven with them. He would need to travel with an adult.

'Where's your mum?' The words came out more fiercely than she would have chosen.

'Haven't got one.'

'She died,' someone said quietly, close to Summer's shoulder. 'Couple of years back.'

'There's just me and my dad.'

The boy had blue eyes. And they were dark with distress—making him look a lot older than he probably was. A lot older than any kid should have to look. Summer had lost her mother. She knew what that was like but she couldn't afford to start feeling sorry for the kid. If she let him touch her heart, it might open the door to everything associated with her father and that was a world of hurt she thought she'd left well in the past.

But how could she not feel the connection? This kid even *looked* like her. Short and skinny, with bleached blond hair that was probably still full of sea water, which was why it was sticking up all over the place in the kind of spikes that Summer favoured for a hairstyle.

The unexpected mix of something so personal with what should have been a purely professional situation was impossible to deal with. Thank goodness Zac seemed to know exactly the right way to deal with it. He had his hand on a skinny shoulder.

'Want to come with us, then? We'll look after you, buddy.'

A single nod. The surfboard was handed over, with some reverence, to one of the lifeguards. The news crew, who'd been filming from a respectable distance, began to move closer. People would get interviewed. Close-up shots of that surfboard would probably be all over the Internet in no time. There could be more reporters waiting at the hospital and they'd be eager to get some sound bites from one of the crew.

Maybe Monty could deal with that. Or Graham, back at the base. All Summer wanted to do was get this job over with and find some way of getting her head around it all. But what was she going to do about the boy? She had a responsibility, whether she wanted it or not, and dealing with that was inevitably going to open a can of worms that Zac would want to talk about. That he had the right to know about, even?

A short time later, Dylan was strapped into the front seat of the helicopter beside Monty, and Zac and Summer were in the back with their patient. They were lifting off from the beach. They were in an environment totally familiar to Summer and heading back to the world she knew and loved.

But it didn't feel the same any more.

It was being shaken and it was impossible to know just how much damage might be happening.

Even Zac seemed different. Was it her imagination or was he treating Jon with even more care than usual? She didn't need reminding to keep a constant watch on his blood pressure and oxygen saturation. Surely he didn't need to keep asking about pain levels?

'It's down to three out of ten,' she finally snapped. 'And we're only a few minutes away from hospital. He doesn't need any more pain relief.'

Zac's expression was sympathetic but it felt like a reprimand. He was trying to do the best for everyone involved here but this was a decision their patient should be allowed to make. Was he providing an example of not letting anything personal interfere with something professional? 'How bad is it, Jon?'

'Better than before.' It was clearly an effort for him to open his eyes. 'Summer?'

It was easy to pretend to be absorbed in the measurements she was recording. To pretend she hadn't heard him call her name.

'Where's my boy?' Jon asked then. 'Who's looking after Dylan?'

'He's up front,' Zac told him. 'Coming to the hospital with us.'

'But who's going to look after him? He's just a kid...'

'Don't worry about it,' Zac said. 'I'll make sure he's taken good care of.'

What? Summer's frown was fierce. This felt wrong. This wasn't what he'd promised in that look. The one that had told her he was on her side and would protect her. He was treating Jon Pearson as if he was his girl-friend's father and not just a potential threat to her emotional well-being. As if this unknown and unwelcome half-sibling was part of her family.

And what did that say about Zac? That he'd think it was forgivable to cheat on your wife for pretty much an entire marriage? That it was okay to pack a bag and simply walk out when you decided that your daughter was old enough to be considered an adult?

'You're grown up now, chicken. It shouldn't matter that me and your mum aren't going to live together any longer. I won't be far away. I'll always be your dad.'

She'd only just turned sixteen, for heaven's sake. She'd been nowhere near old enough to handle her mother's emotional disintegration.

And it sure as hell *had* mattered.

'You're a cheat. A lying cheat. I can't believe you'd do this to Mum. To me. I hate you...I never want to see you again...'

She had seen him again, though, hadn't she? At her mother's funeral, less than a year later. Not that she'd gone anywhere near him. What could she have said?

This was your fault. It might not look like it to anyone else but, as far as I'm concerned, it was murder...

Murder by drowning in the dank blackness of the cloud that had been left behind in their lives.

The echo of her mother's voice was even more disturbing. Concentrating on recording a new set of figures wasn't enough to chase it away.

Blood pressure was ninety over sixty. Improving. At least it was recordable now.

You can never trust a man... No matter how much you love them—it's never enough...

Oxygen saturation was ninety-three per cent. Not enough but it had also improved from what it had been.

There was enough blood—albeit pretty diluted now—to be keeping Jon alive.

'He's going to need blood.' Had Zac guessed her train of thought? 'Do you happen to know his group? Might speed things up.'

'He's O positive.'

'Really? Me, too.'

The coincidence was hardly impressive. 'So am I. It is the most common group, you know. Thirty-eight per cent of people are O positive.'

Her tone sounded off, even to her own ears. Cold, even. She turned to stare at the cardiac monitor.

He was in sinus rhythm so his heart was coping. The heart rate was too fast at a hundred and twenty but that was only to be expected with the low levels of circulating oxygen.

Looking up at the monitor made it inevitable that her glance would slide sideways at Zac but he'd looked away when she'd been making the comment about blood groups and seemed to be focused on checking the dressings over Jon's leg wound.

She couldn't shake that echo of her mother's voice. How could she when her father was lying there only inches away from her?

She loved Zac. More than she would have ever believed it was possible to love someone. And she trusted him completely.

Despite evidence to the contrary? How easily had she taken his word and shut those poisonous whispers from Kate out of her life?

The way her mother had always refused to believe rumours of her father's infidelity?

Her thoughts shouldn't be straying like this in the

middle of a job. She was being unprofessional. She'd never felt like this. Well—maybe just a little—that first day she'd been on the job with Zac and she'd had to make an effort to separate the personal and professional, but that paled in comparison to the wash of mixed emotions she couldn't control right now. A mix of the present and past that was turning into a confused jumble.

Shaking things unbearably. Damaging things.

Nothing was going to be quite the same after this. Including how she felt about Zac?

Maybe that was the worst thing about it.

They were coming in to land on the roof of Auckland General. There would be a resus team waiting for them in Emergency. They could hand their patient over and if it had been any normal job that would be the end of it.

But Summer knew that, this time, it might only be the beginning of something else.

Something that had the potential to ruin her life all over again?

How on earth was she going to cope?

And then they were out of the helicopter and there was a flurry of activity as they got everybody out and ready to move. Summer gathered up the paperwork so she was a step behind as the stretcher started to roll. A nurse had taken charge of Dylan. For a moment, Summer stared at the entourage and it was hard to make her feet move to start following them.

But somehow Zac was right beside her. His side pressed against hers.

'It's okay,' he told her. 'We can deal with this. All of it.'

It was a good thing they had to move fast to catch up with their patient and take the lift down to the emergency department. A good thing that there were so many other people around because otherwise Summer might have burst into tears.

She had no idea exactly how they were going to deal with any of this but she desperately wanted to believe Zac.

There was the most enormous relief in the idea that, this time, she wasn't going to have to do this alone.

They could deal with this.

Together.

CHAPTER EIGHT

ZAC STOOD WITH Dylan in the corner of the resuscitation room, his arm around the boy's shoulders, as the team made their initial assessment of his father. Summer stood on the boy's other side. Not touching him but still close.

He could only imagine the mixed feelings she must be experiencing but she was standing her ground. Being protective of a scared ten-year-old kid who she happened to be related to. It made Zac feel enormously proud of her.

'Do a type and cross match,' Rob told one of the nurses. 'He's going to need a transfusion.'

'He's O positive,' Zac said.

'Thanks, mate, but we'll still have to check.' Rob's glance took in how close Zac and Summer were standing to Dylan but, if he was surprised, he gave no sign of it, with the same kind of professionalism that had stopped any of the team commenting that their patient's name was the same as Summer's. 'Bitten by a shark, huh? Your dad's going to have a great story to tell, isn't he?'

'Is he…is he going to be okay?'

'We're going to give him some more blood and make sure he's stable and then he'll be going up to the operating theatre so they can see what they can do. Try not to worry too much, okay?' Rob's smile was reassuring but he turned away swiftly. 'Has someone got hold of Orthopaedics yet? And where's the neurosurgical registrar? And Summer…?'

'Yes?' Summer responded to the tilt of the ED consultant's head. He wanted a private word. Was he going to warn her that Dylan might need to be prepared for the worst? That he might lose his father?

That she might lose her father again—permanently, this time?

It shouldn't make any difference but it did. There was new grief to be found. A grief mixed with regret and…and something that felt like…*shame*?

'We need to intubate,' Rob told her quietly. 'It's better if you take the lad somewhere else. Is he…is there some connection I should know about?'

Summer's heart was thumping. This was the moment when she had to decide how far she was going to go in opening a part of her life that had previously been out of bounds.

'Jon Pearson is my father,' she said aloud. 'And Dylan's my half-brother. I…I didn't know he existed before today, though.'

'Hmm…' Rob's look was searching. 'You okay?'

Summer's gaze shifted to where Zac was still standing with his arm around Dylan's shoulders. Skinny shoulders that were hunched in misery and fear.

'I think I will be,' she said quietly.

'I'll get Mandy to set up one of the relatives' rooms

for you. She can take care of him if you need a break
for any reason. If there's any way we can help, just say.'

Dylan wasn't happy about being taken somewhere
else.

'I want to stay with my dad.' There was hostility in
the glare being delivered as she and Zac ushered him
out of the resus room. 'I don't want to go anywhere
with you. You're Summer. I know all about you. You
were mean to Dad.'

Summer's jaw dropped. *She* had been mean?

'Um...I didn't know about you.'

'You would have if you'd talked to Dad. Like he'd
always wanted you to.'

Summer tried to push away memories of things she
wasn't proud of. Like the look on her father's face when
she'd turned her back on him at the funeral and walked
away. The letters she had ripped up. The parcels she'd
had returned to their sender. Yes...there was definitely
shame to be found in the kaleidoscope of emotions this
day was creating.

'You don't care,' Dylan continued. 'You don't care
if Dad dies. You don't care about *me*.'

'That's not true.' The sincerity in her words was a
shock because it *was* genuinely sincere. She'd had no
idea how much she *did* actually care, did she? But there
was a huge part of her that still didn't *want* to care.
There was a battle going on inside and it was hard to
know which way to turn.

'He's not going to die, buddy.' Zac's voice was calm.
'What we don't know is whether they're going to be able
to save his leg and we're not going to know that for a
while yet. You can't stay while the doctors are doing
their work and that's why we're taking you somewhere

else. In here. Look, there's a TV and DVDs and that machine has lots of food.'

'Are you going to stay with me?'

'Sure.' Zac's smile was as reassuring as his calmness.

'So *she* doesn't need to stay then, does she?'

'She kind of does.' Zac let the door swing closed behind them.

'Why?'

'Well…she's kind of your big sister.'

Dylan's huff was dismissive and Summer could feel herself stiffen defensively. So what if this kid didn't want anything to do with her? Maybe she didn't want anything to do with him, either. She was just trying to do the right thing, here.

'And we're kind of together, you know?'

'You mean she's your girlfriend?'

'Yeah…' Zac's gaze found Summer's and held it. She felt some of the tension ebb away. Yes, there was a battle going on but she wasn't alone and if she had the choice of anyone to be on her side, she would choose this man.

Dylan's gaze went from Zac to Summer and back again. He shrugged and the look he gave Zac was an attempt at a man-to-man resignation that could have been funny if it wasn't heart-breaking at the same time.

'Guess that's okay, then.'

An hour of waiting brought the news that Jon had been taken into Theatre. Another hour passed and then another. The team of specialists had a huge job ahead of them to try and repair nerves and blood vessels and muscle if they were going to save his leg. Dylan had stopped talking as soon as the decision had been made regarding his company and all Zac and Summer could do was sit there with him and watch the cartoons he'd chosen as distraction.

Shared glances acknowledged how much they needed to talk about but none of it could be discussed in front of Dylan. Even the practicalities of where he would stay while his father was in hospital was something that needed to wait until they had confirmation that all had gone well in Theatre. The young boy seemed oblivious to the tension and frustration that slowly built around him. He shut himself away, seemingly absorbed by the meaningless entertainment, until, eventually, he fell deeply asleep on the couch. Mandy chose a moment a short time later to poke her head around the door.

'Looks like he's out for the count.'

'Yeah. Any word from upstairs?'

'Sounds like it got a bit dodgy for a while. He lost a huge amount of blood. Last I heard, he's stable again and the neurosurgeons are doing their bit.' Mandy took a blanket from the back of the couch and covered Dylan's bare legs. 'Why don't you two take a break? I'll stay in here with him. Even after his dad gets to Recovery it's going to be another hour or two before he'll be awake enough for a visitor.'

Zac stood up. 'Great idea. Let's go and get some coffee, Summer.' She looked exhausted enough to fall asleep herself but the lines of tension in her face suggested that was unlikely to be an option for a long while. She needed to talk more than she needed to sleep, but how much would she be prepared to tell him?

The sensation of being nervous was unexpected but this was a big ask, wasn't it? How close would Summer let him get?

How much did she really trust him?

He couldn't just ask, either. He knew that Summer guarded her privacy. He knew that he would probably get some answers by asking direct questions but he didn't want to do that. The information would still be guarded and the question of trust would not be answered. It mattered whether Summer was prepared to tell him what was important without being asked. Trust was like love, wasn't it? If it wasn't given freely—if you had to *ask* for it—it probably wasn't really worth having.

And it didn't seem as if it was about to be given. They sat in the cafeteria drinking bad coffee in the same kind of silence with which they'd been sitting in Dylan's company. Strained enough to make Zac's heart ache. He wanted to help but he couldn't just barge into a space he might not be welcome in.

It was still the early evening of what had been a beautiful day. Harsh sunlight had faded to a soft glow. How much better would it be if they could be sitting on the beach at Takapuna, watching the sunset over Rangitoto? They'd had their first moments of real connection on that beach and surely it would be easy to talk there. Apart from anything else, Summer needed a break from the emotionally traumatic situation she had unexpectedly found herself in. Some way to reassure herself that her life hadn't suddenly gone belly-up. They couldn't go to the beach right now, of course, but…

'Let's go back to the base,' he suggested.

Summer's immediate reaction was to shake her head. 'I can't leave. Not yet.'

But Zac could see the way her gaze went to the windows and beyond. That the notion of escaping was more than appealing.

'Dylan's being well looked after. He's probably going to sleep for hours, anyway. We don't have to be that long but we could get changed and bring our bikes back here and that way we'll be ready to go home later, when things are more sorted.'

Summer looked torn. 'It's a good idea,' she said. 'You should do that. I'd better stay, in case...in case...'

'I'm confident that your dad's not going to die,' Zac said gently. 'You'll be back by the time he wakes up and it can be you that takes Dylan in to see him...if you want,' he added hastily, seeing the way her eyes darkened with emotion. 'Only if that's what you want.'

'I don't. I told him I didn't ever want to see him again. He...I...' Her voice cracked and she dropped her gaze, clearly struggling not to cry.

It broke Zac's heart. Here was this strong, capable and incredibly independent woman in front of him, but he could see a young girl as well. A girl who'd been unbearably hurt in some way.

Oh...God...had her father been violent to her? Snatches of memory flashed through his brain like a slide show that could be felt as much as seen. The fist that couldn't be avoided. The fear in his mother's eyes. Blood. *Pain...* The knot of overwhelming emotion in his gut was powerful enough to make him feel ill. There was grief there. And a white-hot anger. He had to move. Standing up, he held out his hand to Summer.

'You don't *have* to see him again,' he said, his voice raw. 'And you're not going anywhere alone.'

He loved the way Summer took his hand so readily. The way she kept moving as she got to her feet, coming into his arms as if it was the only place she wanted to go. He held her tightly, pressing his cheek to the top

of her head. More than one group of people in the cafeteria were staring at them. The need to protect Summer kicked up several notches.

'Let's get out of here,' he said softly. 'Just for a bit.'

It was the right thing to do. It was Summer's idea
to see if there was an ambulance crew who might be
clear of a job in Emergency and have the time to drop
them back at the helicopter base and that allowed her
to step back into her own world. They changed out of
their flight suits into civvies and that made it feel as if
the job they'd been to at Piha Beach was really over.
Best of all, they kicked their bikes into life and could
roar through the city, weaving in and out of the traffic,
feeling the freedom of their preferred mode of transport.

No. That wasn't the best of all. This was. Walking
into the green space of the enormous park over the road
from Auckland General Hospital. Walking hand in hand
in soft light, mottled by the canopy of ancient trees, and
feeling the caress of a gentle summer breeze.

It was as good as life could get in this particular moment, Zac decided. And then he changed his mind only
moments later, when Summer's hand tightened around
his and she started to talk, albeit tentatively at first.

'You never knew your dad, did you?'

'No. My mother never even told me his name. The
only father figure I had came into my life when I was
about four and…he was never a dad to me.' He could
have said so much more but this wasn't about his story.
Or was it? Would sharing something that was never spoken about be a way of showing Summer how much he
was prepared to trust her? How much he wanted her to
be able to trust him?

His hesitation made it irrelevant. Or maybe Summer was already lost in her own memories.

'My dad was the best,' she said softly. 'I adored him. Everybody did. He coached all the kids and was the chief lifeguard and a volunteer fireman and the go-to guy for the whole community.'

'Country town?' Zac was absorbing the undercurrent of her words. He could let go of the idea that her father might have been violent and the relief was sweet. But what else could have caused such a catastrophic breakdown in a relationship that should have remained strong for a lifetime?

'A beach community. Tiny. There was never much money but if the sun was shining and the surf was up, it didn't matter. We were all happy. Dad would be running his surf school or the shop and Mum made pots that she painted and sold to the crowds that came in the summer holidays. I had a long ride to school on the bus but that was okay, too. We'd go with salt in our hair from a morning ride and we'd know there'd be time for the sea again after school.' She was silent for a moment. 'I'll bet Dylan's life is just like that. When I saw him on the beach today, he looked like all my friends did at that age. Like I did. I could have guessed who he was before he said anything if I hadn't been trying so hard not to think about who it was we were treating.'

'That must have been so hard for you. I can't believe how well you coped with it.'

Her tone was suddenly shy. 'You helped more than I can say. Thank you.'

Their steps had slowed and now they stopped. Zac drew Summer into his arms. 'You would have managed anyway but I'm glad I was there. I'm glad I'm here now.'

Summer pressed against him for a long moment but then pulled away with obvious reluctance, shaking her head. 'It's not over, though, is it? And I have no idea what to do. It's all this confused jumble in my head. I've hated Dad for so long. I want to hate Dylan too, but he's only a kid. It feels like he's the cause of it all but he's not. It's not his fault and…and he even looks a bit like me…'

Zac smiled. 'He does. He looks like a cool kid.' His breath came out in a poignant sigh. 'I wish I'd been around then.' He lifted an eyebrow. 'Maybe I was. Did you happen to notice a Combi van full of cool teenagers with their surfboards at your beach?'

It made her smile. 'Lots. Did you happen to notice a cool chick with a pink surfboard? My dad made it for my thirteenth birthday.'

The smile vanished. Those big blue eyes glittered with unshed tears and her voice was shaking. 'I miss him… I've always missed him…'

In the silence that followed, they both sat down on grass that was bathed with the last of the day's sunshine. Zac let the silence continue but then decided that he could ask a question now. He'd been invited into that private part of her life. It felt as if she was ready to trust him but he made his words as gentle as possible.

'What went wrong?'

Summer had picked a daisy from the grass and she held it in one hand. With the fingers of her other hand, she delicately separated a tiny petal from the others and plucked it clear.

'We lived for surfing competitions,' she said. 'They were the big, exciting days over summer and there were always huge barbecues in the evenings. Everybody knew each other and they were big social events.' Another petal got plucked from the daisy. 'There was this woman—Elsie—who turned up to a lot of the comps when I was a kid. Mum said she was an old friend of Dad's but she was weird about it. When I was thirteen— the year I got the pink surfboard—I heard a rumour that there was something going on between Elsie and Dad.'

'Ohh...' Zac knew instantly where this story was likely to go. He closed his eyes as if to hold back the distress of a small family about to be broken apart.

'I asked Dad and he denied it. I asked Mum and she said it wasn't true. She got really angry and told me never to mention it again. Dad had married *her*. He loved *us*. He was ours. For ever. She was always a bit over the top, you know? When she was happy, she was super happy but little things upset her. A lot. I didn't dare mention it again.'

More petals were coming from the daisy. Half of its yellow centre had a bare edge now.

'And then, one day—out of the blue—just after I turned sixteen, Dad told me that he had to leave. That he had to go and be with Elsie. That he'd been living a lie and life was too short to keep doing that. He thought I was old enough to understand, but all I could see was that he'd been cheating and lying for years—to the people who loved him the most in the world. I told him I never wanted to see him again.'

A whole bunch of petals got ripped clear. And then the daisy fell, unheeded, into the grass.

'Mum fell to bits. She wouldn't eat. She never stopped crying. I got her to see a doctor and he put her on medication but it was never enough. The pills got stronger and there were a lot of them. Enough for her to take so many that when I came home from school one day and found her unconscious on the floor, it was too late.'

'Oh, my God,' Zac breathed. He reached for Summer's hand and held it tightly.

'She never came out of the coma.' The tears were escaping now. 'They turned the life-support off a few days later.' Summer scrubbed at her face. 'Dad had the nerve to turn up at her funeral but, as far as I was concerned, he was guilty of murder. I refused to talk to him. Or even look at him. And I haven't, ever since…' Her indrawn breath was a ragged sob. 'But I had to, today. And I thought he was going to die and…and I realised I still love him. And when Dylan told me I'd been mean, I realised how horrible I have been. He tried to keep up the contact. He wrote to me. He rang me. He sent me presents. I ripped up the letters and blocked him from my phone. I sent the presents back. And then, when Mum died, I blamed him, even though I knew that wasn't fair. I'm…I'm not a very nice person, am I?'

Summer tilted her face up and her expression broke Zac's heart. It was easy for it to crack because it had become so incredibly full as he'd listened to her story. No wonder she'd believed the accusations she'd heard about him with regard to Shelley after experiencing the pain that deception and denial could cause and yet she'd been prepared to take his word that the accusations were unjustified.

And how hard must it be for her to trust any man?

But she had trusted *him* with not only the story but her own fear about what kind of person she was.

He had to gather her into his arms.

'You're the nicest person I've ever met,' he said

softly. 'And you don't have to do anything you're not ready to do. That includes talking to your dad or taking any responsibility for Dylan. I'll take care of everything.'

He pressed a kiss to the spiky hair that always felt so surprisingly soft. 'I'll take care of *you*,' he whispered. 'I love you, Summer.'

Those words blew everything else away.

It felt as if Summer had been adrift on a stormy sea for the last few hours, in a boat that was being dragged further and further into a storm where it would capsize and she would have no protection from the wild water in which she would inevitably drown.

But those words were an anchor. Something that could prevent the drifting and allow her to ride out the storm and then choose a safe path to find her way home.

They made the pain bearable. They made any doubts evaporate. Zac hadn't tried to defend her father in any way. He understood how hard it had been for her and he was ready to protect her completely. She didn't have to see her father or have anything more to do with her half-brother if that was what she wanted. He would take care of it all.

Those words made her feel safe.

It felt as if her own words had simply been waiting for the chance to escape. To be made real.

'I love you too, Zac.'

It was the moment for souls to touch through the windows that eyes provided. For trust to be offered. For lips to touch gently and linger to seal an emotional troth.

But the safety Zac's words promised gave Summer something else as well.

Strength.

'I think I do want to see Dad,' she said slowly. 'I've let this haunt me for too long. It's been like poison in my life. Probably in my relationships, too. I don't want that any more.'

Zac's smile was gentle. 'No poison permitted,' he said. 'Not for us.'

'I don't want it to hurt anyone else, either. Like Dylan.' The reminder that there was a scared kid curled up asleep on the couch in a relatives' room was a wake-up call. It was time to get back to reality.

'Let's go back.' Summer's limbs felt stiff as she got to her feet. How long had they been sitting there? 'We need to get stuff sorted. Like where Dylan's going to stay tonight.'

'He could come home with me. Gravy's really good at taking care of waifs and strays.'

'But he's not a waif. He's…he's part of my family.' Her breath came out in an incredulous huff. This was going to take some getting used to. 'I always wanted a sibling when I was a kid. Maybe this could be…I don't know…a gift, even?'

'Maybe it is.'

'So I guess I'll take him home with me. There's room on the boat. Flint will just have to sleep somewhere else.' She frowned. 'Except he might not want to. Dylan, that is. He thinks I'm mean. I suspect he hates me.'

Zac took her hand again as they crossed the road to the hospital entrance.

'He just needs the chance to get to know you. And I have a feeling that sleeping with Flint might be a pretty good place to start.'

'Maybe.' Summer smiled up at Zac as they headed

for the lift. 'I think the only point in my favour right now, though, is that I'm your girlfriend. You're the hero who saved his dad. *My* dad,' she added in a whisper.

It still didn't feel real. Her world was still spinning.

It was undeniably weird. But part of that weirdness was very, very good.

Zac *loved* her.

She could deal with anything on the strength of that. Even this.

CHAPTER NINE

ZAC WAS THE HERO, all right.

It was Zac that Dylan chose to have by his side when he walked into the intensive care unit later that evening to see his father—leaving as much distance as possible between himself and Summer.

It was Zac who drew Summer closer to his other side as they reached the bed that was flanked by a bank of monitors, IV stands and the nurse who was monitoring her new patient carefully. Jon Pearson was awake, but only just. He was still weakened by the massive blood loss he had suffered and the medication for his pain made staying awake almost impossible.

But it was Summer that Jon focused on first when his eyes fluttered open and, for the first time in so many years, she met the eye contact—and held it. Neither of them smiled. The moment was too big for that.

But it was a start. A new beginning?

A smile appeared for his young son.

'Still got my leg.' Jon's voice was croaky. 'We'll be riding those waves again soon, kid.'

Dylan was clearly struggling not to cry. He inched closer to Zac and lifted his chin but his voice wobbled. 'Your board's munted, Dad. It got chewed to bits.'

'No worries. I'll make a new one.' Jon closed his eyes and drew in a long breath before he pushed them open again. 'We'll put that one up on the wall. In the shop. People'll come from miles around to see it.'

His eyes drifted shut again. The brief conversation had exhausted him. The glance between the nurse and Zac gave the clear message that it was time for visitors to leave.

Zac put his hand on Dylan's shoulder. 'We'd better head off and let your dad get some rest, buddy. You can come and see him again tomorrow.'

'But I want to stay here.'

'Summer's going to take you home with her. On her motorbike. We found a helmet that will fit you back at the rescue base. She's got a cool bike—it's a Ducati. And it's red.'

The smile for Summer made her think of being out on the road with Zac's bike in front of her. Heading off so that they could spend time together somewhere special. The wave of longing was overwhelming. All she wanted to do right now was be somewhere with him again. Doing something that didn't involve such difficult emotional drama. They had only just declared their love for each other. How unfair was it that it was going to be impossible to spend this night in each other's arms?

Maybe Dylan noticed the look that passed between them. Or maybe he just wasn't impressed by the incentive that had been offered. He ignored Summer and fixed his gaze on Zac.

'Can't I go home with you?'

'Hey...I only live in a house. Summer lives on a

boat and it's really cool. And she has a dog. His name is Flint.'

'I don't like dogs.' The words were sullen.

It was an obvious effort for Jon to open his eyes again. 'Go with Summer, lad. She's…she's your big sister…'

Another moment of eye contact and this time Summer found a smile, albeit a wobbly one.

'I'll look after him, Dad. You rest.'

It was a promise that wasn't going to be easy to keep, Summer realised a short time later when, thanks to the bike ride, Dylan was forced to make physical contact by putting his arms around this unwelcome newcomer in his life. It felt even harder after Zac's bike peeled away to leave her alone in Dylan's company. He had offered to come back to the boat with them but Summer knew she had to make the effort herself. Maybe it was a kind of penance. Or a need to prove that she wasn't the monster that Dylan believed she was—the unknown other child who'd always been so mean to his dad.

Looking after him in a physical sense wasn't the problem. She could give him a safe place to sleep and feed him. Finding him some acceptable clothes might be more of an ask, but she could sort that kind of issue tomorrow. It was the emotional side of things that was far trickier. Dylan had lapsed back into the miserable silence he'd displayed while they were waiting in the relatives' room. She didn't even have a television to distract him with on the boat.

At least there was Flint, who was overjoyed to have company after a longer day than usual, and feeding her dog gave Summer something to do after a tour of her home that took such a short period of time.

'I'll make us something next. Do you like bacon and eggs?'

Dylan shrugged.

'You'll just have to ignore Flint trying to persuade you that he's still starving. He'd do anything for a bit of bacon rind.'

Sure enough, it was Dylan's foot that Flint laid his chin on when they were eating. Summer pretended not to see a piece of bacon rind being slipped under the table.

'Your bed is usually where Flint sleeps,' she told him, 'but I'll put some clean sheets on it and Flint can sleep somewhere else.'

Another shrug but it was clear that Flint intended to share his bed with the visitor when things were sorted for the night.

'Want me to put him somewhere else? Up on deck?'

'Nah.' Dylan climbed into the bed and edged to one side. 'I'm good. There's room.'

Summer took her hand off Flint's head and got a lump in her throat as she watched her dog step politely into the space provided and then curl up beside Dylan.

It was far too soon to offer the comfort of physical touch herself—for either of them—but Flint seemed to understand that that was exactly what was needed.

'Night, then. Just give me a yell if you need anything.'

A grunt indicated how unlikely that was but, as Summer turned away, she heard a small voice behind her.

'Did Zac mean what he said? About going for a swim in the morning?'

'Sure. Are you up for a bit of jogging, though? Flint will want to come and he can't go on the bike.'

Another grunt. 'Bet I can run faster than you can.'

He could. With his skinny legs and arms pumping, he stayed ahead of Summer with Flint close beside him and only slowed to wait for her when they got to an intersection and he didn't know what direction to take. By the time they got to the beach the first light of the day had strengthened enough to recognise the tall figure waiting alone and Dylan took off, even faster. Summer was a little out of breath by the time she caught up.

'You ready?' Zac asked Dylan. 'It'll be a bit cold.'

Dylan shrugged. 'Guess so. But there aren't any waves.'

He was right. Takapuna beach looked like a giant swimming pool this morning, calm enough to gleam under the rising sun. It would have been perfect for paddleboarding if they'd had more time.

'We get waves sometimes,' Zac told him. 'But this is just a wake-up dip. Last one in is a sissy…'

Maybe it was only Summer who noticed the tiny hesitation that gave Dylan the head start. The man and the boy ran into the sea, splashing through the shallow water and then diving as soon as it got deep enough. With a joyous bark, Flint took off to join them and Summer wasn't far behind.

The water was icy enough to make her gasp. By the time it felt bearable, it was time to get out. She and Zac both had to work today and there was a lot to get organised.

Zac seemed to have everything in hand, however, including towels waiting in a pile on the dry sand.

'Gravy's got breakfast ready. Do you like bacon and eggs, Dylan?'

Summer expected him to say that he'd had them already—for dinner last night—but she saw the way his gaze shifted to Flint, who was shaking seawater out of his coat.

'Yeah...bacon's cool.' And then he squinted up at Zac. '*Gravy?*'

It was such a perfect echo of the tone she had used herself the first time she'd heard the unusual name that Summer laughed. 'She's Zac's gran.'

Zac gave Dylan the same explanation as they headed for his apartment.

'Quick shower, then,' he ordered as they got inside. 'And I'll find some dry shorts for you. Might be a bit big, though.'

That shrug was becoming very familiar. 'Doesn't matter. My jacket's dry.'

The bright red and yellow jacket was the first thing Ivy commented on. 'Are you a lifeguard, Dylan?'

'Yep. My dad's in charge of the surf club. I help with Level One—the little nippers. We teach them about water safety and get them confident in the waves.'

Summer had never heard such a long speech from Dylan. There was something about Ivy Mitchell that broke through barriers of age or anything else, wasn't there?

'That's something to be proud of,' Ivy told him as she placed a laden plate in front of him. 'It's a wonderful organisation. I *always* swim between the flags.'

Zac snorted. 'You've never waited till the lifeguards are on duty to swim.'

Ivy looked affronted. 'But if I *did*, I'd swim between the flags.'

Zac and Summer laughed and, to her astonishment, a wide grin spread across Dylan's face a moment later. It was the first time she'd seen him smile. Even better, the smile didn't vanish as his gaze met hers. He even shook his head and then rolled his eyes as if to ask if this astonishing old lady was for real.

Ivy made it easy to organise the rest of their day.

'I can take Dylan into the hospital with me,' Zac said. 'And check on him during the day.'

'He can't stay in the hospital all day,' Ivy declared. 'And he needs some clothes. I'll take him shopping.' She winked at Dylan. 'I love shopping.'

'He needs to visit his dad,' Summer said. '...Dad,' she corrected herself.

The look that flashed between Zac and his grandmother told her that Ivy was already filled in on the fragile relationship but she gave no sign of any judgement.

'Of course he does. We'll go in on the bus after we've done our shopping. What do you need besides clothes, Dylan? A phone? Yes... You need to be able to text your dad. And your friends back home. And Summer, maybe, when she's at work.'

'I'll see what I can do about juggling shifts in the next couple of days,' Summer said. She was being excused from spending time with her father today and it felt like a reprieve. Or did it? 'But I'll drop in after my shift to visit and then I can take Dylan home.'

'Good.' Ivy wasn't going to allow for any more discussion. 'That's settled then. For today, anyway.'

'How long is my dad going to be in hospital?'

They all noticed the possessive pronoun that didn't include Summer.

'A fair while, I expect,' Zac told him gently. 'But we'll look after you, okay?'

'I've got a few days off coming up,' Summer said. 'First day's on Friday.'

'I've got Friday off, too,' Zac said. 'And you might be a bit over hanging around the hospital by then. We could do something fun, maybe.'

Dylan was staring at his plate. There was a pile of bacon rind carefully pushed to one side. Summer wondered how he might be planning to sneak it out to Flint, who was lying on the terrace with his nose on his paws, just inside the open French windows.

'Ever tried paddleboarding?' Zac continued.

Dylan snorted. 'Paddleboarding's for sissies.'

'Careful, mate...Summer's the queen of paddleboarding around here. And I'm learning and loving it.'

Ivy's lips twitched. Had she noticed how often Dylan's gaze strayed towards the doors? 'It's Flint's favourite thing to do,' she said. 'He rides on the end of Summer's board.'

Dylan's jaw dropped. 'No way...'

'Yes, way.' Summer nodded. 'And if you got good at it, he might ride on the end of your board.'

The shrug seemed more like an automatic reflex than something dismissive this time. 'Okay...I'll give it a go. If Dad's okay.'

'Friday's a day or two away,' Ivy said. 'Let's take this one day at a time, shall we? Now, scoot, you two. You've got jobs to go to. Dylan and I need to do the dishes and then go shopping. You'd better give that bacon rind to Flint, Dylan, before Summer takes him home.'

* * *

Day by day, Jon Pearson continued to improve after being moved from the ICU to a private room the day after his long surgery. Visiting became less awkward for Summer as she and Dylan got used to each other's company. While he seemed to accept her presence in his life, though, he wasn't in any hurry to share his father. She had yet to spend any time in Jon's company without Dylan being present and there were often others there as well. A steady stream of friends came from the west coast to visit and, in the first couple of days, there was the excitement of the media interest in the survival story of man versus shark. Dylan was clearly bursting with pride for his dad and that meant he spent as much time as he could glued to the side of his father's hospital bed.

And maybe the lack of any private time with her father was a good thing as they also got used to breathing the same air again. It meant that they only talked about safe stuff. Like their jobs. They could swap stories about dramatic incidents or the kind of training it took to be able to do what they did. Dylan was keen to share his own take on dramas at the wild beach that was his playground. He became more and more interested in hearing about Summer's work, too. Especially if the stories included Zac. There was a bit of hero worship going on there and that was fine. Thanks to both Zac and Flint, Summer had something to offer in the way of being a potential part of his family.

Not spending time alone with her father made life easier for now. Not being able to spend time alone with Zac was less welcome. Oddly, though, the lack of physical contact was bringing them closer on a completely different level. One that was making Summer think more about the future. About what an amazing father Zac would make. He seemed to know instinctively how to relate to Dylan. When playfulness was needed. When a word to the wise was called for. Considering that he'd grown up without a father as a role model for himself, it was extraordinary. But, then, he'd been brought up by Ivy so maybe it wasn't so unbelievable.

The time they spent together on Friday felt like a family outing. Jay was happy to provide paddleboards for them all and, fortunately, it was another day with a sea calm enough to make it easy for learners.

Ivy was on her terrace in a deckchair, watching closely enough to wave whenever Summer or Zac looked up at the house. She was paddling slowly, Flint on her board, with Zac and Dylan not far away. Having been kneeling until he got used to the feel of the board, Dylan was standing up now. He had to be getting tired but he was giving it everything he had, trying to keep up with Zac.

'Hey... Flint...' he yelled. 'Come on *my* board...'

'Go on,' Summer urged. 'It's okay. I won't be offended.'

'Come on, Flint.' Zac joined in the chorus. 'Share the love...'

The big black dog obligingly jumped off Summer's board, making it rock. For a short time, all they could see was the black head above the water and then he was hauling himself up onto a different board. But not Dylan's. He had chosen Zac's. The dog was used to the effort it took but Zac wasn't prepared for how unstable it made his board and he lost his balance and fell off. Flint stood on the board, anxiously watching for him to resurface, and then barked in relief as Zac caught the board. Summer and Dylan were both laughing so hard they almost fell off their own boards.

It was a moment she would remember for ever.

Shared laughter that created a bond. A family kind of moment.

Even the mention of it later made them laugh, lying on their towels and soaking up the sun as they rested tired limbs.

'Wait till I tell Dad how you fell off,' Dylan said. 'You should have seen your arms. You looked like a windmill.'

Summer's smile was more poignant. 'He chose your board,' she said. 'I hope you realise how honoured you are.'

Dylan dug his feet into the sand. 'He was supposed to choose mine.'

'He wasn't being mean,' Summer said. 'Maybe Zac's board was just closer.' She held Zac's gaze, though. She wanted him to know that she didn't believe that. That her dog had chosen him because he was his person now, too. As important in his life as Summer was.

That they were a kind of family already?

It could be like this with their own children one day, couldn't it?

Was she ready to trust that much? To give herself so completely to Zac?

Maybe Dylan guessed where her thoughts were going and felt left out. That might explain the glare she could feel that made her turn her head.

'What's up?' she asked. 'You hungry again?'

Dylan said nothing and an echo of what she'd just said replayed itself, the words taking on a new significance. She sighed. Maybe they weren't becoming as close as she'd thought.

'You still think I'm mean, don't you?'

'Just because you go and visit Dad now doesn't make it all right,' Dylan muttered. 'It's just because he's sick.'

'Summer's not mean,' Zac said quietly. 'I don't like hearing you say that, buddy.'

'She was mean to Dad. I saw him crying one day, when I was little. After one of those parcels came back. I heard him tell Mum how much he missed her. How much he *loved* her.' The emphasis was a statement of how little she had deserved it.

Summer's heart ached. How much time had she missed having a father in her life?

'It's going to be different from now on,' she said. 'I'm sorry about the way I acted. I was...'

'Hurt,' Zac finished for her. 'Summer wasn't that much older than you are, Dylan. How would it make you feel if your dad decided he wanted to go away and make another family? With someone else?'

'She could have come too.' Dylan's feet were almost buried in the sand now.

Zac's hand moved discreetly between the towels. Summer felt his fingers close around hers. Offering support. An ally. Telling her that Dylan might not believe she had deserved her father's continued love but *he* did. Telling her that she had *his* love now as well. She had to swallow hard and scrunch her eyes shut so that the full feeling in her heart didn't escape as tears.

'She had to look after her mum,' Zac said carefully. 'Her mum got sick.'

'My mum was sick.' Dylan's voice wobbled. 'She... she died.'

'So did Summer's mum.'

There was something different this time in Dylan's gaze when he raised it to meet Summer's. Almost... respect?

Zac gave her fingers a squeeze and then let go, as discreetly as he'd made the contact. He must have been able to sense how big this moment was but, yet again, he knew how to lighten things and make it seem no more than a natural step forward.

'It's cool living on a boat, isn't it?'

'I guess. But it doesn't go anywhere.'

'It could.' Summer was happy to move away from anything intense. 'The sails aren't any good but it's got a motor. I turn it on every so often to make sure it still goes. I should do it tonight, in fact. I'll let you turn it on, if you like.'

Dylan didn't respond. He had rolled onto his side and was tickling Flint's tummy.

Zac smiled. 'You didn't really mean it when you said you didn't like dogs, did you?'

A skinny bare shoulder gave a single shrug.

Zac's tone was as light as it had been when he'd mentioned the boat. 'Sometimes, when things are tough, we say—or do—stuff we don't really mean. Sometimes it's good to just forget about them and start again.'

They all lay there in silence after that. Silence that made it easy to hear Ivy's call from the terrace above.

'Yoo-hoo! Are you lot coming inside for some lunch?'

They got to their feet and gathered damp towels to shake the sand out of them. Walking up to the house, Zac took Summer's hand. Flint was on her other side with Dylan close beside him.

The boy looked up at Summer. 'Do you reckon Flint'll sit on my board one day, too?'

It was another one of those moments to treasure. Zac's hand was warm around hers. She had her beloved dog by her side and she knew she was about to make her little brother smile.

'I reckon you can count on that. Maybe next time we go out, even.'

Going out on the boards wasn't going to happen again any day soon. A summer storm was brewing and the next day the wind came up and the sky darkened ominously.

'We'll go and visit Dad after lunch,' Summer said. 'We can go shopping this morning and find him some presents. Some nice things to eat, maybe, seeing as he's feeling so much better. Hospital food's not up to much.'

'Zac said I could go and see where he works and he'd show me some cool stuff. Like the saw they use to cut people's chests open.'

'Did he? Okay...we'll have to see how busy they are in Emergency, though. We can't get in the way if Zac's in the middle of saving someone's life.'

Dylan's nod was serious. 'I wanna do that one day. I think I'm going to be a doctor like him.'

'You could be a paramedic, maybe. We get to save lives too, you know. And being on the helicopter is pretty exciting.'

Dylan's grin was sympathetic. 'Zac gets to do everything. He's the best.'

Summer had to grin back. 'Yeah...I think so, too.'

The best boyfriend. The best lover. And he would be the best father for any children she had.

Oh, yeah…she was so nearly ready to trust that much. Maybe the only thing in the way was to deal with the ghosts still haunting her past.

It was time to talk to her father. Properly.

The opportunity came later that day when Zac appeared during their visit to Jon and told Dylan he could have the promised tour of the emergency department.

'You want to tag along, Summer?' he asked.

'No, I'm good. I'll stay.'

The sudden tension in the room advertised that the significance wasn't lost on anybody. Dylan hesitated, clearly feeling protective of his father. He eyed Summer.

'Is that cool, Dad?'

'It's fine, son. Come back and see me later.'

Summer gave Dylan a smile intended to reassure him that she wasn't about to start being mean. Zac got the message, even if Dylan didn't. His glance, as they left, told her that he was impressed she had chosen to stay and have her first time alone with her father. Proud of her, even?

It was impossible to know how to start. Summer fiddled with the supply of grocery items she and Dylan had chosen to bring in. Fruit and biscuits and ginger beer. She held up a packet of sweets.

'Do you *really* love sour worms?'

'No. But Dylan does.'

'Ah…that might explain the salt and vinegar crisps, too.'

'No. I *do* love them. Might need a beer to go with them, though.'

Small talk seemed to be exhausted at that point. Summer finally sank into the chair beside the bed as the awkward silence grew.

It was Jon who broke it.

'I can't tell you how sorry I am, love. About what happened to your mum. About not being there. I know you think it's my fault that she died…'

Summer shook her head. 'I did, I guess. But I'm a bit older and wiser now. I get that people make their own choices. And I know Mum wasn't the easiest person but…she really did love you…'

'I know that. I loved her, too.'

'Not as much as you loved *her*…'

'Elsie?' Jon's smile was sad. 'That was a very different kind of love. We'd grown up together. We started dating when we were fourteen. We were always going to be together.'

Summer's jaw dropped. 'So why did you marry Mum?'

Jon lay back against his pillows, his eyes closing. 'Elsie's family had moved to Australia and she was a couple of years younger than me. She was going to come back to New Zealand as soon as she turned eighteen. And then we were going to get married.' His breath escaped in a long sigh. 'I was nineteen. Elsie had been away for more than a year and I…I was lonely. Not that that's an excuse but there was this big surf comp and a party afterwards and your mum was there and she…she made it clear how keen she was on me and…'

'And she got pregnant?'

'Yes. I had to tell Elsie and…and she was devastated. Said she never wanted to see me again. It was the worst time. Your mum was in love with me and she said she couldn't live without me and she really meant that. I was scared she'd hurt herself if I left and, besides, there was a baby involved and I wanted to do the right thing by everyone. And then you came along and I found a new kind of love that I thought would always be enough. I didn't think I'd ever see Elsie again but she turned up for a comp when you were about eight or so. And it was still there. The way we felt about each other.'

Summer was silent. How would she feel, she wondered, if she and Zac were forced apart and then she met him again years later? Would she still feel the same way?

Yes, her heart whispered. It would never change.

'We tried,' Jon said quietly. 'And, when it became too hard to stay away from each other, we still tried not to let it hurt you or your mum.'

'Did she know?'

'I think so. But she chose not to believe it. I think she thought that if she simply refused to believe it, it wouldn't be true. Her mental health was always a bit fragile. She had a stay in hospital after you were born with postnatal depression. I had about three months of looking after you by myself and…it might sound horrible but I'd never been happier. You were my little girl and I loved you to bits. I never, ever wanted to make life hard for you.'

Summer had tears trickling down the side of her nose. 'I'm sorry, too. For shutting you out. And the longer I did it, the easier it seemed to just leave it all behind and not go back.'

'Ah…don't cry, love.'

'But Dylan was right. I was mean to you.'

'You were a kid. And you were protecting your mum. That's not something to be ashamed of.'

Jon stretched out an arm and Summer was drawn from her seat and into a hug that took her back in time.

Back to before the tragedy of losing her mother. Back to a time when she and her father had shared so many magic moments. Like the moments she had had with Zac and Dylan so recently. The bonding family moments.

They didn't get wiped out, did they? Maybe they got covered up but you could find them again and how good was that?

'I kind of like having a brother,' Summer admitted when they finally stopped hugging and both blew their noses and regained some composure. 'He's a nice kid.'

'He's very like you were at that age.'

Summer smiled. 'Yeah...he's got seawater in his veins, too.'

'Has it been okay—having him to stay?'

'I think he likes the boat. And he loves Flint. And Zac.'

'You and Zac—is it serious?'

Summer's nod was shy. It was as serious as it could be, wasn't it? She couldn't wait to tell Zac about this conversation. About the moment when she knew she had forgiven her father because she recognised that his love for Elsie had been the way she felt about Zac. That being with anyone else would be living a lie.

'It must be getting in the way a bit, having a kid brother on the scene.'

'It's fine. It won't be for ever.'

'It could be a while longer, though. They say I'm healing well but I won't be up on my feet for a week or so and I won't be going home any time too soon. I'm worried about Dylan missing too much school. I've got friends who've offered to have him stay. Parents of his friends.'

'He'd be worried about you.'

'It's not that far. Someone could drive him over almost every day for a visit. If I send him home, he won't be interfering in your life so much.'

It was unfortunate that Zac and Dylan arrived back in the room at precisely that moment. Just in time to hear those last words.

Zac's eyebrows shot up. Dylan visibly paled.

'Are you sending me away?' he demanded.

'I'm just thinking about all the school you're missing. Come and sit down and we'll talk about it.'

'I don't want to go away. I like being here. I like Flint and…and paddleboarding and stuff.' Dylan glared at Summer and her heart sank. She hadn't been included in why he wanted to stay. Of course he must think she'd been complaining about him interfering with her lifestyle but that wasn't true. She needed to talk to him as well. She cast a helpless glance at her father.

'I'll explain,' he said quietly. 'Don't worry.'

But Dylan's face had shut down. He shoved his hands in his pockets. And then he frowned.

'Oh, no…where's my phone?'

'You had it downstairs. You were taking a photo of the rib spreaders, remember?'

'I must have left it there.'

'I'll go and look. I have to get back to work, anyway.'

'I'll come with you,' Summer said. 'And then I can bring the phone back. You stay here with Dad, Dylan.'

It was a relief to be alone with Zac. 'He's got the wrong idea,' she told him. 'I'd said how good it was having him but Dad thinks he's getting in the way of *us* being together.'

Zac's glance as he pressed the button for the lift gave Summer a jolt of sensation deep in her belly.

'I guess there is a bit of truth in it,' she admitted, as the door closed behind them.

'You think?'

They were alone in the lift. Zac caught her chin with one hand and ducked his head to place a lingering kiss on her lips. By the time the lift doors opened on the ground floor, Summer's legs were distinctly wobbly.

Oh, yes...they needed some time alone together. Soon.

'I had the kit open in my office to show him,' Zac said. 'I reckon that's where the phone will be.'

They had to go through the emergency department to get to the office. To Summer's surprise, she heard someone calling her name.

'*Kate*...what on earth are you doing here?'

'I had to come in with Shelley. Felix broke his leg. It looks like... Oh, it's all such a mess, Summer. I'm so glad *you're* here...'

Kate's gaze shifted to the man by her side and there was no way Summer could avoid this.

'This is Zac,' she said quietly. 'Zac Mitchell.'

The door to the resus area behind Kate opened further and Mandy appeared. Summer could see into the room properly now. A young woman was sitting on the bed. She was crying and she had a small, limp boy in her arms. A boy who had dark curly hair and big dark eyes.

A boy who looked remarkably like Zac?

CHAPTER TEN

A PART OF Summer's brain had frozen.

She couldn't think straight and it was frightening. To be able to do her job, she *had* to be able to think straight no matter how many things were happening at once or how horrible those things might be.

But this was different. This involved a person she was intimately involved with and this time she couldn't step back and try to cloak herself with a clinical perspective, the way she'd been able to do when she had to deal with treating her father.

This was about Zac. And whether she'd been right in following her heart and giving him her trust. It had been given; there was no question about that. It had been given totally in that moment of connection with her father when she'd recognised that the strength of how she felt about this man would last a lifetime.

But even that truth seemed to be outside the anaesthetised part of her brain. Or maybe she couldn't catch it because too many other things were demanding her attention.

Kate had taken hold of her arm and her tone was urgent. 'I tried to call an ambulance but she said she had to take Felix to Auckland General and just put him in the car and took off. All I could do was follow. And now she won't let anyone touch him. Mum and Dad are on their way but...'

Rob was coming towards them, stripping off gloves. 'Right,' he said. 'I'm clear. We've got a two-year-old with a query fractured femur.'

'His GCS is down,' Mandy told the consultant. 'I'm worried about blood loss.'

Rob gave a curt nod. 'Children compensate too well to start with. Let's get a type and cross match stat, in case we need some blood products.'

'Do you need a hand?' Zac's voice was quiet. Calm. It made Summer think of the way she had been when faced with treating her father. At least Zac was managing to function professionally. His brain hadn't frozen.

Rob nodded. 'Hang around for a minute. Just in case.' He turned back to Mandy. 'Has the paediatric orthopaedic team been paged?'

'Yes...' Mandy lowered her voice. 'And we might want to page Psyche, too.'

'What?' Rob was instantly on the alert. 'Why?'

'It's a bit odd. She hasn't let anyone else touch him since she carried him in. She got hysterical when we tried so that's why we got her to carry him in here.'

Rob looked past Mandy. And then took a second look and stepped further into the room. 'Shelley, isn't it? Didn't you work here not so long ago?'

'Hi, Rob. You remember me?' Shelley's tears evaporated as she smiled. 'Not the best way to have a reunion, is it?'

'This is your son?'

'His name's Felix.'

'We need to look after Felix.' Rob moved closer but

didn't try to touch his young patient. 'He's hurt his leg, yes?'

'I don't want anyone to hurt him.' Shelley's hold on the toddler tightened and the child whimpered.

The sound made Summer feel ill. It was the first sound she had heard Felix make and it wasn't the normal cry of a child in pain. She knew to worry a lot more about the quiet ones. Especially when they seemed so quiet and well behaved in a frightening situation. And this injury was serious. She could see how swollen the small thigh was and the odd angle of his lower leg. The colour of his foot wasn't good, either. Urgent treatment was needed.

Kate was still holding onto Summer's arm as she moved closer to Rob so she was forced to move as well.

'There's been a series of accidents recently,' she said. 'Some bad bruises. Shelley said it's because he keeps falling off the new bike he got for Christmas but...'

The look in her eyes said it all. Even Shelley's own family were suspicious that the injuries weren't accidental.

'Trampolines are dangerous.' Shelley's voice was calm. 'I *told* Mum and Dad he was too young to have one but they went ahead and bought it, didn't they?' She bent her head over Felix and rocked him in her arms. 'It's all right, baby. Everything's going to be all right...' She started humming a song.

Rob stepped back from the bed, his face grim. 'Yep. Page Psyche. And we'll go ahead with treatment without signed consent if we have to. Let's see if we can get an IV in and I want to get that leg splinted properly before we do anything else to try and prevent any more blood loss.'

He turned back to Shelley. 'We need you to sign a consent form, Shelley, so that we can treat Felix. You know the drill, don't you?'

Shelley stopped singing. She nodded without looking up. 'That's why I had to come here,' she said. 'I don't think I can bring myself to sign a form that means you're going to hurt my baby. His father can do that.'

'His father?' Rob looked sideways as if he expected to see someone else in the room but there was only Zac, standing near the door, Mandy, who was wheeling the IV trolley closer, Summer and Kate, who leaned in to whisper in her ear.

'I didn't mean to tell her that Zac was back in the country,' she said. 'It just slipped out...'

'Yes.' Shelley raised her head and she was smiling sweetly, her gaze fixed on Zac. 'That's his daddy. Zac. Dr Mitchell.'

It wasn't just Summer's brain that was frozen now. The whole world seemed to have stopped spinning.

'Oh, my God...' The packages containing the cannula and swabs dropped from Mandy's hands.

Rob's jaw dropped.

'Oh...no...' Kate buried her face in her hands.

Zac simply stared at Shelley, his face utterly blank and immobile.

Shelley smiled back at him, the Madonna-like expression completely out of place given that she was holding her badly injured child.

And then, as if given a director's cue, everybody turned to look at Felix. Still pale and limp, he looked back at all these strangers with those big dark eyes. From a perfect little face that was framed by soft dark curls.

The heads turned again, as if at some bizarre tennis match, to look at Zac.

There was no denying that it seemed quite possible he was Zac's child.

Zac's voice was as expressionless as his face. 'I am *not* his father.'

Mandy made an odd sound as she stooped to collect the packaging. 'But…I remember now. Shelley was always bringing you stuff. Cakes. Even flowers…and…' She straightened and looked at Felix again, her words trailing into silence.

Doubt hung in the air. As palpable as thick smoke.

Summer stared at Zac. The numb part of her brain was coming back to life. Painfully. She had had those doubts herself but she had dismissed them on nothing more than Zac's word. On instinct. But her instincts weren't always to be trusted, were they?

She'd believed Shelley when she'd first proclaimed the paternity of the baby she was pregnant with and she'd been wrong about that. She'd believed her mother when she'd said that no man could be trusted and that love wasn't enough. That what had gone wrong in her life was her father's fault. She'd been wrong about that too and look at how much damage trusting her instincts had already done.

All she needed now was the reassurance that she was right to trust Zac.

To love him…

But she couldn't see anything. He could have been looking at Rob or Mandy or Kate. Possibly even Shelley. There was nothing there for her to read and, just for a dreadful moment, fear kicked in. A dreadful certainty that there was something he hadn't told her.

What if he *was* hiding the real truth?

And then something happened that forced an abrupt break to that desperate eye contact.

Felix screamed—a tortured sound that gave way to broken sobbing.

Rob spoke briefly to Zac and then gave Mandy a curt nod and took a tourniquet from her hand. It was past time they got some pain relief on board for this little boy.

Shelley burst into tears as well. 'I didn't mean it,' she sobbed. 'It just *happened...*'

Kate moved to touch her sister. 'It's okay,' she said. 'We're going to look after you. *And* Felix.'

More people arrived in the resus area. The paediatric orthopaedic consultant, who had two registrars with her. Another nurse, who was carrying a paediatric traction splint, and an older woman who didn't have a stethoscope around her neck. The psyche consultant, perhaps? Or someone from Social Services?

Zac was edged further back in the room and Summer couldn't catch his gaze again.

She didn't need that reassurance, did she? This was *Zac* and of course she believed him. Shelley was crazy. She wanted to say something but the noise level in the room was rising and the moment had long gone. X-ray technicians were getting ready to use the overhead equipment. Tubes of blood were being handed to a junior nurse. An IV line was in place and medication had been administered. Felix, thankfully, was now sedated and peacefully asleep.

Stuck in a corner behind Kate at the head of the bed, Summer couldn't even move without disrupting something that was far more important than her need to talk to Zac.

'Do you need blood on standby?' One of the ED registrars was by Rob's shoulder as he was getting the splint ready to go on the small twisted leg. Summer had been asked to provide support when they were ready to fasten the Velcro straps and put the traction on to straighten the leg.

'Yes, please. Just in case. Have we got the type and cross match back already?'

'Yes. And it's good that we checked. He's AB negative.'

Summer's brain raced. AB negative was the rarest blood group there was. And she was pretty sure that the parents had to have the blood groups of A, B or AB.

'That means that someone who's an O couldn't be his father, doesn't it?'

Rob nodded. 'You ready?'

'Yes.' Summer lifted Felix's foot, keeping one hand under the calf. The splint was slipped into place and Rob began to fasten the straps. 'Zac's an O.'

The look Rob gave her was scathing. 'You didn't really think he was lying, did you?'

'No. Of course not. But this *proves* it…' But Summer could feel the colour flooding her cheeks.

She'd meant that it was proof for Shelley's family. For the psychiatrist. But she'd made it sound as if *she* had needed the proof. And she hadn't. But Rob didn't believe that. What if Zac didn't believe it, either? She would never be able to erase that last time their eyes had met. When she'd bought into that collective doubt for just a moment in time because she was so sure there was something he hadn't told her. A moment that could potentially have been long enough to destroy the trust they had built between them. Possibly irreparably. And she couldn't blame him entirely if it did.

She had to get out of here. She had to find Zac.

'I'm sorry, but I've got to go,' she told Kate. 'I'll be back later.'

Pushing her way out of the resus room, Summer scanned the emergency department. An ambulance crew she recognised were handing over a patient at triage. Orderlies were pushing patients in beds or wheelchairs. A nurse was wheeling a twelve lead ECG machine into a cubicle. A group of doctors were standing around a computer screen looking at the results of an MRI scan. There were people everywhere but no sign of Zac.

She went to his office. It was empty, but there, on the corner of his desk, was a mobile phone. Dylan's phone. The reason they'd come down here in the first place. The reason they'd had those brief moments in the lift when he'd kissed her with all the pent-up passion of not having been able to make love to her for days now.

And superimposed on those thoughts was the image of Zac's face and the way he'd looked at her that last time. As if he didn't even recognise who she was.

*Oh...God...*was it possible that that kiss in the lift was the last one she would ever receive from him?

Summer clutched Dylan's phone.

She could ring Zac. Or text him.

And say what? That the blood results were back and now everyone believed him? With the unspoken assumption that that 'everyone' included her?

No. This was too big for a message that could be misinterpreted in any way. Too big for communication that couldn't include body language or touch, even.

In the moment of indecisiveness, the phone in her hand began to ring. For a heartbeat, the wild hope that it might be Zac brought the sting of relieved tears to her eyes.

'Is that you, love?'

'Oh…Dad…'

'Dylan wanted to check that you'd found his phone.'

'Um…yes…'

'I need you to take him home. To collect his things. We've had a talk and I've got friends coming to collect him this evening.'

'Okay…I'm on my way. Just give me a minute or two, yes?'

She had to go back to the resus room first. Rob was amongst the team members who were standing back as a series of X-rays were being taken.

'Rob?' Summer tried to catch his attention discreetly. 'Do you know where Zac is?'

'I told him to go home early. To get himself away from this until it's sorted.' Rob's gaze was on Shelley, who was now flanked by two security guards and well away from her son. He shook his head. 'It's always so much worse when there are kids involved in this kind of crisis.'

Indeed it was. And now Summer had a child involved in what felt like a personal crisis of her own. She raced back to her father's ward. Dylan made no protest about being bundled into his jacket and helmet for the ride home and it took all of Summer's focus to cope with the traffic and blustery conditions as she rode over the exposed harbour bridge. Rain wasn't far off now and it could well be accompanied by a thunderstorm by the look of the turbulent sky.

Dylan ignored Flint when they arrived at the boat, which should have been a warning sign, but Summer had too much else on her mind.

'I've got to go and see Zac—just for a minute,' she told Dylan. 'I'm sure he'll want to see you before you go tonight.'

His look was as scathing as the one Rob had given her not so long ago but she couldn't explain why she had to see Zac face to face instead of ringing him. Or to try and reassure him that Zac didn't want him out of the way and not interfering with his life any more than she did. She wouldn't know where to begin, trying to explain any of it to a young boy, and there simply wasn't the time.

'It'll take fifteen minutes. Twenty, tops. You pack up your stuff and, as soon as I get back, I'll take you back to the hospital so your friends can collect you.'

'Fine.' Dylan turned away from her, the word a dismissal.

It was only a few minutes' ride away but the lower level of Ivy's house had an empty feel to it. Summer kept knocking on the door but the sinking feeling got stronger. Nobody was there to answer it.

A voice came from the balcony above, though.

'Is that you, Summer?'

'Yes.' She stepped back until she could see Ivy peering over the railing. 'I'm looking for Zac.'

'He's not home yet. Come inside and wait for him. This weather's getting dreadful.'

'I can't. I've got to get back to Dylan. If you see him...can you tell him I'm looking for him?'

'Of course.' Ivy pushed wind-whipped strands of hair back from her face. 'Is everything all right, darling?'

Again, Summer had no idea where to begin. She could only nod, emphatically enough to try and reassure herself. If nothing else, the action had the bonus of holding back tears.

If Zac wasn't home by the time she'd taken Dylan back to the hospital and returned, then she would tell Ivy everything. Surely this amazing woman was old and wise enough to be able to tell her how to fix something that seemed to be more and more broken with every passing minute.

It had probably been a little more than twenty minutes when Summer eased her bike into the stand at the marina. She hurried down the jetty to the mooring. Past all the yachts she knew almost as well as *Mermaid*, all of them bobbing on an increasingly disturbed bed of water. Most were empty, waiting for their owners to have some spare time at the weekend. A few, like hers, had people living in them.

Clive was the closest marina neighbour and he was the friend who could look after Flint if she was ever caught out on a job.

He was out on his deck right now, tying things down in preparation for the coming storm. He stopped what he was doing and stared at her, a rope dangling from his hands.

'*Summer!* What on earth are you doing here?'

The odd query stopped her in her tracks. Why wouldn't she be here, on her way to her home?

'I saw you going out. Fifteen or so minutes ago. Thought you must be getting the boat out of the water or something.'

'*What?*'

Summer started running, her boots thumping on the wooden boards of the jetty. She got to the point where Flint was usually sitting to await her return. Beside the bollards that her ropes were always curled around to anchor the boat.

There was nothing there. Just an empty space—the water dark and rippled.

Summer looked out at the harbour. It was already darker than it should be for this time of day. There were plenty of small yachts anchored away from the marina and they were all moving in the wind and the roll of the sea so it took a minute to make sure that none of the movement was as purposeful as it would be if there was anybody on board.

If there was a motor running.

She couldn't see *Mermaid* anywhere.

Dylan had taken her. With Flint on board.

He'd run away.

Thank goodness her brain didn't freeze this time. Summer knew exactly what she had to do. She pulled her phone out and made two calls.

The first was to the coastguard to raise the alarm.

The second was to Zac.

'Summer?' His tone was wary. Had he been reluctant to even answer her call?

'Zac...where are you?'

'I'm at the rescue base. I came in to have a chat to Graham.'

About giving up being a HEMS member, perhaps, so that he didn't have to work with her any more? The thought intruded even if it was completely irrelevant right now—fear for others was overwhelming any fear for herself.

'Dylan's gone. He's taken *Mermaid*.'

'No way… *How?*'

'I showed him how to start the motor last night. And I…' Summer squeezed her eyes shut. This was all her fault. She'd taught Dylan how to make the boat move and then she'd left him alone long enough to give him a head start. She'd known he was upset and *that* was her fault, too. He'd overheard the tail end of the conversation she'd had with their father and he had only been beginning to be ready to share the most important person in his life with the girl who'd been so mean to him for so long.

'There's not much petrol,' she added desperately. 'He could be drifting by now. He doesn't know how to use the radio and he's got Flint on board as well and…' Her voice caught in a strangled sob.

Zac's voice was calm in her ear. Any wariness had vanished. 'Have you called the coastguard?'

'Yes. Of course.'

'There'll probably be a call coming in here soon, then. Monty's on base. I'll ask him whether it's possible to go out in this weather. How soon can you get here?'

Summer was already running back towards her bike. 'I'm on my way.'

CHAPTER ELEVEN

As a doctor, Zac Mitchell knew that a heart couldn't actually break.

As a man, he knew that that was exactly what happened to his heart the moment he saw Summer arrive at the rescue base.

One look into her eyes and he could feel it happening with a pain like no other he had ever experienced.

Of course she was afraid. Her young brother and her beloved dog were out there on an unforgiving sea in a small boat in a breaking storm but—as he held the eye contact for a heartbeat longer—he could see another layer to that fear.

Summer could feel the distance between them.

And she knew why it was there.

She had doubted him. He might love her more than he thought it was possible to love anyone, but how could he commit to spending his lifetime with someone who had doubted him—about *that*—even if it had only been for an instant?

But right now that didn't matter.

What mattered was that Summer needed him and he could be here for her a hundred per cent, even if it would be for the very last time.

He closed the physical distance between them with a couple of long strides and then he gathered her into his arms and held her close enough to feel his heart beating against her small body.

'We'll get through this,' he promised. 'Together.'

The hug was a brief one. They weren't alone, even though most of the day's crew had gone home.

Graham's face was grim. 'The coastguard's boat has been tied up with an incident out on Waiheke Island. They're on their way but conditions are worsening and the light's fading fast.'

'We've got to find them.' Summer's face was white. 'What if they drift into a shipping lane? With no lights?'

The thought of what would happen to a small boat, unseen by a container or cruise ship, was horrific.

Monty looked away from the weather maps and rain radar he had on the computer screen in front of him. 'We'll take the chopper up. Turn on the sun.'

Graham shook his head. 'It's getting marginal for flying.'

Monty's chair scraped on the floor. 'We'd better get on with it, then.'

Summer raced to her locker to grab her gear. Zac was right behind her.

'You don't have to do this,' she told him. 'I would never ask you to put yourself in danger for my sake.'

Zac could only meet her gaze for a moment. 'You would never *have* to ask,' he said. 'And I'm coming. End of story.'

Every minute that passed was a minute too long.

It took time to scramble into the gear they needed for an offshore rescue mission like this. A titanium undervest and Poly-Lycra under-suit and then the specially designed wetsuit. The lifejacket came equipped with a range of accessories like a strobe light and mini flare, a whistle and a knife and even survival rations.

They strapped themselves into winching harnesses even though they knew how unlikely it was that it would be safe to be winched onto a moving target like a boat in this kind of weather. It took more time for Monty to complete pre-flight checks and get them airborne. And then minute after minute flicked past as they circled the inner harbour, working out from the marina where the *Mermaid* had been moored.

There was no sign of any small craft, including the coastguard vessel. Even the larger ferries were on the point of suspending services and the only people going near their yachts were those who were trying to make them more secure as the storm bore down on the city. The flash of lightning on the horizon heralded the first squall of rain that obscured visibility enough to make Monty curse.

'We'll have to abort if this keeps up.' But there was no indication that the pilot had any intention of calling it quits yet and Summer knew that this was the kind of challenge that Monty thrived on. He'd keep them as safe as possible but would also take them right to the edge if that was what was needed to save a life.

The squall passed and the helicopter rode the rough air to move further towards the open sea. They were over the shipping lane between Rangitoto and Takapuna beach now—the track that the big container and cruise ships took to gain entry to the city's harbour. Fortunately, there was no sign of any large vessels. Unfortunately, there was no sign of any smaller ones either.

'The swell's getting big enough to make it hard to see,' Zac said. 'Turn on the sun, Monty.'

The night sun was a light attached under the nose of the helicopter that had the strength of thirty million candles. Below them, the white foam of breaking waves on the big swells covered the inky blackness of the deep water below.

Summer's stomach sank and then rose with every air pocket that Monty negotiated. Her heart just kept on sinking. They weren't going to find the *Mermaid*. It would get thrown onto rocks and there would be no way to rescue Dylan. Or Flint.

'*There...*' Zac's shout was triumphant. 'Nine o'clock.'

'*Where?*' Summer's heart was in her mouth now. 'I can't see them.'

'Wait...'

The water rolled and, yes...there she was, riding the swell. Still afloat but clearly without power. Being washed towards the rocky coastline.

Monty was on the radio instantly, relaying the co-ordinates to both the coastguard and the team ready to mobilise on shore.

'Can you get me down?' Summer's hand was already on her harness, her gaze on the winch cable that would need to be attached.

'Bit dodgy...' Monty's tone was a warning. 'You sure about this, Summer?'

'No.' It was Zac who spoke—the word an appalled exclamation. 'I'll go down.'

'The coastguard's not far away,' Monty said. 'They'll be able to get someone on board.'

'My brother's down there,' Summer responded. She surprised herself with how calm she sounded. 'He's just a kid. He must be terrified.' She caught Zac's gaze and held it. Flashing through her head was the memory of the last time they had faced the possibility of a tricky winch job—when they'd been called to that young forestry worker with the chest injury. When the question of how much she really trusted Zac had been raised. When she'd known how much she *wanted* to trust him and she'd wanted the chance to demonstrate that trust. Wanted the kind of bond that could only be forged by meeting—and winning—a life-threatening challenge.

She should have been careful what she'd wished for...

But here it was.

'Please, Zac...' Her voice was almost a whisper but seemed magnified by both the internal microphone system and the desperate plea in her tone. 'I need you to winch me down.'

He didn't want to do it. She could feel the strength of how much he didn't want the responsibility of her life dangling on the end of a wire. Trying to time the descent so that she didn't meet the deck of the boat as it came up on a rising swell. She could break her legs. Get tangled on the mast. Smash her head against the side of the boat...

He could refuse and that would be an end to it.

But he knew how much she needed to do this.

And he had to know she would only ask because she trusted him completely.

'Okay...' The word was almost a groan. 'I'll do it.'

It was possible to lock into his training and keep things completely professional up until the moment when Summer stepped off the skid to dangle in the air below the helicopter. Monty had just as much responsibility for keeping her safe but it felt as if he had her life in his hands.

And he couldn't let anything happen to threaten that.

Right now, the pain of knowing she had doubted his word was utterly irrelevant. She was trusting him with her life.

And he *loved* her...

How could he have even believed for a moment that he would prefer to live without her in his life?

Nothing mattered other than keeping her safe. Keeping Dylan safe. Even keeping Flint safe because Summer loved him.

And he loved her...

The tense minutes of the descent had sweat trickling down his spine beneath the layers of safety gear.

'Minus six metres.' Summer sounded remarkably calm. 'Five...four...no, five...'

It was so hard to judge with depth perception changed by the artificial light, let alone the heaving sea changing the actual distance. They had to time the swells and wait for the moment when they could—hopefully—get the meeting of Summer's body and the solid deck of the boat exactly right.

And, somehow, they did.

There was an awful moment as Summer fell on landing and slipped across the sloping deck. It looked as if she would go overboard or potentially get caught and he would have to fire the charge that would cut the cable and prevent the helicopter being pulled from the sky. How had she managed to find a handhold and release her connection to the cable at the same time? But there she was, clinging to a handrail and holding the cable clear as she gave the signal to wind it back in.

'Take it up, Zac...' Her words were a breathless but relieved statement. 'I'm good.' He must have imagined the grin because he couldn't possibly see from this distance, but he could still hear the words despite how quiet they were. 'Thanks, mate...'

And then she disappeared into the interior of the yacht and, only seconds later, the lights of the coast-guard boat could be seen approaching. There was nothing more that the helicopter crew could do except provide light as another difficult mission was launched to take the disabled *Mermaid* under tow and get her back to safety.

It was over.

Every bone in Summer's body ached.

Her heart ached now, too. For a while, she had forgotten the finality of the way Zac had looked at her when they'd been in the emergency department with Shelley and Felix.

Fear had taken over. And then the adrenaline rush of the rescue mission. By the time the *Mermaid* had been safely towed into port, the helicopter had long since landed, which was just as well as the storm had well and truly broken. Dramatic forks of lightning and crashing thunder were a background for getting Dylan safely back to the hospital and his father.

He stayed glued to Summer's side as they walked towards the ward.

'Dad's going to be so mad at me, isn't he?'

'No. He's going to be too relieved that you're okay. Like I am.'

The look that passed between them acknowledged the bond that had been forged under circumstances neither of them could ever forget. In the moment she had climbed into *Mermaid*'s cabin to find a terrified boy crouched in a corner with his arms tightly around a big black dog and she had put her own arms around both of them for a long wordless hug.

There were more hugs in that hospital room. And words of reassurance from both Jon and Summer that Dylan wasn't being banished. That they were a family now and nothing was going to be allowed to break that.

Yes. A poignant joy had taken over from the fear.

The dramatic start of the storm had settled into steady, drenching rain by the time Summer and Flint were given a ride home by Monty, who had come to pick them up from the coastguard's base.

And it was then that Summer realised she had no home to go to. The *Mermaid* couldn't be towed back to her marina until the weather improved.

'Come home with me,' Monty said. 'We can collect your gear from the boat tomorrow.'

But Summer shook her head. Because the fear had returned. The overwhelming relief that her brother and her dog were safe was wearing off. The joy of knowing she had a real family again was also being pushed into the background. What if she had lost Zac from her life? She hadn't seen him for hours now. Hadn't heard from him either, but then her phone had got wet during that rough ride back on the coastguard vessel and it was completely dead.

As dead as that dreadful message in the look that Zac had given her when she'd been seeking reassurance? As dead as the future she had started to dream of? One that had included children that they would take to the beach and build sandcastles with. Teach them to paddleboard so that they could stand up one day and wave at their great-grandmother, who would be watching from her deck.

Ivy...

The yearning for the kind of wisdom and warmth and humour that only Ivy Mitchell could dispense was suddenly overwhelming.

'I need to go to Takapuna,' she told Monty quietly. 'Down by the beach. I'll show you which house.'

The rain was so heavy that both she and Flint had runnels of water cascading off them by the time the knock on Ivy's door was answered.

Not by Ivy.

It was Zac who wrenched the door open but that was all he did. He simply stood there, staring at her. She could see the breaking tension in his face. Relief. *Love...?*

'For heaven's sake, Isaac...what are you *thinking*? Get them inside...' Ivy tugged her grandson away from the door. 'Come in, darling. Oh, my goodness. You're completely *soaked...*'

Flint stayed where he was as Summer moved.

'You too,' Ivy ordered and Flint stepped cautiously onto the polished floorboards, puddles gathering under every paw. 'I'll get towels. Isaac, take Summer downstairs to your place. She needs a shower.' She waited until they were both at the head of the internal staircase, Summer's hand tightly encased in Zac's. 'And a proper hug,' she called after them. 'Don't forget your manners. I'll see you both in the morning.'

It was an instruction they should both have been

able to laugh about as soon as they closed the door to the rest of the world behind them but neither of them was even smiling.

Zac pulled Summer into his arms and held her so tightly she couldn't breathe.

'Don't ever scare me like that again,' he growled. 'I thought…. Oh, my God…I thought I was going to lose you.'

It didn't seem to matter that he was getting wet. Or that she couldn't breathe. The hope that this meant Zac still loved her as much as she loved him was enough to survive on. Summer never wanted to move. She wanted to feel his heart beating against her cheek like this and feel his arms around her like the strongest, safest protection ever.

It was Zac who released the hold enough to move and see her face.

'Are you okay? You didn't get hurt?'

'I'm fine.'

'And Dylan?'

'He got the fright of his life but he's okay, too. He's with Dad—waiting to get taken back to the west coast tonight.'

The breath that Zac released was a long sigh. 'And Flint's good. He'll get dried off and we'll be lucky if there's any bacon for us at breakfast. That's all that matters.' His mouth quirked into a crooked smile. 'I'm not sure what Gravy meant by a "proper" hug but a hug is not quite what I'm thinking about right now.'

Summer's gaze dropped from those gorgeous dark eyes to the mouth that she loved almost as much. Her eyes drifted shut as her lips parted to murmur agreement but the only sound that emerged was a whimper of need as Zac's lips found hers.

And, for a very long time after that, the need for a shower or anything else was completely forgotten.

It was a time for a reunion—both physical and emotional. A time to celebrate a bond that could survive testing times and only become deeper.

Stronger.

A time for the kind of honesty that provided the glue for that kind of bond.

'I'm sorry I doubted you,' Summer whispered in the quiet hours of the night, as she lay in the warmth of Zac's embrace. 'It was only for a moment.'

'You weren't the only one.'

'Everybody knows the truth now. And I don't think it was about Felix that made me feel that way. I just couldn't help feeling that there was *something* you hadn't told me.'

'There was.' Zac was silent for a long moment. 'Because it's something I've never told anyone. Nobody knows, except for Gravy. I don't even like thinking about it.'

Summer waited out the new silence. Only her fingers moved where they lay splayed on his chest—an almost imperceptible caress of encouragement. She was being invited into possibly the most private part of Zac's life, here.

'It wasn't the accusation that I was the father of Shelley's baby that shocked me the most,' Zac told her. 'It was the idea that I could have pushed her down any stairs. My stepfather...he was abusive. Violent. I could never hurt a woman. *Ever...*'

'I know that,' Summer said softly. She pressed her

lips against the soft skin close to her face. 'I couldn't trust you any more than I do now. I love you so much.'

'Not as much as I love *you*.' Another soft sigh escaped Zac. 'So much I can't begin to find the words.' He moved, bending his head so that he could place another tender kiss onto Summer's lips. A kiss that was enough to move them onto a new space. One that accepted the past and made it part of a foundation instead of a barrier.

'Gravy's got a dream,' he told her then. 'She wants to live long enough to throw confetti at our wedding and drink too much champagne at the reception. She wants dogs tracking sand into the house and babies playing in the garden and on the beach. She even mentioned a paddleboard or two propped up by the shed.'

'Ohh…' Summer was smiling but she could feel tears gathering in her eyes.

Tears of joy.

'You like that idea too?'

The question was almost shy.

'It sounds like the best idea *I've* ever heard.' It seemed an effort to draw in a new breath and it seemed as if the whole world was holding it with her. 'Do you?'

She didn't really need to ask. She could feel the answer in the way Zac was holding her. The way he pressed his lips against her hair.

But it was still good to hear the words. So, *so* good…

'I don't think I could come up with a better one.' But then his voice took on a wicked edge as his lips found hers yet again. 'Or maybe I can,' he murmured. 'Just for now…'

* * * * *

To my brother, Regina: You are needed!

IT'S ALWAYS BEEN YOU

ELLE WRIGHT

To my mother, Regina. You are missed.

Chapter 1

Dr. Lovely Washington frowned when she felt the sun beaming down on her. Morning already? She patted the mattress, pausing when she felt cool skin under her palm. Drake. She pinched him. He pushed her hand away, grumbling something incoherent.

She smacked him. "Drake, what are you doing in my bed? And please…close the blinds. The light is killing me."

"Whashuleafmelone," he mumbled.

"I won't leave you alone until you get up and shut out the sun," she said, pinching her forehead. "My head hurts. And aren't you late or something?"

When he didn't move, she went to throw the sheet off, then stopped abruptly. Frowning, she patted her bare breasts. Uh-oh. *Where is my shirt*? Reluctantly, she slipped her hand under the sheet, over her stomach, her belly button, her—

She sat up abruptly. "Oh, my God, I'm naked!" Her mind raced to remember how she'd ended up like that. Last night was a blur. They'd booked a two-bedroom suite at the Bellagio because her family reunion was there. Two rooms, two beds. Yet Drake was in her bed and she was naked. "Oh no."

Drake had agreed to come because she hated going to these things by herself, and she wasn't particularly thrilled to face her family alone after her breakup with Derrick. When she needed someone—and she did— Drake was always there. He was her very best friend, since the age of two.

Her night had taken a turn for the worse when she'd received a call from the hospital that she'd lost a patient. Drake had dragged her out onto the Strip to distract her. That was all she remembered.

She held her face in her hands, praying the shooting pain in her head would stop. She remembered something else. Tequila. Lots of it. Peeking through her fingers at Drake, she sucked in a deep breath. She couldn't tell if he was naked. He was lying on his stomach, his bare back gleaming at her in the sunlight. The sheet was draped low. Gently, she lifted the thin material.

"Drake!" she screeched, digging her nails into his back.

He pushed himself up on his elbows. "Ouch! What?"

"Get up," she ordered through clenched teeth. "Now."

He blinked and glanced at her with one eye. "What happened?"

Pulling the sheet with her, she hopped out of the bed. "Look at you," she said, pointing at his bare ass. "You're naked! Oh, my God."

"Oh, shit." He rolled out of bed onto the floor with a loud thump. Reaching up, he pulled the balled-up comforter with him. He finally stood up with the thick cover wrapped around his waist.

There was no movement—just eyes on eyes, heavy breathing and loud thoughts.

"Why are you naked?" Her heart raced as she watched his gaze drop to the bed.

Drake ran a hand through his wavy hair. "Why are *you* naked?"

She swallowed past a lump that had suddenly formed in her throat. "I asked you first," she croaked.

"Obviously, I don't know." He rolled his eyes and pinched the bridge of his nose.

"Why are you nervous?" she hissed. Drake was normally a calm and collected person, but they'd been friends long enough that she could recognize when he was nervous. After all, they'd been best friends for almost their whole lives.

His bloodshot eyes flashed to hers and his forehead creased. "I can't remember. I just remember walking on the Strip doing shots."

"What do you mean you can't remember anything? You're naked!" she shrieked.

He pressed a hand to his temple. "Love, please, be quiet. You're making my head hurt worse. I don't need continuous updates on our lack of clothing."

She clutched the sheet to her chest. Tears pricked her eyes. "Drake, did we…?"

He held a hand up. "Don't say it. There has to be a good explanation."

"But we're both…" She dashed a tear off her cheek.

"Don't cry. That's how we got into this situation in the first place."

Placing her hands on her hips, she hissed, "What the hell is that supposed to mean?"

He covered his eyes. "Pull the sheet back up, Love."

Realizing she'd let it fall to the floor, she screamed and scrambled to pick it up, twisting the fabric around her body. "This can't be happening."

He motioned toward the bathroom. "Put some clothes on, for Christ's sake. This is already bad enough."

"Don't tell me what to do."

"Go in the bathroom," he demanded.

"You go in the bathroom," she countered, clutching the sheet in her palms.

"Love."

"What?"

He stalked toward her and she retreated until the back of her knees hit a chair. Overcorrecting, she stumbled into the seat.

Drake held out a hand and she took it and let him pull her to her feet. Then she shoved him away. "Get away from me, you ass."

He nudged her toward the en suite bathroom. "Look, get dressed. We're never going to figure this out standing here like this."

"I hate you," she growled as she stomped into the bathroom. Kicking the door closed, she leaned against it. A hotel robe was hanging on a hook and she snatched it and slipped it on. Once she secured the tie, she whipped the door open and stormed back into the bedroom toward a now clothed Drake.

His back was to her and he was murmuring curses to himself. She jumped on his back and wrapped an arm around his neck. "You took advantage of me." With her other hand, she yanked his hair.

He fumbled with her weight and they both crashed down on the mattress. She flailed her arms and kicked at him until he grabbed her wrists and pinned them to the bed.

"Calm down," he pleaded. "Stop trying to fight me." The vein on the side of his temple jumped and his biceps bunched as he held her arms above her head.

Love was angry, but she was something else, too. Something that she'd never felt before. Well, tried to never feel before. His hard chest pressed against her soft one made it kind of difficult not to feel aroused.

"Get off of me, Drake." Needing to put some distance between them—because the last thing she needed was to be aroused—she bucked against him.

"Love, would you just…" He sighed, his hooded bedroom eyes boring into hers. *Bedroom eyes*? Her stomach fluttered and a warmth spread over her. She cursed her body for responding in ways she wouldn't dare admit.

Is he doing this on purpose? His eyes stayed on hers, seeming to look straight into her soul. Maybe he wasn't *trying* to turn her on, but he was.

"Promise me." His husky voice seemed to light a fire in her belly. "If I let you go you have to keep your hands to yourself."

"You took advantage of me," she muttered, her voice shaky. The anger she felt was melting under his gaze. Unclenching her fists, she let the tension ooze out of her arms. She chewed on her bottom lip. His breath fanned across her mouth and she couldn't help but entertain the idea of *letting* him take advantage of her.

"We don't know that," he said, snapping her out of her thoughts. "Neither of us remembers last night. You can't say for sure that we did anything but sleep."

"But we were naked," she murmured. *Why am I whispering?*

He squeezed her wrists. "Stop saying that. Let's concentrate on the present."

"Well, get your *naked* chest off of me and I'll try."

He jumped up, leaving her splayed across the bed, angry with her body for betraying her and with her mind for its wayward thoughts. She glared at the textured ceiling and prayed for a time machine that could zap her into yesterday, where Drake was merely annoying— not annoyingly sexy. Would she ever be able to look at him as the friend he was without thinking about his mussed hair and lean physique? Let alone the fine line of hair that trailed down his stomach and disappeared under the waistband of the low-riding sweatpants he'd donned. She tightened the belt on the robe and sat up, smoothing her hair back.

"What *do* you remember?" he asked, in the tone he often used on his patients. Detached.

Obviously, he wasn't as affected as she was. *Ouch.* She cleared her throat. "Lana called. One of my patients went into labor and was admitted to the hospital, possible peripartum cardiomyopathy," she answered, as if she was reporting to her chief resident during rounds. "Instead of paging me, she had paged Blake. The mother insisted on a natural birth, but her heart couldn't take the labor. She died. I was upset that I wasn't there, so you took me out to get my mind off of it."

He lifted his eyes toward the ceiling and muttered a string of curses. "I keep replaying last night over and over in my head. I can't remember how we got in bed. I remember the bar, the shots. You were finally loosening up. When we left Caesars, you were tipsy, so I had to kind of hold on to you. I can see us laughing at random people on the way back to the room. Then we ran into a few of our high school classmates. They asked us to go out with them, but you didn't want to, so we headed back here. Then…" He averted his gaze, swallowed roughly.

She bowed her head and wondered what he'd just remembered. They were friends. Best friends, in fact. They'd grown up finishing each other's sentences. Love knew all of Drake's "tells" and was certain he'd just filled in some blanks.

"The bar and walk I remember," she croaked. "That's about it."

It wasn't a complete lie. She'd been very inebriated, inconsolable over the loss of her patient. Drake had done what he always did—make it better, help her forget.

"Hopefully, it'll come back to us later. For now, we can't assume anything happened."

They'd shared the same bed many times during their lifelong friendship, and nothing had ever happened. Not even an accidental brush of arms. Hell, he'd seen her in her underwear plenty of times. But...

"We were still clearly on our own sides of the bed," he continued, without meeting her gaze. "There's no clue—"

"I feel sore," she blurted out. "My whole body does."

"You were drunk. You could've fallen or something."

Love wondered when Drake had turned into Mr. Positivity. The proof was staring them right in the face. The bed. She scanned the rest of the room before zeroing in on the bed again. Frowning, she walked closer to it and ran a finger over the tiny bright red spot. Closing her eyes, she gasped. "Oh, my God!"

"Stop saying that," he said, between clenched teeth.

"It's blood. There's your clue. We had sex."

"Love, you're not a virgin. The blood is probably from a paper cut or something."

"You don't really believe that, do you?"

He glared at her. "Just...be quiet. Let me think."

"You know we had sex," she muttered under her breath. And the worst part? She didn't remember the details. If she was going to participate in something that would more than likely ruin her friendship with Drake, she would've liked to remember it.

Chapter 2

Drake had a headache. And it was getting worse by the minute. He peered down at the tiny speck of blood on the stark white sheet. *Shit*.

The evidence was there. They'd woken up in bed together naked, she'd admitted her body was sore, and now there was visual proof. Not that he needed it. He knew exactly what had happened between them, but he couldn't say the word out loud. The memories were coming fast and furious with each passing minute, with her standing in front of him in nothing but the hotel bathrobe.

"What are we going to do?" she asked, sitting on the edge of the bed.

"Nothing." He cracked his knuckles, rolled his neck and plopped down next to her. When she scooted away from him, Drake tried to tell himself that he wasn't bothered. "We just have to deal with it. It happened."

She twisted the tie of the robe around her fingers. "I know we have two bedrooms, but maybe you should move into a separate room for the remainder of the trip."

He hated this. Love was his best friend. They'd spent countless hours together, shared many a hotel room and even a bed—platonically. He'd never thought anything else about it—until now. "What's that going to prove? Apparently, we've already seen everything there is to see."

"That's not funny."

It wasn't; he knew that.

"What if…it happens again?" she whispered.

His eyes snapped to hers. "It won't. I'm never drinking with you again."

She lowered her gaze. "You don't have to say it like that," she mumbled.

"How am I supposed to say it?" he asked incredulously. "You're my home girl. We've never done anything remotely close to this."

"We can't say that anymore," she muttered under her breath.

They exchanged glances before turning away. "I guess not," he agreed.

"I hope this doesn't affect our friendship."

"It won't." As much as he hoped it wouldn't, the very conversation they were having indicated that it might. Theirs was a relationship of comfort as much as it was one of respect and unconditional love, not marred by the hurt feelings and expectations that often accompany a love affair. Now, he couldn't even make eye contact with her—a fact that didn't go unnoticed.

"You can't even look at me, Drake."

"Neither can you," he retorted.

Love sighed and stood up. "Maybe I should just hop in the shower."

He rubbed the back of his neck. "Maybe you can soak in the bathtub," he suggested. "It'll help with the soreness."

Without another word, she walked into the bathroom and closed the door. Once he heard the lock click, he fell back on the bed. As he listened to running water, he ran a hand down his face. He needed Advil and quickly.

They'd had sex. But something didn't seem right. What had made this time different from every other time? Why would they choose this trip to get busy? The sight of Love clutching the sheet against her breasts for dear life haunted him. She was scared and teary-eyed. He closed his eyes tightly, hoping to erase the image.

He hoped the bath would relieve her anxieties. Deciding to take a shower himself, he slid off the bed and walked into the second bedroom. The Bellagio was Love's favorite hotel in Vegas and she'd insisted on splurging on the suite. There was a separate living room and two bedrooms—one for each of them. His en suite had a steam shower and hers had a soaking whirlpool tub.

He padded into the bathroom and turned on the shower. After waiting for the steam to fill the room, he stepped in. He placed a hand on the tile and let

the water beat against his back, loosening his tense
muscles.

*His hand massaged her back as they burrowed into
the mattress. Their lips touched in the softest of kisses.
She caressed his face as he suckled on her bottom lip.*

Drake shook his head as if to shoo away the vivid
memories, and lost his balance. When he reached out
to grab the bar, he slipped on the shower floor and
landed on his ass. So much for relaxation. Taking a
deep breath, he sat there and rubbed the water out of
his eyes.

*He brushed his mouth against her chin and trailed
his tongue to the hollow of her neck.*

He scooted back against the shower wall, letting
the water drizzle over him.

*When he looked at her, he felt like he was drowning
in her eyes. He felt his stomach tighten as he smoothed
his hands over her thighs. She moaned and murmured
her approval. He traced the band of her underwear
with his thumb before he slipped a hand inside. He
parted her slick folds with his finger and she purred.
He thought he would explode. He loved to hear her
satisfied groans. Kissing her deeply and possessively,
he lowered himself on top of her.*

Drake leaned his head against the tile as more
memories rushed back to him.

*Love wrapped her long legs around his waist and
they linked fingers, gazing into each other's eyes. He
wanted her unlike anyone else. He wanted to claim
her and make her his forever.*

"I want you," he whispered.

She smiled. "Have me."

He kissed her nose, then her chin. His mouth closed

around her breast and he heard her gasp. His tongue swirled around her nipple until she dug her nails into his biceps. Releasing the nipple, he kissed his way over to the other one, taking it into his mouth and giving it the same attention. Her nails scraped against his scalp as he kissed his way down to her navel.

Drake closed his eyes as his body reacted to the memory. His heart pumped with excitement.

He began to enter her, and—

"Drake!"

He jumped and immediately registered the cold water pulsing down on him. Cursing, he stood up, pushed the shower door open, and stepped out.

The knocking continued. "Drake! Can you hear me?"

"What?" he yelled.

"The concierge is here," Lovely told him.

Swearing, he wrapped a towel around his waist and yanked the door open, practically pulling her into the bathroom.

She tried to regain her balance by grabbing him. Her hair was wet, her face flushed. Her hazelnut-colored skin was still moist. Grabbing her waist, he steadied her.

When their eyes met, she pulled back. "He's out in the sitting area," she said, tugging on her robe.

"Did you ask him what he wanted?" The small opening in the bathrobe gave him a glimpse of her breast and he tried not to look. Really. He didn't want to remember taking it into his mouth. He let his eyes wander over Love's curves. If there was a contest for best female anatomy, she'd win hands down. Her skin was flawless; her hair was like an ebony waterfall.

And she was all natural—no weave, no acrylics, no color contacts and no silicone.

"Drake, did you hear what I said?" she asked.

"Huh?"

"I said he asked for you," she told him. "Said he had something to give you."

Adjusting his towel, he secured the knot. "Can you…?"

"Oh." She hurried out of the bathroom, bumping into the door on the way out.

He slipped his sweatpants back on hurriedly. When he came out of the bathroom, Love was sitting on the bed, shoulders slouched. Grabbing a T-shirt, he pulled it on. He wondered if she'd remembered anything. His thoughts drifted to his roaming hands…her flat, quivering stomach…the sultry moans coming from her full lips. Shaking his head, he strode past her and into the living room.

The concierge greeted him with a wide smile. "Good morning, Dr. Jackson. I trust you had a wonderful night." He shook his hand.

"What can I do for you?" Drake asked.

Love appeared in the doorway. She folded her arms across her robe and leaned against the frame.

Drake shifted his attention away from her and back to the concierge, who was eyeing Love with interest. Drake cleared his throat. "How can I help you?"

The short man coughed. "Oh, I'm sorry. I didn't mean to disturb you."

"You didn't," Drake told him.

"I just thought you might like this," he said, holding out a small box.

Drake grabbed the box and examined it. "What's this?"

The concierge laughed. "Very funny, Dr. Jackson." He patted him on his shoulder. "We rushed this up as soon as it was sized."

Opening the box, Drake gaped at the huge diamond ring. "Why did you bring me this?"

The man shifted. "You ordered it, Dr. Jackson. Last night."

His headache suddenly grew worse. "I didn't order this."

"You and the missus were in the hotel store and you purchased it."

Drake pretended he didn't hear Love's gasp or feel her body leaning up against his back as she gawked at the ring in his hand. "The missus? What the hell are you talking about? I'm not married."

"Uh, sir, you and your wife approached the front desk attendant and asked to purchase the ring from the hotel jewelry store." The man motioned to Love. "It was around three o'clock this morning. You told him you were on your way to your wedding."

"My what?" Drake bellowed, struggling to remember that part of the evening. "This has to be a mistake. I'm not married. And what kind of jewelry store is open at three o'clock in the morning?"

"W-well, you insisted," the concierge stuttered. "Your wife spotted the ring in the display case. You paid for it with your credit card and she gave us her ring size. Trust me, it was a legitimate transaction."

Advil. Better yet, Vicodin. He sat on the edge of the couch and pinched his forehead. Could this day get any worse? It wasn't enough that he had made love to his best friend and remembered only bits of it. Obviously, there was more to last night than sex.

"Are you sure, sir?" Love asked. "Maybe someone stole Drake's wallet and used his credit card to purchase this ring?"

The concierge sucked in a deep breath. "Ma'am, perhaps the problem was too many drinks?"

Drake flew to his feet, twisted the man's lapels in his fists and pulled him closer—nose to nose. "Watch your mouth. Perhaps *you* got the situation wrong." He let him go, shoving him back a bit.

After straightening his tie, the concierge smoothed a hand over his suit coat. "I'm sorry, Dr. Jackson. But you purchased the ring. I'm sure we can pull up the security cameras." He drew an envelope out of his inside pocket. "And this was sent over via courier this morning."

Drake snatched the envelope and ripped it open. Love rested a hand on his arm and he glanced at her. She was stunning, and she smelled like warm vanilla. Forcing his gaze away, he pulled the thick paper out and scanned it. Sighing, he handed it to her.

"Oh, my God!"

Drake rolled his eyes. "You said this was around three?" he asked the concierge.

He nodded. "Yes, according to Bill, the manager in charge. By the way, I wanted to come here in person to let you know that we've upgraded you to the honeymoon suite."

"This can't be happening," Love mumbled.

"Honeymoon suite?" Drake asked.

"Yes. To show our appreciation for your business."

Running his hand through his hair, Drake told him, "I don't need to switch rooms."

"We've already made the arrangements," the concierge insisted. "A bellboy will be here shortly to collect your things and transfer them to your new accommodations."

"This is Vegas." Drake crossed his arms over his chest. "People get married here all the time. Why upgrade us?"

"Well, after the amount you spent in our hotel store, it's our pleasure."

Drake didn't want to ask the question, but he had to. "How much is the ring?" he groaned.

"This is an original design, worth more than the price you paid."

"How much?" he repeated.

"We agreed on a discounted price of $15,000."

Love let out a colorful curse, then covered her mouth.

"Fifteen thousand?" Drake roared. "Are you crazy? They knew we were drinking and they still let me pay that much money for a ring?"

"Like I said, sir, you insisted," the man responded.

"Thank you," Love told the concierge. "We appreciate your hospitality. Can you leave us alone for now? We need a moment." She walked him toward the door. More like pushed him. "And we appreciate the gesture, but the honeymoon suite is not necessary."

"Certainly, Mrs. Jackson," the man said, with a wide smile. "Please let us know if you change your mind."

"We will," she assured him. "Thank you again. Have a good day."

"I will and—"

She closed the door before the man could finish his sentence.

Drake clutched the ring box in his hand. "I spent $15,000 on a ring, Love."

She squeezed his shoulder. "Drake, we'll figure this out. We'll find the receipt and try to return it."

"Good luck with that. They sold it at a discount. It was probably a final sale."

"We have to find your wallet," she said, hurrying into her suite bedroom.

He followed her. She picked a pair of discarded pants off the floor and shoved her hands into the pockets. He checked his coat and discovered his wallet was there. He opened it, leafed through the receipts and found nothing. "It's not here. I'm screwed," he said, dropping the wallet on the dresser.

She propped her hands on his shoulders. "Drake, we got married. We don't remember our wedding. We had sex, after almost thirty years of innocent friendship. Screwed is an understatement. But all is not lost, because we still have our brains. So I say we go find the—" she glanced at the wedding certificate "—Hunk O' Burning Love Wedding Chapel and try to get this thing annulled. Then we can check with the jewelry store."

Love grabbed an outfit and disappeared into the bathroom.

"Okay, Mrs. Chipper, what if this can't be fixed?"

She emerged from the bathroom a few minutes later, wearing a pair of capri pants and a tank top. "I'm not dealing with that right now. The worst has to be over."

Another knock sounded, and they heard a familiar voice from the other side say, "Lovely, open the door."

Her eyes widened. "Oh, my God."

He shook his head. "See, that's where you're wrong. It's not over—not by a long shot."

Chapter 3

"Don't answer that." Love wrapped a hand around Drake's arm. The constant knocking was getting to her, but she could handle it. "Maybe she'll go away."

"Have you met your mother?" Drake asked.

"She can't come in here." Gloria Helen Washington was the last person Love needed to see today. "She'll know what happened."

"How? We're both fully dressed." He peeled her hand off him. "Just act normal." He hurried to the door and opened it.

Gloria breezed into the room. "Lovely Grace Washington, what is your problem? What took you so long to answer the door?"

Love rolled her eyes and crossed her arms over her chest. As if naming her Lovely wasn't bad enough, her mother had added Grace to it. As soon as she was old enough, she'd insisted everyone call her Love. "What is it, Mother? You know it's early."

Love knew she hated to be called "Mother." Gloria wasn't your average stay-at-home mom. As a child, Love could be found chanting during a windstorm watch, and running around in a bright bandanna and a tie-dyed T-shirt. Yes, her mother was a hippie and damn proud of it. Even in her sixties, Gloria still had a carefree way about her. Her gray curls were wild and free, and she wore loose-fitting, flowing clothes at all times. Her mother thought the world would be a better place if everyone embraced love, hence the name.

Growing up had been pretty traumatic for the straitlaced Love. She was the only black kid in the neighborhood who wore sandals in the winter and listened to Jimi Hendrix. Instead of Ring Pops or Now & Laters, Love was forced to munch on celery sticks and snap peas. No hopscotch or Foursquare for her. Gloria thought it best that she recited poetry in the park. And Love hated poetry. Yet, even though they clashed often, Love adored her mother. And she was proud of the independent woman she'd become after the divorce. Her mother went from doting on her husband to owning one of Vegas' premier flower shops. Gloria was famous for her floral creations.

Her mother pulled her into a tight hug. "I've missed you, my baby girl. The rest of the family should arrive sometime this afternoon. Thank you for gracing us with your presence this year. You know, it's been years since you've attended. Everyone always asks about you."

The rest of her family was as colorful as her mother, which often caused a problem for the Love.

For years, the Nelson family gathered on her grandmother's birthday in March for a family reunion. Each year, the reunion alternated between several states to give each leg of the family a chance to plan it. Love had managed to avoid the last several due to school and work, but since the reunion was back in her childhood hometown, her mother had threatened to haunt her in life and death if she didn't attend.

Her mother had obsessed about this reunion for over a year, since she was the only member of the family that lived in Las Vegas. The hosting family always stayed at the hotel with everyone else, and Gloria needed Love's assistance to help make the reunion a success.

"Like I had a choice," Love grumbled, wrenching herself out of her mother's arms.

"Don't get smart." Gloria smoothed her hair back and grinned at Drake. "Hello, Drake. I'm so glad you're here." She embraced him.

"Good to see you, too, Mom," Drake said.

Love's best friend had called Gloria that for as long as she could remember. Drake and Gloria had a loving relationship and Love often found herself on the outside looking in at the two of them. They shared the same taste in food and television, preferring big steaks and fried potatoes with their zombie and sci-fi shows.

"You're looking handsome as ever, son."

"Mother," Love said, cutting in, "I know you want to talk about the reunion, but I have to make a few runs. Then I wanted to visit with friends."

Peering up the ceiling, Love let out a long sigh. She hated lying to her mother. Love was many things, but a liar wasn't one of them. She lacked the ability to make it convincing, even though she'd tried to perfect the skill growing up. Although she had made plans to visit with her friends, she had no intention of doing so now. She had business to take care of, a marriage to annul.

"Love, this is family time." Gloria picked at her daughter's hair with a frown on her face. "Why did you straighten your beautiful curls?"

Love pushed her hands away. "My hair is fine. And I promised them I'd stop by. The last time I came home to visit, I wasn't able to spend any time with my friends."

Gloria dropped her purse on a chair and scanned the room. "This is nice," she said, as if she couldn't care less what Love wanted to do. "Listen, a couple of your cousins really wanted to come but they couldn't afford a hotel. I figure they can sleep in this big ole room with you."

"No," Love said. "That's not possible. Drake is my roommate. The second bedroom is his."

"I can get my own room," Drake offered.

Love glared at him. "Mother, how about I catch the next flight back to Michigan, and they can have this room? Or better yet, I can go stay at your house."

Gloria lived in the Las Vegas suburb of Summerlin South. It was just fifteen miles from downtown. The house held many fond memories for Love and she'd love to get away and sleep in her old room for the night.

"That's not a good idea," Gloria said. "You need to stay and be in the thick of things, with me."

"It's actually okay. I figure I can spend some time in my childhood home, prepare the house for the cookout you want to have there on Sunday." Love scratched her neck and tried to ignore the skeptical look on Drake's face. He must have caught the sarcasm.

"Okay," he said, elbowing her. "I'll book a room for them. My treat."

"Thank you, Drake," Gloria gushed. "I just love you."

"So it's settled, Mother." Love picked up her mother's purse and handed it to her. "I have to finish getting ready now. I have so much to do."

"Wait, I wanted to ask you something. I'm planning a visit to Ann Arbor in a few weeks. Do you have room for your dear old mother?"

Love adored her mother. She really did. But Gloria Washington was a professional nagger. The last time her mom had stayed with her she'd rearranged everything, put all her canned goods in the recycle bin, threw away her favorite socks and insisted Love eat those nasty breakfast bars filled with millet grains.

"Uh…w-well," she stammered, "I would've said it was no problem, but I…it would be awkward."

"Why?"

That one word was enough to make Love hyperventilate. Briefly, she wondered if her mother would accept it if she answered the question with a whopping "because I said so." Or better yet, a big fat "nunya."

"Why, Lovely?" Gloria asked again. "You have a huge three-bedroom condo you're renting all by yourself. Why would it be awkward? Unless you lied to your mother about living alone?"

Love hated when her mom referred to herself in the third person. She struggled to find a suitable excuse. "I meant to tell you sooner. I don't live alone anymore."

"A roommate?"

"Kind of," Love lied. Again. She pressed a hand to her stomach, uncertain why she felt the need to tell her mother she had a roommate. *I have to throw up.* "The economy is rough. I figured it would help."

Gloria's eyes flitted back and forth between Love and Drake. Finally, she placed a hand on her hip. "When did you start lying to your mother, Lovely?"

Damn. Caught already? "Why do you say that?"

"You hate living with anyone. You wouldn't even let Drake move in."

Love shifted her attention to Drake, who was watching her with a smirk on his face. Although he was her best friend, she had turned him down when he'd asked to stay with her while he found a place. Instead, she'd suggested that he book a suite at the Marriott closest to the University of Michigan Hospital, where they were both residents. He was pissed, and didn't hesitate to tell her. Love had assured him it was the best thing for their friendship. She adored him, but there was no way she could live with him. Drake was your typical smelly, messy and loud man. Not to mention a man-whore.

"Mother," Love said. "I didn't want to tell you this, but…" She stalled, running a list of possible roommates in her mind. "Drake *is* my roommate."

He gaped at her.

The room was silent for a few minutes as both of them absorbed this news.

"Drake?" Gloria asked. "That's impossible."

"It's the truth. But I can't really talk about this now. I told you I have plans."

"No, I want an explanation. If Drake is your roommate, you'll never find a man who wants to marry you."

Drake snorted and Love smacked his shoulder.

"When did this end up being about marriage?" she asked her mother. "Wait...don't answer that." It seemed as though these days, every conversation between them contained a reference to the *M* word. "Please, Mother. I promise we'll spend lots of time together. Later. I'll answer all of your questions then." She hugged her. "Love you."

Gloria stomped to the door. "Okay, Lovely. Take care of your business. But we are going to talk about this. And since Drake is your roommate, he won't care if I stay there for a few days. Right, Drake?"

He shrugged. "Sure," he said drily.

Love opened the door to let her out, only to find the concierge on the other side, preparing to knock.

"Mrs. J—"

"Hi!" Love said. "Did you need something?"

"I forgot to give you the receipt from the jewelry store."

She snatched it from him. "Okay, thanks. Bye."

"Who is that?" Gloria asked, shoving her out of the way.

"Mom," Drake interrupted, pulling her from the door. "It's just the concierge. I purchased something and he was bringing the receipt. Thanks again." He pushed the door closed, but the concierge stopped it with his toe.

"One more thing, Dr. Jackson. Just a reminder—this is a final sale."

Love sighed.

Drake muttered a curse. "Fine."

"Thanks for your business, Dr. Jackson. And congratulations again." He turned to walk away and Love let out a sigh of relief—until he glanced back at them over his shoulder. "Please let us know if you choose to take us up on the offer of using the honeymoon suite."

"Honeymoon suite?" Gloria repeated.

"Yes," the man said, tugging at the lapels of his suit as he lifted his chin. "We here at the Bellagio love to cater to our important guests. Nothing more important than a wedding."

"Whose wedding?"

"Do something," Love mouthed to Drake.

"Mom, how about we go get breakfast?" he said, nudging Gloria away from the concierge. "I'm starved."

"Wait a minute," she exclaimed, digging in her heels. "Who got married?"

"Why, *they* did," the chubby man replied with a toothy grin. "They visited our jewelry store to purchase the ring."

"Oh, my God." Love leaned her forehead against the wall.

Gloria turned to them. Tears welled in her eyes, and she fainted.

Chapter 4

Drake watched as Gloria's eyes rolled back in her head.

"Mother!" Love called. But it was too late.

Gloria fell like a heavy tree and nearly slipped through Drake's arms, but he was able to catch her. Grunting, he carried her to the couch. "Get my bag, Love," he ordered.

She sprinted into the bedroom, came back with his medical bag and dropped it on the floor next to him.

The concierge had followed them into the room. Drake glared at him. "You can go now. I'll handle this."

"Maybe I should call an ambulance?" he suggested.

"No, she should be fine. Like I said, I've got this. I'll call if we need anything."

The concierge glanced at Love. When she nodded, he left the room without another word.

Drake assessed Gloria, checking her airway and pulse, while Love propped her legs up on a pillow. Her pulse was strong. "Mom, can you hear me?"

Gloria moaned softly. "Lovely…"

Love knelt in front of her and picked up her hand. "Mom, I'm here."

Gloria's eyes fluttered open. Drake let out a quick sigh of relief. Gloria was many things, but mostly she was as much *his* mother as she was Love's. Gloria had been the only motherly figure he'd had, since he hadn't known his real mother. She had stepped in and filled the gap. Drake had never gotten along with his stepmother, and he'd been grateful that he'd had someone in his life who had supported him through everything.

"Mom, are you okay?" Love's voice pulled him back to the present. "You fainted. Have you been taking your medication? Your insulin? Did you eat this morning?"

Gloria was a diabetic. Over the last few years, she'd had several complications as a result of her illness that had required Love to fly out to Vegas and take care of her. The most recent hospital stay was only a few months ago, and Gloria's doctors had suggested amputation due to lack of blood flow to her legs and feet.

Love had recently told him that she'd been trying to convince her mother to get a second opinion at University of Michigan Hospital, but her mother had declined. Drake knew it bothered Love that her mother lived so far away and seemed to be getting worse.

Drake poured a glass of water and handed it to Gloria, who took a sip.

"I'll be okay, baby." The older woman struggled to sit up. Eventually, she simply leaned on her elbows. "Baby, please tell me…"

Love peered at Drake. "Mom, don't think about anything right now. You need to lie back. No sudden movements."

Gloria shook her head and finally sat upright. "I told you I'll be okay." She smacked Love's hand away when she tried to keep her from rising to her feet. "You need to tell me what's going on. And, Drake, if you don't tell me the truth, I'm calling your father."

The threat of his dad knowing anything that was going on in his personal life was enough to give Drake pause. Gloria had used that threat often on him, growing up. It was the only thing he'd ever responded to. Simply put, he couldn't stand his dad. Life with him had been one disappointment after another. The safe haven that Love and her family had provided had saved him.

Dr. Lawrence Jackson, plastic surgeon extraordinaire, had always been too busy working and having affairs with random women to even care what Drake did in his personal life. What the man cared about was that Drake was surgical resident, studying to take over his own thriving practice. Except Drake never intended to become his father. In fact, he'd worked tirelessly to distance himself from the man who drove him insane with his demands and unrealistic expectations. Instead of plastic surgery, he'd chosen cardiothoracic surgery as his focus, much to his father's chagrin.

The only thing he'd loved about living at home was his siblings—two brothers, one sister and his uncle El, who was like a brother.

The last thing Drake wanted was his father involved in the mess he'd gotten himself into. No doubt there would be a long lecture that would end in him cursing his dad out and Love urging him to apologize out of respect.

"Mother, please." Love stood and straightened her clothes. "It's not what you think. That man doesn't know what he's talking about."

Drake cleared his throat. "Mom, you fainted. You need to relax a bit."

"I'll relax when both of you explain to me how you came to Vegas, got married and didn't tell me."

Gloria's sudden high-pitched screech caught him off guard, and he jumped.

"Why are you screaming?" Love covered her ears.

"Because!" She stood finally, pulled them both into a tight hug, and kissed Drake's cheek. "This is so exciting. Why didn't you tell me? You should have let me know."

There was something about her tone that made him a little suspicious.

Love pulled out of the group hug. "Mom, you don't understand. It—"

Gloria gasped. "We can have a small reception. Yeah. We can do it in June. That will give me enough time." She sat back down on the sofa, then rifled through her purse and pulled out her phone. "June 10 is perfect. Oh my, I have to get out of here. I have to tell your father, Love."

Threatening to tell *his* father was one thing, but

there was no way *Love's* father could know what had
happened. He was, after all, Drake's boss.

Drake nudged Love. "Do something."

She stood there, her mouth hanging open.

"Give us a minute, Mom." Drake pulled Love into
her bedroom and slammed the door. "Love, say something to your mother before she tells the whole free
world," he demanded through clenched teeth. "She
threatened to tell my father. And did you just hear
that she's going to tell *your* father? He'll hop the next
flight, then he'll kick my ass before he fires me."

Love tugged at his shirt. "We have to do something."

Drake muttered a curse. "Ya think? We need a
game plan. First, you need to get your mother."

"Now she's *my* mother. *You* need to handle this,
since you're her favorite."

He threw his arms in the air. "Please, Love. The
man came in here with the receipt for the ring, and
told her that we're married because our drunk asses
actually did that last night. The sooner you get that
through your head, the sooner we'll be able to figure
out what we're going to do to fix this."

She placed her palm over his mouth. "Shh, you're
getting too loud. She'll hear you."

He counted to ten and took a long, deep breath.
"Do you understand why I'm a little concerned right
now?" he asked, when she removed her hand.

"Of course I do. But we don't know the circumstances," Love argued. "We don't even know if this
certificate is legal. And if we really are married, we
won't be after today."

Drake grabbed her shoulders. "That's all fine and

good, but before we figure that out, we need to get your mother under control. And that means coming up with an explanation for the concierge's visit. She's not going to buy one of your crazy, nonsensical lies."

Gloria's loud laugh carried through the door.

He pointed in that direction and frowned. "Is she on the phone?"

Love bolted out of the bedroom and snatched her mother's cell out of her hand. Ending the call with a quick "Sorry, gotta go," she handed the device to Drake. "Mom, who were you talking to?"

"Your aunt. I was just getting ready to tell her about your happy news. She's going to be so excited."

Drake wrapped an arm around Gloria and steered her over to the couch. "Mom, I understand it was a lot to take in at once. But you've got this all wrong."

Her smile faded. "Care to explain?"

He glanced at Gloria. "Yes, you deserve an explanation."

"Aren't you happy that you married my daughter?" Gloria asked, concern evident in her brown eyes.

Drake was torn. The question was a double-edged sword, and any answer he'd give would be bad, in her opinion. He'd always been truthful with Gloria, but he couldn't be now. If he told her the truth—which wasn't an option—he'd be admitting that he'd married her daughter in a drunken state, in a cheesy Las Vegas wedding chapel, and he wasn't happy about it. If he said yes, the response would send her on a rocket to heaven and it would take a miracle to bring her down. There had to be a middle ground. He glanced up at Love, who was staring at the floor. *No help.*

A knock sounded and drew their attention to the

door. Drake hoped it wasn't that damn concierge returning to make matters worse. He stood and followed Love across the room.

She glared at him before she pulled the door open. In front of them, on his knees, with a ring in hand was Love's ex-boyfriend.

Oh, my God!

Love swallowed at the sight of the jerk who'd broken her heart, and the gorgeous ring in his hand.

"Love, you're beautiful." Derrick flashed a dimpled smile. "I couldn't let another day go by without telling you how I feel. I love you. I want to marry you. I want us to have forever."

Love was speechless. She'd dreamed of such a proposal from Derrick Harper when they were together—over a year ago. He was successful, cultured and handsome. He was everything she'd thought she wanted. The life he could offer her was appealing on some level. But the pain that he'd left in his wake still stung. The horrible breakup had devastated her, and she'd gone out of her way to avoid him. In fact, she hadn't seen him since. And now he was proposing? She couldn't believe this was happening.

"What the hell are you doing here?" Drake asked incredulously.

Derrick rose to his feet. The smile he'd been sporting a few seconds earlier turned into a sneer. "Drake. I guess I shouldn't be surprised that you're here."

"Answer the question." Drake's voice was a low growl, and Love knew that this confrontation could turn physical. Drake had never cared for Derrick. The way Derrick broke up with her—with a text—had made Drake's disdain grow by leaps and bounds.

"Derrick?" Gloria stepped between Drake and Love. "You're here."

Love frowned at her. It wasn't a question, and there was no hint of surprise in her mother's tone.

"How did you know I was here?" Love asked him, knowing the answer already.

"You didn't tell her I was coming?" Derrick asked Gloria.

She averted her gaze as a blush crept up her neck to her ears. She pushed a strand of her gray hair behind her ears. "I didn't. But you can leave."

Derrick narrowed his eyes. "What? We talked about this. I flew all the way here."

"Mother, how could you?" Love felt the sting of tears in her eyes.

"I didn't. Your father called and asked for the details of the family reunion. He told me that Derrick wanted to win you back, because he realized he made a mistake letting you go. I'm sorry, Lovely. I should have told you, but I thought I was helping you."

Love couldn't stop the snort that escaped. "Help? You encouraged a man who broke my heart to come to my family reunion and propose? Mother, do you realize that he broke up with me with a text message, after he cheated on me with his colleague for months? That means I wasn't worth more than a few characters."

She felt Drake's hand on her shoulder. The soft squeeze that came next soothed her frayed nerves, and she shot him a grateful glance out of the corner of her eye.

"I've got this," he whispered in her ear. "Harper,

you're out of order. For you to show up, after a year, and expect her to fall into your arms and accept that whack proposal, you must be crazy. It's obvious to me that you don't think much of Love."

"How is this your problem?" Derrick asked, his dark eyes icy.

"Love is my problem. When you don't respect her, I have a problem with it. You've already hurt her enough. I'm not going to stand here and let you try to insert yourself back into her life so you can do it again."

"Drake." Love squeezed his arm. "I'm okay."

He looked down at her, his eyes soft. He shook his head slightly before turning a hard glare back to Derrick. "Get out. Go home. Don't call her again."

Derrick snickered. "Why don't you let Love talk?"

Drake stepped closer to him, nose to nose. "Don't let the fact that I'm a surgical resident make you think that you won't see these hands."

Gloria spoke up. "Derrick, you need to go. It's too late, anyway. Drake and Lovely are—"

"Mother, stay of this," Love snapped. The way her mom had reacted to the news of the marriage hadn't been a shock. Gloria had always shipped a potential Love and Drake union, and she was itching to tell anyone that the two of them were married. Love couldn't let that happen. So far, they had managed to not outright admit it to her, but they hadn't fully denied it, either.

Shaking her head, she turned her attention back to the two men in front of her ready to go to blows any minute. "Derrick, you need to leave. You're not welcome in my life anymore."

"I don't believe you." He held up the ring. "You know we belong together. It just took me longer to realize it. I was stupid, full of myself. Then I realized that you were everything to me. I want to marry you."

"I can't do this," Love said, pulling Drake back out of the doorway. "I'm done." Without another word, she slammed the door in Derrick's face.

Drake barked out a laugh. "That was good. I'm proud of you."

"Lovely, I'm sorry." Gloria pulled her into a hug. "I'm so sorry. I should have never listened to your father. Why didn't you just tell Derrick that you and Drake were together?"

Sighing, Love backed away from her mother's embrace. "Mother, I need a minute. I'm upset and I need to talk to Drake. Alone."

Gloria's shoulders fell. "Fine. I'll go." She gathered her purse and headed toward the door. "I'll see you at the dinner tonight, right?"

Love turned away from her hopeful stare, and nodded. "I'll be there. And, Mom, please don't say a word to anyone about what the concierge said." She didn't give Gloria a chance to answer, but simply walked into the bedroom and closed the door.

Chapter 5

Love sat on her bed and stared at her painted red toenails against the plush beige hotel carpet. It had been several hours since her mother had left. She and Drake had gone to the Hunk O' Burning Love Wedding Chapel, only to find that it was closed due to a "family emergency."

Drake had then sped to the Clark County Courthouse, only to find that it was closed until the following Tuesday due to an unpaid furlough day. Needless to say, Drake was pissed and had cursed during the whole ride back to the hotel.

She heard the door open and looked up to find him standing in the entranceway. "I'm hungry," she said.

"I ordered you something through room service."

She chuckled. Despite how infuriating Drake could

be at times, he still knew her like the back of his hand. "Thanks," she mumbled.

"We need to discuss this." He sat on a chair on the other side of the room, far away from the bed.

"Not if you're going to yell."

"I won't."

Love scooted back and leaned against the headboard. "Let's talk, then."

"We're going to have to carve out some time to fly back and get this taken care of. In the meantime, we just act like nothing has changed. We keep avoiding your mother's questions, and go back to Michigan like nothing happened. I'm not sure we would be granted an annulment, because of the..." He scratched the back of his head.

"Sex?" she interjected.

"Right." He shifted in his seat. "Once it's done, we can tell your mother that it was a big misunderstanding and we're not married."

Love stared at the ceiling, unable to say anything at that point. She wondered if he was going to actually address the fact that they'd had sex, since he'd had a hard time even saying the word.

"I'll take care of the court fees," Drake continued. "I did some research on the process."

As he explained the process, Love didn't let on that she'd done her own research on the way to the chapel earlier. They didn't even have to appear for a hearing in certain cases, and they definitely had grounds for an annulment because they'd been intoxicated at the time of the marriage.

Love picked at the comforter. "We can split the

fees. I think we should hire an attorney to take care of everything else."

He nodded. There was a soft knock on the door. Drake disappeared and came back minutes later with the room service tray. They quietly ate lunch. It was the first time they didn't say anything to each other. They'd always been able to talk, to laugh at and with each other. Now, they were in a sea of awkwardness, and she couldn't take it anymore.

"Drake, don't you think we need to talk about the fact that we had sex? I don't want this to be a thing between us, one that we can't get past. I need you in my life."

He shrugged. "What can I say? We had sex. After all these years, one night of tequila and we did it. I guess I just don't know what to say about it."

Love turned, to find him picking at his food. "I remember."

Drake gave her a sideways glance. "Me, too."

Over the course of the day, she had been able to recall the details of last night, all the way up to the rushed wedding at the gaudy chapel. They had spent the evening visiting casinos on the Strip and drinking. She wasn't sure when it happened, when something had changed between them. She just knew it did, and all of a sudden, they couldn't deny the attraction, couldn't stop touching and kissing each other.

"It was my idea to get married." While they'd watched the fountain display at the Bellagio, Love and Drake had kissed. Things had heated up quickly, and Love recalled how she'd announced that she wasn't having sex again until she was married. That's when

Drake had proposed by singing "Suitelady (The Proposal Jam)" by Maxwell. The rest was history.

"We were pretty twisted," he said softly. "I'm not even sure how I let it happen."

Love wasn't sure why she felt deflated at his comment, but it stung.

"I wanted you," he admitted. "In a way I never thought possible. It was a need I couldn't shake away, or convince myself it didn't exist."

She peered up at him, caught his gaze, before he averted it.

"I remember that part," he added. "I'm not sure how I can forget it. It certainly can't be undone." He stood and joined her on the bed. "But you're more important to me than anybody in my life. I'm willing to try."

A lone tear escaped down her cheek and he swiped it away with his thumb. "I hate myself for doing this, for depriving you of your first wedding. I know how much you wanted that. And you deserve it, with someone who is going to love you and treat you well."

Love closed her eyes. The dig at Derrick was clear. Yet she couldn't help but feel sad that Drake blamed himself. "It's not your fault. I wanted it, too. You were sweet, gentle and tender. And I appreciate that."

He squeezed her hand. "We can do this, right?"

Love didn't know if they could or not. She only knew that she would work hard to make sure it wouldn't destroy their friendship. Instead of answering him, she pulled him into a hug. One of his hands swept up her back and rested on the nape of her neck. Prior to yesterday, that would have been a normal

Drake thing to do. But in the aftermath of the night before, it was doing all kinds of things to her body.

Her instinct was to pull away, but she couldn't let herself do it. Not only would pulling away shine a bright light on the way they had changed their relationship with their actions, but she had to admit it felt good to be in his arms. Drake was the only man who made her feel safe. Her father didn't even have that title. It was only Drake. Regardless of what they did or didn't do with each other, she needed him like she needed her next breath.

"Yes, we can do this," she answered finally, holding on to him even tighter.

After an uneventful family dinner, Drake and Love had settled in for cocktails and conversation with her mother and her aunt. The dance was in full swing, and all around them the Nelson clan was mingling and catching up.

Love and Drake had both let out a sigh of relief earlier that Gloria had kept her mouth shut during the organized program, especially when the MC asked if anyone had any announcements. Now, as they sat at a high top table with her mother and her aunt, Love watched Drake interact with various members of her family. They absolutely loved him, and he managed to charm most of the women in the room with his deep dimples, smooth dark skin and beautiful white teeth. He was dressed in a navy suit with an azure-blue shirt that fit him to perfection, and she noted the way random women had responded to him all night.

"You want to go play?" he whispered in her ear.

She choked on the water that she'd just taken a sip of. "What?"

He flashed a knowing grin. "The slots?"

"Oh." She wiped her mouth with a cocktail napkin. "Nah, not right now."

Love enjoyed the slots. But if heading to the casino floor was anything like the walk into the banquet hall that evening, she'd pass. Drake was a gentleman, so it was second nature for him to keep his hand against the small of her back as they walked. Since her navy blue, knee-length dress was cut low in the back, every so often the tips of his fingers would brush against her bare skin, stirring her nerve endings. It also didn't help that he smelled like spice mixed with a burst of citrus.

Absently, she wondered if it would be this way forever, now that she'd been with him. As much as she wanted to act like it never happened, separating the Drake that held her hair up while she hurled in the toilet in college from the Drake that made love to her at her favorite hotel on the Strip was proving to be harder than she thought.

"Drink?" he whispered.

She could smell the cognac on his breath, and fought against an urge to lean in closer to his warmth. Exhaling, she told him no. She'd stick with water. "You don't have to hang around if you don't want to."

"I'm fine." He finished off his drink. "Your mother did a good job with the dinner."

"She did." Love grinned at him over her shoulder.

He beckoned to the waitress and ordered another drink. Then he turned to Love. "You look nice tonight."

Smiling, she tapped a finger on the table. "You don't have to say that."

"I know," he said simply, with a wicked grin. "I hope they know we didn't plan to be color coordinated."

Unable to help herself, she burst out in a fit of laughter. "I know! I can't believe that happened."

When his distinctive laugh followed, she pressed a hand to her quivering stomach as relief washed over her. They could still relax and make each other laugh.

The clink of glasses drew their attention toward her mother and the microphone she was holding in her hand.

Oh, no.

"Can I have your attention, please?" Gloria began.

The chatter in the room dimmed to a dull roar. Drake dug his fingers into Love's knee.

"I am beside myself with glee because my daughter made it to this reunion. It's been a while and I'm so happy she's here."

Love stood up abruptly, hitting the table with her knee. *Oh, God.* Rubbing her knee, she called out, "Mom, what are you doing?"

"I want to say to Drake that I love you like a son," Gloria continued, as if Love hadn't spoken. "And I'm so happy that you're a permanent part of my family now. I want everyone to congratulate my daughter and her new husband, Drake, on their marriage."

A round of claps and multiple cheers erupted. Love's throat closed up as people swarmed her. Leaning against the table, she searched for Drake in the crowd. She took a few cleansing breaths as her stomach churned. Her throat became dry, and she reached for her glass of water. It was empty. Then Drake was there, behind her, leading her away.

The roar of the crowd disappeared, replaced by the bells of the slot machines, then silence. She struggled to breathe, grasping at her throat frantically.

"Sit here," he said, gently setting her on a hard ledge.

She heard the sound of running water and, seconds later, felt a warm cloth against the back of her neck.

"Love, breathe," he whispered, as his hand closed around hers. "It's okay." He pressed the cloth against her forehead and rubbed her back.

A few seconds later, she felt her airways open up. "Drake."

He knelt in front of her, holding a glass of water in his hands. "Drink this." He held the cool glass up to her mouth, and she gulped it down.

Wiping her mouth, she shot him a smile. "Thanks."

"You have to be careful, Love. It's been a long time since you've had one."

Love had been known to have panic attacks in the past. And more often than not, Drake had been there to pick up the pieces. That was why he—as annoying as he could be—was the most important person in her life. The first time it had happened to her, back in high school, she'd thought she was having a heart attack. Over the years, she had been able to manage them. Drake was right. She hadn't had an attack in a long time, but after the events of the day, she wasn't surprised.

"Did she just do that?" she finally managed to ask.

He nodded. "Yes, she did."

"She's going to come find us." Love imagined her mother searching frantically for them. She glanced at the small room, and realized she was sitting on a toilet. Frowning, she searched his gaze. "You brought me into a bathroom?"

Drake shrugged and blew out a short breath. "I didn't have many choices. You needed to get out of there. And I asked your mother to give us some time."

Love leaned forward, rested her head on his shoulder. "What are we going to do? This is a nightmare."

He leaned his chin on her head and wrapped his arms around her in a tight hug. "We'll be okay. She didn't tell a lie. We did get married, in a moment of obvious lack of judgment. So we have to deal with the consequences."

She pulled away, searched his eyes. There was no panic in them. He was calm, as usual. "How can you not be freaking out about this? What happens when my dad finds out?"

He rolled his eyes and looked away from her. Standing, he took the washcloth and tossed it in a bin. "If your dad finds out, we'll deal with it. In the meantime, we have to tell your mother the truth."

"What truth? That we got married on a whim because we had too many shots and wanted to get our freak on? I don't know if I can do that here. She's so happy, so proud. I'm sure she thought I was vying for spinsterhood, and this just gave her life. Besides, the whole family is here."

And with her mother's progressing diabetes and her recent diagnosis of peripheral artery disease, Love thought that she needed some happiness.

Drake sighed. "So, we wait until after the reunion is over."

"Maybe we should just wait until we can get an annulment. Or a divorce," she added under her breath.

"The fact that my father called my mother to get the deets on the reunion for Derrick makes me think they talk a lot more than I thought. She would definitely tell my dad we got married. He won't be happy with you. He'll kill you."

"What do you suggest we do? We're not going to stay married, Love."

Love looked down at the tile, focused on the grout between the gray, beige and ivory colored squares. "Let's make it through this weekend. When we get home, we'll hire an attorney to take care of it. We can tell everyone that we made a mistake and decided to fix it before our friendship suffered for it. This way, my dad won't be too upset, because he'll think I did this willingly, and he won't take it out on you or your career."

Drake didn't answer for what seemed like an eternity. Love rubbed her thumbnail over one of the sequins on her dress.

"Okay," he said finally. "We'll wait until we're home and divorced to break the news to your mother."

Love stood, then stepped closer to Drake. She tilted her head to meet his gaze. "Drake, I need you to promise me that we won't let this ruin us."

His eyes softened, and he pinched her chin as he had so many times before. "Love, we won't. You're my best friend and nothing is going to change that."

A tear fell from her eyes, and he smirked.

"You're such a baby," he said, grabbing a tissue and holding it out to her. "Get cleaned up, so we can go play the part of a loving couple for a few minutes."

Love went to the mirror and grimaced at her raccoon eyes. "How about we just go back up to the room and let them think we snuck away because we're in newlywed mode? I look like a crazy woman." She eyed him in the mirror. "Hmm?"

"You're beautiful."

He turned her to him and his finger trailed down her nose before he hooked a hand behind her neck and pulled her closer. When his lips touched hers, it felt like a dream. The kiss wasn't passionate, but achingly sweet. It was soft, warm. Just what she needed in that moment.

He pulled away and grinned. "Whatever you want." He brushed his thumb back and forth over her earlobe. "You go on up, and I'll find your mother and tell her that we're turning in. I'll also ask her to not tell anyone else, because we want to make our own announcement back in Michigan."

Love let out a nervous laugh and tried to pretend Drake hadn't just kissed her knees wobbly. "Let's hope she listens."

He wrapped an arm around her and led her out of the bathroom. "I'm praying she will."

Chapter 6

The warmth of Las Vegas had been replaced with a Michigan snowstorm. In March. Ann Arbor was the sixth largest city in "The Mitten," as some people called the state. It was home to the Ann Arbor Art Fair, "The Big House," the annual Hash Bash, Zingerman's Delicatessen and the University of Michigan.

Love had dreamed of attending "U of M" as a child. Maize and Blue was in her soul, running through her veins. Except she hadn't expected Ann Arbor to be so cold, wet and humid at times. She had grown up in Las Vegas, after all.

Still, in her time there, she'd come to love the quaint college town, with its parks, many shops and diverse population. And the food…yum. *I'm so greedy.*

Love walked through the University of Michigan Health System, now known as Michigan Medicine, greeting several people in the halls. There was a flurry of activity as always, with individuals from all walks of life milling around. A musician played on a grand piano in the lobby area and patients readied themselves for appointments. As a medical resident, focused on Obstetrics and Gynecology, Love been assigned to all the many hospitals within the system. Her favorite, of course, was the Von Voigtlander Women's Hospital, attached to the C. S. Mott Children's Hospital. Considered one of the nation's leading medical institutions, Michigan Medicine was on the cutting edge in many specialties, and Love was happy to be a part of it.

The elevator doors opened on floor five and Love rushed out, nearly slipping on the linoleum. Gripping the edge of a nearby counter, she stood still for a minute, taking a few deep breaths. It had been a day since she'd awkwardly said goodbye to her *husband*. They'd successfully finished the reunion weekend without ending up in bed with each other again. Which was a good thing. Well, that's what she kept telling herself, anyway.

Except for that kiss. One kiss, and she'd felt like her world had titled on its axis. She'd been going back and forth about bringing it up. Sure, they'd had sex and got married, but that night of the reunion dinner he'd kissed her deliberately, while sober. Then he'd acted like nothing extraordinary had happened. She hated him.

They'd agreed to talk before she headed into work this morning, but she'd avoided his many calls. After a night of Drake-filled dreams, talking to the man was the last thing she needed.

"Hello, Dr. Jackson."

Love stopped in her tracks and turned when she heard his name spoken, and Drake's low-voiced response. He was grinning, like the flirt he was. And the stupid nurse who'd greeted him was eating it up. There was nothing about the encounter that was abnormal. Drake was well-known and well-liked by the staff, especially the women they worked with. Last week, the overly friendly nurse wouldn't have bothered her, but this week that damn nurse was talking to her husband.

Closing her eyes tight, Love willed the jealousy away.

"How was your trip?" Nurse Annoying asked Drake.

"Good," he answered. "How was your weekend?"

Love rolled her eyes when the nurse flipped her hair and giggled like a teenage girl with a crush before relaying the details of her weekend clubbing and drinking with her friends.

"I was wondering if you liked Thai food?" the nurse purred, reaching out to fix Drake's collar. "There's a restaurant that just opened up around the corner. I happen to be free for lunch, if you want to join me."

Tramp.

Drake and the woman turned to face her, and Love realized that she'd spoken out loud.

"Really?" the nurse snapped.

"I'm sorry," Love mumbled. "That was inappropriate."

"I called you this morning," Drake said to her, an arch in his brow. A signature trait that seemed even more endearing today. "We were supposed to talk."

Love looked at the nurse, then at Drake. "I know." She fidgeted, squeezing her purse between her palms. "I was busy."

"Too busy to discuss Vegas?"

Love motioned to the nurse, who was listening intently. "Can we talk about Vegas later?"

"What happened in Vegas?" the nosy woman asked, folding her arms across her chest. "Wait, you went to Vegas with Dr. Jackson?"

"Actually, Drake went to Vegas with me. And shouldn't you be administering some medication this morning?"

"Rita, I need to take care of something right now," Drake told the nurse.

She actually had the nerve to pout. "What about lunch?"

Love couldn't help it; she opened her mouth and it came out. "Drake, don't you think you should run along and get that infection checked out before it spreads?" She flinched when he pinched her.

"She's lying," Drake assured the nurse. Then, after a scalding glare in Love's direction, he added, "About lunch... I don't think it's a good idea. I don't mix work and pleasure. Sorry."

"Oh, I—I didn't mean a date," she stammered. "I was just asking as a friend."

"Give me a break," Love mumbled.

The nurse backed away and stumbled over a wheelchair. "But I understand, Dr. Jackson. I'll see you around."

Love covered her smile with her hand, but Drake chuckled out loud. And even though he'd blatantly laughed at her and boldly rebuffed her advances, Love was sure the other woman wouldn't hesitate to let him take her to bed. That's just how women were around the handsome, eligible Dr. Drake Jackson.

Love slung her bag over her shoulder and started for the residents' lounge, with Drake on her heels.

His hand around her arm stopped her. "Love, wait."

"Drake, I have to get started. I want to talk to Dr. Hastings about my patient." Since finding out in Vegas about the woman's death, Love had been rolling her entire history with Mrs. Rodriguez in her mind. Her father had once told her to never get too personal with her patients, but she couldn't help it. "I have many questions."

Drake let her go, and ran a hand through his hair. "Love, we can't deal with this if you keep avoiding me. We have to put on a united front here at the hospital."

"Why? No one knows anything."

They'd managed to get her mother to promise not to share the news with anyone else, so Love felt secure in the fact that no one in Michigan would know unless they told them, and they'd decided not to tell anyone.

"Yes, I know. But there is the pesky detail of hiring an attorney to handle the annulment."

She forgot. Sighing, she scratched her ear. "Okay, you're right. Come over tonight and we'll talk about it."

Drake hesitated, tapped his foot against the floor. Nodding, he pulled his phone out of his jacket. "I'll be over after five. I have to go."

He walked away without another word. Love watched him round the corner toward the patient elevators. Nibbling on her finger, she sighed and entered the residents' lounge.

"Hey, you," Lana called, approaching her. "What are you doing here? I thought you weren't coming back for a few days?"

She peered up at Dr. Lana White and smiled. "Hey. No, I was always supposed to be back today."

It was always good to see Lana. Her cousin was like a breath of fresh air in her life. Love had been a lonely kid. Her mother's diabetes had prevented her from having more children, so Lana had been a stand-in sister. She was popular and intelligent and had taught Love all about boys and science.

Lana dropped a file on the table and plopped down in a chair. "Girl, it's been boring as hell without you."

Love set her bag in her locker and quickly dressed in her scrubs. "I wasn't gone that long."

"Did I tell you that my life and my stomach depend on you to be around?" She laughed, rubbing her flat belly.

Lana was a mess in the kitchen, so Love had spent many a night cooking for her. "You're so greedy."

"Hey, there is no shame in my game."

The two shared another laugh. Lana could eat anyone under the table, but looking at her, one would never know that. She was a natural beauty, with perfect skin the color of rich toffee. Her cousin was slender and toned at five feet nine inches tall. For a long time, Love had envied Lana's long legs, silky hair and confident stride. It had taken years for her to feel comfortable in her own petite frame, especially when around her gorgeous cousin. For all intents and purposes, Lana was the only girlfriend she had. It was a bonus that she was also a close relation.

"I saw Drake zoom past me," Lana said. "He barely said two words to me."

Love froze. "Oh? He's probably going to see El." She pulled a bag of veggies from her roomy purse, closed her locker, and plopped down next to Lana.

"El, huh?"

Love didn't miss the interest in her voice. For years, she'd hoped that El and Lana would connect as more than friends. Unfortunately, El hadn't been interested in dating since he'd broken up with his ex-girlfriend Avery. Poor Lana had been crushing on him for quite some time.

They sat in silence for a moment, before Lana stood. She opened the fridge and pulled out a bottle of water. "I'm hungry. I'm gonna head to the cafeteria. Care to join?" She took a long gulp of water.

"I'm married," Love blurted.

Water sprayed out of Lana's mouth onto the floor and the wall. "Damn," she exclaimed, grabbing a napkin and wiping her face. Then she placed a hand on her hips. "What did you just say?"

Love hurried to wipe up the spilled water before meeting her gaze. "You heard me."

Lana wrapped an arm around Love's shoulder and guided her over to a couch on the other side of the room. They both sat. "I heard you, but I don't understand. The Love I know went to Vegas single, and now you're standing in front of me telling me that you're married. Who did you marry?"

Love swallowed, hugging herself. "You have to promise not to tell anybody."

Lana shrugged. "Who am I going to tell?"

"Promise me."

"I won't say anything."

Love tucked her feet under her bottom and relaxed a bit. "After you called and told me about Mrs. Rodriguez, I was beside myself with grief."

"I know. I had to convince you not to come back, remember?"

"Drake took me out to distract me."

Lana bit her lip. "So, what's different about that? Drake is always there to distract you."

"I know, right? But this time we woke up the next morning in bed together."

The blank look on Lana's face told Love that her cousin still wasn't following. "So what? I don't know why, but you two have been known to share a bed. Often. I'll never understand how that worked between you, but hey. To each her own. Not many women can sleep in bed with a man as fine as Drake and not be tempted to…explore. And vice versa." Lana took another swig from her bottle of water.

Oh, boy.

Lana rambled on, obviously ignoring what had to be a sick look on Love's face. Or maybe she just felt sick? "You're a good catch, too," her cousin continued. "Any man would want to be with you. You're gorgeous." She took another swig of her water.

"Naked." Love jerked back when water sprayed on her face. "Damn, Lana. Can't you control your spit reflex?"

"Oh, no. I'm so sorry." Lana grabbed a handful of tissues from the table and dabbed Love's face. "You can't spring something like that on me."

Snatching the tissue away from her startled cousin, Love muttered a curse. "Anyway, long story short, I couldn't remember what happened the night before. But there was evidence of sexual activity on the bed."

Lana frowned. "Evidence? Why do you have to sound like an old episode of *Law & Order*? So mechanical. What kind of... Oh! And you don't remember having sex with Drake?"

"Keep up, Lana. I didn't remember when I woke up next to him naked. I remember now."

"You had sex with Drake," she whispered.

"Why are you whispering? There's no one else in here. Yes, we had sex."

"Was it good?"

Love gaped at her amused cousin. "Stay focused."

"Okay. I'm focused. I'm putting on my doctor's face. Detached and listening Lana here. Answer the question."

Lana placed a hand over her mouth and let out a squeal of...delight? Then she cleared her throat and straightened in her seat. "Okay, you have my undivided attention."

Love hesitated before she continued the story. "Then the concierge comes up to the room with a ring."

"A ring?"

"Yes." Love took a deep breath. "I married Drake in Vegas."

Lana's mouth fell open. "Get out of here."

"Believe me, I wish I wasn't telling the truth."

"You and Drake got busy *and* married in the same night? After all these years of pure, platonic friendship, you just chucked all the unspoken rules out the window and did it?"

Love hung her head.

"This is too juicy not to share."

Love shot her a death glare. "If you say one word, I will kick your ass up and down this hospital."

Lana's hands went up in surrender. "Okay, okay. I won't say anything."

Love pointed at her cousin. "I swear, Lana. Don't play with me."

Lana squeezed Love's knee. "My lips are sealed. Calm down. But you have to admit, this is good tea. Blogworthy. You, Ms. Queen of Control, had sex and got married, while drunk, to your best friend." She barked out a gleeful laugh. "No one would believe me if I announced it on the loudspeaker during rounds."

Lana was right. No one would believe it. Love had to admit that, if she hadn't been there, she wouldn't have ever thought she was capable of being so reckless. She filled her cousin in on the plans for an annulment. "And there's one more thing."

"There's more?"

"My mother found out."

"Gloria knows?" Lana asked with wide eyes. "Oh, God. You must be mortified."

It was no secret that her mother wanted Drake and Love together. She'd just given up on that hope after years spent denying they were anything more than friends.

"And she announced it in the middle of the family reunion."

"Oh, Jesus. Does Uncle Leon know?"

"No, thank God. I convinced Mom not to say anything to my father. But you know her. She is giddy with excitement. And when she's excited, she's crazy."

Though Lana was her cousin on her father's side of the family, she knew Gloria well. She still spent her summer vacations in Las Vegas with Love, even after Love's parents divorced.

"This just gets better," Lana mused aloud. "How do you feel?"

"How do you think? Drake can barely say the word *sex* in front of me, and I can't look him in the eyes. It's a nightmare."

"I think you two should definitely talk about it. It's going to be a huge elephant in the room. Not to mention awkward for everyone else around you. And if you don't want Uncle Leon to find out about it, you best air this before it starts to affect your friendship."

It was a truth that Love had been worried about since she'd landed at the Detroit Metro Airport the night before. Drake seemed normal enough, but their situation was anything but.

"How is Drake acting?" Lana asked, concern in her dark brown eyes.

"He's Drake. Calm under pressure. He doesn't look at me like we had sex."

That fact alone made Love feel totally inadequate. Drake had told her he wanted her, but he never said he'd enjoyed their lovemaking. Just that he remembered it. She knew him. Had seen him when he was into a woman, heard him talk to El about women that he found entrancing and unforgettable. Her worst fear, which really shouldn't even be a fear, was that she was a bland blip on his sex radar. The thought of being one of those forgettable women he never talked about made her feel sick. Especially since everything about that night was memorable for her.

What was more frightening? That he didn't enjoy it, or that she'd enjoyed it too much?

"Love, it's going to be all right," Lana said, as if she sensed the turmoil inside her. "You and Drake will work it out. You have to. Life wouldn't be the same if you and Drake weren't…you and Drake."

Love smiled and leaned into Lana, who hugged her. "Thank you, cousin. Love you."

Love's cell phone buzzed in her pocket. Hoping it was Drake, she grimaced at the sight of her father's number. She unlocked the phone and read the text: In my office in fifteen minutes.

Something told her there was another wrench in her best-laid plan.

Chapter 7

"El, we need to talk." Drake barged into El's office, closing the door behind him.

Dr. Elwood Jackson sighed and told his secretary, "Give us a minute."

Drake hadn't even realized there was someone else there, but he couldn't care. He needed to talk to his uncle. "You need an hour," he said.

"Block my calendar off for an hour," El told the shy woman as she exited in a hurry. When the door closed, El tapped on the desk. "This better be good. You know I'm busy."

Drake took a seat on the couch in the office. It was the one El used when counseling his patients, and he had half a mind to stretch out and start the conversation with "I'm going crazy." Instead he simply said,

"You're a shrink, but you're also the closest thing to an older brother that I have."

El was his father's youngest brother, and technically his uncle. But he was only five years older than Drake, who liked to call him his uncle-brother. El had told him to drop the "uncle" from the title years ago, but Drake used it sometimes to get on his nerves.

"What's going on, Drake?" he asked, leaning back in his chair. "You're acting out of the ordinary."

Drake slapped a dollar bill on the desk. "Now what I'm about to tell you is restricted under doctor/patient confidentiality."

El smirked. "Really? You're paying me a dollar? What the hell is happening?"

Drake leaned forward, his hands flat on the desk. "This is serious, El. What I'm about to tell you is a game changer. And I need your ear and your advice."

El rubbed his chin and nodded. "I'm listening."

Drake managed to get the sex and marriage thing out in one sentence. But it annoyed him that five minutes later El was still laughing. While his uncle-brother snickered at his expense, Drake grew more and more frustrated.

Tapping his fingers against the desk, he finally yelled, "Give me my damn dollar back. You're no help."

El coughed in an effort to stifle his laughter. "I'm sorry. I'm just... I can't believe we're having this conversation."

"Last I checked, me talking and you laughing is not a conversation."

"You're right." El cleared his throat. "Let me get

this straight. You had drunken sex with your best friend, married her, and now…"

"That's it. We're still married."

"Why this trip to Vegas? Why now?"

"How the hell should I know? I'm not sure what happened to turn this into what it is. One minute we're hanging out on the Strip and the next we're married."

"What did Love do?"s

"Freaked out. Especially when her mother announced it to the entire family reunion," he mumbled under his breath.

"What?" El blared. "When did Gloria find out?"

"She happened to be in the room when the damn concierge dropped by with the happy news and the receipt for the $15,000 ring I bought her."

"Fifteen thousand!"

"I can't talk about that. Man, if I wasn't there, I wouldn't believe it. What the hell was I thinking?"

"I'm wondering the same thing."

"Thanks."

"This is not like you, which leads me to believe that a part of you wants to be with Love in some capacity. Do you think that's why you did this?"

Drake frowned. "El, what the hell? You know me. You know Love."

"You're not answering the question. *Impulsive* is not a word I associate with you or Love. Neither are *sex* and *marriage* after years of friendship. I'm just wondering if there wasn't a part of you that's always wanted to be with Love on that level."

Drake thought about that for a minute. Love was beautiful, hands down. And not just physically, but her beauty radiated from within. For years he'd watched men try to get close to her, drawn to those special inner qualities. She was an exceptional cook, she loved sports and she loved him—flaws and all. That meant something to Drake, made him want to deserve someone like her. But he wasn't the type to settle down. He wanted the high life and a high-rise in the city, women in every town and no expectations. Love wanted the small-town life, a husband who came home at a reasonable hour every night, kids, and family vacations. And Drake wanted that for her.

He was wise enough, though, to know that Love had ruined it for any woman he'd meet in the future. He'd always compared any prospective woman to her, and the other woman always lost. But that wasn't something he'd ever shared with anyone else. It was his secret and he'd keep it that way.

"No," he grumbled. "A relationship with Love will not work. We want different things in life. She deserves better than me."

"Ah," El said.

Sighing, Drake shifted in his seat. He hated that "ah" El pulled out during serious conversations. It meant that he surmised something about Drake that Drake would undoubtedly resent.

"In a perfect world, would Love be the one you want? I mean, you both have some weird codependency on each other. She's your girl without being your girl. I know you've been friends for a long time, but it's very telling that the minute your inhibitions were lowered, you slept with her and committed to each other officially. Have you asked yourself why?"

Drake stood abruptly, paced the floor. "Stop asking me questions like that."

"Well, you did pay me."

"To buy your silence, not to prescribe me medicine and be my psychotherapist."

El chuckled. "You do realize that one dollar doesn't even buy you a minute of my time under normal circumstances."

And this was the downside of having a shrink for an uncle-brother. El always tried to find the hidden emotions in everything. Drake was tempted to inquire if El had asked himself all these whack questions. Maybe his uncle-brother wouldn't be afraid to move on from Avery.

"To answer your question," Drake said, "we don't live in a perfect world. Because if we did, I wouldn't be going through this right now."

"Is it possible that you have feelings for Love that go beyond friendship?"

It was a trick question. There was no right answer. If he said yes it would affirm El's suspicions of hidden emotions. If he said no it wouldn't make any sense, since they'd spent the night together rolling around in bed naked.

"She's my best friend."

"Like a sister?"

Drake snorted as he paced. "Hell no." He had a little sister, and knew what sister feelings were. His friendship with Love had never been like that. For starters, he didn't admire his little sister's legs or her cleavage. "But we've known each other since we were toddlers."

He and Love had never crossed a line with each other. Drake had never given her kisses behind the chalkboard in kindergarten, made forts in the backyard so they could play house. No Hide-and-Go-Get-It in the wooded trails behind the school. There was no picking on her boyfriends because he was jealous.

"This is going to sound like a strange question, but did you enjoy it?" El asked.

Drake whirled around. "What?"

"Did you enjoy being with her?"

Drake clenched his fists and stretched his neck. "I—I…" he sputtered. "It was sex. I enjoy sex."

"Once again, you're not answering the question. Did you enjoy being with Love on that level? It's a simple yes or no answer."

"Of course." Drake scowled at El. "Like I said, it was sex."

"Was there anything about the experience that was different than your other sexual relationships?"

"Yes!" Drake blared. "It was different because it was her!" The sheer exhaustion he felt after that admission made him sit back down on the couch. Hard. Arms on his knees, he leaned forward. "I can't stop thinking about it. Once I remembered the details, it's been running through my mind on a loop."

Every kiss, every touch of her lips to his…it still burned there. It wasn't simply making love. They made fire together. Hot, scorching fire that had seared his brain, stayed with him. Seeing her that morning in her snow boots and puffer coat, looking into her expressive brown eyes, had made him want a repeat.

"I don't know what to do with this," Drake admitted. "Things are different. I'm trying to keep it the same but I still feel her, smell her. She's not in the 'can't go there' box I put her in all those years ago.

I've gone there, and I can't flip a switch and pretend I didn't."

El coughed. "Okay, so let me ask you…what are you going to do about it?"

What can I do? Any move he made ran the risk of destroying everything, and he'd promised he wouldn't let what happened ruin them. "Nothing. The sooner we can end this marriage, the better."

The answer wasn't one he liked. He'd have to put some distance between them if their friendship had any chance of surviving. She'd already been hurt enough by Derrick. Drake couldn't hurt her.

His phone buzzed with a message, breaking him from his thoughts. When he saw who it was from, he groaned loudly.

"Who is it?" El asked.

"Her dad." Drake glanced at the text again: My office now. "I have go. I'll call you later."

Walking to Dr. Leon Washington's office was like walking the plank. It wasn't that Drake hated him. It was quite the opposite. Drake's own father was a lousy one, and Dr. Leon had filled in a lot of gaps for him as a child.

Drake's parents had never married. His mother was one in a long line of mistresses that only served one purpose in life for his father. When Drake was born, his father took custody of him, and he could count on one hand the number of times he'd actually seen his mother. He'd met her once after his kindergarten graduation. The second time was an unplanned incident at the mall when he was a teenager. He hadn't even recognized her when he saw her but she had walked up to him and gave him a hug and a kiss before she disappeared from his life for good. He'd found out she died a few years later.

His father's wife never showed him love. He figured it was because he was the constant reminder of the man's infidelity. There was the kind nanny and the housekeeper. Then there was Gloria. His father and Love's dad were colleagues and the two families spent a lot of time together. Dr. Leon had taught Drake how to drive, how to change a tire. He'd helped him study for the MCAT and wrote letters of recommendation to medical school.

Somehow, Drake knew that marrying his daughter was a different story. The elder man, his boss, had made it clear that Love was off-limits. Yes, Dr. Leon was firmly in Derrick's camp, as evidenced by the fact that he'd sent the fool to Vegas to woo Love back.

Drake rounded the corner toward Dr. Leon's office and slowed when he spotted Love pacing outside the door.

"Love?" he asked, approaching her. "What are you doing here?"

"What are *you* doing here?" she asked.

"Your dad texted me and told me to come."

"Me, too."

"Great," he mumbled.

She looked up at him, tears swimming in her eyes. "Do you think he knows? What do I say?"

The relationship between Love and her father was strained, had been since Leon divorced Gloria, married his mistress and moved to Michigan. It was partly because of his high expectations of his daughter, but mostly because of the divorce and everything that had happened afterward. Her parents had had a contemptuous relationship, but the one thing they'd never argued about was her. Her father had never fought for her. He was completely okay with summer and holiday visits, which infuriated Love.

She'd once shared with Drake that she knew her father was overbearing, but a part of her always wanted to please him, even though he didn't deserve her loyalty. She even went so far as to date a man handpicked by her father. Derrick. The asshole who'd cheated on her for months.

Drake ran his finger down her cheek, and she leaned into it. There was nothing he wouldn't do to stop her tears. Even lie, cheat or steal. "Don't cry," he whispered. "It could be a total coincidence that he asked to see us both. Don't worry, until we have something to worry about. Besides, he won't take his anger out on you. I'll be the one doing cholecystectomies for the foreseeable future."

She giggled. "Stop making me laugh."

"You know I'm right."

"Probably. He won't even give you those gallbladder surgeries. You'll be lucky if he lets you scrub in on an appendectomy."

"My bet? I'll be stuck in the ER intubating patients all day or on central line placement."

She nodded. "Ready?"

He knocked on the door. When he heard Dr. Leon beckon them to come in, he opened it. He expected to see Love's father with his head buried in a chart, or writing on the whiteboard in his office. Instead, Drake froze when he saw Derrick Harper sitting comfortably in front of the desk.

Dr. Leon stepped forward and met his gaze, the

frown on his face telling Drake this wasn't a friendly visit. "Well, well," he said. "If it isn't the newlyweds."

"Daddy?" Love said, her voice shaking as her gaze moved between Derrick and her father. "What's going on?"

"You tell me," Dr. Leon said, gesturing for them to take a seat.

Love held on to Drake's hand and squeezed it tightly. Her father was a formidable doctor, in and out of the operating room, but what distinguished him from other surgeons was his willingness to teach. He'd mentored students across the country. Right now, though, he didn't look so amenable.

Dr. Leon ran a hand over the stubble on his chin and let out a heavy grunt. "Since you're not talking, how about I start?" He pointed at Derrick, who sat with a smug look on his face. Drake wanted to kick his ass. For the life of him, he didn't understand what Love had seen in the man. He was a jerk, plain and simple. And Drake knew jerks, because he was an ass on a good day. "Imagine my surprise when Derrick told me what happened in Vegas when he arrived to propose. Not only did he walk into you and Drake sharing a hotel room, but he overheard your mother announcing to a roomful of people that you're married."

Drake glared at Derrick.

"What?" Love said. "You were there?"

"I went to the dinner to talk to you," Derrick said. "I left when your mother announced the marriage."

"And you couldn't wait to come back and tell my father?"

"Never mind that," Dr. Leon said. "Why? Are you pregnant?"

Love shook her head. "No. We'd never… I mean, it's not like that."

"Drake?" Dr. Leon said. "Care to say something? I believe you owe me an explanation."

"I do. But I'm not talking about this with him in the room." Drake couldn't believe he'd basically told his boss to kick someone out of his office. "This is between me, you and Love. Not Derrick."

Leon glared at him. "Listen, you married my daughter without so much as a call for permission. After everything I've done for you."

Love gasped. "Daddy, don't—"

Drake glanced at her out of the corner of his eye. "Love, let me handle this." He met her father's hard gaze with one of his own. "With all due respect, sir, this isn't about you. It's about me and Love. He doesn't belong in this room."

"Who do you think you're talking to?" Derrick asked incredulously.

Drake stood. "Did I stutter? I meant what I said."

"Well, luckily, this isn't your office." Derrick sneered at him.

Drake looked at Dr. Leon. "I've known you for a long time. You're like a father to me, especially since my dad couldn't be bothered. I think I deserve a chance to talk to you without an audience."

"If you have something to say, say it," Dr. Leon challenged.

Drake squeezed Love's hand when she gasped. "Dr. Leon, the fact that we're even having this discussion stings. I thought you knew that I would never intentionally hurt Love."

"I don't think you'd intentionally hurt her," Dr. Leon responded, his voice flat.

Drake couldn't figure out why the older man, his mentor, was choosing to treat him as if he was no better than a random guy on the street. He knew Dr. Leon wouldn't be happy, but this was another level of disdain that he'd never expected. Love's father was stern, not overly affectionate, but he'd never been a jerk. It rankled Drake, made him want to confront the older man, his job be damned.

"I know my daughter, and there is more to this story."

It was laughable that Dr. Leon was standing in front of him, telling him that he knew Love. "I understand that you think you know your daughter, but when are you going to admit that I know her just as well—probably better? I know what she wants out of life, and I will do my best to make sure she realizes her dreams. As I'm sure she'll do for me. There is nothing I wouldn't do for her." It was the truth, and Love knew it. That's why he could be found watching chick flicks on a Saturday afternoon, or visiting every single new art exhibit in the area, or snoring through off-Broadway plays. "And I don't really care what anyone else has to say about it, because I've got her."

Leon stared at them, long and hard.

"I'd love to continue this conversation," Drake told him. "But I need you to ask that fool to leave."

Dr. Leon held his ground. "Derrick is family."

The comment stung, especially since Drake respected Leon, modeled his professional career after him.

"Family?" Love said. "Really, Daddy? Drake is family, legally now. I know you're upset, but he *is* my husband. Derrick is not, and never will be because he broke my heart."

"Lovely Grace Washington!" He bit out the words like she disgusted him. "I'm your father and you will respect me."

"When are you going to respect *me*, Daddy? This man cheated on me and broke up with me via a text message. But you don't seem to give a damn. Maybe because you did the same thing to Mom."

"Lovely!" Dr. Leon shouted.

"No. I can't believe you're even entertaining Derrick after what he's done."

"This is the first I'm hearing of it," her dad argued. "You told me things just didn't work out between you and Derrick."

"Well, now you know. Do something about it."

Drake wasn't surprised Love had his back. She always did, willing to go into battle for him at any time. "Calm down," he whispered against her ear as he massaged her shoulders. "This isn't helping."

Love jerked out of his hold. "No. I'm sick of being calm. Daddy, since you love Derrick so much, you marry him."

Then she stormed out of the office, slamming the door behind her. Turning on his heels, he went after her.

"Drake?" Dr. Leon called to him.

He stopped at the door, but didn't turn around.

"We're not done yet."

"We are today," Drake said. "I need to go see about my wife."

Chapter 8

Love burst into the lounge area carrying her patient charts and her dreaded, ringing cell phone. It had been ringing nonstop since she'd stormed out of her father's office that afternoon. Frustrated, she never even looked to see who was calling. She was pretty sure that Drake, her mother and Lana were among the many callers. But she didn't care. She wanted to be alone.

In five minutes, she'd be safely outside in the frigid air. Anything was better than the hospital at that moment. She'd finish her chart notes at home. Luckily, she didn't have appointments that day. Love pulled her bag out of the locker and dropped her phone and files inside.

She didn't stop stuffing her bag when she heard

the door open and close behind her. Instinctively, she knew it was Drake. "Go away."

"Love, we have to talk."

She groaned when a traitorous tear escaped. "No, we don't. I'm done talking today. I'm going home. Alone."

"You can't just run away."

She turned around, glared at him. "Why not? I need some distance between us right now."

Because she couldn't tell him that the way he was willing to go up against her father, his boss, for her made her swoon inside. She slung her bag over her shoulder and headed toward the door.

"Wait," he called.

When he caught up to her, she turned to him. "Just let me go, Drake. I have to go."

"Why are you flipping out on me? What did I do?"

"You didn't do anything, Drake. I'm irritated. And you know I hate to feel this way."

"We're in this together."

She peered up at the ceiling. Last week, her life had been boring but she loved it. Today, her life was anything but boring and she was unraveling at a rapid pace. "I can't do this right now."

"Stop being emotional. I need you to talk to me, like you're Love and I'm Drake."

"Drake, please. I'm tired, and you're damn right. I'm emotional." As she talked, a different type of energy took over. Anger. "We are married. When I envisioned holy matrimony, I pictured a white dress, fresh flowers, soft music, my friends and family surrounding me, and my father walking me down the aisle. I wanted to *remember* the most important vows I'll ever make and look back with fondness at my wedding pictures on my silver anniversary."

It seemed odd to others, but after Derrick broke up with her, she'd wanted to abstain from sex until she found the man she was going to marry. She'd promised herself that the next time she made love to anyone, it would be her husband. Her goal was to replace bad sex memories with good ones, lasting ones.

"Not only did that not happen, my father basically said he didn't give a damn that the guy he wants for me is the asshole of the century. My mother is running around planning wedding receptions." She ticked off the reasons on her fingers. "And my best friend, my husband, is acting like we're going to just get over the fact that we had sex and got married on a whim. As much as I'd like to believe that this will be a story we share with our real spouses someday in a fit of laughter, it's unrealistic."

"Love—"

"No, Drake. There is nothing you can say to make this better right now. Please back off. I want to be alone."

"Okay," he said simply.

That one word infuriated her even more. Pivoting on her heels, she stalked off and slammed the door behind her.

Twenty minutes later, she was in her home, climbing into bed. Closing her eyes, she took in the fresh linen smell. Her emotions were playing mean tricks on her and she couldn't take it.

She had no idea what she was going to do. Drake had been her best friend forever. There was little they didn't know about each other. But his presence was making it worse, with his kind eyes, and the way he cared about her. It was distracting, and she needed to get a grip.

Her father had hurt her. She'd purposefully with-held the real reason she'd broken up with Derrick. Instead, she'd chosen to downplay it as two people who'd grown apart and couldn't take the weight of a long-distance relationship.

In reality, long distance suited her just fine. It was the infidelity that had made her blood boil. And the lies had sealed his fate. But instead of taking it like a man, he'd chosen to end it first with a short, harsh text message.

To have her father simply shrug it off like it didn't matter devastated her. It shouldn't have surprised her, but it did.

Her parents' divorce had been absolutely the worst period of her life. Drake had spent countless nights holding her as she cried herself to sleep. Her father had moved to Michigan during her freshman year of high school, the same day her boyfriend had dumped her for not putting out. Drake had stolen a fifth of tequila from his father's stash and shown up at her house to keep her company.

Smiling, she recalled her first foray into the world of tequila. They'd spent hours talking about nothing and taking shots, before she'd hurled on his brand-new sneakers. There would be many more nights of them being there for each other. When Drake received word that his mother had died, she'd been the only one who could console him.

The sound of her phone buzzing drew her out of her memories. She glanced at it and read Drake's text:

I know you're pissed. I'll give you a few hours, then I'm coming over for dinner. Make something good. I'll bring dessert.

She couldn't help the small laugh it elicited. He always could cheer her up. Then she typed in her response: I'm not cooking. But I want a decadent and expensive dessert.

Love turned her phone off and rolled over on her side. A nap was exactly what she needed. As she lay there, her eyes feeling heavy, she prayed sleep would come sooner rather than later. Yawning, she burrowed into the down pillow.

"I, Lovely, take you, Drake, to be my lawfully wedded husband."

"I like the sound of that," Drake murmured against her lips. Nipping at her ear, he whispered, "I, Drake, take you, Lovely, to have and to hold from this day forth. Forever."

His mouth brushed against hers before kissing her fully. The searing kiss that followed curled her toes, it was so good. His lips were soft, but firm. And she was lost in him.

"Did we really just do this?" she asked, peering into his hooded eyes.

"Yes." He swept his thumb under her chin, down her neck.

Her eyes fluttered closed as he kissed her eyelids, her nose, then her mouth. "Drake, did we make a mistake?"

"If we did, it's the best mistake I ever made."

He kissed her again, pulling her flush against him.

Without warning, he picked her up and carried her out of the chapel.

Love's eyes popped open, and she sat upright as their wedding night replayed in her dream. Again. Every detail filled her mind—from the touches, the kisses, the— *Shit.*

He'd kissed her with a sweet tenderness she'd never felt from him before, and she'd wanted him like no other man before him. It was a perfect wedding kiss, one that could and should go down in the record books. He'd at least given her that. As butterflies tickled her stomach, she relived the moment they'd come together, him inside her, filling her completely. A soft moan escaped from her parted lips at the memory. It was everything. He'd made it everything.

Squeezing her eyes—and her legs—closed, she screamed into her pillow. How the hell was she supposed to look at him and not think about it?

A little while later, Love shuffled into the kitchen. Opening the fridge, she pulled out a casserole pan, humming to herself when she looked down at the delectable vegetable lasagna she'd made the night before. She'd been so wired from thinking, she'd decided to put that energy to good use and cook.

Her phone rang and she looked down at her mother's face staring back at her. *Not going to answer that. Not now.* The last person she needed to speak with was her giddy mom, Gloria. Most conversations with her ended up being about Love's lack of companionship or her mother's lack of grandkids. But that was before the eventful reunion. Now that she'd gone and married Drake, she was sure the conversation would turn to wedding receptions and the six grandkids Gloria couldn't wait to have. This event was bound to be a spectacle.

Despite her mother's weird ways, she'd made a name for herself as an event planner for many years before retiring to open a flower shop. Love admired her for not letting the divorce send her to the bottle or catapult her into a sinking depression. Gloria Washington had made great strides to become a formidable businesswoman. She'd started out with a few small jobs creating floral displays for her neighborhood church. One Sunday, an executive at the Bellagio Hotel in Vegas had visited the church for a function. The visitor had been so impressed by the display, she'd insisted on meeting Gloria. That meeting had turned into a job at the hotel in the Sales and Catering Department. Gloria's career grew from there, and she eventually went out on her own and opened her own shop.

Even now, no matter how she was feeling, her mom managed to get out of bed every morning and make it to work. Love couldn't be more proud.

Love checked her voice mail and text messages just in case it was an emergency. No messages, so it must not be important. *I love you, Mom. But I still don't want to talk to you.*

Cutting a hefty piece of lasagna, Love set it on a plate and put it in the microwave. While it warmed, she went to the wine rack and pulled a bottle of pinot noir from her reserves. Once she'd poured a nice glass for herself, she swirled the liquid around and took in the fruity, yet earthy, aroma. Love took a sip and let it rest in her mouth a moment before swallowing. Perfect.

The ding of the microwave signaled it was time to eat and she hurried over to retrieve her dinner plate. She heard the front door open and close, but stayed put. She knew it was Drake. He was the only one who had a key.

Her phone rang again, and she was tempted to answer if only to stop the constant calls. Out of the corner of her eye, she saw Drake stroll into the kitchen and slide a box onto the countertop. She didn't have to look inside to know what it was. The box was from her favorite bakery. Distracted, she almost didn't see the hands reaching for her plate of lasagna.

Love smacked the back of one. "Don't you dare. Get your own piece."

"Damn. Okay."

"I knew I was asking for it when I gave you a key. You're always letting yourself in and helping yourself to my food. Maybe you should leave a twenty on the counter for groceries."

"Ha. You're funny." He pulled his wallet from his back pocket and slapped a crisp twenty-dollar bill on the counter. "You know I don't eat homemade meals unless you cook for me."

Love ignored the cash and the man in front of her, and finished her glass of wine. She burped. "Get that dirty money off my counter." She cut another piece and put it in the microwave.

Once again, her phone chimed. "Is that your mom?" Drake asked.

"Why?"

"She called me and asked where you were and why you weren't answering her calls."

Great. "Did you tell her I was asleep?"

"I did."

She pulled his lasagna out of the microwave when it was done and set it in front him. He'd refilled her glass of wine and poured one for himself. They settled in for a quiet meal.

"So, I called the chapel today," Drake told her. "Everything is legit."

Love knew that. Her dreams proved that much. They'd gotten married in a cheesy, gold trimmed chapel by a minister in an Elvis costume for heaven's sake. It was too odd to not be true.

After a few minutes, Love said, "Did you know you're the third man I've had sex with?" Drake choked on his food, covering his mouth with his napkin. She waited until he finished chewing before she spoke again. "I realized that we've never been the type of friends to talk about sex—especially my sex life."

"Maybe it's because sex should be kept between the two people having it?"

She tilted her head, assessing him. Drake was her best friend for a reason. Sure, he was loud, annoying, and he could be a jerk some days. But he was sincere, sweet and loyal every day. She smirked. "Still, we've shared so much with each other and it's never come up. Weird, huh?"

For some reason, she couldn't stop staring at him, letting her eyes wander over the clean lines of his face. He was focused on everything but her, yet she found herself entranced by the mere strength of him—his strong hands, the tiny scar under his right eyebrow, the way his dark rinse jeans hugged his thighs, the tattoo on his arm that poked out from beneath his short-sleeved shirt. He was a beautiful man. She'd never really appreciated it before, but it seemed to be all she could think of in that moment.

"You're staring," he muttered, pushing his food around his plate.

"Sorry." She finished her second glass of wine and moved to the sink. As she rinsed the dishes, she heard him stand up and walk over to her. Pausing momentarily to breathe, she glanced at him out of the corner of her eye as he leaned his hip against the sink.

"Love, I'm sorry."

She swallowed. "Why?"

"I can't help but feel like I took advantage of you that night."

"Is that what's been bothering you?"

He nodded, crossing his arms over his muscular chest.

"We were both drunk, Drake. It's not an excuse, though, because we both know better. I make it a point to tell the women I see every day to watch their alcohol intake. But things happen. If I had to get drunk and throw my inhibitions out the window, I'm glad it was with you." Their gazes met. After swallowing hard once again, she said, "I mean, it's good that I had sex with you and not some random guy in a bar." *Shut up, Love.* Except she couldn't stop talking. "I'm just saying…well, I trust you more than anybody." *Just stop talking.* "And it wasn't like it was bad sex. It was good."

He picked up her hand and entwined his fingers with hers. "It was," he agreed, his voice low and husky. His thumb traced the length of hers, and her nerves stirred. "But don't you wonder why we chose that night to…"

"Have sex?"

He nodded. "We've been friends for almost thirty years. It's not like we haven't been drunk together before. Why this trip? Why now?"

"Does it have to mean something deep?"

"Shouldn't it?" He squeezed, and her gaze dropped to their joined hands. "You're a beautiful person, not the type of woman that any man—including me—should take to bed without it meaning something."

"Do you love me?"

He gaped at her and she couldn't help but laugh.

"Drake, it's not a trick question. I'm not asking if you're in love with me. Do you love me?"

"Of course I love you. You already know that. You're the most important person in my life."

"Then it means something. We can't dwell on it, though, so let's move forward."

Drake arched a brow. "And ignore that it happened?"

"Not exactly. I don't think we could ignore it if we tried."

The room descended into silence. He stood there, his eyes locked on hers, his hands holding hers. He inched closer to her.

"Love?"

At that point, she wasn't sure why she'd even started the conversation. It was bad enough that just being near him was doing all kinds of things to her body. "Yes?" she said, her voice coming out more whispery than she'd intended.

His thumb swept over her palm. "I know what you're trying to do, but it's not that simple."

Oh, God. He smells so good. His cologne washed

over her and she couldn't help but lean closer to get another whiff. Today he smelled like black pepper, leather and wood.

"I don't think it's going to be so easy to move on from this," he added.

She looked at his fingers as they drew tiny circles over her wrist and up her arm. Her heart beat in her ears as a warmth spread from her belly to her toes. He was talking, but she had no idea what he was saying. She was too entranced with his mouth, the feel of his breath on her skin. Her eyes wandered down his neck to the top button of his shirt.

Stop picturing him naked, Love.

"But you're right," he said.

Confused, she frowned and peered up at him. "Huh?"

He chuckled, and she couldn't help but smile. Touching her face, then her neck, she let out an airy giggle. *Breathe, Love. Focus.*

Drake was quiet now, studying her when she looked into his brown eyes again. And he was closer. It was almost like he could read her mind.

Oh hell, why do I want him to kiss me?

Then he did. His lips met hers in a soft kiss, one that seemed to steal her breath.

Wait, Love. The warning in her head was clear. She pushed him away. "Drake, what did you just do?"

He rubbed his chin, a frown on his face. "Uh, I kissed you."

"Yeah, you did. Why did you do that?"

"Because you wanted me to."

His answer was so matter-of-fact that she backed up a step. How the hell did he know that? "You can't just keep kissing me like that. You did it in Vegas, too. Just kissed me for no reason."

"You were upset, and I wanted you to feel better."

"So you kissed me?"

He sighed, rubbed his forehead. "I don't know. It just felt like the right thing to do at the time."

"And today?"

"I don't know," he repeated.

Love's curiosity got the best of her and she asked, "And how do you know I wanted you to kiss me?"

He shrugged, shoving his hands into his pockets. "I can't describe it. I can always tell when a woman wants me to kiss her."

"So you just do it?"

"Of course not."

"In this case you did."

"It's you. I kissed you because *you* wanted me to."

She opened her mouth to respond, but the words didn't come. His question to her earlier roared in the back of her mind. *But don't you wonder why we chose that night...?* It had to mean something that they'd had sex, married each other.

"Why?" she whispered.

"You tell me."

She sucked in a deep breath. "Maybe..."

"You want me to kiss you again, don't you?"

Love paused, shocked at his question. Not because he was being his confident, cocky self, but because he was right. She did want him to kiss her again. She wanted it more than she wanted her next breath.

"Yes," she admitted with a sigh.

She trembled as he stepped into her, pulling her to him for another kiss. His mouth moved over hers with

short, languid movements. His tongue swept into her
mouth and tangled with hers, drawing a low moan
from her throat. His hands roamed over her back, over
her butt. She felt a buzz between them, and then the
heat of his nearness was replaced by a chill.

When her eyes opened, he was staring at his phone.

"Love, I have to take this. It's the hospital."

He stepped out of the room before she could for-
mulate a response.

What had just happened? He ran off to answer his
phone in the middle of a kiss, one that had curled her
toes and made the hairs on her arms rise.

Her eyes darted around the kitchen until they lit
on the white box on the counter and she hurried over
to it. Opening it, she moaned at the sight of the deep-
fried beignets. Picking up two, she stuffed both in her
mouth, all the while thinking that eating beignets was
not the only thing she wanted to do with her mouth.

Chapter 9

Drake leaned against a wall in Love's living room. He'd been off the phone for five minutes, but still wasn't able to go back to her in the kitchen. Because he'd kissed her. Twice. And he'd wanted to go in for thirds and more, but his phone had been his saving grace.

It wasn't anybody important, just another resident with a question on one of the patients he'd doctored that day. But it was a welcomed interruption because things were on the verge of going way left.

Drake leaned against the couch. El's words rang in his ears. His uncle-brother had surmised that sex with love had to mean something. And he was right.

He'd spent the last several nights turning every moment over in his mind, trying to find the difference. There was no clarity, no epiphany that would explain how they could go from being best friends to married within the span of twelve hours.

They'd slept in many a bed together. He'd seen her in her underwear more than a few times, had knocked back shots several nights, and still...no sex. Nothing. Now, he couldn't stop imagining it. He remembered how she'd looked beneath him, how her bare skin had felt beneath his hands.

He was tempted to leave right then and there, but he wouldn't do that to her. Groaning, Drake walked over to the wet bar on the other side of the living room and poured a healthy glass of cognac.

If he went back into the kitchen, looked at her standing there in those cute little shorts, with that damn bun in her hair, he was liable to kiss her again—or more. Everything had changed. She'd told him they needed to move past it, but could they? He doubted it, since he couldn't stop wanting her.

Yet even as he warred with himself over his next steps, he knew he couldn't run from it. With other women, if things got too hot, he'd walk away. Simple and painless. Love wasn't other women, and walking away wasn't an option. She was his closest friend, the best woman he knew, and now she was his wife.

Drake finished the contents of his glass in one gulp and walked into the kitchen. Love was standing at the island, her head down. Had he hurt her by walking away in the middle of that kiss? It wasn't his greatest moment, but that phone call had offered a reprieve, given him a chance to think before he made another impulsive decision.

"Love, I'm sorry."

The fact that she didn't respond was odd. If he'd

pissed her off, she'd lash out. If he'd hurt her, she'd
cry. But her lack of response was not like her. He
stepped closer, caught a glimpse of the open box in
front of her.

"Love?"

Finally, he reached her and turned her around to
face him. His friend, his wife, was standing before
him covered in confectioner's sugar. Her cheeks were
stuffed with beignets and the box was…empty?

"You ate all of the beignets? I bought half a dozen."

A burst of powdered sugar flew into his face when
she opened her mouth to speak. "I'm sorry," she mumbled almost incoherently.

He picked up a napkin and wiped his face. "I can't
believe it." Her lips and chin were white with pow-
der. He poked one of her cheeks, and another puff of
sugar flew out. "You're going to pay for that in the
morning, ya know?"

She nodded, chewing rapidly. He poured her a glass
of wine and pushed it toward her. Once she'd successfully swallowed the beignets, she gulped down
the entire glassful.

"Don't laugh."

He covered his mouth. "I'm not laughing. I'm
shocked."

"I couldn't resist." She grabbed a towel and
scrubbed her mouth with it until her lips were red.

He gripped her wrist. "Stop."

"I'm so embarrassed." She tucked a stand of loose
hair behind her ear. "I couldn't stop eating them."

"You have some…" Reaching out, he wiped sugar
from the side of her mouth.

She touched where his finger had been. "I must look a mess."

"Not even a little bit."

Her eyes softened, propelling him forward until they were almost touching. He framed her face with his palms, brushed her cheeks with his thumbs. Her sharp intake of breath spurred him on. Leaning forward, he nuzzled her nose with his.

"Drake," she whispered.

The smell of sugar and dough on her breath mixed with the exotic scent of her perfume made him ache with need. Soon, he couldn't see the room around him or hear the sound of the ice maker dropping a round of cubes into the freezer. Everything simply faded away and Love was the only thing he was aware of.

"Are you afraid of what you're feeling?" he asked her.

She swallowed visibly and nodded.

"But you don't want to deny it?"

Love's answer didn't come in words. That didn't matter, though. He was fluent in her body language, and he'd heard her response loud and clear. She wanted him, too.

He skimmed her jawline with his fingertips, watched her eyelids flutter shut. "Talk to me, baby." He laid a hand on her chest, felt her heart beat fast beneath his palm.

Opening her mouth, she said, "Drake, I—"

Unable to stop himself, he leaned in and licked leftover sugar from her chin. Her lips parted more and he took full advantage, pulling her into a deep kiss. Her body was flush against his, her softness melding into his hardness as if they were meant to be like this with each other. She moaned low, raked her hands through his hair, digging her fingernails into his scalp.

He wanted to explore every inch of her skin, see her in the throes of passion, immerse himself in her. Her body was fuel to the simmering fire building inside him. Her lips were soft, welcoming, addictive.

Lifting her up, he set her on top of the island. Eventually, he had no choice but to pull back, breaking the kiss to breathe. With hooded eyes, she looked at him as he lifted her shirt up and off. The strap of her bra fell over her shoulder and he slowly pulled it down. He took her nipple in his mouth, circling it with his tongue and suckling until she cried his name. He swept his hands over the quivering skin of her stomach before he brushed his lips against her navel and dipped his tongue inside.

Love's head fell back as she sighed. "Drake, please."

He traced the waistband of her shorts with his tongue before pulling them off. He groaned, seeing the tiny piece of lace she had on underneath. After running his finger over the fabric, he gripped the elastic and pulled it off, leaving her exposed, open for him.

Drake dropped to his knees, brushed his finger over her slit. She was slick with yearning, writhing under his touch. He massaged her to a quick climax, enjoying her hoarse cries as her orgasm ripped through her. He didn't even give her a chance to come down from her high before he leaned in and tasted her, swirling his tongue around her clit before taking it in his mouth.

It didn't take long before she came again, this time so long and hard he had to fight his own release. But there was so much more he wanted to do. He wanted to take his time, love her thoroughly.

Standing, he cradled her in his arms and carried her into the living room. Laying her on the couch, he peered down at his satisfied wife. She was glorious, glowing. He unbuttoned his shirt and tugged it off.

Love reached out and unbuckled his belt, sliding it free. She unbuttoned his pants and tugged them and his boxers off. Her eyes flashed as she took in every inch of him, her palms smoothing over the muscles of his legs and lower abdomen before squeezing his erection.

Drake groaned before he grasped her wrists. "I don't want to come in your hand, baby. I want to come inside you."

Love fell back on the cushions, pulling him with her. Nestled between her legs, he kissed her forehead, her nose, then finally her mouth, biting down on her bottom lip as he pushed inside her. They started slow, familiarizing themselves with each other and finding a rhythm of their own. As they discovered their groove, the pace quickened and soon they were racing toward completion.

As much as he needed the release, Drake wanted to savor this moment. She was everything. And he was all hers. There was nobody else, no expectations or obligations. They were in sync with each other. He had never experienced anything even close to this, and he wanted it to last as long as possible before the weight of reality crashed down on them.

With that in mind, he whispered, "Let go."

That was all it took. He watched her as she came. It took everything in him not to let her milk his release from him. He bit the inside of his cheek as waves of pleasure washed over her.

A few seconds later, she opened her eyes and smiled. He felt a shift near his heart as his chest tightened. She was so damn beautiful.

She ran a knuckle down his cheek. "I can't believe we did this again."

Placing a finger over her lips, he said, "I'm not done with you yet."

Her eyes widened as he started moving again, thrusting in and out of her like there was no tomorrow full of explanations and excuses. This time, their lovemaking was slower, deliberate.

"Look at me," he commanded softly.

He knew he was close, but he wanted her with him when he came. With their gazes locked on each other, they found their release together.

Drake gave himself over to Love in more ways than one, and he knew there would be no turning back.

Drake woke the next morning still on the couch, with Love wrapped around him like a warm blanket. And he couldn't think of anywhere he'd rather be. Which, frankly, scared him to death.

"Drake?" Love's voice was soft, unsure. Definitely not groggy with sleep. "Are you awake?"

"Yes," he admitted.

She lifted herself up on an elbow. "We had sex again."

Sex? That was definitely not sex. Drake had had plenty of sex and none of it was even remotely similar to what had happened between him and Love. "Are you cold?"

She glanced at him. "Did you hear me?"

"I heard you," he murmured.

She fingered a fold in the throw he'd draped over them. "Can we talk about this?"

Not with your naked body pressed against mine. "Maybe we should get dressed."

Unfortunately, she didn't take the hint and move. "Drake, this isn't what I expected. We made love."

"Well, we are married." He knew his attempt at humor didn't work when her chin quivered. He squeezed the tip of it between his thumb and forefinger. "I'm sorry."

She dropped her forehead against his chest, and he tickled the back of her neck.

"It's complicated," she murmured. "We've yet to talk about this marriage and lawyers and the divorce. Instead, we had sex again. I'm worried we just changed things once more."

Their lovemaking had been intense, a game changer for him. And he definitely wasn't ready for the change. "Love, I'd like to think that we've been friends long enough to withstand anything that comes our way. We're adults, and we made an adult decision last night."

She glanced up at him. "What now?"

He brushed his thumb over her eyebrow. "I honestly don't know. And it's kind of hard to think about that when you're lying against me like this."

She laughed then. It was a full, throaty laugh that seemed to lodge itself in his heart. Love was beautiful on an average day, but the after-sex-relaxed-bedhead Love was stunning. She was perfect.

"You're my best friend," she said.

He swept his palm over her shoulder and squeezed. "Nothing is going to change that."

"You're worried."

"Who said I was worried?"

"You don't have to say it."

Distracted by her and the need to be with her again, he sat up. She held the blanket to her chest and slid off him so that he could stand. After dragging on his pants, he turned to her. "If I'm worried, it's because I don't want you hurt. Not because I'm worried about our friendship."

"We slept together, Drake. How do we come back from that? It's not like we can magically not be attracted to each other."

She stood and slipped on his shirt, which looked damn good on her. So good, he imagined taking her again with the shirt on. "We don't. We adjust to it. Like you said, we can't take it back. It's like an amputation. We'll miss the way it was before, but we'll learn to live differently."

"I say that to my patients who've just lost loved ones."

"I know," he said. "It applies here, too."

She chewed on her thumbnail. "What if it happens again?"

He'd asked himself the same question a million times since she'd put on that shirt. He knew it was going to happen again, he just didn't know when. "It won't," he lied. "We won't let it, okay?"

"And you can just go back to normal?"

Nope. "Well, I want to try to figure this out. You're too important to me not to try and work on it."

She walked closer, peered up at him with sad eyes. "Are you sure?"

He wrapped his arms around her, and she burrowed into him.

"I need you, Drake."

They stood like that for a while, swaying to their own music. "I'm here, Love. Always."

A hard knock at the door interrupted their tentative peace. Love frowned. "Who could that be? It's so early."

Drake buttoned Love up in his shirt. She smoothed a hand over her hair as he walked to the door. There was another knock before he got there and he paused when he saw who was on the other side through the small window. *Shit.*

"Who is it?" Love asked, tugging at his shirt.

Without answering her, he opened the door. "Mom."

"Mom?" he heard Love say behind him.

Gloria breezed into the condo like she owned the place. "Drake, you're here. Be a doll and grab my luggage. Lovely, I've been calling you."

"Mom, what are you doing here?" she asked.

Drake dragged the three heavy suitcases forward. "Are you moving in or something?" He met Love's mortified gaze.

"Silly," Gloria said with a grin. "No. I just wanted to spend more time with my daughter. I've finally decided to get that second opinion from a U of M doctor, like you've been suggesting. Plus, we have to get started on the wedding festivities."

The color drained from Love's face, and Drake walked over to her. *"Are you okay?"* he mouthed.

She placed a hand over her heart and shook her head.

"Wait! Oh no," Gloria said with a gasp.

Drake looked at her. "What?" He followed Gloria's gaze toward the couch, then Love, then him, and realized she was connecting all the dots.

"Oh my," Gloria said, clasping her hand over her heart. "I'm sorry. I interrupted something."

Love glanced back at the couch and her eyes widened. "Mom—"

"It's cool, Lovely. You are newlyweds. I guess I should have booked a hotel room. It's just that usually I stay with you, and I was looking forward to bonding time."

"Mom, you know I don't have a problem with you staying here. It's just—"

"Oh good," Gloria said. "I'll just use the downstairs bedroom. You won't even know I'm here. I promise."

She pulled her cell phone out and placed a call. Drake and Love stood speechless as she connected with an old friend, made plans for dinner and gushed about her now married daughter. When Gloria clicked off, she yawned and announced she was going to take a nap because she hadn't been able to sleep on the red-eye.

It wasn't until they heard the slam of the downstairs bedroom door that Love said, "We're screwed."

Nodding, Drake said, "I know."

Chapter 10

The hospital elevator door opened and Love zoomed out and down the hall toward the lounge. She had to think. She was still married to Drake, and they hadn't even hired an attorney yet, hadn't talked about getting an annulment or divorce since they'd returned from Las Vegas. And her mother was there, staying with her—and Drake.

It had been a week since Gloria had shown up on her doorstep. Drake had moved in temporarily, to keep up appearances. Every night they'd retreated to bed together. Every morning Drake woke up, showered and dressed, leaving before the crack of dawn. Yes, they slept in the same room, but Drake had insisted on sleeping on the floor. She suspected he hadn't done much sleeping, but she hadn't called him on it. Things had gone quiet between them. A week before, he'd made her climax so many times the memories made her quiver with yearning. Yet they still hadn't resolved anything.

Love had kept busy carting her mother around during her off time. They'd already seen several specialists, and the diagnosis had been confirmed. It was peripheral artery disease, or PAD. Oftentimes, patients with PAD confuse their symptoms with neuropathy or something else entirely. As a result, it's often undiagnosed. In her mother's case, Gloria thought she was just "getting old" and failed to tell her doctors *all* of her symptoms.

They'd worked with a nutritionist on a diet plan that Love hoped would help control Gloria's diabetes. Next, they were set to see a surgeon to discuss the amputation recommendation that Gloria's Nevada doctor had given. The thought of her mother losing a foot and a leg made Love sick to her stomach, and she was willing to do anything possible to prevent it.

"Love?"

She froze, turning slowly. Derrick stood there smiling at her, with a bouquet of flowers in his hand. "What are you doing here?" she asked him.

He held the flowers out to her. "Peace offering?"

Love scanned the area, noting the interested glances from the nurses and other staff on the floor. The news of her marriage to Drake hadn't hit the hospital ticker yet, but she'd made it a practice of not bringing her personal life into the job. Every second of the day, a staff member was involved in some mess at their workplace. The hospital really was a den of scandal, fodder for the next television medical drama.

Derrick was dressed in a slim-fit blue suit with a

mini check pattern. He wore his clothes well, spending thousands on tailoring and ties. His slate watch and his bald head gleamed under the hospital lights. As he approached her, she instinctively backed up a step, needing to keep some distance between them.

He stopped in his tracks, lowering his extended hand and letting out a heavy sigh. "Can we go somewhere?" he asked under his breath.

Clutching the strap of her bag, she considered him for a moment. There was a time when she'd have done anything for Derrick. He was everything she'd thought she'd wanted in a man. They had the same goal of settling down in a suburban area and starting a family. While Drake dreamed of nightlife in the big city, Derrick was satisfied spending evenings at home, each of them working on their laptops next to each other on the couch. They'd been happy together. Well, she was happy. So happy that she'd never batted an eye when he'd announced he had taken an assignment in California for a year. She'd actually encouraged him to go follow his dream. The Harper family owned and operated a medical supply company. He'd spent years proving that he could take over the reins from his father, and it had paid off nicely when he'd stepped into the vice president of supply chain and logistics role, in their Michigan office.

As hurt as she'd been, she could look at him now and still see the amazing man he was. He'd made mistakes—a lot of them—but he wasn't a bad guy. Never had been. And she wasn't totally blameless in the downfall of their relationship. She'd promised monthly visits, but had canceled all of them due to some work thing or another. In reality, she'd been content in the long-distance relationship, and not inclined to make visiting him a priority. She'd been distracted with work and her patients. And he'd begged her for time. Eventually, he'd found someone who'd given him the time Love wouldn't.

It still didn't make it right that he'd cheated. Or the tactless way he'd ended it with her. The breakup had devastated her, knocked the wind out of her. He'd hurt her beyond words, and forgiveness was a long way off.

"Derrick, I think we've said all we have to say at this point. You made your choice. It's been a year, and you can't come waltzing back in here with a ring and flowers like you didn't break my heart."

The flowers were beautiful, though. The large, colorful arrangement featured a variety of blooms in magenta and orange, including several snapdragons, her favorite. Since they weren't in season, she figured he'd paid a pretty penny for the bouquet. The fragrance wafted to her nose, and she took the bouquet from him, inhaling the sweet scent. It reminded her of bubble gum. Memories of nights in her mother's greenhouse assaulted her. She'd spend hours inside, immersing herself in the different smells as she'd studied. It was her peaceful hiding place when her parents were divorcing. Drake had often met her there, held her as she'd cried.

The thought of Drake made her spine stiffen. He'd been so distant lately, and she felt helpless. So much had happened between them, it was hard to figure a way around everything.

"Love, please. Ten minutes. That's all I'm asking for," Derrick said.

"I know you want to talk, but it's not possible," she

told him. No matter what happened with Drake, she had to find a way to send Derrick away.

Sighing, she continued, "You worked with my father to manipulate me. Do you know how much trouble you've caused?"

Love hadn't seen her father since that day in his office. The day she'd defended Drake and their relationship before storming out. She had attempted to mend fences with her dad, but his secretary had informed her that he'd left town for a conference.

"That's why I wanted to talk to you," Derrick said. "I was wrong to go to your father. I was upset and jealous. During our relationship, you'd always told me you and Drake were only friends. I never believed that was all it was, but I dealt with it because I loved you and wanted a life with you. Then you *married* him, Love."

She glanced around to make sure no one was within earshot. The last thing she needed was to be the subject of the hospital rumor mill. Derrick had seemed skeptical when she'd described her friendship with Drake to him before. The two men had never really gotten along, which made it difficult in the beginning of their relationship. Derrick had told her several times that he thought Drake was in love with her, and she'd refuted his claims fervently.

"It made me rethink so many moments in our relationship," Derrick continued, shoving his hands into his pockets. "I want to believe that what we had was real, but seeing you with him, watching the closeness between you two, pissed me off. There is a level of understanding and acceptance between you that we never had. Part of me knew that's why you never really cared enough to visit me in California. You didn't need my companionship because you already had his. He fulfills that for you. Yes, I handled it all wrong. I hurt you, which was the last thing I ever wanted to do because I care for you so much. But you hurt me, too, Love."

His words hit her in her gut. Swallowing roughly, she nodded. "I know. But we can't go back and undo that now. Too much has happened."

Derrick bowed his head. "I still love you."

Before Love could respond, a voice came from behind her. "Unfortunately for you, that doesn't matter now."

Love whirled around. Drake was standing behind her, a chart in one hand and a cup of coffee in the other. "Drake? Where did you come from?"

He shot her a wary glance, before turning his attention to Derrick. "I know Love has told you to leave her alone. Yet you're still here. And with flowers this time. Where's the ring? Ready for a repeat of Vegas? Instead of a door slamming in your face, how about my fist?"

"Drake," Love croaked. "Stop."

But Drake wasn't paying her any attention. He was focused squarely on Derrick, his jaw set in determination and his eyes full of ire.

"I would comment, but I don't think you want to hear what I have to say," Derrick said.

"You're right, I don't want to hear anything you have to say."

Derrick stepped forward, his nostrils flared. "You don't want none, Drake. So I suggest you walk away."

Love gasped. Did Derrick just take it there? She

wedged herself between them. "Hey, please stop this. I'm at work."

"You heard her, Harper," Drake taunted. "We're at work. Go somewhere else, and take those damn flowers and that sorry-ass apology with you."

Derrick let out a humorless chuckle. "Feeling threatened?"

Drake shrugged. "Nah, man. I know the history between you two. All of it."

"You know nothing about me. I'm even going to venture to say you don't really know anything about my relationship with Love. Maybe a few things, but not everything. You forget, I know Love, too. She's not the type to share everything."

Drake frowned, caught her gaze for a minute. His eyes softened a bit before he turned a hard glare back toward Derrick. "I know all I need to know, and let me tell you something *you* may not know. I don't care about the relationship you and Love *had*. I just care that you know it's over."

"Maybe," Derrick said simply.

"Definitely," Drake countered. "At the end of the day, you're standing here proposing a reconciliation with *my* wife. And you don't see the problem with this?"

Love vaguely registered the whispers around her. She met the eyes of several of the staff around her, as they registered the "tea" that Drake just poured. Her days of flying under the radar at work were over.

"Drake," she muttered under her breath. "We have an audience."

He peered down at her, a small smile on his lips. "I know," he said. "I don't care."

"I care," she snapped. "We have to work here."

His jaw tightened. "Fine. Handle this, then." He motioned toward Derrick. "Because if you don't, I will."

Drake turned to leave, but she gripped his wrist, halting his retreat. "Don't go. We need to talk."

"Not here, and not in front of him."

Sighing, Love glanced at Derrick. "You have to go."

"Can we meet for coffee later?" he asked.

"No, she can't." Drake's voice was louder this time. "You don't want this kind of problem with me, man. If you don't get the hell away from her—"

Love whirled around, her eyes darting about the floor. She knew what that meant. Although Drake was from a wealthy family, he'd been in several fights in high school due to his hot temper. The boys had tended to try him because they'd thought he was a soft rich boy who would take it. "Drake, go in the lounge. I'll handle this, and we'll talk." When he didn't move, she added, searching his eyes, "Please."

The kiss that followed caught her off guard. It wasn't sweet; rather, it was hard and possessive. His tongue pushed past her lips, and his hands were in her hair, holding her to him. She moaned as he devoured her mouth with passion in front of the entire floor. She felt that kiss from the top of her head to the tips of her toes. Electricity sizzled around them and she had no choice but to give in to his demanding mouth. Then it was over and he was walking away from her.

On shaky legs, she looked up at Derrick, handing him the flowers. "I'm sorry, Derrick. You have to go. Drake is my husband, and you need to respect that."

Pivoting on her heels, she took a steadying breath, and left Derrick standing there.

Drake paced the lounge area, after kicking everybody out. The last person, one of his colleagues, had just scurried off when Love walked in, locking the door behind her.

"Drake, what the hell was that?"

He didn't have an answer for his behavior. The only thing he knew was the blinding jealousy, the burning sensation in his chest, when he'd encountered the two of them standing so close together. The flowers in her hands, and the way she'd looked at the other man. Despite what Love had said, it was obvious to him that she still felt something for Derrick. Just thinking about it made his stomach clench.

He'd been reckless, confronting Derrick the way he had in front of the staff, his colleagues. It would be fodder for the gossips for weeks, but he didn't care at that moment. The only thing he'd cared about was putting his fist through Derrick's face.

"Drake?" Love's voice pulled him out of his thoughts. "Talk to me."

He shook his head, resuming his rapid pacing back and forth. "I can't right now."

"Why are you so angry?"

"Why aren't *you* angry? He doesn't even deserve your time, but you gave him plenty of it today."

She recoiled as if he'd slapped her, her hand flying to her mouth. "How long… What do you think you saw, Drake?"

"It doesn't matter. You were falling for it, even though you didn't want to."

"I wasn't. I told him to leave, that too much had happened."

He'd heard her words, but he could read her better than she knew. He knew when Love was wavering, when she was doubting herself and her decision, and when she was attracted to someone. He'd seen the way she eyed Derrick as he approached, the appreciation in her eyes. It had taken every ounce of restraint in him not to kick the retractable banner about cardiac health that he'd cowered behind in order to eavesdrop. Eventually, he hadn't been able to take it anymore and had stepped forward, if only to let the other man know that Love was off-limits.

"Listen, Love. Whether you believe it or not, he won't give up. And you know why? Because you gave him an ear, you accepted his peace offering and engaged in a trip down memory lane."

Realization dawned in her pretty brown eyes. They were eyes that had haunted his dreams in the past week, made him retreat inward to deal with the gamut of emotions he'd experienced since he'd made love to her a second time.

"I told you," she said. "Everything is different between us. And you promised it wouldn't be."

Averting his gaze, he studied the scratch on the tile, the one he and Love had put there months ago when they were moving the heavy table to the other side of the room.

"We have to talk about this, Drake."

His heartbeat quickened when she grabbed his hand and squeezed. When he looked into her eyes, he knew he was lost. She was right; everything had changed. He couldn't pretend anymore that he didn't want her. "I can't do this right now, Love. Seriously."

He glanced at his watch. His worst fears had been realized when he'd been relegated to scrubbing in on appendectomies. Before Dr. Leon knew he'd married his daughter, Drake had been on track to scrub in with Dr. Benjamin Porter on an off pump coronary artery bypass surgery. Instead, Love's father had assigned another less skilled resident to the coveted spot.

Love's chin trembled and she stared down at her hands.

Guilt slammed into Drake like a Mack truck. "I'm sorry," he mumbled. "We'll talk. Just not here. We can have dinner tonight, and discuss it."

She bit her lip. "I can cook, if you'd like."

Drake had managed to avoid being in the kitchen alone with her over the past week. He didn't think he wanted to take the chance of showing his ass again this soon. "Maybe we can go out to our spot."

The Mexican restaurant by the mall was their favorite place to eat out. Love was enamored with the gooey queso dip, and he appreciated the strong drinks. He definitely needed a stiff one if they were actually going to have this conversation.

She smiled, and he found himself responding with one of his own. He leaned in, as if he didn't have any control of himself.

"Drake." The way she said his name, a mixture of a soft whisper and a groan, made him want to pin her on that table and make love to her right then and there.

"Love," he said, his voice low and unrecognizable even to his own ears. He swallowed past a lump that had wedged itself in his throat.

"Your phone is ringing."

He jerked back, pulling his phone off its clip. He'd been so entranced that he hadn't even felt the vibration. The 911 on the screen was his cue to exit. "I have to go." Good thing, too. There was no telling what would have happened if they hadn't been interrupted by the page. "Meet me at the spot at five o'clock?"

She smiled when he pinched her chin. "I will. See you soon."

Hours later, Drake was on his way to meet Love when he heard a familiar voice call his name. His day had sucked. The afternoon spent in the emergency department intubating patients had put him in a sour mood. But he'd rather be flipping burgers than dealing with the man behind him.

"I see you're on your way out," Dr. Lawrence Jackson said. "Don't you have some time for your father?"

Drake turned to face him. "Dad. What brings you here?"

Although his father was on staff at the University Hospital, he'd been traveling in recent years, consulting on cases at several top hospitals and delivering fiery speeches at medical schools across the nation.

"You would know why I'm here if you'd answer my many phone calls."

Drake's father wasn't one for a random check-in call or visit. There was always a reason behind his actions. Drake had spent most of his childhood avoiding the man, especially once he'd realized that nothing he did would ever be good enough for him. He'd worked his butt off in school, graduating at the top of his class at every stage of his education. But because he'd cho-

sen to explore cardiothoracic surgery instead of joining the family specialty, his plastic surgeon father had
made it clear that he had no use for him.

"I'm busy," he told him. "Boards are soon, and I've
been preparing for them."

"And getting married."

Drake paused, unsure how to respond. He guessed
the gossip mill had churned all day after his display
earlier. "Dad, can we talk about this later? I'm on my
way to meet Love."

"Your wife." His father shook his head slowly, staring at him with a stony expression in his eyes. That
familiar look of disappointment seemed etched on
his face. "When did you decide to ruin your life and
career, son?"

Drake sighed heavily. "What makes you think I've
done that?"

His father explained the phone call he'd received
from Love's dad earlier in the week. The two had actually conversed about the "monumental" mistake
their offspring had made in getting married. Dr. Leon
had apparently gone on about how Love was his baby
girl and he didn't want Drake breaking his daughter's heart.

"Is she pregnant?" his father asked.

Drake shook his head. "Are you crazy? No."

He regretted his words and tone the minute he'd
used them. But his dad tended to take him there. Every
lecture, every criticism served to put him on the edge
of a small window ledge.

"Watch your mouth," Dr. Jackson warned.

Drake shifted, rubbing the back of his neck. "Why

would you even say that? That would imply that I only married her because she's having my baby."

"I had to ask. Leon is wealthy, but he's not of my stature."

His father's air of superiority rankled Drake. There were all these unwritten rules for a Jackson. Too bad there weren't rules against knocking up a woman that's not your wife, then basically paying her to give up custody of her child to his unfeeling father. That's what Dr. Lawrence Jackson had done to Drake's mother, after all. And although he'd never had the chance to really know his mother, Drake had always imagined how different his life would have been if his father wasn't such a domineering jerk.

The only contact he'd had with his mother's family was a maternal grandmother who'd visit from time to time. Grammy had been a breath of fresh air for Drake and when she'd died of a heart attack, he had become fascinated with the heart. It was that experience that lead him to declare his desire to go into cardiothoracic surgery, to the utter displeasure of his controlling father.

"Dad, you like Love."

That much was true. His father, always one to point out everyone's flaws, had never given him any indication that he didn't like Love. In fact, he'd doted on her when they were near each other, offering her drinks and laughing heartily with her.

"Oh, I think she's a lovely person. But I don't agree with this farce of a marriage. Especially if it is going to hamper your ambitions. Leon already told me he moved you from a few key surgeries as a result."

"And what did you say to him?"

Heaven forbid, his father would actually defend him. Drake and his siblings were an afterthought, a means to an end. As long as they did what he told them. His younger twin brothers were also surgical residents, studying plastic surgery. And his youngest sibling, his sister, was in her final year of undergraduate studies at University of Michigan. Her goal? To become a part of the family's thriving plastic surgery practice. Drake and El were the only two who'd deviated from that preordained plan. El had chosen to go into emergency psychiatry.

The Jackson family was a pillar in the Ann Arbor area. His father and grandfather had perfected the art of philanthropy and had spent countless hours and dollars building up the family name. Drake's dad had moved to Las Vegas for work, and had honed his reputation in the health care field, having privileges in several Vegas area hospitals.

When Drake graduated from high school, his father decided to move back to Ann Arbor, even though he was rarely in town.

"Actually, I suggested that he get out of his feelings and reinstate you to your rightful place on the surgical resident team," his father told him. "I will not have him jeopardizing your career over this unfortunate mistake."

The word *mistake* lodged in Drake's head. The thought that his father considered Love a mistake made him want to smack him. "Don't call her that. She's not a mistake."

"I didn't call *her* a mistake." His father checked his watch. "There is a fund-raising event next week.

They are honoring me with an award. You are expected to attend."

There it was. The real reason for his visit. "I can't be there," Drake told him.

"You will be there. It's not a request. On Monday, Leon wants to meet us for lunch. I told him you'd be there, as well. Get out of your feelings, and do what you need to do to get to where you want to be. Listen, I wasn't particularly happy when you defied my wishes, but you are still better than any of those incompetent residents in the general surgery program. You have a fellowship to win at Johns Hopkins, and intubating patients and performing appendectomies won't cut it."

Drake scanned the area, catching a few curious glances from others. "I have to go."

"To dinner with me," his father said smoothly. "I have a late flight and we have business to discuss."

The man strolled toward the elevators, winking at a nurse and giving a curt nod to another doctor, before turning expectantly to Drake.

Reluctantly, Drake followed him, sending Love a quick text, letting her know he'd see her at home later.

Chapter 11

Love rubbed her eyes and craned her neck toward the sound of her blaring phone. Frowning, she reached over to the nightstand to answer it. Only it wasn't there. The ringing continued. She opened an eye and noticed the flashing light coming from her open purse, in the chair. *Damn.*

She silently prayed that whoever was calling wasn't dying, because she had no intention of getting out of bed to answer it. Jumping, she pitched a pillow toward the offensive sound and covered her face with another one.

When the ringing stopped, she thanked God and pulled the comforter over her head. Unfortunately, the caller was persistent, and the phone sounded again. Love rolled out of bed and landed on her butt. Growling, she crawled over to her purse, dumped the contents on the floor and grabbed the phone. "What?" she yelled.

"Lovely Grace Washington!"

Oh, my God. "Hello? Hello?" She pushed the end button and hung up on her father. More than likely he wouldn't fall for the lost signal excuse she was about to give him, but she wasn't prepared to talk to him, especially after their last conversation. She needed to gather her thoughts.

She glanced at the mound of folded blankets on the small love seat at the far end the room. Drake wasn't home yet and it was—she glanced at the clock—11:00 p.m. Earlier that evening he had canceled their dinner with a simple text and nothing else. Now awake, she tiptoed down the stairs to the living room, then the kitchen, hoping she wouldn't wake her mother who was in the downstairs bedroom. No Drake.

Where the hell is he?

Love hurried to the bathroom and turned on the shower. She'd fallen asleep waiting for Drake, and now she was concerned that he hadn't called. After trying his cell a few times, and getting his voice mail, she decided to go to the hospital to see if he was there.

Stepping into the hot shower, she moaned. The water felt so good against her weary skin, but she had to make it quick. Her father was bound to call back any minute and she had no choice but to talk to him.

Once she finished, she stepped out and wrapped a huge bath sheet around her. Turning to the mirror, she wiped the condensation off and ran a comb through her hair.

"Love?" Drake called from the other side of the door.

She flung it open. "You're here."

He swept his gaze over her body, then turned away. "What are you doing up?"

She grabbed his arm and drew him back. "I was going to head to the hospital to find you. My father called. I hung up on him."

"You what?"

"Where were you? I tried to call you a few times."

"My father showed up at the hospital, and we went to dinner. Argued a little, then I went back to the hospital to check on a patient before I came here."

A pang of guilt shot through her. She knew Drake had a volatile relationship with his dad, and that the older man's visits often ended with a bad argument. "I'm sorry. What is he in town for?"

"Fund-raising event." Drake shook his head. "And you should know your father called him."

A heavy feeling settled in her stomach, and she leaned against the bathroom sink. "Wow. My dad certainly didn't waste any time. How did that conversation go?"

"Well, they both agree that we made a mistake in getting married. Both feel that our decision is detrimental to our careers. Basically, your father doesn't think I'm good enough for you, and neither of them believes that we're capable of living our lives without their guidance and instruction."

She pulled her towel tighter against her chest. Swallowing, she said, "Drake, I'm so... I feel like this is my fault. After all this time, I've tried to give my dad the benefit of the doubt, but he's not the same man that I grew up with. He's controlling and dismissive.

He shouldn't have said the things he did to you, or your father."

"You are not to blame for your father's actions, just like I'm not for mine."

"I know it hurts you, because you care about him." Love knew the respect and admiration Drake had for her father. Learning that none of that mattered now had to be a blow. "I'm so angry with him."

"Don't be," Drake said. "You can't control his reaction. But we do need to talk about this. And not just gloss over it."

"Do you want something to drink? Or eat?"

He shook his head. "Not really." He tugged his shirt off and shuffled into the bathroom. "My father has requested our appearance at the high society fundraiser next Saturday. He's getting an award, and has to make it appear that the Jackson family is loving and supportive of each other."

"Well, I'm not coming to that."

He looked over at her. "I know you hate events like this, but I need you there."

Love's stance softened at Drake's sincerity. She knew it would be hard for him to be around his father, in the type of environment that always made him feel like a fake. He'd grown up feeling like he was "daddy's little secret," and Dr. Lawrence Jackson had never done much to correct that assumption.

His siblings were cool, and Love enjoyed hanging out with all of them. But they didn't have the same baggage as Drake because they were born of marriage, albeit marriages to different women.

Dr. Law, as Love called him, had been married three times. The twins were born to his first wife.

His arrival in the home had caused many a problem, because Drake was the result of a torrid affair. Dr. Jackson's wife at the time resented Drake, even though he was not to blame for the heartache she'd suffered. She'd made life hell for him, and that's why Love was so grateful for her loving mother, who'd never hesitated to show Drake love and understanding.

Drake was proof that money wasn't everything. His life was anything but charmed, even though he was born with wealth and status simply because he had the last name Jackson.

Love relented. "I'll be there."

"Thank you."

"I know how you feel about your father. This is the worst possible time for him to be in town, while we're trying to figure things out."

"Yeah, well, it is what it is."

Drake made quick work of brushing his teeth and washing his face. And Love found herself staring at his broad, well-defined shoulders, his ripped back, his strong arms, and toned abs. His pants hung low on his hips, giving her a glimpse of the thin line of hair disappearing under the waistband of his black boxer briefs.

"Do you still want to talk?" he asked. The smirk on his full lips let her know that he'd caught her staring. Again.

Eyeing the door, and rubbing a hand through her wet hair, she answered, "Um, sure."

His slow, deliberate gaze over her body sent a shiver of awareness to her core. "Don't you think you should put on some clothes?" She opened her mouth to respond, but stopped short when he added, "Or I could take mine off so we're equal."

She let out a nervous laugh and stepped away from him, tripping over a shoe in the middle of the floor and tumbling backward. She landed with a loud thud on her butt. Jumping up, she struggled to regain her composure as behind her, she heard Drake chuckle. Her face and neck burned as she entertained the idea of bolting. She couldn't turn around and face him. Her chest tightened, and a tingle swept up the back of her neck and across her cheeks. Rubbing her arms, she took in a deep breath.

He wasn't laughing anymore. In fact, the room was too quiet. Love leaned against her dresser and listened for any sign of Drake in the room behind her. She heard him draw closer to her, until he was right behind her. She smelled the faint scent of his soap and the minty toothpaste he'd just used.

She felt his nose against the back of her neck, then his lips as he brushed them against her sensitive skin.

"I'm sorry," he muttered, pressing another kiss to her back. "I shouldn't have laughed. I think I like that I make you nervous."

"It's not funny, Drake."

"You're right. It's not a laughing matter."

Instinctively, she knew he wasn't talking about her fall anymore. He confirmed that when he whispered, "You're driving me insane, Love. This past week has been torture for me, staying in this room only a few feet away from you, not touching you like I want to."

"I didn't know what you were thinking," she admitted. "We barely saw each other. You disappeared on me, and it scared me."

He rested his chin on her shoulder. "I know. It scares me, too."

It was unlike him to be so vulnerable with anyone. She hated that their situation was pulling them both out of their normal routine with each other. There had never been any awkwardness between them. She was never nervous around him. But now...

"You smell so good," he breathed against her skin, before sucking her earlobe into his mouth.

"Thank you," she whispered.

His soft laugh made her hot, and the way his hands roamed her body ignited the fire. He picked up her hand and kissed the back of it. "I want you."

She let out a shaky breath. The admission sent her heart soaring right over the cliff edge she'd been holding on to as if her life depended on it. She was falling hard for her husband, and her emotions frightened her with their intensity.

"Drake, we should probably talk, like we said we would."

He squeezed her hips, brushed his erection against her butt. "I know we should, but...it's very hard to do that when all I want to do is make love to you."

"Maybe we should sit on opposite sides of the room?" she suggested.

Drake sighed and retreated to a chair on the other side of the bed. "You're right. Let's do this, because we really should deal with it."

She couldn't figure out if he was being sarcastic or serious, especially since she hadn't looked at him yet. Reluctantly, she turned around to face him. His eyes were dark, almost black as he assessed her. The heat in them scorched her already tingling skin.

Pulling on the robe that was lying on her bed, she shimmied out of the towel, tied the belt around her waist and sat down. "Okay, where do we start?"

"With the obvious," he replied. "We had sex."

He'd finally said the word without averting his gaze. She smiled to herself. "Really?" she asked sarcastically.

"That's where we should begin." He glared at her. "We've been friends for years. Why now? What made that night different?"

"I don't know," she murmured, crossing her legs. Earlier, at the hospital, after the confrontation with Derrick, she'd taken a moment to really look at him. The Drake she knew would have never let someone push his buttons the way Derrick had. "I wish I knew."

"Me, too. It's not like we've had underlying feelings for each other, near kisses or almost moments over the years. It was out of left field."

"I've seen you checking me out."

His eyes flashed to hers. "What are— I didn't. I mean, I've appreciated the gifts God gave you, but I didn't want to do you."

She shrugged. "Well, I think you're an attractive man. So it's not that far out of the realm of possibilities."

"I want us to be okay, Love. I almost could have believed we'd be good after the whole marriage and wedding night. But this week, that night…it was a choice we both made to go there again. I'm not so sure we can be all right after this."

Her stomach rolled. "But you said—"

"I know what I said, Love. I married you while we were both intoxicated, and we got busy like we had no care in the world or concern for the conse-quences. That was bad enough, but I seduced you in your kitchen the next week. I kissed you in front of our coworkers. You went against your father for me. I can't wrap my head around this. I feel like I'm the bad guy that your dad thinks I am because I couldn't see past what I wanted for the good of our friendship."

"Wait, I'm a grown ass woman, Drake. You didn't make me have sex with you."

"You're sweet. You're like Little Red Riding Hood."

"And you're the Big Bad Wolf?"

"Exactly." He threw his hands in the air.

She giggled. "Come on, Drake. You're not some predator luring sweet little ole' me into your lair for a little dessert and some cookies."

"You're smiling again. And this isn't funny."

"It is funny." She scooted closer to him, until she was in front of him. Kneeling before him, she placed her hands on top of his. "I was a willing participant in everything, including the other night. I wanted you, just like I wanted you a few minutes ago. Now if you ask me why, again, I don't know."

"It was good, Love. I want it again, too."

She felt a blush creep up her face. "Yeah, it was. I think it's because we were in sync with each other, which isn't new. We always work well together."

He frowned. "That's a weird way of looking at it."

"Well, I've had a lot of time to think about it, while you were avoiding me."

"I don't know what to say."

There really was nothing to say, Love mused. He stroked a finger over her brow, and she leaned into his touch as he caressed her face. "That's the problem.

We can't change what happened, or even explain why. We just know that we both enjoyed each other, and we'll remember this for the rest of our lives. What we should talk about is our next step. How are we going to move forward?"

"How do you propose we do that when we're sleeping in close quarters? The attraction is palpable."

"I guess the real question is, are we going to stop?"

His eyes widened, then narrowed. "Do you want to stop?"

She bit her lip, tucked a stray hair behind her ear. The answer to that question was an enthusiastic "no." But she couldn't say that to him. Could she?

"Let's sleep on it," she said instead. "We don't want to make another rash decision."

He seemed to accept her answer. "Right. Well, I'm going to go downstairs and do some work." He stood, and helped her to her feet. Her robe fell open and she closed it quickly. He fingered the opening, brushing his knuckle over her nipple. "Don't sleep in that. In fact, why don't you wear those ugly ass pajamas you bought last Christmas with the feet in them?"

She laughed. He'd teased her mercilessly about her bunny pajamas. She'd found them at Macy's and couldn't resist. Apparently, they were coming back in style. "That would be a no. I haven't worn them again because they're so hot."

"Like the woman wearing them."

Her breath caught in her throat. "You're making me high."

He offered her a bemused smile. "Join the club." He leaned and whispered against her ear, "You don't want to know what I'm thinking right now. So I'm going to go downstairs. I'll see you in the morning."

Love was getting whiplash from the back and forth between them. But she'd happily buckle up for the ride if it meant preserving what was best about them. She couldn't live without him.

Chapter 12

The sound of Love's alarm interrupted a steamy dream about Drake. She sat upright in the bed, and noted the empty room. Disappointed that Drake had disappeared on her again, she hurriedly dressed and made her way downstairs quietly. She didn't want to wake her mother at four thirty in the morning, but she had a busy day ahead. Besides work, today was the appointment with her mother's surgeon.

In the kitchen, Love pulled a travel mug out of the cabinet and inserted a K-cup into the Keurig.

"You're up early."

She yelped, holding her hands to her chest. "Drake? You scared me. What are you doing up?"

He stood and stretched. "Fell asleep studying."

The smell of caramel, vanilla and coffee filled the room, and her mouth watered. Love was a coffee girl.

Having her morning cup of joe really was the best part of her day. She picked up her mug and replaced it with an empty one. "You want a cup?"

Drake nodded. "Thanks."

She put two slices of bread into the toaster and pulled out the peanut butter from the pantry. "Breakfast?"

"Nah. I'll grab something on my way to work."

"Sure? I can scramble a couple eggs for you."

He moistened his lips, held eye contact with her for a minute, before turning away. "I'm good. It's too early."

She held his mug, filled with his favorite breakfast blend, out to him. He took his coffee black. She shivered at the spark that passed between them when their fingers touched as he took the offered cup of coffee.

Clearing her throat, she told him, "I've been thinking about our fathers. We're doing the right thing, sticking together. They can't know the sordid details of our wedding. It would just make matters worse."

With her mug in her hand, she blew on the coffee and took a sip. She'd planned to have a talk with her dad today, to make sure he knew where she stood.

"I agree. What happens when we file for an annulment or divorce?"

She snorted, doubting a judge would grant them an annulment now. The only thing in their favor was they were both intoxicated at the time. But even then, their history would make it hard. "Have you thought about which attorney you want to use? Maybe we can use Jared?"

He rolled his eyes. "No."

Jared Williams was a friend that she'd met when

she'd treated his twin sister, Sydney. She'd just broken up with Derrick, and "Red" had been charming and attentive. It was exactly what she'd needed at the time, but it didn't go anywhere, since Red was hopelessly in love with another woman.

"You do know that nothing ever happened between me and Red, right?"

"That's beside the point," Drake said with a shrug. "Red doesn't even practice family law. Why would we use him?"

Love sighed. It was foolish to hope there was a tiny bit of jealousy on Drake's part. She should have known he was being his practical self when he'd dismissed Red so quickly. "Right," she muttered under her breath. "Do you want me to ask him if he can suggest someone?"

"You could. Are we in a rush?"

The loaded question caught her off guard. "I don't know. You brought it up, so…"

"I asked a question, Love." His gaze locked on her as he took a sip of his coffee. It felt like a caress, like his hands were on her, touching her body. "I'm not saying I want to go out and hire someone right this second. We have a lot to consider. For one, my job. I haven't seen any real action in the OR since we made this announcement. Even though your father doesn't like us being married, I feel like if we get a divorce, he will really believe that I took advantage of you."

"Is that the only reason?" She tapped her fingernails against her mug and braced herself for his answer. They'd only agreed on the fact that they were attracted to each other. Staying married was another story.

He set his mug down on the counter. "Take off your clothes," he commanded softly, prying her mug from her clutches and setting it on the countertop, along with his.

She opened her mouth to protest even as she unbuttoned her shirt. No words followed, just soft breathing from both of them. Apparently, she wasn't moving fast enough, because he grabbed the waist of her jeans and pulled her to him to finish. He pulled her shirt off slowly, then unzipped her pants and peeled them off at an even slower pace. It was almost like torture, and he knew it. Love wanted to beg him to rip them off. Her body was on fire for him, needing him, wanting him.

He leaned his forehead against hers. "You're so damn beautiful. I don't know if I'll ever grow tired of touching you, kissing you."

"You haven't kissed me yet."

He caught her bottom lip with his mouth, lingering there before moving to her top lip. They shared short, soft kisses for a few seconds before it grew more frantic, with tongue and teeth and groans and hisses. She held him to her, her fingers gripping his scalp as she fought to stay on her feet. He made her legs weak, her mind cloudy, but she was all in.

She pulled his shirt off and pushed his pants down. "Drake, I want this," she murmured against his mouth. "Make love to me. Now."

He released the band holding her hair up, and her curls fell over her shoulders. Sweeping them to the side, he bit down on her neck, before sucking the tender spot until she had to stifle a cry. Somewhere in the haze of desire she remembered her mother asleep in the guest room. But not for long. As Drake blazed a trail of kisses up her neck, to her jawline, her chin, then her mouth, she could think of nothing but him. His arm wrapped around her like a steel band, and lifted her against him, coaxing her to wrap her legs around his waist. This time, instead of taking her to the couch, he carried her up the stairs to the bedroom, kissing her the entire way.

The taste of him made her dizzy with need. Her mind screamed to stop this before they ruined everything, but her heart and her body wanted him.

Gently, he lowered her to the bed, brushing fingertips over her trembling skin. Drake was the musician and she was his instrument, and he played her like an expert. He knew her, remembered the places that made her squirm with pleasure. Kissing her below her ear, he whispered, "Tell me how you want it."

Love wasn't shy, but she'd never taken the lead in lovemaking. She'd been content to let her partner take control. Drake made her want to please him, because he'd spent so much time making sure she was satisfied.

"How about you tell me?" she asked, arching her brow. "What do *you* want?"

He rested between her legs, ran his tongue over her parted lips. The hard evidence of his arousal pressed against her inner thigh. "You. That's all."

Love searched his eyes. There was no hesitation, no doubt. His hand slipped between them, into her wet heat. Her mouth fell open with a soundless cry as he circled her clit with his thumb, teased her, tempted her. Her hips rocked against his hand as his finger slid in and out of her. She was so wet for him, so gone. The pleasure took her over, warmed her from the inside.

She needed a release, and it didn't take long for her to spiral out of control and fall over the cliff as a climax tore through her body.

Love burrowed into the soft mattress, sated and drowsy. She placed a kiss on his neck, ran her tongue over the bulging vein that signaled his struggle to hold on, to not push forward inside her. His head fell to her shoulder and she tickled the hair at his nape, hugging him to her.

Seconds later, as he placed wet kisses against her ear, her shoulder and the base of her neck, she opened her eyes. He stared down at her, a sexy smile on his lips that seemed to ignite the ache between her thighs. She was consumed by him, as if he'd crawled inside her and taken over her body and soul. She wanted more, needed it to survive, like she needed sunlight or water.

As if he'd read her mind, he smoothed a hand down her side, over her waist to her knee, and raised it to wrap around his hip. Gripping her leg, he rested his length against her opening. She pushed up, tried to take him in, but he didn't move.

"Drake, please."

"Tell me how you want it," he repeated.

"I… I don't know."

The tip of his rock-hard erection pressed against her. "Love." His mouth met hers again in a soft feather of a kiss. It was vulnerable, needy. "I *need* you to say it."

The way he'd said her name, the way he implored her to tell him how she wanted to be loved, shook her resolve. There was a longing there she hadn't noticed before. Drake needed her to give him permission, to make it okay to love her in this way.

The line they'd crossed a couple weeks ago was gone. There was nothing standing between them, nothing in their way. She could give in and let this be what it was, or deny him. It was her choice, always her choice.

"Love." His hand tangled in her hair, pulled gently, urging her to make the decision.

Swallowing, she kissed his chin, then nipped it with her teeth. "I want you nice and slow."

She cried out as he filled her, the sound muffled by his mouth over hers in a demanding and passionate kiss. He held still, giving her a chance to adjust to his size, before telling her, "Your wish is my command."

An hour later, they lay joined together in a tangle of limbs. Love was nestled against Drake, her face against his chest. "I'm so late for my shift."

She felt the rumble of laughter underneath her cheek. "No, you're not. You're always two hours early. You still have time."

Propping herself up on her elbow, she kissed him. "I better go," she said against his mouth. "I have to shower again and get over to the hospital."

"I won't be there for a few hours."

"Can I ask you a question?"

He cocked his head to the side, raising his eyebrows. "You have to ask?"

Love ran her thumbnail over a scar on his chest. "Yes, I do. This is a serious one."

Drake groaned. "No, we can't go all serious lying in bed naked. I don't want to ruin the moment."

She sat up, holding the thin sheet against her body. "I have to ask."

He held her hand, ran his finger over the pulse point in her wrist. "Go ahead."

"Drake, I hate that your father makes you feel the way he does. Have you ever considered telling him how you really feel?"

"He already knows, Love."

"How could he?"

"I told him, when I was a senior in high school. I found out he'd never stopped sleeping with my mother. He'd lied to me for years, allowed me to believe that he had no connection to her and didn't know how to get in touch with her. They'd seen each other every single time he visited Reno, or she came to Vegas. And that wasn't even the worst part. He supported her financially, all the way up until she died."

"What?" A weight settled in her gut at his admission. "How could he?"

"Trust me, I've asked myself that same question many times since then." Drake explained that the argument started when Dr. Law broke the news of Drake's mother's death. It had spiraled from there, with the two men almost coming to blows. "The worst part was he didn't see where he was wrong. Still doesn't."

Drakes eyes watered, and her heart broke for him. She thought back to that time. Drake had been angry, withdrawn. She'd assumed it was grief over never knowing his mother and hadn't pushed him to open up to her. "I'm so sorry."

"There is nothing for you to be sorry for."

She felt the anguish radiating off of him, the despair at finding out that his mother had been in touch with his father but had never reached out to Drake. "I blame her, too. She could have demanded to see you. All those years, she had access to you and didn't take it."

Love climbed on top of him and hugged him. When his arms wrapped around her tightly, she closed her eyes. Love wasn't sure what she'd say to Dr. Law when she saw him again. She just knew that she wouldn't let him make Drake feel bad for being himself.

"It hurt," he confessed, his voice cracking. "I hated him for it. I lived in that house feeling like I was his dirty little secret, that I would never be good enough for him. He'd told me all these horror stories about my mother, and I accepted what he'd said because I didn't know her. He lied to me over and over, didn't even think he owed me the truth." Drake kissed Love's her forehead.

"Well, that's on him. He did owe you the truth, Drake. And you are good enough."

She looked at him then. Tears welled in her eyes and their gazes held. He brushed a tear from her cheek. "You know why I believe that now?"

"Why?"

"Because of you. You have always seen the best in me, been my biggest cheerleader. The support you've given me is invaluable. I don't know what I would have done without you." Another tear fell. "That's why we can't let whatever this is get between us."

"We won't," he vowed. "We can't."

An hour later, Drake sat in the living room drinking another cup of coffee. Love had left only a few minutes earlier, after he'd bared his soul to her and made love to her again.

They'd turned another corner that morning, lying in each other's arms. He'd shared something with her that he'd never told another person, and it felt good to be honest with someone about his mother and father.

Drake had never been an insecure person, except when his father was involved. It had taken him a lot of years to get over the revelation that his mother just never wanted him. The fact that she could willingly sleep with a married man while ignoring her own kid made him grateful that he'd never gotten to know her. He was certain she would have destroyed his life if she'd been a part of it.

"Hey, Drake," Gloria said, entering the room. He smiled at his surrogate mother. Gloria was beautiful, full of life. He remembered how fast she used to move when they were children. She'd never stop moving, always picking up extra jobs and making sure she was in the right places.

The Gloria of old was in stark contrast to the woman in front of him. Her gray hair was neat and she still had that gleam in her eyes, but her steps were slower. She wasn't moving as fast, due to her limp. Love had explained what was going on, and he'd agreed to drive Gloria to the hospital that morning for her appointment.

Diabetes was controllable, but it could be debilitating. He prayed that Gloria wouldn't have to lose a limb.

"Hey, Mom." He stood and helped her to the couch. "How are you feeling?"

"Well, I've seen better days, son."

"I figured we'd stop and get breakfast on the way to the hospital. Is that okay with you?"

The older woman smiled. "You don't have to put yourself out. Besides, I don't have much of an appetite. They've got me on a new medicine, and it's making me queasy."

Concerned, Drake asked, "Did you tell your doctor?"

She shook her head. "Not yet. I plan to mention it today. We have a call scheduled for after my appointment with the surgeon."

Drake wondered if Gloria would consider moving to Michigan. He knew Love would feel better if she was closer. But he suspected Gloria would rather walk over hot coals than move here, especially since her business was thriving. She'd had to trust her shop to her employees for once. Knowing Gloria, that had to be hard on her. He couldn't say he blamed her for not wanting to move, though. It wasn't his ideal place, and definitely not somewhere he'd planned on staying.

"Make sure you keep me posted. I'm glad you're here, though. I feel better knowing that you're getting a second opinion."

Drake had never understood how she'd fallen in love with Dr. Leon. They were nothing alike. Gloria was quirky and spontaneous, while Love's dad was deliberate and serious. When they'd split up, it had been traumatic and sad. As a permanent fixture in their home, Drake remembered what they were like in love with each other, had seen the stolen kisses and playful swats on the butt. He'd heard the declarations of love and the banter between them. Somewhere along the line, it had disappeared and been replaced with bitterness and resentment, arguments and manipulation.

Aside from the good times between Love's parents, Drake had never seen a thriving and happy relationship. The ones he'd seen had all ended with broken hearts. He'd figured it was because people expected things of their mates and when those expectations weren't met, the trust faltered. It was what scared him the most about being with Love.

Love was Drake's best friend, and he wanted her. He wanted her more than he'd ever wanted any woman before, more than he wanted to scrub in on a thrombectomy this afternoon. But that didn't necessarily mean he was willing to throw all his sensibilities out the window to risk winding up like Gloria and Dr. Leon, or his father and every single stepmother he'd had.

"Tell me the truth," Gloria said. "What's going on between you and my daughter?"

"We're trying to figure things out." Drake wasn't sure how much he wanted to tell his mother-in-law.

"I can ask you because I know you'll tell me the truth. Lovely likes to dismiss me, keep her life under wraps."

"You know your daughter. She's always been very private."

"This marriage—how did it happen?"

He shifted in his seat. "It just kind of did. I realized that my life was better with her in it and I popped the question." The lie rolled off his tongue so easily, it shocked him. But he went with it.

"I didn't hear you mention love. Do you love her?"

"I do." There was no confusion. Drake knew he loved his wife. Again, it still didn't mean they'd end up together. He'd rather be without her romantically than lose her altogether.

"I worry about her, ya know? I'm getting older, Drake. I want her to be settled already. She's so closed off to certain things. That's why I'm so grateful she has you, because you've opened her eyes to possibilities. You wade out in the deep end while she stays near the shallow end. Since she was a child, I've always tried to make her see the glory in living life on her own terms. I want her to stop and smell the snapdragons."

He barked out a laugh. "I think she'll be okay. She's driven, goal oriented."

"Like her father," Gloria mumbled, a hint of disgust in her voice.

"But I've seen her free, unbothered. She is your daughter, too."

Gloria smiled sadly. "I didn't want Love to be an only child."

This was news to him. "Really?"

"I miscarried three babies after God blessed me with Lovely. She's my little slice of heaven on earth. I'm so proud of her, and I know you'll take good care of her."

"Mom, you're scaring me. What's going on with you?"

She shrugged. "Nothing. Just thinking back on my life. It didn't work out with her father and me, but I never want her to give up on love."

Drake glanced at Gloria, took in her tired eyes. She was sick, possibly facing major surgery. Of course she'd be concerned about where her daughter would end up if she wasn't around. That was normal. But he hoped that time was many years away.

Chapter 13

Love opened the door and stepped in. "You called?"

Her father sat at his desk, pen in hand and a stack of files in front of him. She recalled how hard it was to be his daughter at times, and how she'd almost buckled from the pressure her first year of medical school.

It seemed like Love had had to fight for everything, including her medical school acceptance. Her father was old-school. He believed in hard work and had refused to give her preferential treatment when it came to her admission to the program. She was expected to work twice as hard and get in on her own merits.

Love had tried to pretend that her father's refusal to help her in any way with school hadn't bothered her, but it had and still did. The man in front of her was well respected in the medical field, but all she'd ever wanted was his love and attention.

Rubbing the stubble on his chin, he gestured toward the chair in front of his desk. "Have a seat."

"I'll stand."

Dr. Leon, as everyone called him, used to be her hero and the most important man in her life. But that had changed somewhere around the time he'd left her mother and moved hundreds of miles away. He'd disappointed her time and time again, almost made it impossible to meet his lofty expectations. Yet she still hated to let him down.

"Why did you do it?" he asked after a few tense moments of silence.

"It seemed like the right thing to do at the time," she answered.

"Are you pregnant?"

"You already asked me that, and I told you no. I'm not sure why you're having such a hard time accepting my choice to marry Drake?"

"I've racked my brain over this, and I can't understand why you'd do this. Why would you throw your life away on a relationship that will never work?"

"You don't know that."

"Lovely, you're my daughter. I know you. You've wanted the big white wedding since you were a little girl. Yet you settle for a quick Las Vegas ceremony?"

"I know you're upset, but Drake is my husband. We're together, and I want to give this a chance. For once, why can't you support me?"

"Maybe I'm old-fashioned, but I expected any man that wanted to marry you to come to me first. You're my only child, Love. I would have liked the honor of giving you away."

"I'm sorry you weren't there, Daddy. I know Mom

wanted to be there, as well. But Drake didn't force me to marry him. He didn't do anything I didn't want him to do. Please understand that."

"I'm sorry, I don't understand it. And despite what you may think, I only want the best for you."

"If you can't see that Drake *is* what's best for me, I don't know what to tell you."

"Love, I just don't agree."

"Well, I'm glad it isn't your decision to make." She crossed her arms. "I mean, it's not like you don't know Drake, Daddy. He's the same person you took under your wing all those years ago. You taught him how to ride a bike, for Christ's sake. You were more like a father to him than his own."

"You're right. He is the same person I've known for years. Last I checked, Drake was looking for a career, not a wife. And that was just last month. He wants the high life, fly-in surgeries, penthouse view, guest lecturer. He wants fame and notoriety. You are fundamentally different people. This marriage will be over before it starts."

Love swallowed rapidly as her father ticked off the many reasons a relationship with Drake wouldn't work. She had to admit they were all reasons that ran through her mind daily. "You don't understand him. He would never hurt me."

"That's where you're wrong. I do understand. Mark my words, you'll end up heartbroken when he wakes up one morning and realizes he wants more."

It felt like a slap, and Love swayed on her feet. The words did more damage than she wanted to admit. The fact that her own father made it seem like she could never be enough for a man like Drake stung, but not more than the fact that she had wondered the same thing countless times over the past few weeks. Her father's words served only to heighten her own fears about their fate, especially since she'd fallen for Drake as hard and fast as he'd made love to her last night.

Frowning, she observed her father. A question had niggled at her mind for years. She'd never understood why her parents had divorced, and listening to her father just then, it all made sense. Clearing her throat, she asked, "Is that what happened with you and Mom?"

"This isn't about me and your mother."

"Isn't it? How else can you explain how mean you've been about this? I get it, though. You don't want me hurt. But Drake won't hurt me."

"He will," her father insisted. "You can't say what he won't do. Look, I like Drake. He's a talented doctor with a long career ahead of him."

"Then why are you punishing him at work?"

"I was angry, disappointed. I've remedied that as of today."

Love closed her eyes and sent up a silent "thank you, Lord."

"I respect him as a person," her father continued. "He's just not the man I want for my daughter."

"And Derrick is?"

"Lovely, he's a good man."

"He cheated on me. I can't believe you're pushing him on me, even knowing the truth."

"People make mistakes. But I know that Derrick is sorry for what he's done. He's honest about his shortcomings, humble. And I appreciate that about him."

Love shook her head, rolling her eyes at that ass-backward reasoning her father had thrown out. It pissed her off that the man who'd been larger than life to her at one point couldn't admit the real reason he was so against her marriage.

"Daddy, I wish you could see Drake the way I do." He opened his mouth to speak, but she forged ahead. "And I wish you'd stop making him like you, when that couldn't be further from reality. Yes, you hurt Mom. But that doesn't mean Drake will make the same choices. The fact that you expect my husband will treat me the way you treated my mother pisses me off. It not only insults my intelligence, but it hurts that you assume I'm not good enough to keep a man like Drake happy."

"Love, baby girl, that's not why—"

She nodded, praying the tears wouldn't fall. "It is, and it hurts. So, no, I won't take Derrick back. I'm married to Drake, and until you can respect that, we don't have anything else to say to one another."

Love stomped out of the office once again. She waited until she was on the other side of the closed door before she sagged against it, finally allowing the tears to fall. The only person breaking her heart at that moment was her father. She pulled her phone out of her pocket, tempted to call Drake. He was her safe place, after all.

Her phone rang before she could dial, though. Staring at the screen, at the familiar number, she decided to answer. "I'm glad you called. I need to see you."

Lunch at the hospital offered a wide variety of choices for a starving Love. She'd decided to go with something fattening after the argument she'd had with her father. With a plate of cheese fries and a juicy double cheeseburger, she headed toward the far right of the huge cafeteria, waving at a few friends on the way.

As she approached the table where he sat, Derrick was typing furiously on his phone. They'd eaten lunch at that table many times over the course of their relationship.

He smiled when he saw her, standing to greet her. Derrick placed a chaste kiss on her cheek and waited until she was settled before taking his seat again.

Eyeing her food, he chuckled. "Bad day?"

Love popped a fry in her mouth, moaning at the cheesy goodness. "You don't want to know the day I've had, Derrick."

"Try me."

"Daddy."

He nodded, seemingly understanding without a wordy explanation. "Another argument, huh?" He snatched a fry from her plate.

She shot him a sideways glance. "Can you say understatement?"

"Love, I'm sorry."

Her eyes flashed to his dark ones. "What are you sorry for?"

Derrick lifted his hands, then let them fall. "For hurting you, and then waltzing back into your life like you owed me something."

Love sat back, watching him as he explained that her father had tried to convince him to stick around and help drive a wedge between her and Drake. She was livid, had half a mind to send her father a "breakup" text, disowning him. He'd enlisted her ex to destroy her marriage. What nerve!

Derrick reached out, placed a hand on top of hers. "It's no secret that I don't care for Drake, but I respect your decision. I told your father that, as well."

Surprised, Love smiled, glad that she hadn't been completely wrong about Derrick. "Thank you."

"For what it's worth, I hope Drake can make you happy."

She flipped her hand over and squeezed his. "I know it's hard for you to say that, but I appreciate it. I wanted to see you because I felt like I had to be honest with you."

"I'm listening."

"Even if there was no Drake, I couldn't be with you." She felt his hand go slack in hers. "It's not to say I don't care for you, because I do, even after everything that's happened between us."

Love had a light-bulb moment as she sat across from the man she'd thought she'd spend the rest of her life with. As good as they were together, it wasn't enough for her. And Drake…even if they filed for divorce tomorrow, she'd never be the same. She'd been forever changed by this experience, and she was no longer willing to settle for less when she'd felt what true passion could be.

"I've changed," she admitted softly. "The person I am now is not willing to just accept everything someone gives her. I can admit that I played a huge part in the demise of our relationship, but I can't be with someone I don't trust. Long-distance relationships are hard, but I felt like you owed me more. And I just had to tell you that. I think you're a good man, but I'm not in love with you anymore. I hope you understand."

"Actually, I do. It's a hard pill to swallow, but you're right."

They sat for a minute in an awkward silence. Love wondered what he was thinking, but decided not to ask. They'd pretty much said it all, and she was ready to close the book on that chapter for good.

"So, are you going to eat those fries?" he asked.

She giggled and picked one up, pointing it at him. "Wouldn't you just love for me to say no."

"Seriously, I'm hungry."

They spent a few more minutes catching up, before he had to leave. He hugged her, and walked out of her life.

Drake watched his wife have lunch with her ex with narrowed eyes.

"Are you just going to let him worm his way back into her life?" Gloria said, elbowing him in the side.

He flinched, rubbing the spot she'd hit. "Damn, Mom. That hurt."

"Drake, that is your wife. You need to go over there and get your woman."

"They're just eating," he told her, more to convince himself than his pushy mother-in-law. "I can't keep making scenes at work. I told you about what happened the other day."

During their car ride that morning, Drake had confessed that he'd made a fool of himself at work and had since been tormented by his colleagues. His uncle-brother, El, had lead the charge, blazing on him every time he saw him. His younger brothers had also joined the group, making sure they mentioned his possessive ways every time they ran into him in the hall.

Drake noted the way Love laughed, and was entranced at the way her head fell back when she did so. She enjoyed Derrick's company, that much was clear. And he hated it. He hated him.

"Hey, I'm all for giving zero—"

"Shh," he hissed, before she finished her sentence with an f-bomb. Gloria and he had an understanding. There wasn't much he couldn't say to her, but he wanted to keep it clean.

"Hey," she repeated, placing a hand on her hip. "Don't shush me. You know I'm right."

"You're right," he grumbled reluctantly. "I'll talk to her later. Don't worry."

They watched as Derrick stood and hugged Love. Before Drake realized it, he'd stepped forward, halting in his tracks when Derrick rushed out of the cafeteria.

Gloria hooked her arm in his and pulled him toward Love, who was finishing her burger. "Hey, Lovely," she said, taking the empty seat across from her daughter and forcing him to take the seat beside her.

Love shot a glance at him. "Hey." She smiled at her mother. "Hi, Mom. How are you feeling today?"

"Better," Gloria said. "Especially now that Derrick is gone. I hope he's gone for good. Lovely, you really shouldn't be eating all that cheese. It will mess with your stomach."

As Gloria went on about cheese and the digestive system, Drake swept a hand up Love's leg and squeezed her thigh.

"Lovely Grace, are you listening to me?"

Drake chuckled, knowing that she had tuned her mother out.

"Sure," Love lied.

"I still want to throw you and Drake a reception."

Drake dug his fingers into Love's thigh. He'd spent the morning avoiding talk about a reception, but it seemed Gloria wouldn't be deterred.

"Mother, I don't think it's a good time," Love told her.

"I'm not going to deny that I was hurt when I found out about your hasty wedding. But I've moved past it. By the way, I heard you and Drake in the kitchen last night."

Drake choked and rubbed the back of his neck.

"Mother, please." Love covered her ears. "Oh, my God. I'm so embarrassed," she muttered.

"What? You know I have ears like a hawk," Gloria said innocently.

"Oh, God," Love grumbled. "Make it stop."

"Okay." Gloria folded a napkin into a little square, like she used to do when they were children. "Anyway, I had to look at myself in the mirror. I swore I'd never be as old-fashioned as my parents were. I didn't intend to raise my child the same way they raised me."

"Mother, you're nothing like your parents."

Drake knew the history. Love's grandparents had co-pastored one of those Southern Baptist churches in the backwoods of Tuscaloosa, Alabama, before moving to Las Vegas to start a ministry in what they called the den of sin. Her Nana and Papa didn't understand when Gloria showed up pregnant out of wedlock, and they disowned her. They hadn't even shown up for the wedding a few months before Love was born.

"So I can't be too mad you went and eloped without me or your father there," Gloria said. "But I can say I'm ecstatic that you married Drake. He's perfect for you. And in an effort to prove to you that I'm really okay with this decision, I want to give you two a reception."

"Mom, you have a lot going on right now."

"She's right, Mom," Drake agreed.

Gloria could need surgery, and he didn't want her stressing about something that didn't matter to him. He knew Love felt the same way.

"Can we table this discussion for after your appointment today?" Love picked up her mother's hand and kissed it. "I want us to focus on getting your health under control, right, Drake?"

"Exactly," he agreed. "If you want to help, fry me some chicken for dinner."

Love glanced over at Drake, who shrugged and ate one of her fries.

Gloria gave them a watery smile, stood and pulled them both into her arms. "I love you, my Lovely. You, too, Drake. You have made me so proud." She gave them each a kiss on the forehead before pulling back. "We have to go. I want to use the bathroom before my appointment."

As Gloria walked off ahead of them, Drake and Love followed at a good distance. He leaned into her. "I saw Derrick."

"You did," Love said, a sneaky smile on her plump lips. She was so ready to be kissed, and he wanted to push her into one of those little nooks and do it. But he'd promised himself he'd keep his hands to himself at work. It was becoming harder by the minute, though.

"Why was he here?"

She raised a brow. "Are you jealous?"

"Pretty much," he admitted.

She laughed, and his mouth went dry. "That was honest."

"I know no other way to be."

Nodding, she told him about her visit with her dad and the subsequent lunch with Derrick. "It was time to let him know, in no uncertain terms, that we are over."

Drake couldn't deny he was glad Love had handled Derrick, even though he still wanted to knock him out.

Love stopped in front of the restroom her mother had entered, and folded her arms over her chest. She grinned up at him, biting her lip. "I like that you're jealous."

He couldn't help it; he reached out and rubbed her bottom lip with his thumb. It took everything in him not to kiss her right then and there, gawkers be damned. "Well, I don't like when you laugh with other men."

She gasped. "You're hilarious. Am I supposed to be serious all the time, Drake?"

"When you're not with me."

She shoved him playfully, but he grabbed her wrist and pulled her to him. It was strange being like this with her in the hallway outside the cafeteria. Anybody could see them, but he didn't care. He imagined how she'd taste right then, could almost hear the breathless way she said his name when she was coming for him.

He leaned in closer, his hands tightening around her waist. His gaze lingered on her mouth, before he pressed his lips against hers. She pulled him against her, taking control of the kiss and prying his lips apart with her tongue. A low moan escaped from his throat.

Or was it hers? He honestly didn't know where he stopped and she began, they were so close.

Someone clearing a throat behind him put a halt to what was sure to escalate. He'd already spotted an empty nook to his left.

Love giggled against his mouth and they slowly backed away from each other. Gloria was standing with a hand on her hip. Around them, a few people clapped, and Drake took a bow.

"I'm going to go," he said, when the applause died down. He could still taste Love's lips, and fought back a groan. He hugged Gloria and placed a kiss on her forehead. "Bye, Mom." Then he turned to her daughter. Brushing her hair back, he whispered, "I'll see you later, Love."

She waved at him, and he saluted her, then left.

Chapter 14

Love tapped her foot against the tile as she replied to an email. Her mother sat on the exam bed, rambling on about how she was sick of doctors scheduling appointments for a certain time, then not even walking into the room until an hour later.

"Lovely?" she called. "Are you listening to me?"

Love gave her a grin. "I'm sorry, Mother. I had an urgent email. What were you saying?"

"Never mind." Gloria waved a dismissive hand. "You always do that—tune your poor mother out."

The fact was—and she was ashamed to admit it—she rarely listened to her mother completely. It was a big problem because her mom had a habit of sneaking things into the conversation when Love wasn't paying attention.

"Mom, I'm sorry. You have my undivided focus."

"I'm scared," Gloria whispered, tears welling in her eyes.

Shocked by the uncharacteristically emotional admission, Love scooted closer to the bed. Throughout her life, she had seen her mother loud, frantic, nosy, sweet, but never scared. She rubbed her knee. "Aw, Mom, it's going to be okay. No matter what, I'm going to take care of you."

It was the least she could do, because Gloria had always put her first.

Gloria dashed tears from her cheeks with both hands. "When your father left me, I tried my best not to let you see how devastated I was. I didn't want you to witness that and think all relationships were bad. I worried about you for so long. You'd be so wrapped up in school, and I wondered if you'd ever actually let yourself start to live. I wanted that for you so badly. I wanted you to be able to be free, because I wasn't."

Love found herself wiping her own eyes, as her mother continued, "To see you happy, and in love, makes me feel like I didn't fail you."

"Mom, please." Love leaned forward and embraced her. "You did not fail me. You've been there for me through everything. I don't know what I would have done without you." She held her gently as she cried into her shoulder. Love wasn't sure what was going on, but it frightened her.

"Lovely, I won't be around forever. It does my heart good to know that you will be well taken care of when I'm not here."

"Stop talking like that, Mom. I'm going to do whatever I have to do to make this okay, even if that means moving you to Michigan so that I can take care of you."

Gloria laughed. "Yeah, right. You'd hate living in the same house with me."

Love let out a shaky laugh of her own, grateful that her mother found anything funny. "I would, but I love you more than I love my solitude."

"Solitude? You have none of that now. Drake is there."

Love paused. Her mother was holding on to her marriage for dear life, it seemed. "True. It's been an adjustment."

"Don't be too hard on him."

Love smirked. She remembered when she'd refused to let Drake stay with her years ago when he'd been looking for a place to live. Now, he was living with her, sleeping with her. He had a toothbrush in her bathroom, underwear in her drawers.

What a difference a wedding and good sex made.

"I have a confession to make," Gloria whispered.

Curious, Love pulled back and met her gaze. "What is it?"

"When I first found out you and Drake were married, I thought you were up to something. I couldn't believe it. I even considered a drunken night might be the reason."

Love laughed. Loudly. "Wow, Mom. That's…something."

"I know. But watching you two together made me realize that you really do care for each other. You're in love."

Love thought about that for a moment. She did love Drake—really loved him. Not just because he was

Drake but because he was *her* Drake. Her husband. And she wanted it to stay that way.

It was hours later when Love got back to work. She opened the door to exam room three and stepped in to see her favorite patient. "Hi, Sydney."

Sydney Smith, her friend Jared's twin sister, looked up from a magazine and smiled. "Dr. Love."

They hugged. Normally, Love wouldn't do that with a patient, but Sydney had become a friend. The two had clicked immediately when Love had had the pleasure of delivering baby Brynn.

There was nothing more rewarding than being in the delivery room. Love enjoyed helping mothers bring babies into the world. Early on, she'd vowed to help women with conception problems and little or no access to health care realize the dream of having a child. It was her passion, and her ultimate goal was to open a specialist clinic devoted to women's health.

"What brings you in, Syd?" Love asked, taking a seat on the stool. She quickly docked her tablet and signed in to the system.

Syd sighed, her hazel eyes flashing. "I think Brynn is going to have a little brother or sister."

Love gasped. "What? So soon?"

Syd's little one was only two years old, and it had been a rough pregnancy. She'd ended up on bed rest for two months leading up to the harrowing birth of her daughter.

"Is Morgan ecstatic?"

Morgan and Sydney had an adorable, devoted relationship. There was no hiding the love they had for each other. Love had been honored to attend the wed-

ding, right there in the hospital chapel. Love recalled
the despair in Syd's eyes the day they'd brought him
in with a life threatening gunshot wound, after an attempted robbery. It had been touch and go, but Morgan
eventually pulled through and popped the question a
few minutes after he'd regained consciousness.

Ironically, Drake had been a first year surgical resident in the OR during Morgan's surgery. The two men
had become cool after that, often meeting for basketball at the gym during the week.

Syd crossed her legs, her wedding band sparkling
under the lights. "Girl, you know he is, but I'm not
so sure I'm ready to go through another pregnancy.
It was hard, and I was miserable."

Love laughed, and typed a few notes into her tablet. "Are you concerned about being able to carry to
term again?"

It was a common fear for women who'd had difficult pregnancies.

Syd bit her lip. "It's crossed my mind. I don't want
to spend my entire pregnancy worried. Then, too, my
business is booming. We just expanded our current
building, and we're scouting spots in Canton. It might
not be the best time to have a baby. Brynn is a handful already."

Love nodded. Syd owned the Ice Box, a restaurant in the neighboring town of Ypsilanti. The city
was named in honor of Demetrius Ypsilanti, a Greek
revolutionary leader, and was the home of Eastern
Michigan University. Love spent a lot of time in Ypsilanti, whether she was eating at one of the many res-
taurants in Depot Town or hanging out at Sydney's
bar with Drake.

"I understand," Love assured her. "But let's start with a pregnancy test. There's no point in worrying yet. You don't know if you're going to have a bad pregnancy, so we can't make assumptions."

Syd sighed. "Right. Let's do it."

Love pulled up Syd's medical records and skimmed them. "I want you to head down and get your blood drawn right after your appointment. I won't do an ultrasound or anything until we get a positive test."

"Thanks, Love."

Love prepared a lab requisition and wrote a script for prenatal vitamins. "Anything else going on?"

"Nothing much. How are things going with you? Last time I saw you at the bar, you were drowning your sorrows with your best friend."

Love snorted. "That was a while ago."

"It was. He's a hottie, by the way."

Grinning, Love tugged at her ear. "We got married a few weeks ago."

"Are you serious?"

"Yes. It wasn't planned. It just kind of happened."

"That's awesome, Love. Are you thinking of starting a family soon? Because I'm going to selfishly ask you to hold off until I have my baby."

Love barked out a laugh. "Girl, you don't have to worry about that."

"You never know. I mean, kids were the last thing on my mind when I started seeing Morgan. And then it just happened."

Love clicked on the calendar of her tablet. Her period wasn't due for another week or so, but Syd was right. Essentially, they'd done nothing to prevent a pregnancy. The few times she and Drake had had sex, they hadn't used a condom. Love was on birth control, yes, but she'd seen that fail time and time again.

Her hands trembled as she finished with her notes. The thought of being pregnant herself was enough to make her rethink everything. Making love to Drake was becoming one of her favorite things to do. So much so that she'd been counting down the hours until she could see him again. But they had to take better precautions, because neither of them was ready for a baby.

"Love?" Syd called.

Shaking herself out of her thoughts, she offered her a small smile. "Sorry. A lot going on right now." Not wanting to get into the details of her marriage, she explained about her mother instead. "My mom is in town dealing with some health issues."

Her mother's appointment with the surgeon had gone well. He'd determined that amputation should be a last resort. In the meantime, he set up Gloria on a new treatment he was hyped on. Gloria had sobbed openly at the news.

Love still wanted her mother to consider moving to Michigan, or at least staying for an extended visit. But Gloria was stubborn, and hadn't budged.

"We should really catch up over drinks soon," Love told Sydney. "Well, I can drink and you can have apple juice and pretend it's cognac."

They both laughed then.

Syd stood up and took the form from Love's outstretched hand. "Thanks. I'm going to head to the lab and then go to work. Please let me know as soon as you get the results."

"I certainly will."

The two said goodbye and Love started toward the office. Along the way she pulled out her phone and typed a text to Drake: What if I'm pregnant?

Drake stumbled and almost took an L in the middle of the floor. His *wife* had sent him a text asking what would happen if she were pregnant. Hell, the thought was enough to send him straight to the bar. But he was scheduled to scrub in on a surgery in a few hours and wanted to study a bit beforehand. Dr. Leon had sent him a curt email reminding him of his obligation to the hospital, informing him that his recent change in marital status would not grant him any favors, and letting him know that he'd be assisting him with a heart transplant.

Drake had hoped to talk to Dr. Leon again, but it was obvious the older man didn't want much to do with him outside of work. He suspected the recent change of heart had more to do with his father's demands than anything else, which pissed Drake off. But at least he knew where he stood with his mentor now.

He stared at the text, dissecting the words. *What if I'm pregnant?* Drake was hit with a dilemma. Should he go to her and ask her what she meant, or send a lighthearted text like "stop playing around. LOL."

Deciding against both options, he typed: We'll talk later. He hesitated for a minute, deleting and retyping the same message at least three times. Sighing, he hit Send and dropped his phone into his pocket.

A few minutes later, he was knocking on El's office door.

El swung the door open, a pinched look on his face.

"You do know that I actually have a job that I do on a daily basis."

Pushing past his uncle-brother, he made himself comfortable on a little bench by the window. "We need to talk."

"You're lucky my appointment canceled." El took his seat, crossing one ankle over his knee. "What do you want?"

"Love might be pregnant."

El stared at him, a blank expression on his face.

"Say something," Drake said. "Wait." He pulled a dollar out of his lab coat and slapped it on the desk.

El shook his head. "In a minute, I'm going to recommend you spend a few days in the ward. Take that damn dollar back." He picked the bill up and flung it at Drake.

The weightless paper didn't make it far, landing on the floor in front of the desk. "Keep it. I need to know you won't tell anyone about this."

"I'm a little insulted that you feel the need to constantly swear me to secrecy, as if I make a habit of telling your business."

El the psychiatrist would never even think of sharing a patient's stories with anyone. El the uncle-brother would definitely spill the beans at the wrong moment, like a family barbecue or something. Of course, he wouldn't do it maliciously. It was just what "big brothers" did. El had tormented him and his younger siblings for years. If that meant embarrassing them in front of everyone and their mama, El couldn't resist at times.

Drake jumped to his feet, pacing the room with long, impatient strides. "We haven't talked about a divorce," he confessed. "It's kind of an afterthought. When we left Vegas, we were committed to ending this marriage as soon as possible. And we haven't even hired a lawyer. What does that mean?"

What Drake didn't add was that he wasn't as miserable as he'd imagined he would be. Being married to Love wasn't awful. It was actually pretty damn good. "It's only been a few weeks, but it feels right to me, like this is the way it's supposed to be between us."

"You slept with her again," El said. It wasn't a question.

Drake glared at him. "How the hell do you do that?"

"Occupational hazard."

"More than once." Drake pinched his nose, feeling overheated. "I'm not sure I can stop at this point."

"Are you in love with her?"

It was unrealistic, plain and simple. They'd been married for only a few weeks, had never even been on a real date. But he was sure he was. Hell, he'd probably always been a little bit in love with her. "It's impossible, right?"

El shrugged. "Not really. Not with your history with Love."

"I guess not, but it's still weird." The feeling only seemed to intensify as the days passed.

"Love is a beautiful person, bruh."

Drake smiled to himself, thinking about his wife. Love was beautiful and intelligent, and she took good care of him. She was the best of both worlds. "What happens if this doesn't work out?"

He didn't expect a verbal answer. It was El's style to just let him talk until he figured it out himself. So when his brother said, "Why would you go into this thinking it will fail?"

Sighing, Drake told El about the confrontation with Love's father. "The man has a point. I suck at being committed to any woman. If I mess this up, I not only lose my job, but I will destroy the best relationship I've ever had. She's my best friend, my confidante, my support. Do I risk that for an uncertain outcome?"

"I think your question should be, how can you not? Look, love isn't easy. You know that. It hurts, but when it's good, it's really good."

Drake knew El was speaking from experience. Even though things hadn't worked out with El and Avery, his uncle-brother still believed that love was worth it. "You're right."

"Are you afraid to fail, afraid to take a chance on Love?"

"It's not like I had a good role model on being faithful and committed to one woman." Drake had made it a point to date wide and far. His father had set the example for him. But El's assertion that he was afraid to take a chance on Love was wrong. One thing that Drake always did was bet on Love. She'd never failed him. That alone made him want to be what she needed, whether it was with her or without her.

"I don't want to disappoint her. If I hurt her, I hurt me."

"Don't you think Love knows that about you?"

He didn't even blink before answering, "Yes. She knows everything about me."

"And she loves you, anyway."

That she did. Drake bent down, picked up the dollar bill and dropped it on El's desk. "You earned that today."

"Get the hell out of here."

Drake barked out a laugh. "I do have to study. I better get to it."

"Wait, all this mushy talk, and I conveniently forgot to ask about this whole pregnancy thing."

Drake told El about Love's text, and his uncle-brother snorted in amusement. "Wow, you two are made for each other. I'm assuming Love is on some sort of birth control, correct?"

Pausing, Drake thought about that for a moment. They'd never talked about it, but knowing her, she had it under control. He nodded. "I guess. I can't see her not being on the pill or something."

"Well, I suggest you definitely have that conversation. Can't have any Drake Juniors running around the hospital."

"Shut up." The thought of a mini-Drake or a little Lovely was uncomfortable, but a pregnant and glowing Love was appealing on some level.

"Hey, I'm just saying…"

"I gotta go. Basketball tomorrow?"

"Sure thing. Are you going to that fund-raiser next week?"

Drake groaned, unable to hide his disgust. "I am, unfortunately."

"Tell me about it. I won't be there long, though. One of my patients will need me."

Drake waved a dismissive hand. "And you know that already?"

"Yep."

Drake snatched his dollar from the table. "I need

this back to buy a bag a chips out of the vending machine."

Drake made plans to meet El for breakfast in the morning, before heading to the gym. Then, he gathered his things and went to see his wife. They had to talk.

Chapter 15

Love sat on a swing in the park next to her condo rental, a beer in hand. The day had been longer than she'd hoped, and she'd needed a breath of fresh air and solitude. It was cold as hell, but she was bundled up. And she wasn't pregnant. Thank God.

She peered up at the endless sky. The chill of the night was somehow overshadowed by the magnificence of the stars. One of her favorite things to do was visit the planetarium. Love was a proud nerd. Astronomy was one of her favorite subjects in school, and she'd spent hours at the College of Southern Nevada Planetarium as a young girl. Even now, as an adult, she would walk over to the University of Michigan Museum of Natural History and sit in the planetarium. Nothing beat the real thing, though. And the clear night above her was proof that God existed.

Drake pulled into his parking spot, and she watched him hop out of the car and grab his things. He was so confident in everything he did, from school to work to driving. They hadn't talked much since she'd sent the dreaded text earlier. His three-word response only served to ramp up her anxiety about their situation.

She could admit that she wasn't as experienced as he was with the opposite sex. While she hated to think of him with other women, even before he was with her, she knew he'd had many lovers. She'd had only three: terrible sex with the popular jock in high school, Derrick, and now Drake. Bad-sex guy had ruined her first time by behaving like a jerk during and after. She wasn't even sure why she'd done it. She didn't even like the guy that much.

Love took another swig of her beer and tugged her favorite Michigan hat over her ears. Drake had given it to her for her birthday a few years earlier. He'd had it specially made for her. It was blue, with hashtag "Hail" in gold writing across the front. It was a University of Michigan thing, short for "Hail to the Victors," the Michigan Fight Song.

Drake spotted her on his way into the building and headed over to her. "What's up?" he asked. "You do know it's forty degrees outside."

She smiled at him. "I'm bundled up."

"Did you bring an extra?" he asked, gesturing to her beer.

Pulling one out of her coat pocket, she handed it to him. "Of course."

He set his stuff down, and sat in the swing next to her. "Long day."

"Tell me about it."

They swayed in their swings for several minutes, in a comfortable silence. Drake broke the ice first when he said, "You're not pregnant, Love."

Giggling, she finished off her beer. "I know."

He glanced over at her, sending a bolt of awareness through her body. "What was that about?"

She toed the dirt below her and hooked her arms around the swing chains. "I guess I panicked. Sydney came into the hospital, thinking that she was pregnant." The results of Syd's test had already come back positive. Love had called her friend personally to deliver the news.

"Good. I'm sure Morgan is happy."

Syd had cried uncontrollably on the phone after she gave her the results. Initially, Love didn't know how to react, whether they were tears of joy or not. Eventually, after the tears subsided, Syd exclaimed that she was happy and couldn't wait to meet her new bundle of joy.

"He is," Love told him. "The whole situation got me thinking. We haven't really discussed sex. We just keep having it."

Drake laughed then, a low, husky chuckle. "Actually, I don't think we've had enough," he said with a wink.

Love pushed him away from her. "Ha ha. I'm trying to be serious here."

He tapped his beer bottle against his thigh. "Fine. I'm being serious with you."

She twisted in the swing until she was facing him. "You should know that I am on birth control."

"I figured you were."

Love had thought about how to broach the subject

of the marriage and what they were ultimately going to do about it. But the selfish part of her wanted to enjoy him for a little while longer, before they had to start thinking about lawyers and court dates.

"Do you think we're past the point of no return?"

His eyes flashed to hers, locked on them. Love sucked in a deep breath, waiting for him to say something. Words didn't come, though. Only silence, for what seemed like an eternity. She wanted to look away, but couldn't force herself to break the trance.

"Drake," she finally croaked, clutching her throat. "Are we—"

Before she could finish her sentence, he grabbed the plastic-coated chain of her swing, pulled her to him and took her lips in a searing kiss. She gripped the chains, held on for dear life as he kissed her hard, parting her lips with his tongue.

He broke the kiss first, leaned his forehead against her shoulder. "Love, I want to be honest with you. At this point, I'm not sure I want to let this go."

Her heart soared at his admission. She'd been thinking the same thing. The more time she spent with him, the more she wanted to spend with him. Thoughts of late dinners, weekend getaways, Top of the Park in the summer, with her resting between his legs while they watched a movie on the big screen… she envisioned it all in her mind. She found herself thinking about him, even when she should have been studying or listening at lectures. It had been only a few weeks, but he'd branded her.

"I'm glad you said that," she said. "I feel the same way."

He closed his eyes, letting out a heavy sigh. "Good."

"Good."

Drake stood up and tossed their empty bottles into a nearby recycling bin. He walked over to her, ran the back of his finger over the tip of her nose. "You're cold. Let's go in. I'll warm you up."

"Not yet. We have to race."

He grinned. "You're silly. We may have done that when we were kids, but I'm too old for that now."

"You act like you're ready for Geritol. Sit down."

"Okay." He sat on the swing. "Ready, set, go."

Just as she did when she was a kid, Love pumped her legs, propelling the swing higher. The brisk air against her cheeks and the sheer happiness she felt from doing something so simple and free with Drake made her feel giddy. As their swings moved higher, she screamed with glee. He was going to beat her to the top, as he always did, but her dismount would clinch the score.

"You ready?" he asked, from way above her.

"Go ahead."

Without warning, he jumped, soaring through the air to land on the dirt. He stumbled, but remained standing.

"Yes, you suck," she teased.

"Just jump, woman."

At the apex of her next swing Love kicked forward, flying up, then down. When she hit the ground, it was a perfectly stuck landing. She did a fist pump and took a bow. "Yay! I still got it."

Catching her breath, she beamed up at him. He

rubbed her shoulders. "I can admit when I fall short. You did good, baby."

She wasn't sure when she'd started being his "baby," but she'd take the endearment gladly. She rose up on the tips of her toes and brushed her lips against his. "Race you home," she murmured against his mouth before taking off.

Drake turned off the lights in the kitchen and started up the stairs. They'd spent the evening watching a movie with Gloria and eating popcorn. Since Gloria had insisted they all spend "family" time together, Drake hadn't had a chance to cozy up with Love the way he wanted. It was his turn now.

Opening the bedroom door, he halted at the sight of his *wife* standing before him in nothing but a pair of thin lacy panties.

"Drake!" She folded her arms over her bare chest, covering herself. "You should really knock."

"It's too late for shyness, Love. I've seen everything." He burst out in a laugh, tugging his shirt over his head, then set his watch on the nightstand.

A pillow against the back of his head knocked him forward. He rounded on her, picking up a throw pillow and tossing it at her. She ducked easily and ran to the other side of the bed. They stood facing each other, her chest heaving as her eyes shone. Love picked up another pillow, raised it above her head and swung it at him. He grabbed it and pulled, but she didn't give up easily.

"Let go!" she ordered.

"Don't hit me," he warned.

She eyed him, her grip tight on the pillow. "Let go."

"You let go."

It was a battle of wills, and she had the upper hand. Only because she was basically naked. Her smooth brown skin was waiting to be touched, caressed… kissed.

"Come here," she demanded, with hooded eyes.

He released his hold on the pillow and circled the bed. Hooking a finger into the waistband of her panties, he tugged her forward. Sweeping his hand over her chest, then her shoulders, he watched her eyes darken with desire for him. The control he had over her in the bedroom was like a drug. There would never be a better high. The more she gave him, the more he wanted.

Before he could kiss her, though, she smacked him in the head with that damn pillow and bolted toward the master bathroom. He jumped on top of the bed and caught her, wrapping his arms around her waist, and pulled her against him.

Laughing, Love told him to put her down. She snorted, gasping for air as he spun her around and dropped her on the bed.

Love rolled over on her back, fanning herself. She pointed at him. "The look on your face…" She dissolved into a fit of laughter again.

He climbed over her, between her legs. Grabbing both her thighs, he yanked her forward until he was pressed against her heat.

He trailed kisses down her neck until he reached her breast, pulling her nipple into his mouth and sucking until she cried out his name.

She tugged at his hair, urging him up and kissing

him with an urgency. He pulled back first, smirking when she cursed in frustration.

A pretty pout formed on her lips. "You're playing with my emotions."

"Are you ready?"

Love nodded, and her tongue darted out to moisten her lips. Drake mimicked her action, running his tongue over her full mouth before he kissed her. He groaned into her mouth when she rubbed him through his pants.

"You have on too many clothes," she mumbled.

She helped him unbutton his pants, and he kicked them and his underwear off at the same time. Settling between her legs, he placed a soft kiss on her lips and pushed inside her. He held still, relishing the feel of her. It was too intense, almost too much.

"You're so beautiful," he whispered.

She grinned. "You are, too."

Drake kissed her forehead, her cheeks, then her chin and finally her mouth. "I love you."

The words left his mouth before he could stop them. His pulse raced as he wondered if he should backtrack. Had he ruined the moment?

She arched her hips against him, taking him in farther. He stifled a groan, tried to hold it together.

"I love you, too."

A whimper escaped as he moved, slowly at first, taking his time to work her into a frenzy. She squirmed beneath him, writhing as the thrusts grew more intense. He was ready to let go, but he needed her with him.

Gripping her hips, he flipped over on his back. She sat astride him, her hands planted on his chest and her hips grinding down on him. He sat up, smoothed a hand up her back. She wrapped her arms around his neck, and they rocked together, giving themselves over to each other.

"Let go," he said, guiding her movements.

Slick with sweat, they picked up the pace. Her fingernails scraped his back, and he bit down on her shoulder. She groaned, long and hard, as her orgasm ripped through her. He felt his release build, then he exploded with her name on his lips.

Later, they sat facing each other, her legs flung over his. Moaning, she said, "This is so good."

"Want more?" he asked.

"Yes, please."

He fed her another spoonful of banana pudding. After they'd made love a third time, she'd told him she wanted something sweet to eat. He'd sneaked down to the kitchen, careful not to make too much noise and wake up Gloria, and pulled out everything he could find. In the bed with them was a bowl of banana pudding, a slice of lemon pound cake, a brownie and Jell-O. He broke off a piece of cake and popped it into his mouth.

"How is it?" Love asked.

Drake scowled. It wasn't the best cake he'd ever tasted, but he liked to support entrepreneurs. One of the patient techs had ideas to start a cottage industry baking cakes and wanted him to be her taster. "Not good."

Love wrinkled her nose. "I told you to stop buying food from those people at the hospital. You never know what their houses look like. They could have bugs." She shook her head. "Yuck."

"I'll try anything once." He squeezed her thigh, leaned in and kissed her. She caressed his face as they deepened the kiss.

When she pulled back and dipped her spoon in the red Jell-O, he took a minute to look at her. She was a vision, with her hair wild and free. His oversize shirt hung off her shoulders, exposing her bare skin.

They ate in silence, devouring the food in front of them. Finished, she fell against the mattress. "Woo, that was yummy."

He set their dishes on the bedside table and lay back next to her. They stared at the ceiling, seemingly in their own thoughts.

"Drake?" she asked, rising up on her elbow and looking down at him.

"Hmm?"

"Did we just declare our love for each other?"

Chuckling, he confirmed that they had in fact done that. "I meant what I said."

"Why do you love me?"

He shook his head. Leave it to Love to ask the hard questions. "I've loved you since I was two years old."

"Drake, that doesn't count. We were in Pull-Ups."

"It counts, because I feel like you being my best friend has contributed to the way I love you now."

"How so?"

"I loved you before we were us, and I love you more now *because* we're us."

"Aw, you're so sweet. And corny." She laughed.

"I'm glad I can still make you laugh."

She wrapped her arms around his waist and snuggled into him. "What do we do now?"

From his experience with Love, he knew he had to

let her set the pace. He knew what he wanted, and he didn't second-guess it. They were taking a big leap, but he was ready to jump, as long as she was with him. The easy way they were with each other confirmed that they could make it work. The awkwardness of the morning after their wedding had disappeared. Love was comfortable with him, invested in them.

"We take it day by day," he said. "Are you good with that?"

She pressed her cheek against his chest, kissed him right above his heart. "Yes, I am."

He heard the growl of her stomach. "Are you still hungry?"

"Oh, my God, that is so embarrassing, and so not sexy."

"I can try to cook you something."

"I want to live to see tomorrow." She giggled. "I have a taste for fish and grits, but it's too late to eat. I'm already going to pay for this dessert break."

"Aw, shoot. I must have put it down if you're talking about making my favorite meal."

She pinched him. "Shut up. Go to sleep. I'll make you fish and grits tomorrow."

The room descended into silence again. He squeezed her tight. "Good night. I love you."

"Love you, too."

Chapter 16

The Cadillac Club, an exclusive society, hosted a fund-raiser for the hospital every spring. Each year they awarded countless scholarships to prospective college students at the Annual Beau/Debutante Ball for high school seniors of color. They were also what Love considered a black elite social group.

Ann Arbor had a large population of affluent African Americans—doctors, lawyers, business owners and executives in local companies. True, they donated money to countless charities, but in doing so, some of them looked down on the people they were trying to help.

The Jackson family—more specifically, Drake's grandfather—was a founding member of the club. They were honoring his father with an award for philanthropy, and Love had promised Drake she'd be at the gala—even though she hated events like these.

Formal dinners were not her idea of fun, especially when it was an event that served one main purpose: to provide affluent individuals with a venue to act superior to other people. Love preferred low-key events. She'd rather be chilling in a bar with a bowl of peanuts and a big screen TV than attending a tense, stuffy dinner.

As she and Drake walked into the ballroom, his hand on the small of her back, she felt extremely uncomfortable. It had been a week since they'd declared their love for each other, and things were good. But they hadn't yet been around Drake's father together.

They'd spent the last week in a little bubble, holed up in bed or sneaking off at work to have lunch together or make out in the residents' lounge.

Love shifted, pulled at her gown. "I do not want to be here," she grumbled.

"We won't stay long," Drake whispered against her ear. "You look beautiful, though."

He'd told her that countless times already that evening. And she felt beautiful. Dr. Law had sent a limousine to pick them up, because heaven forbid one of his sons show up in a car. She'd been on edge for the whole ride, until Drake made her come so hard in the back of the limo she couldn't think about anything but him.

Sighing, she asked, "Promise?"

"I'm counting down the minutes till we leave."

The ballroom was gorgeous. The dusty rose and champagne color scheme was elegant and timeless. It was obvious the club had spared no expense to ensure everyone enjoyed the party and would be talking about it for months. Waiters walked around with trays of champagne, floral arrangements graced each tabletop, silver gleamed in the chandelier lighting. Everything seemed to sparkle. Love was impressed.

"Hey, bruh." Drake's younger brother Ian, one of the twins, approached them. The two men embraced and Ian gave Love a kiss on the cheek. "Hello, sister-in-law."

Love winked at him. He was like a little brother to her, too. "Hi, brother-in-law. You look good."

"And if you weren't married to my brother, I might have to take you home for the night."

"Watch it," Drake warned.

"Hey, I call it like I see it, and your wife is wearing some dress."

Love thanked Ian for the compliment. It had taken her hours to get ready. She hadn't been able to decide on what to wear. She'd purchased two gowns because she'd been torn. In the end, she'd chosen the black one. Nude mesh fabric with beaded accents created an illusion of a sheer back and side panels. It fitted her like a glove. Her hair was swept to the side in a delicate updo. From the moment he saw her, Drake hadn't been able to keep his eyes off her.

"Dad was looking for you," Ian murmured to Drake. "He was ready to send me out to fetch you."

Drake shrugged. "He knew I was coming. Where's Myles?"

Ian shrugged in turn. "Hell if I know. Probably working."

Myles was Ian's twin brother, but the two could not be more different. Ian was carefree, while Myles was closed off, serious. Of all the siblings, Myles was the most like Dr. Law. The twins were only seven months younger than Drake. Dr. Law had had two women pregnant at the same time.

Ian was dressed in a charcoal gray tuxedo, his short hair and beard groomed. He and Drake were around the same height, while Myles was a little shorter. Love took a moment to admire her husband in his black tuxedo. She loved a man in a suit and Drake wore one well. Love hadn't encountered a Jackson man that wasn't fine. Even Dr. Law was a devastatingly handsome man.

Ian nursed a tumbler filled with an amber-colored liquor. She suspected it was scotch. That was his drink of choice. "I was subjected to lecture two million ten about how he has high expectations for my career, and I should stop volunteering and focus on school," Drake's brother said drily.

Ian spent time volunteering with the Red Cross. Love had worked with him on several projects, and she appreciated his heart for service. Dr. Law could learn a thing or two from his sons.

"Where is Melanie?" Drake asked.

"She's out of town," Ian said. "Claimed she had to attend a conference in Seattle. I think she's full of it."

Melanie, or Mel, was the youngest of the Jackson brood. She was happily enjoying her college years, partying and traveling without a care in the world.

"Aw, I was hoping to see her," Love said.

"Hello, family." Myles, with his hands stuffed in the pockets of his heather-gray tuxedo, stepped up to them. He kissed Love on the cheek and shook Drake's hand. "I see the gang is all here."

"I'm glad you finally left the hospital," Love told him. Myles stayed at the hospital more than required. "It's time you live your life."

"Congratulations on the wedding," he replied, changing the subject. "I'm shocked. All these years, and you just up and decide to get married. I don't get it."

"You sound like Dad," Ian said. "I'm glad you did it, Drake. You got a good woman."

Drake wrapped an arm around her waist, pulled her closer and placed a kiss to her temple. "I know. You don't have to tell me."

"Well, if it isn't my boys," Dr. Law said as he approached. "And my new daughter-in-law." He greeted his sons with handshakes and gave her a hug. "Good to see you, Lovely."

She smiled. "Same to you."

Love couldn't help but feel some type of way about Dr. Law after hearing about how he'd lied to Drake about his mother for all those years. She wanted to give him a piece of her mind. One day, she'd get her chance.

"Drake, I have some colleagues I need you to meet."

Love smiled when Drake shot her a look as he followed his father away. She scanned the ballroom and spotted her own dad on the other side of the room. She'd expected him to be there. He was a member of the club, although not as prominent as Dr. Law.

Love walked over to the bar and ordered a club

soda. She wasn't in the mood for alcohol. She had an early shift in the morning.

"Hello, Lovely," her father said. "I was wondering if you were going to try and avoid me tonight."

She turned to him. "Hello, Dad."

He hugged her. "You're beautiful."

"Thank you."

"Where's your husband?"

Love didn't miss the sarcasm. Her father was still salty with her and Drake for getting married. "He's with his father. Dad, I really need this to stop. I hate fighting with you."

He let out a heavy sigh. "I'm sorry."

"Are you?"

"I am. I shouldn't have said or done the things I did. You're my daughter, and I love you. I just want you to be happy. Can you forgive me?"

Love eyed him. "Can you promise to leave Drake alone?"

There was a long silence, and Love wondered what he was going to say next. Was this an act?

"I promise."

She hugged her father, shutting her eyes when his arms closed around her. A hug from Dr. Leon Washington was a rare thing, and she savored it. "Thank you, Dad."

Drake stood on the far side of the ballroom, a letter from Johns Hopkins in hand. They'd accepted him into their cardiothoracic surgery residency program. It was a fellowship that he'd applied for last year, before Love.

Two months earlier he wouldn't have hesitated. But now...

"What are you going to do?" his father asked.

Drake's dad had given a lecture at Johns Hopkins and run into the chief of surgery while there. The two were old friends, and the other doctor had given him the letter to hand deliver to Drake.

Scratching his forehead, Drake shook his head. "I don't know."

"You've worked for this."

Drake was skeptical about his father's sudden show of support. He could see right through him. This was about Love, plain and simple. "I'm married, Dad. I can't just up and leave. I can continue here."

"Son, this is a huge opportunity. You can't pass something like this up."

"Don't tell me what I can or can't do. All of a sudden you're concerned? I wonder why I find that hard to believe."

He caught a glimpse of Love walking toward them, and tucked the letter in his inside jacket pocket.

"Hey, babe," she said.

Drake hugged her, kissing her brow. "Hey."

He couldn't stop looking at Love. Her beauty glowed from within. When he'd first seen her dressed and made up earlier, he couldn't breathe. It overwhelmed him at times, the way he loved her. The thought of leaving her made him sick.

"I spoke with my dad," she said.

He glanced at his own father. "I'll talk to you soon." He led Love away without another word to him. "How did that go?" he asked her.

"It went well. He apologized."

"That's good."

She eyed him curiously. "Are you okay?"

Drake wasn't sure if he should tell Love about the acceptance letter, especially since they'd decided to try and make their relationship work. But he'd never lied to her before, not about anything serious. Sure, he'd told her on a number of occasions he hadn't eaten her food, but this was big. Taking that fellowship would put them in different states for three years. Even if they did decide to try and make it work long-distance, the odds of them succeeding were low.

"I'm fine, just irritated with my dad," he told her. It wasn't an outright lie, just not the entire truth. "Let's take our seats. Dinner will start soon."

Drake and Love joined Ian and Myles at a table. His father was seated at the adjacent table with his current wife.

"What do you have a taste for?" Drake asked Love, frowning at the menu card in front of him. He hated these highbrow events. The food always consisted of rubbery chicken, overcooked beef or dry fish.

She hummed. "Um… I'm thinking the chicken dish. What about you?"

"The rib eye."

"Okay, get your steak and we can share my chicken. I have to save room for my cheesecake."

Drake nodded, distracted by the skin peeking out through the slit in her dress. He reached out and brushed a hand over her knee. "I want to take you home."

"Yeah? I want you to take me home. But we have to stay, at least until your father gets his award."

"Drake?"

He turned at the sound of his name being called. Howard and Dawn Harris approached the table. Though the couple were colleagues of his, he couldn't stand either one of them. They were nothing but trouble, and had caused many problems at work.

"Is that you, Love?" Dawn said in a saccharine tone.

Love smiled brightly at them. "Yes, it's me."

"You clean up nice," Dawn said.

Love tapped a finger on the table. Drake knew she couldn't stand Dawn, either. "How are you two?" she asked.

Drake picked up his glass of cognac and raised it in greeting. "Hi, Dawn. Howard," he said drily.

"We're good," Dawn replied. "I didn't know you'd be here."

"Why not?" Drake asked. "My father is winning the award of distinction."

"I heard that you two are seeing each other now." The other woman folded her arms over her chest.

"We're married," he said. "Happily. But you know that, right? You've been the one spreading rumors about us around the hospital."

Love's eyes widened, but she played along. "Which is surprising to us because you don't know anything about our relationship."

Dawn's cheeks turned red and she nervously clutched her purse strap. "Who said I did that? I rarely even think about you."

Love piped up, "Oh, how wonderful. I don't think about you, either."

Without another word, Dawn pulled Howard away in a huff.

Drake smiled at Love. "You're brilliant."

She looked at him, her eyes sparkling in the dim lighting. "Well, you married me. I guess that makes you brilliant, too."

Chapter 17

Love looked up when Drake walked into the bedroom. "Hey," she said, setting her pen down on her book. "You're home earlier than I thought."

"Yeah, I'm tired." He undressed, then slipped on his pajamas.

He sat on the edge of the bed, bowed his head. She crawled toward him and hugged him from behind, pressing her lips to his cheek. "Do you need anything? I made dinner."

Drake kissed her hand, held it against his mouth. "You are too good to me. I don't deserve you."

"Yes, you do. We deserve each other." She brushed her lips against his. "I can warm up some food for you."

Some women hated the thought of taking care of their men, but Love embraced it. She loved cooking for Drake, and making sure that he was eating well. It was relaxing to her, and not that different from how she'd been with him before everything changed.

He shook his head. "No, I'm good. I ate at the hospital."

It wasn't like Drake to turn down food. Especially food she made. He loved her cooking. It had been a busy week for them, and they'd barely seen each other. All week Drake had been acting distant, too. She couldn't figure out why, though. Part of her worried that he'd reconsidered everything. When she'd asked him, he told her he was just tired. She'd known him long enough to know when he wasn't being entirely truthful, which concerned her, because he'd never lied to her before.

"Are you sure you're okay?"

"I'm fine, Love." He stood up. "I'm going to take a shower."

The next morning, Love woke up to an empty bed. Drake had withdrawn the night before and it really concerned her.

She walked downstairs, hoping to find him in the kitchen or the living room. No Drake. Just then, she heard the front door open.

Drake rushed in with a cup of coffee. When he spotted her, he shot her a stiff smile.

"Hey," he said, dropping his keys on the table. "What are you doing up so early?"

Love shrugged. "I was looking for you. Where'd you go?"

"I went to the hospital to check on a patient."

Love couldn't tell if he was lying about the patient,

but something was definitely wrong. "Do you have to go back?"

"Not for a couple hours. I came back to get some sleep."

Love stretched and walked over to Drake. Wrapping her arms around his shoulders, she kissed him. "Want to watch TV or do me?"

Drake smirked. "I'd love to do you, but I'm going to choose sleep." He smacked her lightly on her butt, and disappeared up the stairs.

Sleep wasn't even an option. A feeling of dread took over as she wondered what had happened to Drake to pull away from her.

Later on, Love stuffed Drake's tuxedo pants in a bag. She'd decided to take his suit to the cleaners when she took her dress. He'd already left for his afternoon shift.

She racked her brain trying to think about everything that happened at the ball. But nothing seemed out of the ordinary. She was tempted to talk to El. Maybe he'd be able to shed some light on things. But she didn't want to involve anyone else. Her mother had once told her not to bring other people into her relationships. Whatever happened between her and Drake was between them.

Shaking her head to clear her mind, she checked the pockets and heard the crinkle of paper from the inside pocket. She pulled an envelope out and noted the return address: Johns Hopkins. The urge to open the envelope reared its ugly head. Love wasn't the type to spy on her man.

She reasoned with herself about it. Drake *had* been acting strange, ever since they'd left the fund-raising event. She was taking his tuxedo to the cleaner and the letter happened to be in his pocket.

Giving in to temptation, she pulled out the contents and scanned them. Her heart dropped. Swallowing hard, she read the letter again.

Johns Hopkins?

She didn't want to jump to conclusions, but her father's words came to mind.

Last I checked, Drake was looking for a career, not a wife.

Love choked back a sob. Had her dad been right all along? Drake had been there, fully vested in their relationship…until the acceptance letter arrived.

You are fundamentally different people. This marriage will be over before it starts.

Pressing a hand against her throat, she considered calling Drake, confronting him with the evidence that he'd lied to her. Except he didn't lie, he'd omitted.

Mark my words, you'll end up heartbroken when he wakes up one morning and realizes he wants more.

Her father's words still stung, because Love had known it was a possibility, even then. But she'd chosen to believe Drake when he said he wanted to be with her, that he loved her.

Love stuffed the letter back in the envelope and set it on Drake's pillow. He'd see it when he got home and have no choice but to mention it. She heard the door shut downstairs and figured the conversation was going to happen sooner rather than later.

When Drake entered the room, she asked him, "What are you doing back so soon?"

"I forgot I don't have a lecture this morning. I figured I chill out with you for a while." He walked over to her, leaned in and kissed her. "Want to get some lunch?"

She shook her head. "No."

Frowning, he asked, "Are you okay?"

"I was… I was going to take your tux to the cleaners." She picked up the envelope from his pillow and held it out. "This was in the pocket."

Drake lowered his gaze.

"Were you going to tell me that you got accepted to Johns Hopkins? Or were you just going to leave without telling me?"

Sighing, he sat down on the edge of the bed. "It's not what you think."

"Isn't it? You've been distant. And then I see this. What am I supposed to think? I've been asking you for days if everything is all right. You've been lying to me for days. I thought we were working toward something here."

"Love, I was going to tell you."

"After you accepted the offer?"

"I haven't accepted the offer. I'm not going to."

"Why? You've wanted this for years. Why wouldn't you take it?"

"Because… I love you. I'm not going to just leave."

"But you considered it."

"Of course I did. It's Johns Hopkins."

"Take it."

His eyes widened. "Love, I'm not taking it."

"Please do."

The fact that the minute she read the letter, she'd immediately thought the worst about Drake didn't sit right with her. It was indicative of a greater problem.

Lack of trust. She'd been burned before, and she didn't want to get hurt again.

"Don't do this," he said. "Don't push me away because you're scared."

"I don't know why I thought we could do this, Drake. All I know is if we continue, I might wind up hating you. It's bad enough that because of me you're turning down a job you've always wanted. And I'm not willing to do another long-distance relationship. Bottom line, my dad was right. We want different things. It's good that we know that now."

"What?" Drake jumped up, staggered back a few steps. "I can't even believe you're going to use your dad's words against me. I'm not that guy. I'm not him. I would never hurt you."

"You wouldn't try. And I love you for that. But I think it's best we end this now, before we ruin each other." Love walked into the bathroom and slammed the door.

Drake pounded on it. "Love."

He kept knocking, calling her name, begging her to talk to him. But Love just leaned against the panel and cried silently.

Drake knocked on the door, waited until he heard "come in" before opening it.

Dr. Leon was seated at his desk. "Drake. What brings you here?"

"I wanted to believe that you'd get over it, that you'd accept me." Drake paced the office. After Love had barricaded herself in the bathroom, he'd stormed out and driven around, turning everything over in his mind.

It was curious timing, receiving the acceptance letter from Johns Hopkins. Almost too coincidental. Then it made sense. His own father hand-delivered the letter, the same day Love's father apologized and asked for forgiveness…? A call to the admissions office confirmed his suspicions. His father had worked with hers, sending over glowing recommendations to their friends at Johns Hopkins, calling in a few favors, and voila!

Drake had just left his dad. He'd yelled at him, not just about this, but about everything that he'd ever done to hurt him. And like every other time his father felt like his back was against the wall, he'd responded in kind. It had been a waste of time, talking to someone who didn't know how to listen. Instead of arguing with him any longer, Drake had walked away and now he found himself staring at the man that he'd *thought* was better than his father.

"I don't know what problem you have with me, but I would have never hurt your daughter. I love her too much. I wanted a life with her, and I was willing to give that fellowship up for her. But I guess I should congratulate you. Because of your interference, your manipulations, she ended it. You got your wish. Your daughter will not be married to me much longer. Maybe she can take that asshole Derrick back so he can cheat on her again."

"Drake," Dr. Leon said.

"No, you don't have to say anything. I'm going to Baltimore. Love made the decision for me. You're happy, huh?"

"Drake—"

"Tell me something." Drake hung his head, took

a deep breath and faced Dr. Leon. "When did you start hating me so much? What did I ever do to you? I thought we were better than that. You were more important to me than my own father."

"I don't hate you."

"Then what is it?" Drake threw his arms out in frustration. "Why?"

"You were right. Love was right. I look at you and I see myself. And my protective instincts kicked in. I didn't want my daughter to fall in love with someone like me."

Drake let out a strained snicker.

"It doesn't mean that I don't care about you, son. I do. I still think this may be the best thing for both of you. This way you can follow your dream. You worked hard for it."

His dream. Yes, he had dreamed of a Johns Hopkins fellowship, followed by a prolific career. But now a woman dominated his dreams. And his every thought.

"Great," he said with no emotion in his tone. "Just so you know, though. None of that matters to me."

Chapter 18

Love was miserable, and it was all her fault. She'd been so scared of being hurt that she'd hurt herself in the process. Drake had told her that he wasn't going to take the job, had begged her to listen to him, but no... She couldn't hear him past the roaring in her brain. The truth was she'd been happier with Drake, as his wife, than she'd ever been in her life. It was like she'd been looking through a peephole for her entire life, but when he kissed her, when he loved her, it was like he'd opened up the window to her soul. Who knew that her best friend would be the man she wanted to spend the rest of her life with?

Then she had to go and mess it up. She'd sent Drake packing when it was the last thing she wanted to do. The worst part? He'd actually left, walked out of her life.

Love had always made fun of silly women who

took to bed after a breakup. She'd thought that would never be her, until it was. Dr. Lovely Grace Washington was licking her wounds, eating cookies and ice cream bars and potato chips—and nothing else. All junk food, all day. The last time she'd looked at herself in the mirror, her hair was a mass of naps on her head, she had chocolate on the corner of her mouth and crud in her eyes. That was yesterday. She could only imagine what she looked like today.

She'd tried to rationalize it. Drake was her longest friend; they'd cut their teeth together. She had every right to mourn the end of their relationship, especially since it could also be the end of the friendship. Love complicated things. *Love sucks.* Pun intended.

It had been three days and his smell still lingered on her pillow, the soft scent of wood and leather. She burrowed her nose into the cotton and closed her eyes. It was distinctively Drake and one whiff made her feel safe and secure, like he always had.

Being with Drake, being loved by him, was like a Pandora's box. She'd let him into places she didn't realize she had. He'd opened up a part of her that was under lock and key. It was magical and terrifying at the same time. How could she live without that? She loved him so much, she literally felt an ache low in her belly.

She checked her phone every minute, hoping to see a message from him. Even a one-word text would be okay. The first day, after she'd told him it was over, they'd run into each other at the hospital. He'd brushed past her, going out of his way to avoid eye contact, acting almost as if she was contagious.

During morning rounds, he'd busied himself talking to a first year resident with big boobs and a huge crush on him. Love wanted to choke her. She couldn't avoid the whispers, the stares. Everyone was speculating the worst—that he'd cheated on her, which couldn't be further from the truth. So she'd called in sick the next two days. She was a coward.

Lana had texted her, phoned her, then finally burst into her room last night. Her cousin ordered her to "get her ass out of that bed," but Love simply rolled over and turned up the television. Eventually, Lana relented, giving her another day to sulk before she called in the big dogs. Not that Love knew who the "big dogs" were. Not even her mother could get her out of her room, and she'd tried countless times.

"Lovely?" *I spoke too soon.*

Gloria limped into the room and sat beside her on the mattress. Love felt bad that she'd basically ignored her mother for two days, especially since she was still a sick woman. Love wanted to be there for her. Tomorrow. Yes, she'd get up and go to work tomorrow.

Familiar hands massaged her shoulders, rubbed her back. "You have to get out of this bed. You've been in here for two days."

"I will, Mom. I'll get up tomorrow."

Gloria let out a heavy sigh. "Your father called."

"I don't want to talk to him." She was pissed at her dad.

After Drake moved out, her father had called and asked her for forgiveness. Confused, Love had played along, asked him why he did it, as if she knew what "it" was. She had no idea what he was talking about. When he'd confessed to coaxing the admissions department at Johns Hopkins to consider Drake for the fellowship, her anger had soared to new heights. It was the first and only time she'd ever cursed at her father, then she'd hung up on him.

"You may not believe him, but he is sorry."

Love looked at her mother. "Why are you defending him, Mom? He doesn't deserve that from you."

Gloria tapped her foot on the carpet. "Love, what happened between me and Leon wasn't all his fault. You know that? It takes two people to make a marriage work and two people to destroy it."

"That doesn't make any sense. One person can ruin a relationship." She should know. She'd just done it. "He cheated on you, Mother."

"Yes, and that sucked. But our marriage was over a long time before he cheated. We just hadn't made it official, because of you."

Love gasped. "What? You two seemed so happy."

"Because that's what we wanted you to believe, babe. Sometimes a relationship is not meant to last a lifetime. Talk about two people whose lives were going in different directions. We grew apart. By the time he cheated on me, I'd already fallen out of love with him. I was just biding my time."

The revelation shocked Love to her core. She'd blamed her dad for being a cheating jerk. Well, he still was a cheating jerk.

"When I talked to him today," Gloria continued, sweeping a cookie crumbs and empty Fruit Snacks wrappers into her hand and throwing them into the small wastebasket beside the bed, "I told him to forgive himself, because I already did. Your father isn't a bad person. He's just misguided."

"And controlling," Love added.

"Very. But his heart was in the right place. He was really worried about you. He apologized to Drake."

Hearing that he'd done so meant a lot to Love. She was sure it made Drake feel better.

"I did light into him, though."

Love wiped a tear from her cheek. "Why did he do it?"

"I'm not even sure he knows. I think what it boils down to is you're his baby girl. No one will be good enough for you in his eyes. All he sees is the potential for hurt, and when you were born he made a vow to never let anyone hurt you."

"*He* hurt me. He manipulated me and my marriage."

"I know. There's no excuse for his behavior, but I do believe he's sincere in his apology."

"I love Drake, Mom. I want him to be happy, have everything he wants. Marriage and kids were never on his must-have list. It was stupid to even get involved, but we went in at full speed instead of being cautious. Now look at us. Barely speaking, barely friends. I hurt him."

She'd heard the tears in his voice as he'd begged her to open the door for him that morning it all fell apart. And she'd stubbornly refused, thinking she was doing what was best for both of them.

Gloria squeezed her hand, pulled her into a tight hug. "I know you. I know Drake. You'll always be friends. It's awkward and hurts now, but it won't be like this always. All is not lost."

Love wasn't so sure. She wanted to believe their friendship could survive. They were stupid to try and change the dynamic so fast. They hadn't thought it through, and they would suffer for the rest of their lives.

"Listen." Gloria pulled Love to her feet, patted her crunchy hair. "You need to get out of this bed and take a shower. You are ripe, daughter."

Love laughed. "I bet you've been waiting to say that since yesterday."

"I have, but I figured I'd give you some time before I pulled rank." Her mother held her face in her hands. "You and Drake need to talk before he leaves the state. I spoke with him yesterday and he's flying to Baltimore today to look for a place. His flight leaves at three o'clock. Now, if you want this friendship that you care about so much, go get him before he leaves."

Her mother was right. She couldn't let Drake leave without telling him she loved him. He had been so much of her world, a huge part of her life. They'd done everything together, been with each other through every life moment that mattered. And one thing stayed constant. They never gave up on each other. She had to get to him.

Love picked up her phone and dialed his number. No answer. Muttering a curse, she hung up and dialed again. It went straight to voice mail. *Damn*.

"Mother." Love ran into the bathroom and started the shower. "Want to ride with me? I have to get to Drake."

Gloria grinned and clapped. "I'm so glad you actually listened to me for once."

Love hugged her. "I love you. I don't know what I would have done if you hadn't been here."

"Lovely, I'll always be here for you. Can I plan that reception now? I've been itching to get started on it."

Love laughed and shook her head at her persistence. "Fine, Mother. If Drake takes me back, you can plan anything you want. I'll be down in ten minutes."

But it was only nine minutes later that Love was speeding toward Drake's apartment, cutting through traffic like a madwoman. He lived in a huge apartment by Interstate 94, far from the hospital, which was why he was at her house, eating up her food, more often than not.

She arrived at the apartment and let out a huge sigh of relief that his car was still parked in his spot under the carport.

Love parked haphazardly in one of the visitor's parking spots outside his place.

Wasting no time, she jumped out of her vehicle. "I'll be back, Mom."

"I'll wait here," Gloria said.

Love ran to the private outdoor entrance to his unit. But when she raised her hand to knock, the door swung open and she tumbled inside.

Drake grabbed her waist, steadying her. Just that contact made her stomach tighten and goose bumps spread up her arms.

"Love?" he asked. "What are you doing here?"

El stepped out from behind him. "Well, well, well. You came. I thought I was going to have to go over and coordinate an intervention." She quickly realized that El was the "big guns" Lana had referred to.

Love winced, her gaze darting back and forth between the two men. Her husband was a sight for sore eyes, dressed in dark jeans and a pale blue button-down shirt. He looked good. She leaned in to catch a whiff of his cologne.

"Did you just smell him?" El asked, amusement flickering in his eyes.

Drake shot him a sideways glance. "Can you leave us alone?"

"Not before I say this. You two need to get it together." He turned from Drake to Love. "You made it here first. We were on our way to your place."

She drew in a sharp breath, meeting Drake's gaze. "You were?"

He nodded.

El slipped out and joined her mother, who was now standing outside Love's car watching everything unfold. "Fix it," he yelled over his shoulder as he crossed to Gloria.

Love smiled sheepishly. "I guess they're sick of us, huh?"

"Pretty much."

Love motioned toward the inside of the apartment. "Can we sit down?"

He wordlessly led her in. Drake's apartment was modern, as opposed to the traditional style of her condo. He didn't like clutter, so there was very little furniture in his place, only what he needed. The pieces were was sleek, the design clean, the colors neutral, with only a flash of color here and there.

It had been months since she'd been at his place. She picked up a throw pillow as she sat on the sofa with him. "I like this," she said lamely.

"You bought it."

"Oh," she said with a quick roll of her eyes. Deciding that now was the time, she added, "I wanted to catch you before you went to Baltimore. I feel like we need to talk, sort things out."

"I'm not going to Baltimore."

Her eyes snapped to his and her heart raced. "Really?"

"I turned them down."

Love smiled and tears filled her eyes. "I... Why?"

"You know why."

"But you gave your resignation at the hospital."

"Your dad offered me my position back. He called this morning, apologized to me for interfering."

"I know." She still couldn't believe her father actually apologized to Drake. Especially since he rarely admitted when he was wrong. "I'm shocked."

"I know, right?"

Love picked at her pants, focused on the corner of the rug. Basically she looked everywhere but at Drake. "I'm glad you didn't take the job."

"Why?"

She met his gaze then, and didn't look away. "I want you to stay. I want to work this out."

Drake let out a shaky breath. Over the past few days, he'd imagined this conversation a million times. Except he'd always thought he'd be the one making the overtures. But now his wife was at his house, telling him that she wanted to be with him.

"I realize how wrong I was," she said. "That I can trust this. I can trust my feelings for you, and yours for me. Because they've always been there. I was just afraid."

"Of me?"

"Of us."

"And you're not anymore?"

She shook her head. "I want you to get rid of your apartment, and let's make this official."

A smile tugged at his lips. "Are you proposing to me?"

Laughing nervously, she shrugged. "Would you accept?"

He stared at her, marveled at the way she nibbled on her lip. When he inhaled, she smelled like lilacs and peaches. "What do *you* think?"

"I don't know. I mean, I want to hear what you have to say. You're just staring at me."

He hooked a hand around her head and pulled her into a kiss. She slid her arms around his neck, pressing herself against him and melting in his embrace. It felt good having her in his arms again.

She drew away first. "Is that your final answer?"

Drake chuckled. "If you'd seen me over the past few days, then you'd know it is."

He'd been the "asshole of the century" according to his little sister. She'd overheard the fight between him and his father, and tried to be there for Drake. Unfortunately, she'd caught the brunt of his anger because she was the closest. He'd eventually run her away, but not before she gave him a piece of her mind and punched him in the arm.

Love had been stuck in his head like a melody. Many times he'd been tempted to drive to her house and lock her in the room until they figured everything out, but he'd always convinced himself to leave it be. And now that she was sitting in front of him, putting her heart on the line, he realized that him moving to Baltimore without her would have never worked, anyway. She'd made it clear that she wanted to complete her residency in Ann Arbor a while ago. There was no way he would have been able to live without her. He was hers for the taking.

"Marry me, Love."

Her mouth fell open. "What? We're already married."

"No, for real."

Drake wanted her to have the wedding that she'd always dreamed of, complete with cake, bridesmaids and a white dress that he hoped fitted her like a second skin.

"You're serious?"

"Trust me, I've never been more serious."

She beamed at him, and he closed his eyes to soak in the warmth of her smile. When she looked at him like that, his whole world opened up.

Since she was being honest, he figured he'd tell her some truths. "Love, you're the only one for me. There is no one else that I would rather…get rid of my apartment for."

Love smacked him on the knee playfully. "You're silly."

"I want to say those vows again, in front of our family and friends, sober. And I want to have a redo of our wedding night, sober." He picked up her hand, brushed his lips against her fingertips, over her palm, then her wrist. Then he pulled a ring box out of his pocket.

"Drake?"

He swallowed before he opened it. The ring he'd purchased in Vegas had been sitting in his safe since they'd arrived home. It was time that she wore it. Slipping it on her finger, he kissed it before he kissed her.

"I love you," he murmured.

"I love you more." She winked. "Yes, I'll marry you again, in front of everybody and their mamas."

They stood, and he pulled her into another kiss.

"Drake," she panted a long while later, tearing her mouth away from his. "We can't do this here. My mom is waiting outside. El is, too. Let's finish this later."

"Hopefully, not too much later." He nibbled on her earlobe.

"You're crazy."

"You love it."

"Oh. One thing," she said, holding up her index finger.

Frowning, he asked, "What?"

"You can't ever leave again."

Drake let his gaze travel over his wife's face. "You don't have to worry about that. I won't."

"Good."

"Good."

She slid her hand into his, lacing their fingers together. "Let's go, then."

Epilogue

One month later, Drake and Love renewed their vows in front of their families and friends. Both fathers were in attendance and on their best behavior, and Love's mother had planned an elegant, yet simple reception.

The ceremony was quick, because they'd already gone through that. They'd written their own vows. And Love had cried like a big baby when Drake told her that he'd follow her anywhere, go through anything, as long as she was with him. There was no minister, just them talking to each other as if there was no one else in the room.

When he'd kissed her, the crowd roared with applause—until Gloria muttered "stop" under her breath, three times.

It was a memorable day, filled with laughter and

tears. Once everyone left, Drake whisked her away to their honeymoon in Saint Thomas, paid for by Dr. Law. It was, according to him, the least he could do.

They'd spent the first hour making love on their private beach, which had always been a fantasy of hers. And they'd just returned to their suite from dinner.

Love stood outside on the hotel balcony, letting the sea breeze caress her face. Weddings were fun and everything, but she never wanted to do that again. Between floral arrangements, caterers, invitations and color schemes, she was exhausted. But she wouldn't have changed anything for the world.

"Where did you go?" Drake asked, stepping outside and sliding his arms around her waist.

Tilting her head back, she kissed his chin. "Just wanted some fresh air. Can you believe we got married—again?"

"Twice within three months. Go figure."

Drake had been her pillar of strength during the hasty planning. She'd come home countless times with tears in her eyes and surrender on her brain. But he'd soothed her, plied her with wet kisses, massages and more.

"Come back to me," he murmured against her mouth. "You're so distracted."

"Just thinking about everything we've been through. It's been a wild few months."

"I wouldn't change a thing."

"Not even one tiny detail?"

He leaned back, eyed her with curiosity. "Are you trying to give me a hint?"

"Well…" She turned in his arms and snaked her

arms around his neck, pulling him down for a quick kiss. "We've been right in front of each other the whole time. Don't you think about what would have happened had we got our heads out of our asses years ago?"

"No." He buried his face in her neck, laved the sensitive skin under her earlobe with his tongue. "I think if we'd discovered this years ago, it would have ruined us. We had to wait for the right place and time."

And that was why she loved him. He was calm, dependable and rationale. And sexy as hell. "Drake?"

"Yes, Love."

"I love you." She yelped when he picked her up and slung her over his shoulder.

He smacked her on her butt, and she laughed with delight. "How about you love me in bed, all night?" Dropping her on the mattress, he bent down, placing a lingering kiss on her swollen lips. "I love you, too... Mrs. Jackson."

* * * * *